the Santa Pageant

LILLIAN BARRY

Broccoli & Basil Books

Cover art by Annalise Jensen

ISBN 978-1-7395300-0-6 (paperback)

ISBN 978-1-7395300-1-3 (ebook)

ISBN 978-1-7395300-2-0 (audiobook)

www.lillianbarry.com

Author's note

This book contains discussion of emotional abuse within a past relationship, the aftermath of a broken engagement including the reappearance of the ex, and one flashback.

It also features emotionally immature parents (of adult characters); mentions of polycystic ovarian syndrome, infertility, and postnatal depression; mentions of C-PTSD, RSD, anxiety, and undiagnosed ADHD; some lesbophobia and biphobia; misgendering; ableism; gaslighting; divorce; strong language; sex between consenting adult characters; pipe smoking; and consumption of alcohol. There is also ableist language used to hurt a main character. If you need to, please take care.

This book takes place in a post-pandemic 2023; at time of writing, I had imagined the threat of SARS-CoV-2 would be "over." I made allusions to hand sanitiser and occasional masking, presuming them to be basic health considerations now incorporated into daily life. I mentioned the pandemic in the past tense, as important context to characters' backstories. None of that really holds true. However, I would like to believe in that world, so that is the world I have written.

This isn't an angry book that brings retribution on the perpetrators of abuse—there are other writers who do that better. This is the book where we learn that we deserve love and gentleness after all, and perhaps offer love and gentleness to ourselves.

Friday

10 days till Christmas

1

Effie was no architect (only a structural engineer by education, and a disgruntled fool by occupation), but she would've designed the Pollack way different.

When you repurposed a derelict fish market as a shopping centre, you kept the historic façade, right? You didn't smother it in aluminium mesh and spray-paint silver the centuries-old granite. In Effie's opinion, whoever's choice it had been to lean into the fishy aesthetic deserved a good harpooning.

Tragically, it was too late to scrub the Pollack clean. The grand opening of the new shopping centre was in ten days' time, when the winner of the Santa of the Year Pageant would cut the ribbon with a gigantic pair of scissors and a rainbow of glovèd hands would applaud them to a sense of self-actualisation. The Pollack's new look was here to stay.

Of course, that pageant-winning, scissor-wielding, ribbon-cutting Santa wouldn't be Effie.

She was, in fact, alone, gazing up at the Pollack on that wet Friday afternoon, on the jut of reclaimed land on the North rim of the bay. She worked in the carpark there ("worked" in the sense of "got paid to do nothing"). Beyond the low, seaweed-crusted walls, a dull sea lapped up the raindrops. To the South, through a forest of swaying masts, was the faint shadow of the Castle out in the bay, and Town curved around it all, rising roof upon roof up the cliff. Guernsey, beautiful Guernsey, potato-peel-pie-whatever-the-heck Guernsey.

Effie doodled "Pollack" on her clipboard in various attempts at cursive and thought about the Pollack and its joyforsaken carpark as a metaphor for her and her life. A misunderstood curiosity on a grey plain of tarmac and rain. The seven lonely hours she'd survived in the carpark today clung to her, thicker than the stench of seasalt, and, even worse than that, the one hour remaining before 5pm.

She had so much more to give than this. It was almost bursting out of her.

"Oi, you!"

Sopping strands of hair slapped both eyeballs as she turned away from the sea and back towards Town. A Christmas shopper marched across the carpark. Towards her.

"What are you doing with my car? Are you some—"

Oh, Santa save her. Not another suspicious resident. Wearily, Effie waved her clipboard.

Despite the translucent paper and running ink, her assailant recognised her as A Professional. They flipped from attack to defence, scissors to rock in an instant.

"—some, uh, parking inspector? Is there a problem?"

They halted. Five or six lengths of tinsel looped their neck, Poundland tags attached, and they clutched a transparent sack from the fancy-dress shop containing what appeared to be a Santa suit. But their ankle-length beige coat with its *they/she* pronoun badge didn't disguise their short figure…and the shadow from their umbrella couldn't hide their face.

"…Effie?" said Effie's once-upon-a-time best friend.

Effie was barely a beat behind. "Tove?"

They stared at each other, tasting the rain, and it was like no time had passed since they were standing by the lake at Winter Ball in the heady scent of the honeysuckle, about to (or so Effie thought) tell each other how they really felt.

Effie's workday gloom transformed into a soft excitement that pattered in her chest like snowflakes on a skylight.

"How've you been?" they said at the same time.

Effie laughed nervously. "I'm good." She considered pouring the contents of her mind in a messy offering at Tove's feet—she was very soggy and wanted to go home; a completely irrelevant memory of Tove writing the first thirty digits of pi on her skin in Sharpie was prickling up her arm; did Tove want to hang out after work? (oh rats, she was babysitting tonight)—but she couldn't shake the feeling that her ex-friend wouldn't give a shit about anything she had to say.

After all this time, after all the resolutions Effie had made to prevent what had happened at Winter Ball ever happening again…she was back where she'd started, unable to tell Tove a bloody thing. Convinced Tove didn't want to hear it. Convinced nobody wanted to hear it.

Tove nodded, as if to confirm her suspicions, and a tease of auburn hair snuck out from under their beanie, just like it used to fall from their ponytail in PE. "Seriously though, what are you doing to my car?"

"It's…a survey."

In a parallel universe, Effie would simply ask Tove when they parked, for how long, and how often; but the paid parking initiative she was developing for the new shopping centre was nasty politics. Not to be discussed with random people she was best friends with, kissed once, and hardly saw again. Instead, she hung out in the carpark all day jotting down their registration numbers like a complete loser.

Her stomach knotted at the idea that Beanie Tove might think Clipboard Effie a loser. She imagined the knot was a shoelace to be untied, and unravelled it in her mind, forcing herself to relax.

"Here's my supervisor's card, if you want to give him a ring and ask," she said all business-like, the same as she did for all the various pestering old creeps and science-sly mums who thought she was stealing their personal data. Which, in fairness, she sort of was.

But Tove dropped a heavy "Oh" between them that stalled her intentionally unhinged Cheshire cat grin.

"Oh," Tove said.

Although Effie's thesis was all about archways, nothing could've prepared her yearning, sapphic soul for the way Tove's eyebrows rose and curved and tightened at the business card.

"Oh, you're one of *them*... Never mind."

Tove swept past before she could ask who *them* was, umbrella spraying her wet-dog-style as they collapsed it. As Tove rummaged for their keys, fumbling with bags and umbrella, their beanie rode up their forehead, threatening to jettison itself.

"Tove—" Effie began.

And the hat fell to the ground, mercifully on a dryish spot between puddles.

Effie lunged forward to pick it up; so did Tove. Their foreheads cracked. Tove (always the less sturdy of the two of them) went flying, and Effie pitched sideways to catch them in her arms.

For a moment she saw stars: the person she'd once thought was perfect dappled her vision. Her arm circled their waist. They were soft beneath their coat, the curve of their ass pressing against her leg, the scent of their tea-tree shampoo cutting through the rain, the scratch of their tinsel scarves itching her cheek. An image reflected in their eyes: Effie heroic, Tove adoring.

Then Tove blinked, looked down, and everything shattered.

Effie had trodden on it. The hat. Tove shoved her away with a squeal of rage.

Effie lifted her foot. The beanie was crushed into the concrete. A boot print, huge and muddy, flared like the ruinous brand she left on every good thing she touched.

"I see your feet haven't gotten any smaller," Tove snarled. "What's next, step on *me*? Go on. Dig your heel in. Make me bleed."

Well, now Effie was completely bewildered. "I trod on your hat, not your heart. What's up with you, Tove?"

Tove flinched like Effie had given them a carpet burn. "Nothing. I overreacted."

There *was* something up with them. The old Tove was aloof, maybe abrasive. But morbid, angry fantasies about being stepped on (and not in the good way, apparently)? Effie wasn't so sure.

The hat with its massive mudstain taunted her on the ground between them. When Tove bent down to fetch it, Effie had to clench her fists and squeeze her eyes shut lest she give in to impulse and they cracked aching heads a second time.

"Is it machine washable?" she asked instead.

Flapping the mistreated accessory against their thigh to scatter the rubble caught on the cotton, Tove shot her a look dirtier than the underside of her foot. "You offering to wash it?"

"Sure. And until it's clean, have mine." Effie whipped her own pastel pink bobble hat off her head and thrust it Tove's way, snatching the scuffed beanie for herself.

"Your hat is soaking."

"Wet or filthy, your choice." The offhand flirtation was up and out before she could bite it back.

"God. I forgot you were like this."

"Like what?"

"*Weird.*"

Oof. Like the juice of squished cranberries, all her sunny self-confidence dribbled away, now thick, sharp, with humiliation. She clung to the dregs, fearing where she'd be without her own raw self-belief.

"Weird good or weird bad?" she urged.

With a withering look, Tove took the two sides of her hat and jammed it on their head. "I'm keeping this, by the way. And you can keep mine. So we're even, and you can consider this goodbye."

And that was that. Always driving people away. Should've kept her mouth shut.

Tove gathered their bags and fallen umbrella and slid into the silver Ford Fiesta. The tinsel was draped over the back seat like a drunken passenger and the Santa suit rode shotgun. Tove didn't acknowledge Effie's sidestep to let them pull out the space, but their golden-brown eyes met hers in the mirror as they drove away. Effie used to think Tove's eyes held boundless laughter, but now they looked completely empty.

So much for one kiss one time.

Effie was one of those people who was never happier than when she was engaged on some big project, or "Grand Plan," as she called them. She'd treated her job like a Grand Plan at first, until she'd realised how boring and inconsequential it was.

She left her dreary carpark at 4:57pm, enjoying the delicious rebellion of those three extra minutes as she caught the early bus. Starting Sunday, the Pollack Committee had planned a week-long party in her carpark before the Opening on Christmas Day, and Effie was taking the whole week off—partly because she couldn't bear to miss the festivities, but mostly because the pop-up ice-rink would take up all the parking spaces, and a parking surveyor couldn't survey an empty lot.

The horizon was dark by the time she reached her stop, but her sister's gentrified estate was anything but dark. The neighbours went ham on the Christmas lights, honey-drizzled gammon compared to Town's supermarket sandwich slices.

Effie rang the bell.

The door opened and a tall, blonde woman, a handful of years older, flung be-bangled, jingling arms around her.

"Yikes Effie, your hair looks awful!"

"Thanks, I guess," drawled Effie. "What's up? Have you been pre-drinking?"

"Only apple juice." Her sister pulled her out of the rain. "Settle my tummy before all the techbros go off on the financial and moral glories of AI art."

Effie mimed gagging. "If I were there I'd be taking swings, breaking algorithms, starting a revolution. Apple juice, huh? Do you have to stomach this event sober?"

"Don't be silly. There's an open bar."

Lalla uttered a tense laugh that Effie assumed she'd provoked by being leftie and uncomfortable and, well, *silly*, so decided to ignore.

"Now," Lalla went on, "there's leftover shepherd's pie on the counter ready to heat up. Heather is eating her tea in the kitchen. And I'm serious about your hair. You must use my hairdryer. It's induction, tell me how you like it and I'll get you one for Christmas. I've changed our bed, so you can have our room as soon as Liam gets out...he's looking for his dice, ridiculous man."

"He's taking his dice on holiday?"

"I want peace and quiet while I'm having my mani-pedi at the hotel tomorrow night, so Liam decided he might as well go to D&D as usual. Oh, speak of the devil."

Liam sauntered down the stairs in a suit and skinny tie, saving her from making a poorly conceived joke about straight couples. She'd never get over her sister's taste in baby-faced men, but Lalla beamed at him. Nobody else could make her smile like that. And Lalla's smile was all that mattered.

Effie turned away as they did their little dressed-up, pre-party, flirty bit. The one that went, "I can't wait to show off how kissable you are tonight and then literally kiss you in front of *everyone*." She was happy for her sister, but a pang hit when she took in Lalla's nice two-bed house, her pre(co)cious seven-year-old daughter, her uncontroversial heterosexual marriage. She always felt uneasy, like she might ruin it simply by being there.

"You're still alright with Heather for the weekend?" Liam asked while he helped Lalla adjust her coat over her precariously low-cut dress. "Call anytime you need, yeah?"

"Don't worry, I've planned it all out! Pudding prep tonight, Santa grotto tomorrow—and on Sunday it's the first round of the Santa pageant." She'd been planning it all week.

"Let's go, Liam, she'll be fine." Lalla tugged him out the door. "And don't forget our suitcase!"

"Pog your heart out, champ," Liam called like the cringey e-boy he was at heart.

And then they were gone.

"'She'll be fine,'" Effie muttered. "Who's *she*? The cat's mother?" She didn't babysit for gratitude. She did it because she could, and because Lalla relied on her, and because she wanted to be the best sister she could be. And because it scratched that itch to Create and Execute a Grand Plan. But a bit of respect wouldn't go amiss.

She went through to the kitchen, where her niece was eating mash and beans. "Hi, Heather!"

"Hey, Aunty Effie!" Heather put her spoon down to wave.

"Are you looking forward to our Christmassy weekend?"

"Sort of, sort of not." Heather reached for the notebook on her lap and slammed it down on the table. "Just look at this!"

Effie craned over the most indecipherable chart she'd ever seen in all her years in STEM. "What?" she asked.

Heather huffed an impatient noise. "I tried to tell our fortunes from the clouds. But it rained all day, and it just came out as a big cloudy mess."

The shapes in the notebook certainly looked like a big mess.

"Well," Effie said brightly, "it doesn't matter, because the Christmas pudding will take care of our fortunes."

"How's a pudding supposed to do what Heather Herring could not?" Heather tossed her hair like haughty girls do in movies.

"When we stir it, we each have to make a wish."

Narrowed eyes. Sceptical. "What kind of wish?"

"I can't tell you, it's all yours. What's something you really want for yourself?"

Heather gnawed a knuckle as Effie unpacked the bag of pudding ingredients she'd dropped off yesterday. "Pssht, you can have my wish."

"How about some toys? Rollerskates? A trip to Disney?"

"I don't *need* those things."

"Well, do you want them? It's okay to want things. You deserve good things, even if you don't need them. So, what do you want most in the world?"

"To make everyone happy."

"That's really sweet of you, to wish everyone could be happy."

"No, I want to *make* them happy. Me. And take credit for it."

Effie had to take a moment to process whether Heather's dream was selfish or unselfish. "Okay. Sure. That's a good pudding wish."

"But puddings can't grant wishes. That's what I'm trying to tell you. You have to make them happen yourself."

"Of course puddings can grant wishes. You have to give them the chance."

"Aunty Effie, I *do* love you," said her niece, "but you're very silly."

Five minutes into Effie's weekend of babysitting and her niece was already poking at her like a pigeon at a picnic. Lalla would tell Effie *don't be silly* with Heather in earshot, Heather would shoot that same popgun, and *pow! pow!* now Effie felt like a squashed tit. She could attempt to make Heather respect her by playing the age card or whatever, but no one liked to be told "sit down because I have more LifE eXperIENce than you," and Effie knew that because her family pulled that one all the ever-loving time. What wouldn't she give for someone in her life who *liked* her? A friend, if you will.

A friend like Tove, whose muddy beanie was a hard lump in her pocket.

Once Heather had finished her tea, and Effie had done her damnedest to wash the beanie in the sink, they made the pudding in a big red bucket. Currants, raisins, dried apricot, nuts, flour, treacle…it all went in at once, and then they located Lalla's most humongous spoon and prepared to make their wishes.

Heather went first. She shut her eyes, stirred, and muttered her wish under her breath. Effie managed not to laugh as she wished for a pair of rollerskates and a little brother—but sure, maybe she was wishing somebody else some rollerskates and a little brother.

Then it was her turn. She took the spoon.

The moment she closed her eyes, Heather's socks zizzed across the floor towards the bag of sugar on the counter. It was now or never.

"I want my friend Tove back," Effie thought, without even really meaning to.

She opened her eyes in time to see the sugar teeter over the counter, a cascade of saccharine snow about to shower the entire kitchen, and her niece in the centre of it licking her sweet-coated fingers.

In the split-second before chaos, Tove's empty gaze from earlier flashed across Effie's retinas. Despite today's standoffishness, Tove was the best friend she'd ever had, the only one who'd gotten her that Taylor Swift perfume for her fourteenth birthday even though she'd asked literally everyone for it. Even if Tove couldn't give the love she'd once wanted, their friendship would mean the world. With Tove on her side, Effie could endure her family's barbs, her unfulfilling job, the knowledge that she sucked at everything she tried and drove everybody away in the end. Less obnoxious, less lonely, more *wanted*. That's how they used to make her feel, before the kiss that scared Tove off and ruined their friendship.

Effie wanted to tell Tove she'd changed since then. She'd learned to tone down her Effie-ness and bottle up her impulses for other people's comfort. But after today, she wasn't sure she'd learned a thing. Perhaps she wasn't as scared of what other people would think of her as she used to be—she knew what they thought, more often than not—rather, she was afraid they were right. Today proved that. Time and distance had revealed Tove's true thoughts: they, too, thought Effie was weird. And because she'd once trusted their opinion above all others, it felt like the beam supports had crumbled from her temple of self-belief.

Something had to change. She needed a Grand Plan. And fast. She'd put herself out there and show everybody she was good for something. One last Grand Plan.

But she didn't have time to make one, because then she was covered in sugar.

2

That was the thing about Effie. She made Tove want to scream.

Tove would be minding their own bleeding business when after ten years of dead silence, the mistress of unsubtlety herself would accost them in a freezing carpark and say their name. That is, *Effie's* name fell out *their* mouth first, but in their defence they didn't know it was in there.

Clawing back rage was all Tove could do. With wet hair plastered to her forehead and a goofy look on her face, Effie was the same as ever. She invited them to let loose, to join her unruly agenda of earnestness and trust and thoughtless flirtation. Tove was the only one who knew the truth, and they'd learned the hard way: Effie couldn't be trusted, not one ounce. She would bring her great big foot down on their hat and mash it into the mud. She would act like she returned their love, and then say absolutely nothing at the critical moment.

Frankly, the audacity of saying their name in that tender, heartfelt tone, right before ruining their favourite beanie, it made them sick. Hat or heart, it was all the same.

In fairness, their name was the only thing Effie knew about them nowadays. What she didn't know was that the way she said it went against everything Tove had worked and fallen for since Effie had rejected them at Winter Ball so, so long ago. They simply didn't hear their name like that anymore. It stoked the unvoiced scream deep inside them.

Effie made them want to let out that scream.

So they left Effie in the carpark, a lone figure staring after them through the rain, and drove home with steamed-up windows. By the time they cut into the stony drive at their mum's, they'd forgotten the carpark, forgotten if Effie's presence there was reality or a product of their complex-post-traumatic brain fog. The pink bobble hat on their head smelled of someone they used to know. But inside were only echoes of their name, over and over, in a voice they didn't want to hear anymore.

Rage displaced now, tears tingled in their eyes.

They sat in the car for a good twenty minutes, watching the spiky grasses splay and bend over the dunes under the weight of the raindrops, and swallowing the sobs that clogged their throat. Eventually they were neither sad nor angry, and only then were they ready to go indoors.

"Do you want something for that?" said their brother as they opened the front door.

"Jesus!" Tove jumped back into the rain. "What are you doing here?"

"Watching you." Alasdair perched on the windowsill beside the door, grinding coffee by hand.

"Jesus," they repeated. "Can't you do that somewhere else?"

"Well, no, I'd have to be here to see you drive up and sit in the car staring at a giant shit for half an hour."

"A what?"

"The enormous bird splat on your windscreen. That you've been staring at for the past million years."

"Since the dawn of time, actually," they snapped, "while we're exaggerating." It was their turn to peer out the window as they slammed the door and kicked off their sopping shoes. They'd forgotten to remove their pronoun badge before coming in, so they turned the lapel inwards when they hung up their coat. "Wow, that is a big poo."

"Yeah, I asked if you wanted something for it. Spray? Cloth? Spoon?"

"Wow, funny."

"I'm surprised you didn't see it."

"Windows are transparent, monkey man."

"Not if they're covered in poo."

"I'm going to find Mum," Tove decided, as they should've done the moment Dair opened his mouth.

There was nobody in the kitchen or the living room, where they dumped their shopping spoils. Tove found their quarry in the bedroom upstairs, half-in half-out of the little door into the eaves like a volunteer at a magic show. Mum flashed a rabbit-in-floodlight glare at their limp "Hello," as if she really did think she was about to get chopped in two.

"Tove, just the woman I want. Please would you fetch the Christmas decorations? You're nimbler than me."

Tove scowled at being called "woman," a word that didn't sit right anymore. Like their name, it had been used too often in exasperation. And anyway, what made them "woman"? If it was their tits and vagina, and the submissive, pliant fiancée role they'd played for their ex, they didn't want the word.

Tove didn't like the hypersensitive, hypervigilant self they had become, but it was the self they were stuck with for now.

And that wasn't Mum's fault. It wasn't Effie's either, but seeing her today brought a lot of hurt flooding back and, since they probably wouldn't meet again, she was an easy person to pin everything on. Screw you, Effie, for existing and telepathically making their mum call them a woman.

Tove sighed. They were fairly sure their mum would understand, or at least respect, their queerness, but they weren't ready to open themself up to being probed.

Avoiding that conversation, they crawled into the eaves and retrieved the Christmas decorations, sliding the boxes along the rough boards and sucking splinters out their fingertips.

"I can't believe you kept this junk," they commented when they stumbled on a porcelain set of angels playing instruments.

"I kept them for you," Mum said. "You absolutely loved these angels."

Tove undressed the topmost angel from her bubblewrap. She was tall with bobbed golden hair, soft eyes reflecting the yellow light from the single bare bulb in the eaves. Like Effie, if Effie had ever played a harp in her life.

"They don't mean anything to me," they said, returning the angel to her box. "You could've got rid of them years ago."

"Maybe you're not sentimental, but I am."

Tove was not always kind or forthcoming to their mum. This fortitude in the face of their refusal to emotionally engage always came as a surprise, a welcome one. They could be nicer, if they only knew how.

"Your favourite was the angel with the trumpet," Mum went on. "You wanted to play the trumpet since you were tiny."

"Yep," Tove said.

"You haven't played in a while. There your shining Felicity sits, forlorn in her case, untouched by your loving hands."

"Oh my god, Mum."

"Why don't you go carolling for late-night shopping next Thursday? You used to do it every year." Dair spoke from the bedroom door, still grinding his coffee.

A sick feeling stabbed at Tove's stomach, which they halted with a sharp "No."

"Don't you miss it?" Dair pressed. He and Mum were one and the same, all feelings and memories. Always trying to get inside and find buttons to push and levers to pull, to mould you into what they thought your happiness looked like. "You haven't played at all since you got back from Germany."

"So?" Tove growled. They'd never played their trumpet in Germany, though they said they did. They didn't know if they'd ever play again.

"We just worry you aren't doing much at the moment, Tove," said Mum.

It was true: Tove had barely left the house since coming back from Germany, except to go food shopping, and knitting group on Tuesdays. Prodded like a stuffed bird, they decided to give up their secret plan in order to buy some peace on the trumpet thing. "Joke's on you because I am doing something this week. I'm entering the Santa pageant."

"You're what?" Mum was incredulous.

Dair just laughed.

"There's a contest to pick a Santa to cut the ribbon on the Pollack shopping centre on Christmas Day. And I'm entering."

"Why?" asked Dair. "I thought you didn't care for that corporate shit."

"Language!" snapped Mum.

"Corporate shite," corrected Dair, earning himself a glare.

"I don't. I'm furious, actually," Tove said. "This new shopping centre is going to destroy local trade. Did you know every single shop in there is going to be a chain? The stakeholders are all big-shot UK CEOs. It's such a mess."

"So what? You're going to refuse to cut the ribbon and therefore the shopping centre can't open? You're going to take it down from the inside?" mocked Dair, brotherly nemesis supreme. "I'm still laughing about the idea of you in a Santa suit. Is that what you were carrying earlier?"

"Shush, Alasdair," said Mum. "Tove will make an excellent Santa. But are you sure, darling? It doesn't seem like you."

Those presumptive phrases poked the nasty gremlin inside that wanted to lash out at everybody. What did "like you" mean? What was "like them"? Tove felt like the scattered crumbs from a half-eaten cake, like there wasn't much of *them* left. Even Effie had noticed. "What's up with you, Tove?" she'd asked. Tove had been half inclined to tell her, to fall into the arms they used to think looked so strong and steady. Too bad she, too, had taken her cake and left.

"I have a plan," they informed their family, cramming the gremlin back inside their chest. "I can't take down the shopping centre, and I'm not interested in cutting the ribbon. But there's going to be a lot of publicity for the pageant, and I have a plan to make the most of that."

Mum's brow creased even deeper. "Publicity? That's not your…I mean, you keep yourself to yourself…"

"I'll be fine," Tove said. "Besides, the Santa suit is gigantic. I'll be basically anonymous behind the beard. Most people won't even realise it's…me."

In small communities like the Island, every social decision you made had consequences. Mum had a point: audiences were not Tove's forte, especially when they were actively trying to escape a certain social decision they'd made six months ago. Nevertheless, they'd considered this, and knew they could do it.

Now all they had to do was reassure their mum, whose worry lines etched a big X in their resolve.

"I'm having a practice run tomorrow," they declared. "Santa grotto. Nine quid an hour."

Mum nodded. "I'm proud of you," she said. "You always surprise me. Let me know if I can do anything to help." Her brow relaxed.

Tove exhaled, relief stirring the tension in the room. "I was hoping for free rein of the car."

Dair sputtered behind Mum's back as she said, "What a great idea. Shouldn't be a problem, should it, Alasdair?"

He grunted in defeat. "I need a lift to and from D&D tomorrow. That's all."

"Done," Tove said.

And there. They'd told their family about the pageant, dodged the whole trumpet thing, and nobody was trying to stop them from doing what they wanted. There was nothing standing in their way, or nothing they could predict, and wasn't that the scariest part of it all?

Saturday

9 days till Christmas

3

Effie would rather be almost anywhere than cooped up in her lonely flat on a Saturday morning, and today that was great, because she wasn't cooped up in her lonely flat. Actually, she was in another carpark in the rain, but this time with Heather, queuing for the Santa grotto at a local barn. Fortunately she was a big fan of *Frozen*, otherwise the fifty squealing small girls dressed as Elsa would be really, *really* getting on her nerves. Which they totally weren't. Not at all.

"I'm hungry," said Heather. She claimed she was too old for her Elsa dress, but that didn't stop her wearing an antler headband and a clown nose. "We've been here *hours*."

"We can give up if you like," Effie said, hopefully.

"It was your idea," Heather grumbled, stubbornly.

In all her whopping seven years, Effie's niece had never backed down on anything—and Effie certainly never had in her own twenty-five—so they continued to stand there, dazzled by a rainbow of twinkly lights refracting in the rain, all reds and purples and greens and golds, with the chatter of the queue muffled by their hungry silence.

Eventually they reached the barn door, and an elf with a clipboard pointed Effie to a grotto booth like it was a festive vaccination clinic. Of course they had multiple Santas in multiple grottos, what was she thinking?

At the entrance, which was really a cow-stall swing door with some fake ivy taped around it, Heather flourished a finger. "You wait here," she instructed. "I want Santa to myself."

Effie envied her niece's natural self-assurance. But that didn't quench the burn of being looked down on, not to mention being left out of the fun. Nor did it neutralise the unmistakable stench of cow.

"It's okay," soothed the clipboard elf as Heather marched into the stall. "You can see and hear everything from here."

They were reassuring her—frankly she'd forgotten these Santa substitutes were all old dudes who might or might not be sleazy as hell. She zeroed on the red-and-white bastard whose knee Heather was about to sit on.

...And it wasn't a dude.

Not even an old one.

It was the same goddamn eyes from yesterday, that bore through her in the mirror. The golden-brown eyes she used to know so well, like the Venus pools of sunset they used to swim in, like the burnt batter of chicken nuggets they used to feast on, like the glowing amaretto shots they used to neck under the stairs in their dad's booze cubby.

It was Tove.

Effie's heart pounded like sleighbells in a Christmas song. She hunched to hide herself. Inside the stall, Heather chattered away at the only person Effie had ever loved.

"I want everyone to be happy all the time, you know," Heather whined. "Is that bad?"

"Well, I don't think it's that simple." Tove's windchime voice rippled down Effie's spine. "If you were happy all the time, what would the happiness mean? Don't the bad moments give meaning to the good ones?"

"You know what I mean, like on average happy. Wouldn't that be nice?"

"Maybe. But at the same time, people aren't unhappy for no reason. You can be sad because you're depressed, or sad because you're broke or sick, or sad because you had a bad day."

"I wish there was no reason to be sad."

"Now this," said Tove in the same tone they'd used to explain quadratic factorisation to Effie in Year 8, "is the classic Problem of Evil in philosophy. And the truth is, there is no real point to the badness in life. We do what we can to bring happiness, right, but to a certain extent we have to accept our unhappy feelings and our vulnerabilities. Not every story has a happy ending. And that's normal."

"Kinda suss if you ask me," said Heather. "Who are you anyway? You're not Santa."

Effie nearly pissed herself trying not to laugh.

"I'm the Santa you've got today," said Tove, curt through their fake beard. "Sometimes Santa is queer and that's that."

An escaping gasp flew over Effie's shoulder into the stall. Pointlessly she flailed after it, as if she couldn't simply play it cool and nobody would be any the wiser.

"Oh," said Tove, as Effie stumbled through the swing doors, cheeks hot as a log fire.

That one dry syllable stoked the flame and she tripped over words that didn't need to be spoken. "Sometimes Santa is queer?"

"Please Effie, I didn't have you down as the queerphobic parent." Tove stared her down, scalding her already bright cheeks.

Heather slid off Tove's knee and crossed her arms. "She's my gay aunt, not my mum."

The reminder that somebody else was present stung Effie to resistance. "Why are you being so doom and gloom to a kid anyway?" she challenged. "You're wrong that being happy all the time would make it mean less. That assumes there's more value to things that are scarce, whereas Heather is right—happiness in abundance *is* a good thing. Especially at Christmas. And maybe some stories *do* have happy endings."

"Oh no. You're one of those true meaning of Christmas nutjobs, aren't you?"

"No, but I'm not the one dressed as Santa. What's that about?"

"I have my reasons. What about you? Why *aren't* you dressed as Santa?"

There it was. The light, teasing tone she knew so well. But even then, she never understood if Tove was laughing with her, or at her. The rift between her hands and Tove's defiant, blistering lips sizzled and tightened. Never mind yesterday's rejection. Effie wanted to grab them, kiss all the bullshit out of them.

"Well," said Heather, placing her hands on her hips like a tiny, terrifying CEO. "Who are you really, Santa Scrooge?"

Tove pouted. "If you must know, I'm getting in Santa practice for the start of the pageant tomorrow."

Effie's world froze like a homemade ice-pop. "You're doing the Santa pageant?"

"Yep."

There was nothing to say. Nothing that could possibly explain why Tove, who had apparently become a complete killjoy since their schooldays, was entering the pageant…and Effie was not. The familiar shame of inadequacy rose like bile in her throat.

"You don't have a hope of winning anyway," sneered Heather. "Santa is an old man with a real beard, so there."

The cheeky brat! Lord help her, Effie couldn't let that go.

"What about me? If I entered, could I have a hope of winning?" Surely, if Heather wouldn't support a stranger, she'd have Effie's back. And that would prove her old man theory wrong.

"Absolutely not," Heather maintained. "You're a lesbian."

"Excuse you," Effie snapped. "I'll win the damn pageant and cut the ribbon on the new shopping centre on Christmas Day. Just you wait."

"Wait, what?" Tove stood abruptly, the suit hanging loosely off their shoulders. They grabbed their waistband in the nick of time. "Now you're entering too?"

"I don't see why not." It was perfect. She'd show all the belittling weenies in her life she was worth paying some mind. Then maybe Tove would want to be friends again. It was exactly the Grand Plan she'd been looking for.

"You're both ridiculous," said Heather. "Let's go home." And she sauntered out of the stall.

Effie assessed the situation. *Tove* was clutching their waistband and giving her evils. *She* was looking for some sympathy about this insufferable handful of a niece she was supposed to be babysitting.

She gave up. "I better go. Kids and Tamagotchis…not the same."

"Tomorrow, I suppose," Tove returned.

"It's a date!" she agreed thoughtlessly.

With those loaded words, that one, long-ago kiss came flooding back. How she was a single chin-caress away from telling Tove she liked them. And when the moment escaped her, she never had another opportunity.

God, she'd missed Tove's face so much, even the look of outraged astonishment they were giving her right about now.

Effie turned tail and legged it after Heather.

After popping by her flat to feed Melchior, her extremely meow-y BFF, Effie spent the rest of the day raiding Lalla's craft drawers and trying to come up with an outfit plan.

"You could do sexy swimming Santa," said Heather, holding up an old red bikini that had somehow made it into Lalla's fabric collection.

"I'm sorry, what?" Effie choked on the mouthful of string she was using to measure her collar.

"It was on TV."

"What does your mum let you watch that has a sexy swimming Santa?"

"Oh, it was on something Mummy was watching when she was doing the ironing. Santa was wearing…hm…I think they were called garters…"

"You know what, never mind."

Heather's eyes narrowed. She knew Effie knew she knew and Effie hated that she knew it. But this was Lalla and Liam's problem. Not Effie's.

As far as Santa inspiration went, Lalla's craft materials sucked. She made earrings with wire and seaglass and sold them on Etsy, she wasn't a bespoke tailor.

"I think Daddy has an old Santa suit," Heather said at length.

Effie sighed a sigh of condolence for the thousand safety pins she'd just spilled onto the floor. "Why didn't you say before? Where is it?"

"In his cupboard."

The horrible third-hand Santa suit turned out to be, in fact, *hers*. She'd worn it to that ill-fated Winter Ball ten years ago. As Drama Prefect, she'd emceed the raffle and couldn't resist dressing up, part of another long-ago Grand Plan. The crowd's boos inevitably made her regret it, as well as her mother's attempts to cram her into a ballgown before finally saying, "Well, what you wear is your choice." But it couldn't be that bad, because Tove had kissed her anyway. Effie took a moment to remember the ghost of Tove's hands tugging at her belt, how her felt sleeves draped over their bare shoulders as she clasped their head to kiss them. Tove's dark green halterneck felt like silk. Their skin, like water. "You look good in red," Tove had said. The Santa suit was sentimental. Effie didn't know how Liam had stolen it, but sewing up the long cuffs would serve him right.

"What do you think?" she asked Heather after trying it on.

A shrug. "I'm hungry."

"Again? You're always hungry."

"So feed me, *adult*."

"Really? Don't you care if I win this thing?"

"No?" Heather itched her nose. "This is your thing, gay Santa."

A tuft of pink fur on Lalla's desk sharpened into focus. "That's it, it needs to be more gay. That's why I'm doing this, to show you Santa can be lesbian. *Anyone* can be lesbian. And a lesbian can be anyone, and *do anything*."

Effie had watched too many sad lesbian movies when she was first getting to grips with her identity. It had been horrifying to imagine her sexuality in conflict with her inner optimism. She didn't want anyone else to lack queer joy in their media and role models, or to think their life would be sad and tragic forever.

Heather yawned. "No, I get it. The Santa person earlier said sometimes Santa is queer. It's fine. I agree."

How could she, after personal reflection, come around to Effie's viewpoint? After all that anguish earlier? Annoyance tingled her hair, static from the felt Santa suit. "But you don't believe I could win."

"The winner is voted by the public," Heather explained as if she didn't know that already. "On TV shows, it's always the straight old guy who wins the vote. Or *maybe* the hot person—but you can't change who you're not."

Effie bristled, wishing she weren't the only person on earth who thought herself hot, even though her kid niece would definitely not be her choice for a second. "If you accept that Santa could be queer then why the hell am I doing this?"

"Nobody's *making* you. But maybe you want to do it? Maybe you want to show that mean Santa from earlier that you're good enough to do the things they do. Maybe you want to hang out with them all week and kiss a bunch."

"I don't know what you're talking about."

No seven-year-old had any business being as astute as Heather. (Or maybe they did; maybe they were all like this and adults only got progressively better at ignoring what they didn't want to confront.)

"If you're going to be like that then you might as well make me some tea." Heather wagged her finger, looking and sounding exactly like Lalla.

Effie's phone rang as she was chucking freezer food in the oven and feeding the Christmas pudding with rum.

"Hello?" She tucked the phone into her neck.

"I hope it isn't too late to call."

It was Effie's mother. The phone crunched her ear as she cringed.

"You have nine minutes before I have to flip the fishfingers," Effie said.

"Big girl food, is it?" Mum condescended, starting strong and rich like she always did. This was where they got it from, Lalla and Heather to boot.

"They're for your granddaughter," Effie snapped, lying because she was most certainly going to eat some of them, and feeling guilty about using Heather to escape being patronised.

"Goodness, it *is* big girl food. How old is she now, six?"

Effie sighed. "What's up, Mum?"

"Oh, only checking if you're joining your dad and I for Christmas this year."

"Of course. Like every year."

"Well, it would be fine if you'd made other plans. But it's always as well to check."

"I wouldn't make other plans on Christmas. It's family day. Right?"

"Yes, exactly! Glad we're on the same page."

"Me too." Effie wondered, sometimes, if they were in fact on the same page. Or reading the same book.

Her dad mumbled something in the background, and Mum uttered a tinkling laugh. "Don't be silly! Or I'll have to give you a— Sorry, that was your dad."

Her obnoxiously cute parents bruised her heart. Although not all that present in *her* life anymore, they were fully committed to the belief that they were meant to be together, and would be for the rest of their days. The least she could do was give them their moment, considering she'd already ruined it once before.

"What are you up to this evening?" Mum asked. "I need something to tell my friends. They're always asking what you do and it's a bit of a bother that you don't have a proper job or a relationship or even a hobby."

"I produced the harvest pantomime." Her most recent Grand Plan had been fun, but she'd struggled to sell enough tickets to break even. Even her family didn't come to watch. The theatre company hadn't invited her back for the Christmas panto.

"That doesn't really count, does it?" said her mum in a scrunched-nose voice.

Effie's eyes stung. Her own mother thought her boring, and she had a creeping fear she was right. Now, though, she had the pageant! Maybe soon, she'd be friends with Tove again! Still, she couldn't tell Mum about those things, because neither of them was real yet.

She opted for something safer. "I'm babysitting while Lalla and Liam have a staycation weekend."

"And how are you getting on with Heather?"

"It's great, she's great." She refused to talk shite about Heather. Her niece's attitude might give her a headache, but so it should.

"She did seem very grown-up and self-possessed last time I saw her."

"And when was that?" Pointlessly, she bit back the bitterness.

"Your sister emailed a copy of her yearbook photo at the start of term. I show it to all my friends when they come over to watch *The X Factor*."

Starkly and suddenly, Effie realised she'd had a lot more fun hanging out with Heather today than she was calling her mum right now, even though it had been a while since they'd spoken.

In her memories, her parents were different. It wasn't something she wanted to interrogate too hard, or she might end up concluding she was the one who'd changed. Mum was there, and she wanted to believe she'd be there if she ever needed her. That was all that mattered.

"Hey, Mum," she began, "hypothetically, if I were to go on a show like *The X Factor*, do you think I could win? Or do you think I wouldn't have a chance because I'm gay?"

The tinkling laugh crackled once again through the speaker. "Oh, my dear, it has nothing to do with your sexuality."

Effie warmed, briefly, but the next words made her stomach drop.

"I don't think you'd be very good at a show like that, do you? You don't have the talent. At singing, at acting, at *playing the part*. And if you're not good enough, if they don't *like you*, nobody's going to vote for you."

A much meaner version of Heather's *you can't change who you're not.*

Effie's characteristic optimism drained from her body, leaving only pain. *You break up happy couples. You drive your friends away. If you can't sell panto tickets, you don't have a hope in hell of bringing people together to vote for you.*

And then the optimism returned, flooding back in contrary hysteria.

"I have to deal with these fishfingers," she said. "Thanks, though. For calling. I'll be there on Christmas Day."

She hung up.

She finished Heather's dinner, inhaled her own in four bites, and then put on some sketch comedy while she tinkered with the Santa suit. Savagely she sewed ribbons and bells and sequins in all shades of pink and orange; ferociously she threaded rainbow-striped shoelaces into her combat boots. She threw it all in the washing machine with a buttload of pink dye.

She would be the gayest Santa. And she would win the pageant, if only to spite everyone who doubted her.

"I *am* good enough," she declared to the empty room, "and they *will* vote for me."

4

There was a lot of Effie in Tove's mind when they finished up at the Santa grotto and headed to the Holly & Ivy to meet Dair, having promised to drive him home after D&D. Effie and her niece. Effie and her declaration to enter the Santa pageant. Effie and her gigantic feet, both literally and figuratively, that she was entirely unable to keep out of their business and their cowstall.

In all honesty, thinking about Effie wasn't such a chore. It was a break, actually, from their usual fixations. Even though she'd screwed them over a long time ago, and they could never truly trust her again, it was interesting what she'd become.

It was also interesting to their brother's friends, they soon found out, what they'd become.

"Little Tove, all grown up!" exclaimed Shane, Dair's oldest friend, slapping them on the shoulder.

"Still little though," snickered Dair.

Yes, Dair. Cheers for noticing their perfectly satisfactory five foot two. His comments made them feel smaller.

Tove greeted their brother's friends through gritted teeth. "Shane. Liam." The other chairs at their table were pushed back, empty, which meant their session was over and the other members of the group had left. A small pile of dice wallowed in a puddle of condensation between their pint glasses. "You going to be long?" they growled at Dair.

"Ten or fifteen. Join us for a bit?" A dorky software developer who worked from home, Dair left the house about as often as Tove did, which wasn't much, so they decided to let him have his ten or fifteen.

Shane scraped his chair back. "What do you want, chick? Bud Light? Rekorderlig? I'm a bit skint for Guinness."

"I'm driving," Tove snapped. "Just get me a lemonade."

"Right on!" Shane headed to the bar with the empties.

"Wow, Tove. He's only being nice."

Tove rolled their eyes. "He's a flirt! He called me chick. But I guess you wouldn't recognise a flirt if they kissed you on the mouth."

"That's not flirting, that's just assault."

"Sure, and maybe I don't want to flirt with anyone either. It's just games, games, games. Games till I could cut off my ring finger and never risk getting engaged ever again."

"You don't mean that," said Dair.

"Maybe I do." Tove didn't, actually, mean it. More than anything, they wanted to learn how to connect with other people again. But instead they kept starting shit, like now, and couldn't reel it in once they'd begun.

They darted a belligerent look around the pub, searching for eavesdroppers, and caught Liam's gaze. He looked away.

"Of course you know," Tove jabbed. "Even if you weren't invested in my ruinous relationship, you must know the whole story from my traitorous brother."

"Come on Tove," said Dair, "what am I supposed to say when people ask how you're doing? What fun things is she up to in Germany? Oh, she's back here? How come?"

Honestly, Tove would rather people knew about their catastrophic break-up. It was easier to not have to explain. "Nah, tell them the truth," they relented.

"Not like you tell me the truth," Dair grumbled. "All you ever say is you weren't right for each other, but do you think I buy that when you sit there swinging at anyone who so much as perceives you?"

That's what they were afraid of mostly: people knowing too much. They couldn't have everyone finding out how fucking unhinged they were. Better to keep everyone at arm's length with a normal amount of unfriendly and sadistic. At least, their therapist said it was "normal": the traumatised brain working as it should to protect itself. "Normal but eventually maladaptive" was the caveat. Tove was deliberately ignoring the "maladaptive" part at present. Being a cold bitch was better than exposing their eggshell heart to others' duplicity and impermanence.

"Look, getting unengaged isn't even that unusual," said Dair. "Everyone does it."

"It's true," Liam piped up. "My uncle got unengaged three times and unmarried four."

But Tove wanted to be special. That way all the pain they'd gone through in the effort to not get unengaged, and then the excruciating shame of failing, wouldn't be for nothing.

When Shane returned with the drinks, they took theirs outside. Dair's pestering, Liam's doe-eyes, and Shane's flirting were giving them the heebie-jeebies. They weren't ready to flirt with boys who were too skint for Guinness.

It was only half true, they realised as they glided into the smoking area out back, the cold December air grasping their throat. They ventilated into their glass to keep their mouth and nose warm, lemonade speckling their lips with its fizz.

They were more or less over the break-up. Dating again wasn't a horrible prospect. After six months alone, they were lucid enough to understand that their ex was a piece of shit, and they had a good idea now of how they'd like to be treated, and what they'd do differently in the same situations.

What they weren't over was what their therapist called emotional dysregulation, rejection sensitivity dysphoria, intrusive thoughts, social anxiety, and so on... So long as you're doing the healing work within yourself, these things don't preclude you from dating again, she said—because Tove had asked—but they might make it difficult if the people you date don't understand or want to understand what you're going through. "Are you open," she'd asked, "to being understood?" Tove didn't know how to answer that. They couldn't see themself telling Shane how fucked up their brain was, even though it wasn't his fault they had countless triggers and didn't even know what they were till they started spiralling.

Or Effie. She and her niece were two peas in a pod, with all their talk of happiness as if it were really that easy. No way in hell would she acknowledge the bad stuff in their brain. She'd just say good things were on the way or whatever. Tove ached to yell at her that happily-ever-afters weren't real. That was what controlling partners told you, to make you mistake the worms in your belly for butterflies.

"You look like you are thinking sour thoughts," said a voice that could well be in Tove's head.

They swivelled to find Santa smoking a pipe at one of the collapsible outdoor tables. He couldn't really be Santa—of course—but with a big bushy beard and rosy cheeks, along with the complete outfit, he was straight out of a picture book.

"Hello," Tove said, mentally readying a getaway back to Dair.

"I don't mean to disturb you if you don't want to talk to a strange old man," Santa rumbled, "but you do look as though you could do with cheering up."

Tove shrugged.

"Would you like to hear a story?"

Sure, why not?

"Once upon a time," began Santa, "there was a small bear who loved to make tiny books out of paper and glue. Tiny, tiny books no bigger than your thumbnail or mine. And the fairies, well they loved the bear's books. They asked him to make more. So the bear, all excited, packed up his things and left his family to make books for the fairies. He made mysterious books and romantic books and scary books for the bravest of the fairies."

Cold seeped through Tove's jeans at the knees—the worst place—urging them to leave this bizarre conversation already. But something kept them listening, maybe an eerie sense that this Santa knew exactly what they needed to hear.

"However, after a little while of making his tiny books, the bear realised the fairies weren't very nice to him. They became more and more demanding, and expected him to make more and more books of all different sorts. He wasn't even allowed to keep any books for himself anymore. The fairies weren't very nice to him at all."

"I get it," Tove interrupted. "It's me." They were bear and their ex was fairies.

Santa coughed through his pristine beard. "Even worse, working so hard on something so tiny was affecting the bear's eyesight. His eyes became tireder and his vision became blurrier, and soon he could barely see the things in front of him. But at least he knew how to make the tiny books. He could make them with his eyes closed, and in fact he thought that was all he could do now."

"What happened?" Tove asked despite themself.

"Even though the bear couldn't do anything except make tiny books, that was the one thing he didn't want to do anymore. So he left the fairies' workshop. And he stumbled about in the dark for what felt like an eternity. There, after a long, long time of searching, the bear's family found him. They gave him a pair of spectacles, and the bear could see again, though it took a long while to adjust to all the colours and shapes of the world again. He discovered that those who loved him were not like the fairies. They gave him other books, bigger ones. And the bear found out that he didn't have to make tiny books at all. He could make big books, bear-sized books, books that matched himself and didn't hurt his eyes. And so he did make them."

"And is he a famous author now?"

"No. The story is made up. But I hope you had fun with it."

Santa patted his tobacco with his pipe tool, extinguishing the last of the smoulder. And stood. And turned to leave.

"It was nice to meet you," he said. "My name is Bryan; keep an eye out for me on TV over the next week—I'm intending to win the Santa pageant."

"Oh, me too," Tove said.

Santa Bryan scrutinised them like he was looking for a lie. But, all courteous, he said, "Then I wish you the best of luck."

He swept out, leaving Tove with their lemonade and the story of the bear who made tiny books, and a deep sense that there were people in this world who wouldn't betray their trust, who might love them truly.

If only they could tell who those people were.

Sunday

8 days till Christmas

5

Effie's big day dawned with sunshine, the first ray of cosmic benediction in weeks. She was in such a good mood she remembered to take her hormone pill. She wasn't very good at remembering to take it, but at least she didn't need it for birth control. It was only to make her body marginally more habitable.

"What do you think?" she asked Heather while they munched on croissants from Nice Crumb, the bougie bakery down the coast from the Pollack carpark. "The sunshine, is it a sign?"

"Dunno. No clouds to tell from."

"Big flaw in your whole fortune-telling shtick."

"Sometimes we aren't meant to know what's in store for us," Heather said sagely.

"Uh huh." The sun brought hope, and in all seriousness, Effie couldn't imagine what could possibly go wrong today.

The Pollack carpark had transformed into a party place overnight. Besides the pop-up ice-rink, there was a large stage near what would be the shopping centre entrance, a refreshments marquee, a fire pit, and awning-ed stalls lining the carpark perimeter. Someone with either wings or a tall ladder had been very busy hanging lights and banners between the lamp posts. Despite the sunshine, there was fake snow everywhere, a battalion of drones swooping in every now and then to top it up.

"Wow, this is way nicer than the grotto," Heather cooed. "No wonder I was told to take this week off work."

"Weird they didn't ask you to help. Don't you work for the pageant?"

"No. The pageant is a marketing campaign for the new shopping centre. And the carpark is a utility for the shopping centre but privately contracted out. And I work for the contractors. And my boss works with the government."

"So what do you *do*?"

"I stand here all day and write down car licence plates. I'm supposed to make a round of the carpark every twenty minutes. So we know who's parked here and for how long."

"Sounds pointless. You should get a real job."

Effie seethed in the solitude that came with knowing jobs were not real—or certainly none of the trash jobs she'd ever had.

The longer she did it, the less she believed in the point of her current job anyway. Basically, her boss was propositioning a geolocation-based paid parking model. But to make the pitch, they needed a profit projection. And to do that, they needed to know how many people parked here a day, and for how long. That was where she came in, earning peanuts to do something (menial data collection) that had nothing to do with her area of expertise (structural engineering). She was overqualified, and only a temp anyway, and would likely never have a "real job."

It was nearly ten o'clock and Effie had to register by ten. "Now," she said, "can you see your friends? I can't bring you with me."

"I'll check the group chat."

Heather flaunted her phone. Effie contemplated seven-year-olds with smartphones and how at that age she'd carried round her keyring of jelly aliens wishing she had a pearl-pink flippy phone like Lalla or a Blackberry like their dad.

She tagged after her niece, picking through the gathering crowds to the ice-rink. Heather squealed and leaped for her friend group: Avril, her bestie; Zooey, whose hair was dyed purple for the holidays; and Barney, a boy who wore Dondozo facepaint like a full face of make-up.

"Your aunt is entering the pageant?" Zooey exclaimed.

There were some frantic whispers Effie couldn't make out.

"Okay," said Avril, turning round and squaring her off, "but you're a girl. And you're too young to be Santa."

"I've never been so insulted in my life," Effie declared. "There's no one better *suited* than I am." She gestured at her outfit, which, if she said so herself, was excellent.

They exchanged glances. Christ, was there anyone in the world who didn't look her up and down and find her wanting?

"It's her idea of a joke," explained Heather with a scorn that withered Effie up like Shrinkle art.

She shook the bells she'd sewed painstakingly onto her Santa sleeves. "Tell me I'm not Santa enough when I'm literally a walking jingle bell."

"Sorry," said Barney, "but there's a guy at the Santa registration table who has a way better costume."

On the stage was a quirked-up eyeful wearing what could only be a custom-made Santa suit. There was nothing fancy-dress or pound-store about it; exquisite and velvet, it shaped the curve of every muscle as if made by angels. He bent like a million-dollar drinking straw over the registration table, and whipped off his hat and hand-braided beard.

The seven-year-olds gasped.

"Whoa, he's gorgeous!" cried Zooey.

"He's like a perfect turkey dinner," said Heather in a tone of dark, horrifying intentions.

"Isn't he too *young*, like me?" Effie said helplessly. "My god, are you all lovestruck?"

"Aren't you?" asked Barney, almost companionably, while the others gawped.

"I'm a lesbian," Effie told him. "I don't fall in love with men."

"Oh." He paused as if filing away the information for later perusal. "I'm not a lesbian. I can imagine myself falling in love with girls *and* boys. Definitely people like that guy. I hope he's the real Santa."

"Good for you." Effie sighed.

It was coming up on ten o'clock.

"Heather, I have to go. Stick with your friends and text if you need. Okay?"

"Can I have a tenner for the ice-rink?"

Effie eyed the ice; she'd seen what it had done to Amy March in IMAX. Lalla would kill her if Heather hurt herself. But there were ample adults in high-vis jackets circling the rink and a first-aid stop by the skate counter, plus Zooey's dad was hovering inconspicuously ten metres away. Most importantly, Heather's pout threatened an incoming sulk.

She pulled a twenty from her purse. "Ten for skating, ten for emergencies. Or roasted chestnuts. Or toffee apples." She let herself smile. "I hope it's fun."

She watched them bounce away before turning to the stage. To put the Grand Plan into action.

Hot Santa was still filling in his registration form when she arrived, but he didn't look up.

"Hi, here to register?" said the attendant.

"Yes. I'm Effie."

"What an interesting name. Is it short for anything?"

"Effie, short for the effing best Santa, thanks for asking."

Fortunately, they laughed. "Nice to meet you, although I'm contractually obliged to let you know this is a no-swearing contest. Keep it PG for the cameras."

"Got it. No swearing, I *swear*."

"My name's Nowell with a W. They/them pronouns. I'm the production team lead on the ground, so you'll see a lot of me this week. Now, if you could please fill out this form."

As usual, Effie ended up with a pen and a clipboard in the Pollack carpark. Only this time she was doing it for herself. The form wasn't complicated, just the usual stuff—are you eighteen-plus, do you have any medical conditions, will you give up your firstborn child for a skein of gold?

"So if I'm nearly twenty-nine"—Hot Santa fixed his entire concentration on her without a word of warning or introduction—"which year was I born?"

"I don't know," she shot back.

Effie was tall too, and she got the impression he wasn't used to someone meeting his eyes on the same level. Apparently it reminded him of his manners.

"Good morning, I'm DuBois, would you mind helping me?"

"Hi," she said. "I'm Effie, and if you don't know your birth date I can't help you."

He heaved a sigh. "Thought that might be the case. Thanks anyway."

Like a clockwork toy, the wintry himbo twirled back to his clipboard. Jewellery clinked against his pen, a huge signet ring gleaming on his middle finger. Ah yeah, she already knew this guy through and through.

At that point her phone crooned with a text from her mum, asking was she still vegetarian. *Oh fuck off*. She shoved her phone back into her big Santa pocket. Never yet in her life had she gone vegetarian, she'd just refused to eat the turkey one year because it had been smothered in the world's smelliest mustard.

"That was mean," chided DuBois.

"What? Oh." She'd definitely said *fuck off* out loud. "I guess it was mean." She resolved to send an extra-nice text later explaining that she wasn't vegetarian and she'd eat the turkey no matter what fresh condiment hell awaited her.

She finished her form long before DuBois, even though he'd started first, and Nowell shooed her to a marquee behind the stage—the "green room," they called it.

Inside was a bench where four other Santas sat, facing a wall of Perspex screens, behind which was a painted backdrop of a snowscape and a festive-looking log cabin with smoke rising from the chimney. There was a carved chair, a host of lights, and a massive camera on a tripod. She'd be damned if it wasn't a reality TV confessional booth.

"Join us," called a middle-aged woman from the bench. "What's your name?"

Time to meet her fellow contestants!

Effie approached the bench and the impulse to perform came over her. "My name"—she did a little tap dance and twirl—"…is Effie." Her huge sleeves flopped over her jazz hands.

The woman's lips quirked with what Effie hoped was amusement. "Alice. Pleased to meet you." She was sharp and curt and her face betrayed an excellent skincare routine.

On either side of Alice were two old men, one thin and one fat. "Hello Effie, my name is Bryan," said the thin one, at exactly the same time the fat one said, "Good day to you Effie, I am Bryan."

Bryan and Bryan?

"A pleasure to meet you," Effie said.

"The pleasure is mine." And they both offered their left hands to shake at the same time—which, absurdly, she did, giving Bryan her right hand and Bryan her left hand.

The fourth person on the bench she already knew: Tove, drowning unmistakably in their gigantic red suit like a costume of Jonah-in-the-whale.

"Long time no see," Effie remarked.

Tove folded their arms.

A good joke wasted. What a shame. The old Tove would've laughed.

"Ah, you two know each other," said Bryan—okay, this was the fat one, with bright, rosy cheeks and a storybook vibe, he was Bryan #1; the thin, twinky one was Bryan #2.

"We went to school together," Effie explained. "We—"

"We don't know each other *well*," Tove interrupted. They looked down and away.

Effie stared. Not well? Not *well*?! Bloody hell, they'd seen each other's boobs! Didn't Tove remember that day at Petites Rocques beach? Effie had suffered an unfortunate nip-slip while reaching for the sun-cream, and Tove full-on flashed both their tits to make her feel better. How had they gone from best friends to strangers? How had Effie let that happen?

At that moment DuBois arrived, flushed and breathless from his ordeal with the registration form. Nowell was right behind him, launching into a welcome speech before he'd sat down. Effie, distracted, heard approximately none of it. Mercifully, Nowell handed out a booklet explaining the contest rules.

ISLAND SANTA PAGEANT 2023

Sponsored by the Pollack Shopping Centre Group

Welcome, competing Santas! Complete challenges and earn the public vote to become Santa of the Year!

The challenges are as follows:

Monday—Fundraiser and sleepout. Bring a tent and spend the night in the carpark. Contestants are encouraged to raise sponsorship money for a local homeless shelter. Any contestants who do not last the night will be eliminated.

Wednesday—Live interview. We will invite a friend or family member to join you for a live interview on Channel News.

Thursday—Craft sale. Pick a craft of your choice. You will have £100 for materials and 3 hours to produce as many saleable items as you can, then 1 hour to sell them. The contestant who makes the least money will be eliminated.

Friday—Secret challenge… Come prepared for anything.

Saturday—A second chance! If you've been naughty this year, now's the time to make amends.

Sunday—Christmas Eve delivery. Deliver five presents to five locations around Town, and return to the Pollack. The contestant who crosses the finish line last will be eliminated.

Monday—Christmas Day! Local children will vote for their favourite contestant. The contestant winning the most votes will cut the ribbon on the new shopping centre, and their corporate sponsor will receive prize money.

"I'm sorry, *corporate sponsor*?"

Nowell stopped whatever they were saying to glower at her. A vein ticked ominously in their forehead. "Yes, you will be sponsored by one of the chain shops that have a lot in the new shopping centre."

"Do we get to choose?"

"As I was saying, there'll be a meet in the refreshments marquee at half past the hour, and you'll talk with the sponsors and pick one to affiliate with."

"Cool, thanks." Effie reread the page. Nowell couldn't blame her for not listening. Sometimes words meant nothing until she could see their shapes in her mind. Sometimes words meant nothing when she was hot from the memory of her definitely-platonic ex-friend pulling down their bikini top.

"The first interviews will be directly after lunch," Nowell went on. "These ones will be on the stage rather than the set in the green room, so make sure you're ready to introduce yourself to the live crowd as well as Channel News on TV, although the broadcast won't be till tonight."

"Oh lord."

Someone nudged her in the side. She assumed they wanted her to shut up, but when she raised her eyes, Bryan #2 smiled encouragingly. "Take it easy, Effie. I can tell you have an electric personality inside that suit. Lesbian colours, is it? Or am I mistaken?"

She let out her breath in a whoosh, like an Atlantic wind filling a windsurfing sail. And then instinctively began to overshare. "You're dead right. That's why I'm here. To show my niece that Santa can be lesbian."

"Naturally, Santa could be anyone."

"No one really believes I can do this. Or that I'm any good at anything, really. So. I'm here."

"Very brave of you, Effie. Very brave indeed."

Effie glowed. She had no living grandparents, and it wasn't like her own parents were this nice to her.

"See how far you go, Effie. You might surprise yourself. As well as everybody else."

Everybody else. Effie's attention drifted back to Tove, only this time with no thoughts of the beach or the sun-cream or the prettiest tits on the planet. Why were *they* here? Why were *they* entering the Santa of the Year Pageant?

At half ten Effie and the Santas waddled into the refreshments marquee, six red-suited guppies into an ocean of sharp-dressed sharks. Each shark was a representative from one of the big chain shops that would be occupying the new shopping centre. There was a slew of prize money for the sponsor whose Santa won the pageant, so it was in their interests to schmooze.

"I hate this with every fibre of my being," said Tove as the other Santas dispersed to begin conversations.

"Same," said Effie. "What a scam. Hopefully this is only a formality."

"I cannot be affiliated with any of them."

Although not much of Tove was visible under the Santa suit, they were as rigid and tottery as a Swingball post.

"Why don't we team up?" Effie suggested. "We can share equipment and data and get a leg up on everyone else like we used to do in biology lab. And I can talk to the sponsor people so you don't have to."

"No. You're… I just…can't handle this." Tove swivelled on their heel and marched out of the marquee.

Wow. They'd quit this thing already, they wanted to hang out that little. Astonishing human. Effie couldn't believe she'd ever speculated they liked her back.

"Good morning."

Effie jumped. A middle-aged white man stood far too close.

"My name is Dirk, senior marketing officer at Phantasm Sunglasses. Would you be interested in finding out a bit more about us?"

"What?"

"You're entering the pageant, no?"

"Yes."

"Terrific. We have a vision for a young single mum who wants to be Santa of the Year to bring joy to lots of other children and you would be a great fit."

Yikes. Maybe Tove had the right idea getting out while they could.

"Hello there! Oh, I'm sorry, I didn't realise you were already engaged." A young brown woman with chaotically mismatched earrings cut in front of Dirk. Effie recognised the gesture from her clubbing days. Here was her saviour.

"Not at all," Effie said. "Which shop are you from?"

"Ultraspeed. We do mostly sports clothing but some fashion. My name is Ranjula." She flapped the lapels of her navy fleece, showing off some cute embroidery of a little paraglider and the words "Island Paragliding Club" across the breast.

Effie liked Ultraspeed's anti-chafe sports leggings; she could probably be persuaded to re-embrace her inner gym freak with some free stash.

"I'm Effie," she said, so chill she almost convinced herself she had no ulterior motives. "Do you want to sponsor me?"

Ranjula grinned. "First I have to ask how you're intending to present to the public. I overheard something about a matriarchal Santa who's the mother of all and I'm not sure how that would align with our company values. As a mother myself, I strongly feel that sort of presentation has to come from you the contestant, rather than your PR team. What do you think?"

"It actually sucks considering I can't have kids—not easily, anyway. Ovarian cysts, am I right?" Effie rolled her eyes at the sunglasses man. "No, I'm here to prove to my niece that Santa doesn't have to be a straight old dude. I'm the lesbian Santa the world deserves."

"That sounds perfect! We'd be delighted to sponsor you."

Sunglasses man snorted and made a beeline for Alice, who donned a no-bullshit face at his approach. Effie admired a woman who could handle herself. She also admired someone like Tove, who knew what they couldn't handle—the fact that Effie herself was that un-handle-able thing was disheartening, but she'd overthink that later.

So she grabbed free lunch from the buffet with Ranjula, swapping numbers and chatting a while longer. There was no contract, nothing to sign, all she had to do was tell Nowell her choice of sponsor.

After lunch were the interviews. The Santas would be introduced on stage one by one, so they wouldn't get to see each others' interviews until they were televised that evening.

When it was Effie's turn, Nowell found her scarfing the last of the shortbread on the buffet. "Time to go," they said brightly. "Are you ready?"

"Was I supposed to prepare something to say?" said Effie through a mouthful of crumbs.

"Just be yourself. But like I said before, keep it PG."

"Roger that."

Nowell stepped on stage first and the crowd quietened.

"Next up, it's Effie! Come and show us why you're here, Effie."

She scaled the steps onto the stage, adjusted her posture, and strode over. Nowell was in the centre with a microphone and some cue-cards, and a few hundred Christmas shoppers and revellers arced around the stage like a patchwork tree-skirt. Effie wasn't daunted—she'd spent enough of her university Fridays doing comedy sketches in the biggest lecture theatre's free slot after lunch—but she wondered how it'd be for Tove, who used to freeze up when teachers asked them questions in class. That said, she hadn't seen them since they'd stormed out earlier. It really looked like they were gone for good.

"So Effie, give us an idea of who you are and what you do." Nowell tilted the microphone, and Effie checked she was facing the crowd.

"I'm Santa, and I'm here to make sure you're using your hand Santa-tiser after touching those nasty fishing poles over at the Hook-a-Reindeer stall."

The crowd laughed and groaned in a way she'd missed. Exhilarated, she scrambled for her next joke. "You laugh, but there are free sanitiser stands everywhere, for all you who haven't been sleighing attention!"

The crowd laughed again.

"Alright Effie, what are you doing here today? Why do you want to be Santa of the Year?"

"Okay, bear with me. So I took my niece to the Santa grotto yesterday, and was really caught off guard when she told me I couldn't be Santa because I'm a lesbian.

"Santa Claus isn't a universal concept, and actually our understanding of him has been mashed up over and over again, throughout time and many different cultures. So it's weird that in all the books I read as a child, Santa is always this old guy. See, I believe anyone could be Santa. He's not necessarily a dude who rides a flying sleigh pulled by reindeer. Are you Santa?" She pointed at a boy at the front of the audience. "Are you?" A teenager stood near the back of the crowd, arms folded. "You could be. And so could I. Santa could literally be a gay woman, like me. And I want to prove it."

"How interesting," said Nowell, "maybe you're right. And do you think that's how you'll win the contest?"

"Well, like my grandfather—a lovely old man with a big bushy beard who left me the family business, by the way—always told me, you have nothing to lose. Believe in your elf!" (Obviously her dead, ordinary grandfather had never said or done anything of the kind.)

Nowell's eyelids drooped momentarily as if to hide an eye-roll. "Now tell me, do you know what your talent is going to be for the craft challenge?"

"Of course." Effie hadn't thought about it at all. "I can bend wire into animals, like a balloon artist. I call it merry Christ-moose!"

"Very original," commented Nowell. "And tell me who's sponsoring you through the pageant?"

Effie described Ultraspeed, rattling off the spiel Ranjula had given her. It hurt, but this sponsor stuff was only a bump on her road to victory.

"How will you approach the other contestants? Do you think you'll make any friends? Or do you see them as enemies?"

Now this was an interesting question. "I'm not sure. I have a history of whirlwind friendships and then getting dropped for someone better, but I think…" and she imagined Tove watching her on TV later "…I hope I can make a real friend this time." Even if that friend wasn't Tove, who'd made their disdain clear. Maybe she was better off without Tove. Less competition. Less distraction.

Typically, Effie's loyal lesbian heart found it harder to let go.

6

An old fishing pier unrolled behind the shopping centre, below the sea wall encircling the Pollack site. After rushing out of the refreshments marquee, Tove came here, to escape all those pumped-up marketing egos hoping to put their names on their Santa suit. They couldn't see why someone else should win the prize money when they'd be the one doing all the work. Embarrassingly, the discovery that this very corporate pageant featured unavoidable, insurmountable corporatism made them want to ugly cry.

Maybe they should've told Effie it wasn't her that had them overwhelmed and ready to run. Or…maybe it was just her. Her and her kind, unexpected offer to team up. It was kindness they couldn't believe they deserved, even though Effie had never really been one for ulterior motives. Not secret, conscious ones anyway. She couldn't hide her feelings for shit.

Either way, between Effie and the marketing goons, they couldn't stay in that marquee.

So they'd fled, and found the old fishing pier instead. Relieved to find the land reclaim project had left it untouched, they squatted on the steps and asked themself if they were cut out to be in the pageant. The answer, really, was no.

While they waited for the adrenaline to fade, Tove watched the tide lapping at the granite. Soon the pier would be underwater. They set a challenge: if they could walk down the pier before the tide came up—and not merely walk, but strut like it was a goddamn catwalk—then they could do the pageant.

You haven't a hope. All they see is a child in a big red coat. Nobody will take you seriously.

They yanked their hat over their ears to block out the whispers in their head. It was easy to believe, when half their thoughts were in his voice, that all they needed to do was run far enough, fast enough, to escape him. Yet, looking around, they were alone. He wasn't near them now; the source of the bad thoughts was themself.

Of course, that wasn't strictly true. Because with their phone balanced in their lap, a week-old message preview topped their lockscreen notifications.

It began, **Hey, it's been a while**

The preview, if they dragged downwards, would show another seven lines. Whatever came after that, they'd have to open the message to see. And if they opened the message, they'd have to reply to it. Or at the very least, they'd have to confront the question of whether to reply.

They realised they were still clutching their hat, weighing it down with their arms. Their other secret was that underneath the oversized Santa hat was a pastel pink bobble hat—Effie's hat, to be precise. They'd die if Effie knew how her hat wrapped their head in a warm hug, massaging their temples and holding their brain in place. It smelled of her. Ten years, and she smelled the same. She smelled of safety, of childhood, of a time before the slow crumbling of Tove's soul. They were bolstered, almost restored, by the reminder that they were once a different person with friends and hobbies and hopefulness.

Effie was still too gorgeous and overwhelming to even think about. Her hat, though, they'd take that.

The sea began to kick the occasional wave over the side of the pier, sending spray to tickle their eyebrows. Their self-imposed challenge had a fast-approaching expiry.

They read the rest of the message preview:

Hey, it's been a while… I know you left in a hurry, and I understand why, after what I put you through… I hope you are doing well, wherever you are. I am doing okay – I have a new coworker, a very sweet and timid woman, who reminds me a bit of you, hence I have been thinking about you. Now this may be a bit off the wall, but Christmas is coming up, and since it is a time to love one another, I wondered if

They bristled, as they always did, when they read those faceless words. They itched to open the message and discover what their ex "wondered," though they had a good guess. He wanted them to forgive him, perhaps take him back. He was going to apologise for "what I put you through."

It wasn't an apology they wanted to read. Many controlling and manipulative people, they had learned, had a way with words. Tove's ex, in particular, had spent years studying Tove specifically, and they had a long track record of giving in to him. Although they'd been broken up six months, they couldn't trust themself to react logically to anything he said.

Sweet and timid their ass. Worn down and gaslit, more like. Maybe his new coworker was the same.

What reading the message preview did was reignite their desire to participate in the pageant. Frivolous and profit-driven as it was, they didn't want it to be game over. They had a mission. They didn't want to hear "Christmas is a time to love one another" ever again. Respectfully, they would like a few people to think twice. That was all. They didn't need to win the pageant or anything, just get far enough to make their point.

They got up. They had to clamp their Santa pants to their hips with their elbows, but managed a swagger as they stepped out along the pier. In reality, with the water spooling across the walkway, it was less like working the catwalk and more like walking the plank, but a sense of confidence rushed through their veins nevertheless. They wanted to face this. They *could* face this.

Five minutes later they slipped past the bustling refreshments marquee and into the green room, where Nowell was listing instructions to a stage crew. Nerves tightened in their stomach at the thought of speaking to the wailing crowd outside later, so they sat on the bench and waited for the queasiness to pass—and for Nowell to notice them.

"Hello," Nowell said a short while later, as the crew hopped to it. "Have you found a sponsor?"

"I can't," Tove told them. "It goes against everything I stand for."

"Huh." Nowell peered down, towering and unsympathetic. But then they folded their clipboard under their arm and slid onto the bench. "What's up?"

Tove's breath hitched. *Don't. Cry.* "I have a different idea." If they admitted how they felt, there'd be no escaping tears. So they did the next best worst thing: admitted what they wanted.

When they were done explaining, Nowell smiled. They placed a hand on Tove's shoulder, so light they couldn't feel it through their thick suit. "I think I can make that happen," they said. "It's not against any rules as far as I know. And if it is, I think I can plead a case to the big dogs."

"Thank you." Tove exhaled, relaxed for the first time that day.

"I do think, however, that you'll have to play up your motives for entering the pageant. That's what will get this passed. Narratives make reality TV more entertaining."

They swallowed. "I'm not playing anything up. I'm just doing the best I can do."

"Sure." Nowell didn't understand why they had to clarify, but at least they weren't arguing. "I'll have to make a phone call before your interview, so you'll be on stage last. Will you be ready?"

To project their voice over a few hundred uncaring heads? Definitely not.

But, remembering the message on their phone, this would be a piece of cake compared to explaining themself to that one person determined not to listen.

"I'll be ready," they promised. "Can I watch the other interviews while I wait?"

"Sure, I'll find you a seat in the wings."

And that's how they ended up in the dark beside the stage, watching Effie stride under the lights like an equestrienne in a period drama. Her confidence oddly calmed them, as they relinquished their attention to her. While she was making puns to boo at, stirring them almost to smiling, there was no temptation to brood on their problems.

It hit them, really hit them, that they and Effie, and all their messy past, and their personal frustrations with how glib she was in direct contrast to their inner turmoil, were all jumbled together in the pageant drama now. They were rivals as well as long-lost friends.

Friends? Was that on their mind? Could they ever possibly become friends again?

The bubble of anticipation in their chest took them by surprise. They might have to confront their feelings about Effie after all—before, maybe, they confronted the message in their phone, and Christmas, and themself. Maybe, some part of them whispered, Effie could help them tackle those things, like she'd offered two hours ago, like they'd wanted years ago.

Effie was the only person whose help they'd ever wanted.

7

After hanging out with Heather and her cronies at the Pollack all afternoon, Effie simply had to feed Melchior once again.

The indignant meowing began the second she put the key in the lock. *You've been out all weekend? Weekends are our time.* Effie placated her girl with love and scritches and the promise that she'd be back this evening for proper. After a while Melchior got bored and headed to the window to make quacking noises at the seagulls on the flat roof below. Even though Effie knew she would, it was still a relief to be forgiven.

"Quack, quack!" went her cat.

"She's got the wrong bird!" Heather cried delightedly. "She's just like you."

"What's that supposed to mean?" Effie demanded. "I've never even had a girlfriend."

Heather scowled, her lack of understanding translating into annoyance. "No, I mean she's weird like you."

"And what makes me weird?"

"You have literally no friends. There's got to be a reason for that."

Effie wished for a way to turn back time so she never asked. She didn't need Heather to notice how goddamn alone she was. She didn't need anyone commenting on it as if she didn't lament every day what her life had become. She just wanted someone to like her, what had a girl to do?

"Get your shoes on," was all she said. "I've got to get you home to your parents so I can be truly alone once again as I'm meant to be."

"Don't be like that," Heather chided.

But Effie didn't take the bait.

Lalla and Liam were back from their staycation weekend. Effie was dying to be rid of her social duties, but her unstoppable niece convinced her parents to put off their TV catch-up and watch the pageant interview broadcast, and she decided to stay. After all, her cold flat didn't have a TV licence.

She soon regretted it. Not one of her relatives was rooting for her.

"Your puns are dreadful," Lalla said as she dropped her "sleighing attention" one. "Why did you do that?"

"I am hilarious," Effie countered, upset that her sister couldn't say anything nice about her ever.

Lalla looked rough, claiming a stubborn hangover from Friday's work do, and taking it out on Effie. "I don't know why you bother trying to be funny."

That one stung like seawater on a grazed elbow. "I *am* funny. And I know it, so don't try to tell me otherwise."

"She is funny." Liam defended her half-arsedly at best.

It only got worse when Bryan #1 took to the stage.

"Now he's the storybook Santa," said Liam. "Even his beard is real. Mark my words, he'll win."

"Were you even listening to TV me moments ago?" Effie said. "*I'm* going to win."

Bryan #1 proceeded to compliment Nowell's button-up shirt because it "would make top-notch curtains." Liam was about to eat his words, but it turned out Bryan #1 was a retired carpenter and he was going to make a doll's house for the craft sale.

"Would you like one of those doll's houses if they look nice, sweetie?" Liam asked Heather.

Her eyes lit up like Christingle candles. "Yeah, maybe."

"Will you buy my craft too?" Effie said pettily.

"Sure, what are you doing again?"

"Wire animals. I just said it on telly."

Lalla groaned. "Oh no, you need my help, don't you?"

"I was going to ask another day, but yeah. Please?"

Lalla was excellent at making earrings. She'd do it for a living if it sustained their lifestyle—a mortgage, a kid, meal-kits twice a week, and an annual holiday, which even to Effie, who had none of these things, didn't seem exactly frivolous.

"Text me in the week." She waved Effie away.

Heather snickered.

Effie felt like a fool. She'd leave if she didn't think they'd backtalk her for being "sensitive" as soon as she shut the door. Not that she cared overly much, but with only her own self to reassure her, eventually she'd believe they were right.

Next up was Alice, power-granny extraordinaire. She was early fifties, had three children and eight grandchildren, volunteered for a medical charity for twenty years, and since retiring had climbed such notable earthly appendages as Kilimanjaro, Mont Blanc, and Mount Kenya.

Bryan #2 followed smoothly. Like an evolved, futuristic Santa, he wore a practical Santa costume that looked more like a spacesuit. His craft was remote-control toys and he made drone-building tutorials on TikTok. He wasn't a traditional Santa like Bryan #1, but he'd fly with Heather's generation—that is, if she and her friends weren't already enamoured with DuBois…

"I want him to win *so bad*!" she squeaked when he appeared on the screen.

DuBois prattled about his horse, his motorboat, his upbringing in the gated neighbourhood on the cliff overlooking Town, where everyone had private pools and guard dogs. Then he revealed that his craft was baking.

Liam and Lalla rolled their noses. They were that special brand of self-made millennial who hated young, generationally rich people for being younger and richer than them, and because they wanted everyone to suffer the same as they had to get where they were. Since Effie hadn't really made a life for herself yet, she only, mostly, uncomplicatedly hated DuBois for being rich.

But she had shaken hands with a marketing officer from a large chain that very morning, so her anti-capitalism was feeling rather shallow.

It felt even more shallow when Tove—still in it, apparently—told Nowell and the audience that instead of picking a sponsor, they'd partnered with a local charity who'd get the prize money if they won. There had been no reason for Effie to worry about their stage fright; although not the most animated, they spoke well. Sort of like stop motion, rigid but deliberate and kind of fascinating.

Liam squinted at the TV. "Is that… It must be."

"What?" Lalla asked.

"My friend's sister, Tove. She recently came back to the Island after…I don't know, it was a strange story."

"Tove? Effie had a friend called Tove when she was a teenager. Eh, Effie?"

"Yeah, same person."

Effie avoided Liam's questioning eyes in the reflective glass of the booze cabinet. She wanted to ask about the "strange story," but couldn't. She was fifteen again and trying not to mention Tove's name in case her family somehow guessed they'd kissed. Even though no one knew she was gay at that point. *Because* no one knew she was gay at that point.

She hated that after she left, Liam would tell Lalla the "strange story" and Effie would never be any the wiser. She felt trapped, in the same way as back then, when Tove had said nothing, and she'd opened and closed her mouth, and they'd stared at each other until some random boy called Aaron who was another girl's date stumbled on them there in the honeysuckle. He came to piss, he said, and Tove, breathless as if using him as a desperate excuse to get away from Effie, said *I'll help you find somewhere.* And then they vanished, and a few weeks later he'd dumped his girlfriend and was going out with Tove.

That was the entire story. Effie didn't interfere, how could she? Barge into their brand-new exciting relationship and say *hi Tove I like you and also I'm gay, how about you?* They had a *boyfriend.* They had their happily-ever-after. And not with her. What was a life-changing kiss for Effie had to have been a mistake for Tove.

Effie was glad she hadn't spilled her lovestruck guts back then. Today she'd suggesting teaming up, and gotten brutally shot down. It would've been that times a thousand.

"So why are you in the pageant, Tove?" asked Nowell on TV.

"I'm here to give visibility to people who don't like Christmas. We're not all Scrooges. For some of us, Christmas-time means trauma—cold nights when we couldn't afford heating, a bereavement or loneliness when we were supposed to have our loved ones around us, or maybe we become depressed at the passage of time represented by yet another Christmas. Not to mention the many people who don't and never have celebrated Christmas. Some of us dread the words 'Happy Christmas.' Because what's happy about it when you're reliving some of the worst days of your life? If that's you, I see you. What you feel is real. I hope the rest of the year treats you better than Christmas does."

Effie was stunned. Who was this twenty-five-year-old Tove, with the cold passion and the anger? Their pixel-sharp stare raised goosebumps. Conviction made them radiant. Beautiful.

"This society puts too much pressure on us to be happy at Christmas," Tove went on, "and I would like to see more helping of the vulnerable people in our society, rather than the wilful ignorance which comes with the rituals and gluttony we've all gotten used to. That's the love and generosity I want Christmas to mean to me. That's what I would like the figure of Santa to mean to you."

Monday

7 days till Christmas

8

Blissfully, the house was empty.

Once upon a time, Tove would be sneaking into their parents' room to try out Mum's make-up. In their teens, it would be stealing sips of alcohol from under the stairs. In the apartment in Germany, they'd set an alarm for when they expected Aaron to return, and spend the time doing something *they* wanted to do. Clean things the way they liked them cleaned; message back the friends he didn't like; stare at their trumpet and remember playing it; mostly, though, they'd nap away their feelings.

Today, although napping always sounded nice, they had another plan. Tonight was the sleep-out. They would be spending the night in the Pollack carpark. And for that, they needed a tent.

First port of call was the eaves. Upstairs was littered with dilapidated boxes full of Christmas decorations, the same ones they'd retrieved on Friday, when Mum called them "woman." Tove pushed them away and crawled into the eaves. If any of the family owned a tent, it would be here.

With rising adrenaline, they pushed and pulled storage boxes, restacked them, decimating Mum's filing system. At one point a nail snagged their hair. As a follicle ripped from their head, the detached strand glinting above them, they fought a panic attack that had no business being as intense as it wanted to be. Before continuing, they ran downstairs and yanked Effie's hat onto their head, tucking all their hair inside it. Then they searched onwards. Right at the back in the shadows they found a deep box that could conceivably hold a tent. Although it weighed nothing, it was a struggle to tug it into the daylight, and when they did, it threw them for a loop.

TOVE CHILDHOOD, the top of the box read in thick black marker.

Crap. A pulse of anger streaked to the centre of their brain. How could Mum keep something like this, when they'd spent a decade trying to shed their "childish tendencies"? Again there was Aaron's voice in their head, telling them, "Let it all go. You don't need any of it."

It was funny to think that, after all the pieces of themself they'd snapped and binned, all the bridges they'd burned in the name of love, and how close they'd been to that perfect, isolated marriage, they had ended up in their mum's house after all, faced with all the things they'd left behind.

They were calmed, actually, by the idea that there was something left—something they had before they knew Aaron, or even Effie. Perhaps if they opened this box, they could find something they'd lost long ago.

They pried open the wings.

Colour burst from the box. A hundred soft toys sprung up and spilled down the sides, free at last. Parrots and bears and penguins and their beautiful round Wailord. Oberon, the ash-brown

Guernsey Teddy gifted to them by their mum as a baby, their oldest and most precious friend. They ploughed their hands into the mountain of faux fur. The curves, the varying firmness, the shiny plastic of eyes and noses—each touch was familiar. Every furry face was one they knew in their sleep. They revisited each one, trying to remember all their names. Clutching Oberon to their chest, they wondered if he was the bear from Bryan's story. Had Oberon been making tiny books for the abusive fairies all the time Tove had been with Aaron? They resolved to take extra good care of him from now on. He deserved all the niceness and gentleness in the world.

All of a sudden, they knew what to do.

Tove piled the toys back in the box and bumped it down the stairs to their room. There the work began. Toy by toy, they patched over the memories of their broken relationship. No more dent in the wall where Aaron had punched above their head. No more books he used to ridicule them for reading. No more bare bed, the site of many a night of make-up sex that never truly erased the hurt—not to mention the night they decided to move to Germany, to escape all the other people in their lives, who, he'd convinced them, were trying to sabotage them. (Perhaps they were.)

All of it was hidden by toys.

A sense of peace washed over them as they worked. It was a distraction, sure. Temporary relief from all the things they were trying to work through in therapy. They didn't care how temporary. This room had not felt so safe in years.

At the bottom of the box was a tiny toy keyboard. Their first musical instrument.

Out of curiosity more than anything, they switched it on and tried a key. Astonishingly, it played. They pressed another key and then another. The sound was tinny, and it only played four notes at a time, but their heart beat like a drum as they made music once again. They played nursery rhymes, simple chords, silly ditties from songs they knew backwards and upside down.

There was nothing more natural, and yet they couldn't help but desire more than toy keyboards.

They reached for their trumpet case under the bed, unlatched it and lifted the lid. They stared at their instrument. Polished and golden, Felicity shone back.

They hooked their thumb into the ring and placed their fingertips on the valves. They compressed easily. Even though they hadn't played in years, they'd been caring for her all this time, oiling the valves, greasing the slides, polishing the lacquer. They couldn't bear for her to fall into disrepair. It was like a ritual. Felicity was…one of those things they couldn't fully leave behind, even though Aaron wanted them to.

They picked up their girl, testing her weight. Their arms and fingers weren't as strong as they used to be.

With a deep breath, they brought her to their lips.

A shudder zipped through them and their teeth clanged on the cold metal, drawing blood from their lip. They dropped their trumpet back in the case and snapped it shut, heart racing.

Urgency took hold, like they were missing something, like there was something they were supposed to be doing before touching their trumpet. Something they had to figure out.

That's right. They needed a tent.

And it hit them. Effie would be looking for a tent too.

They recalled her offer to team up. The way they'd responded—saying "no" and rushing out—filled them with remorse. She was inviting them to trust her, and they'd buckled.

Effie's words from the interview yesterday rang in their ears: "I hope I can make a real friend this time."

This was it. They felt ready. Ready to reach out. Ready to try. *Here I come, world. Please be nice.*

9

Although days off were great, making a change from the past sixteen Mondays, Effie was quickly realising her week off wasn't going to be the wild, ice-cream and *Shrek*–packed one she'd imagined when she booked leave. She was going to have to actually do stuff.

Tonight was the fundraiser. There was a seminar open to the public at five o'clock with some events to raise money for a homeless shelter. Then everyone would leave and the six Santa contestants would spend the night in the carpark.

She was digging through drawers in search of her thermals when a muffled *ding* from the bed drew her attention. As usual, Melchior sat on her phone the way a bird incubates its eggs, purring ominously. She loved the warm little rectangle that vibrated sometimes and made her belly feel nice.

"Alright, scheming moggie," said Effie.

Melchior blinked and mewed, kitten-like, acting all cute to confuse Effie's executive function.

Effie shook her head, refusing to be baited. "You've made a fatal miscalculation." She put her hand out, and as Melchior leaned into it, transforming from a loaf to a croissant, swiped her phone from the jungle of fur.

Melchior sad-meowed as she checked the notification.

A Facebook friend request from Tove. Effie read and reread the notification, scarcely taking the words in as her phone shook in her trembling hand. She vowed never to dismiss this notification, with the same conviction she'd vowed as an eight-year-old never to wash the finger Floof the Rabbit had licked at the petting zoo.

Hold on. Tove had really unfriended her sometime in the last decade. Some nerve!

While stroking Melchior to appease her, Effie accepted the request—after all, being petty about it might cost her...well, whatever it was Tove wanted.

Sure enough, a message appeared in her inbox moments later: **Hey Effie, do you have any spare tents kicking about? Embarrassing I know but I haven't been camping recently. Or ever.**

Effie clicked her tongue, and she swore her plants heard because they looked at her funny with their non-existent eyes. She hadn't even thought about the tent.

I don't have a tent either but I know where to get some

Tove said, **I'll pick you up after lunch?**

The idea of Tove picking her up—in their car—to hang out—sent Effie's heartbeat into a frenzy. She had to reply, and quick, before they changed their mind. **Meet me here at 3**, she texted, and sent the location of the hairdresser under her flat.

By three o'clock she'd lunched, packed a bag of necessities, and made sure her fridge was stocked with everything she'd want to eat tomorrow after the sleep-out: milk for tea, ingredients for apple and chestnut soup, and bacon for her hangover/sleepless night special: the infallible bacon sarnie.

She apologised profusely to Melchior that she'd be gone for yet another night and rushed downstairs to where Tove's Ford Fiesta hummed in the street.

"Hello." She swung into the passenger seat and slammed the door. "How are you?"

"Navigate me," said Tove by way of reply. Their expression was impenetrable.

"We're going to the outdoor adventure store. Retail outlet up north."

"Oh that's easy, why didn't you say before?"

"Didn't want you going without me. You're my ride."

"Watch your mouth, passenger. My car has a merciless eject button."

"What, your like 2006 Ford Fiesta?"

"Yep, hotrodded to hell."

"Which button is it?" Effie teased, hovering her finger over the knobs on the ancient sound system. "This one? *This* one?"

"Get off!"

Tove swatted her hand away, knocking the power knob. The radio came on, and it was Nowell's voice advertising the event today. Tove reached to turn it off.

"Leave it on if you like," Effie suggested. "It's cool."

Together they listened to Nowell's pattering, occasionally interjected by the interviewer, a local radio personality. Effie listened out for her name, and for Tove's, but they were talking about the seminar.

She grew bored after a while. "So. You deleted me on Facebook?"

"Yeah." Tove didn't miss a beat. "You were never supposed to know. We weren't ever going to meet again."

"I wouldn't have unfriended you."

"So? We're not like each other. And that's okay."

"But why did you? I thought we were…friends."

"Look, it's not personal. I hate Facebook—all the bleeding weddings and babies and wine emojis and racism and bad memes stolen from Twitter, and did I mention the *weddings*, hell no. I try to keep my friend list clean at the very least, so I don't have to see my preschool bully marrying the prick who chewed my aqua-blue gel pen in Year 6."

"You have a *really* short friend list, Tove."

"Well how many of your Facebook friends do you ever speak to? All 800 of them?"

"No, but I keep people I like and might want to hang out with in the future."

"*Really*?" It wasn't quite an incredulous *really*, or an exasperated one even, but the kind of *really* you say with a squint and a sceptical smirk.

"What do you mean by that?" Effie asked.

"Just saying, but you haven't messaged me once in the past decade."

"How could I, you deleted me on Facebook, remember?"

"Which you only found out today, because you never checked."

"It's not like you tried to reach out either."

Tove honest-to-dog grunted.

"So what's up? Did I do something?"

They halted at some traffic lights, and Tove's side-eye pierced Effie's defences. Their gaze had that same empty look as Friday in the carpark.

"Do you really want to push this?" they said.

"Yes."

"Fine. You thought we were friends. So did I. But then everything happened all at once and then you were gone."

What was she supposed to say to that? Tove's scowl radiated blame, but Effie was still missing half the story. Half of their shared story, but also half of *Tove's* story. If Effie was really supposed to shoulder the frustration they were firing at her, she was going to need more details. Did they have so few Facebook friends because they hated Facebook, preferred keeping the numbers low? Or were they…well, isolating themself? A bit of both? How were either of those things her fault? What was Tove holding back?

Effie's belly bubbled with the discomfort of having forced something she wasn't ready for. She floundered for something else to talk about. "So do you use other social media?"

"I prefer Instagram to Facebook. Still bad, but bearable."

"Let me guess, too many weddings?"

No response.

"Oh well, let's add each other on Insta, and then you can unfriend me on Facebook again."

"Super funny, Effie."

They hated *all* her jokes. God, they were worse company than her family.

"I'll tell you who you remind me of," Tove remarked, this time unprompted. "Romola Garai in the 2009 BBC adaptation of *Emma*."

"What?"

"You know, big forehead, absurd charisma you don't even know how to wield, using your charm to cover up your social faux pas."

"My what?" Effie repeated.

"And I have to say, your performance is electrifying. Stellar acting. I'd almost be taken in by your utterly magnetic personality."

The sarcasm shot pain across Effie's body. Her mother telling her she was boring was like whiplash; Tove telling her she was pretending *not* to be boring was a butcher's blade slicing and dicing the vulnerable pieces of her heart.

"If I take you at face value," she said, barely keeping the wobble from her voice, "can I take that as a compliment?"

Tove left her hanging with a scoff.

On the radio, Nowell was talking about the next round of interviews, which would take place Wednesday evening.

"That's right, we're inviting someone close to each contestant to tell us a bit more about them."

Tove's fingers clenched on the steering wheel. The leather squeaked under their tightening grip.

Effie secretly inspected them. Maybe it wasn't that their eyes looked empty, but when they showed no other expression the purple patches under their lashes grew darker. Even so, if she averted her gaze, Tove had the same aura as ever: they glowed in some real, essential way that had nothing to do with the facts of the past or the present, and more to do with how their soul had persisted after all these years even without Effie watching. Tove was a whole person. They'd had ten years of growing and learning and experiencing...just as Effie had.

Again, she tried to engage. "Who do you think they'll get on for you? For that interview on Wednesday?"

"Oh my *god*, give it a rest already."

So Tove really had messaged earlier intending to hang out in silence. In fairness, Effie had been kind of provocative. Anyone could've guessed that everything she wanted to talk about was a sore point with Tove, a person who was plainly blighted by her existence.

And it dawned on Effie that it was shitty to enter the pageant in the first place, when Tove obviously didn't want to be anywhere near her.

"Hey, I'm sorry—" she began.

"For what?"

Their curt tone pinched the words from her tongue. "Uh..." She fumbled for what she was trying to say. "I... Um... Sorry for talking." Now she wasn't certain what she was even apologising for. Tove was the one who couldn't meet her halfway. After all, *they'd* messaged *her* that morning.

"Just forget it."

Apology declined, Effie had one idea left to get a conversation started. One more try.

"Okay, what *do* you want to talk about?"

Tove's deathgrip on the steering wheel loosened. "I'll tell you what I don't want to talk about. My family and friends, my past, your past, your apologies. The list is not exhaustive and I reserve the right to add to it at will."

Their teasing tone tickled the special spot Effie kept for them in her soul. No matter how irritable they were, how changeable, the Tove she was friends with was still there. Still *here*. So what the hell had them tearing holes in her?

Deep breaths, Effie. Be honest about how you feel. And then, whatever Tove says, respect their boundaries. Effie shuddered, knowing this could be the end.

"I'd love to get to know you again," she said, taking the icy plunge, "but if you don't want me to try, that's cool."

Tove's lips—the left side, the side she could see—twitched ever so slightly upwards. "You can try," they said. "Good luck though. I'm not very friendly."

Effie couldn't speak for the way her heart was thumping. This might be the only encouragement Tove had given since they'd run into each other on Friday. And what did it take? Honesty, earnestness, showing respect for what *they* wanted.

"Noted," she said.

"Some say I'm a real bitch."

Effie studied them. The mood had shifted again, away from her, and drifting into the aether. Their faraway expression reminded her of how Lalla used to get sometimes in the months after Heather was born. Postnatal depression, people called it. Effie used to visit her and Liam's poky flat after school and do her homework between laundry loads. Lalla was there, of course, although it didn't seem like it most of the time. After a while Effie learned some grounding exercises and figured out how to use them with Lalla, and eventually Lalla went to see a counsellor, and Effie went to uni, and they didn't really speak of it again.

There was something about Tove now that seemed untethered in the same way, like they were floating through space—a particular space maybe, one where people, or someone, called them "bitch."

"I'd never call you that." Effie spoke softly but firmly. "Unless you were, like, *into* that in a kinky way. I'm not, particularly, but, well, I'd bend for the right person."

Tove's sharp intake of breath cut the air and they seemed to gather themself back into their body and being. A tiny laugh escaped their lips on the exhale.

"You really cut to the chase, don't you?"

"It's my superpower."

"But you're not a kinky Santa?"

Effie snorted. "Sure I am, if your kink is Christmas and cunnilingus and saying *please* and *thank you*. Compassionate, gentle sex that's so breathtakingly, intimately festive."

"I'm not into degradation either," Tove said quietly. "But I think I could get behind politeness and respect. Is that your other superpower?"

It had started as a joke, but Effie blossomed at the idea that she and Tove might be making some kind of implicit sex pact, that their preferences might align. Still, she couldn't take it to heart. Tove didn't *really* want to sleep with her. She kept the jovial tone as she replied, "That and my third superpower, which is giving the best head of your life. Jingle bells or no jingle bells."

Tove's eyes widened into round rings of scandalised amazement. Their expression was exquisite; their cheek muscles could hold up a bridge.

"You looked like you were a million miles away a moment ago. Glad to see you're back."

"I cannot believe your go-to grounding technique is talking about eating pussy."

They said it so casual, so unafraid: "eating pussy." Effie bit her lip, afraid of the hunger growling in her soul. Tove was always like that—they'd take what you said and pry your jaw open and feed it back into your mouth, make you own it. They'd make you want to own it, if only so they might come back and make you do it all over again.

"It worked, didn't it? I'm a master at scaring the living daylights out of people who pass as allocishet."

"Whoa, hold it! Four superpowers isn't allowed! Prohibited, in fact!"

"You try taking a single one of those away from me," Effie challenged.

Her heart slammed against her chest. She'd wondered if Tove would fly off the handle at "people who pass," but there was no reaction. No reaction from the they/she who'd kissed her back in the bushes at Winter Ball.

God help her, she might be falling for them all over again.

10

"Cheerie!"

Crap. Spotted! Tove made themself extremely busy with the pricetag of a tent as a worker in the outdoor store approached their loitering ass.

"Hi, can I help?"

"Hello," said Effie.

Effie! That traitor, bringing a stranger into their fold to ogle at their ineptitude.

"We're looking for tents," Effie said. "Do you have anything cheaper than the ones on display? It's only for one night."

Tove felt themself emotionally shrinking. As Effie took the lead on the conversation side of things, they did their semi-regular scope-out of the store, checking for—well, checking for people they knew, memories that could be triggered, existential threats conjured from within their mind.

"Wait-here-I'll-be-right-back," said the worker.

As Effie waited, Tove took her in, up and down. She stood in idle animation, swinging her arms loosely, but otherwise vacant in the way she gazed straight ahead. A clockwork toy, lonely and nervous and waiting for someone to interact with, someone to play with her. Familiar affection bloomed in Tove's chest, like the warm bubble of sound from a cornet. All at once they regretted being so rude in the car. Here they were, wanting to make Christmas better for the people they didn't know, and they were ignoring the people right in front of them!

Oh, she was looking at them too. When did she turn her head?

"What's up?" Tove asked softly, something like an apology taking shape under their tongue.

"Hm, uh, I was wishing I had a dishwasher," Effie rattled, nonsequitur as ever. "That said, you should, uh, see my jacuzzi bath—"

"Hello, are you looking for an affordable tent? We have some collapsible models."

They both startled. A different, older worker, with a badge reading STORE MANAGER, held out a bundle flatpacked into a circle.

"Perfect," Tove faltered without looking at the bundle. They felt snuck up on, and guilty for not paying attention to their surroundings even for that split-second. Effie really had them in their own falsely comfortable little world there.

"Wait," Effie intervened. "Are you sure you don't want something better, Tove? Warmer?"

"The tent's just for optics." Tove shrugged. "This is fine. But we'll need two tents."

"It's big enough for two," the manager explained.

Tove's cheeks flamed, and when they looked over, a flush crept up Effie's throat like a sunrise reflected in brass.

"That's not it," Effie insisted in a rush. "We're doing a sleep-out tonight for the homeless shelter. Would you be interested in donating?"

"Ah, you're the Santas! I saw you on the News last night."

Oh, she was good. Effie was *good*. This was exactly what Tove wanted—a chance to do something worthwhile with the visibility they got as a Santa. They couldn't believe they hadn't thought of this. And Effie—unreliability personified—had.

Steeling the molten anxiety in their stomach, Tove recited the stats they'd heard on the car radio and explained where the money would be going. Five minutes later, the manager agreed to sponsor them both for the night, as well as donate tents and winter sleeping bags to the shelter.

"Whoa," Effie hissed as they wound through the aisles to the exit with their two collapsible tents in hand. "So while I was trying to make banal conversation in the car, you were actually listening to the radio? And then to convince the manager to donate? I'd love to be the kind of person who helps people."

Tove was shaking from how hard it had been to stand there and ask the manager for something. "You literally are. It was your idea to ask them to donate, remember?"

"Sure, but I couldn't follow through like you did."

"You totally could," they said, almost aggressively. "You were always good at being there for people." *At being there for me*, they didn't say. *Until you weren't*, they extra didn't say.

"Nah, I'm no good at helping people. Who am I helping anyway? No one needs my help."

She couldn't be serious. Self-deprecation did not become someone as naturally kind and selfless as Effie. "What do you mean? Loads of people need help. Even the ones who you think don't. So why not *your* help?"

"Well, how do I help them? What do I really have to offer?"

"Literally anything, Effie. C'mon, you're good at this when you're not telling yourself you're not."

Tove led the way to the car, but Effie hung back until they opened the passenger door for her. As if she really thought they'd drive off without her.

"So..." she began as they revved up, "how can I help *you*, Tove?"

They'd thought she'd never ask. "Help me get through this pageant. I want a shot at winning the final vote. I want to get as far as possible, and do what I can throughout the process to make Christmas better for everyone." *Which, apparently—but kind of obviously—you are better at than me.*

"Before, when I suggested teaming up, you said no."

Tove thought back to the moment Effie had asked, in the marquee surrounded by marketing reps. How their heart pounded and their head fogged. "That was a mistake," they said carefully. "I needed space."

They felt the scrutiny of Effie's eyes. Was she curious? Suspicious? Apprehensive? Tove couldn't tell. Was she...*hurt*?

The answer rang true in a way Tove couldn't quite comprehend. They were prickly and self-absorbed, they knew that much. Effie probably had good reason to feel hurt.

"I'm not sure, but I think I've been treating you rather unkindly," they said. "I'm sorry. I'll try to do better."

A happy glow seemed to spring from Effie's being and spill out from the inside, sweeping Tove into its brightness. Wow. If this was what being kind to Effie felt like, Tove could get used to it.

"If it's not too late," they added, "I'd like to take you up on the offer. To team up. You help me with the pageant, I help you with...well, what do you need?"

Effie smiled and smiled. "Like I said before, I'd really, really like to get to know you. The now you. The new you."

Tears prickled behind Tove's eyes. "I'd like to try that." They hoped they could keep on top of this kindness thing before their gremlin started acting up again. Before they remembered why their and Effie's friendship had ended the first time.

"Then," said Effie, surprising them with an electric touch to the elbow that totally did not have them close to slamming the brake, "let's start now! Let's get hot chocolate in the arcade. I know a place."

And because her eagerness threw Tove's baseline misery all off kilter, they agreed.

Thanks to Nowell, the Santas could make use of the freshly paved staff parking at the Pollack for the week, so Tove parked behind the new shopping centre, intending to leave the car there for the night. It was only four, and there was plenty of time before the fundraiser began, so Tove let Effie lead them down the High Street to the Victorian covered arcade.

"I can't believe they built a new shopping centre when we already have this," Effie mused, gesturing at the clouded glass roof, the painted archways. "I hope this place keeps its business."

"Even if it does, it would be cool to have something like this in, say, the foyer of the shopping centre," Tove remarked.

"Yeah," agreed Effie. "They could invite local traders to have stalls and pop-ups. There are ways to support local craft and small businesses while making retail more accessible, you know?"

"If it were up to me I'd scrap the entire Pollack project."

"You would?"

"I can't bear to think about who's going to get all the money this thing makes."

"But at least we'll be able to buy comfy sports leggings on-Island now, right? I hate online shopping. Nothing ever fits."

Tove shrugged. They hadn't bought anything except food since they'd returned to the Island six months ago. That didn't make them morally superior, they realised, it just made them sad and unemployed.

Effie stopped at a booth which smelled of sweets and childhood. "We're here. You like hot chocolate, right? But do you like lavender? Orange? Cinnamon?"

"That sounds gross." Tove chuckled, feeling fifteen again and like they were hanging out in Town after school.

"Just one at a time, duh."

Tove ordered a dark hot chocolate with oat milk and Effie got an orange hot chocolate. Effie tapped her debit card, and instead of arguing, Tove thanked her. Perhaps it was the conversation they'd had in the car, but there was something comfortable and inevitable about letting Effie take care of them. Tove used to know her so well that they almost didn't have to worry about the usual bullshit. Effie's main crime was leading them on—failing to follow through after an out-of-this-world-good kiss. So long as they didn't get too attached, she couldn't hurt them.

They wandered the arcade together, blowing on their steaming cups. An upright piano huddled in a dark corner under the iron stairs. **PLAY ME**, read a sign on the music rack. Effie made a beeline and rested her cup on the piano case while she adjusted her scarf.

"For god's sake don't leave a ring on the wood," Tove implored.

Effie slid her paper napkin under the cup. "Do you ever play these days?"

The lack of presumption in the question almost had them spilling the truth: they'd touched keys that morning for the first time in years. And boy, was Tove itching to feel the sound of an acoustic piano ricocheting through their bones.

"I'm rusty," they said, placing their cup beside hers.

"Don't worry, I'm not listening," said Effie.

And before they could second-guess themself, they slid onto the stool and laid their fingertips on the keys. Cold... But their hands were warm from holding the cup. They pressed middle C and the hammer struck a chord in their soul. The sound shimmered, not perfectly in tune, but it hummed under their skin. It was good to be in the dark under the stairs; there was no spotlight, and even though the whole arcade would hear them play, nobody would come looking for them here.

They glanced up at Effie, who looked behind her in mock surprise.

"Still not listening," she promised.

So Tove played *In the Bleak Midwinter*. The warm F major, sad treble grounded by bass that moved in when needed, swelled into the space beneath the stairs and beyond. They sang the lyrics softly over the notes. It came to them easily—more easily, even, when they stopped overthinking the keys and raised their face to Effie's, locking eye contact as the notes surged between them.

When the last chord faded to nothing, Effie drew in a shuddering breath. Tove thought she might say something nice, but instead, choking on laughter, she said, “Did you just misgender Jesus?”

“What?” Tove snapped.

As they spoke, they heard the last line of the song in their head as they sang it moments ago: *Give her my heart.* Fuck. They did misgender Jesus. Effie on the motherfucking brain.

They grabbed their hot chocolate, now cool enough to drink, and hid their blush in the steam. “Thought you weren’t listening.”

“Can’t help what I hear.” Effie shrugged, then sighed. “Much as I love…I’d love to hear more, we ought to get back to the Pollack.”

“Right.” Tove hushed the vibrations in their veins. “Let’s go.”

11

There were lots of people at the fundraiser, speakers and donors and regular people alike. Effie's sponsor Ranjula was there, talking animatedly with a homeless shelter rep. She caught Effie's eye and winked, and Effie learned later that she'd made a donation of Ultraspeed clothing on behalf of the company.

Effie listened carefully to the seminar, remembering how Tove listened to the radio in the car. She wondered about what they'd told Heather at the Santa grotto, about doing your best to bring happiness, but accepting that unhappiness existed. Yet they wanted to help others all the same. Was their cynicism a guise? Self-protection? Like Effie's own corresponding guise of optimism?

Effie learned that there was a growing number of people without stable or affordable housing on the Island, just as there were lots of empty flats in Town being hoarded by vulture funds and landlord surrogates. Half the shelter volunteers' job was advocacy, and the rest was practical support. They were putting on a walk-in event on Christmas Day for homeless and other vulnerable people, and since their facility didn't have a proper kitchen, they were currently fundraising to buy microwave meals for the event.

When dusk fell the crowd headed home. Nowell and a few camerapeople settled down in the back of a van with a big wired heater. Then it was just the six contestants in their Santa suits. Effie had envisioned the six of them climbing into their tents and peeping through the flaps like cats in Santa hats, dozing with eyes half-open as they warily ogled each other. But watching Tove crawl in and zip up, she had to face her disappointment. Even if everybody else remained unzipped, Tove was the one she wanted to exchange thumbs up with during the night.

"So what now?" she asked the general vicinity.

"Sleep," said Tove's tent.

"Goodnight!" called Bryan #2. Bryan #1 had already taken his teeth out, but he waved from the nest where he'd cosied up in his wife's crocheted blanket. Alice continued arranging her tarpaulin as if she'd done this before. (She probably had. This stuff was required at power-granny bootcamp.) The only other Santa still loitering about was DuBois, who Effie caught sneaking guiltily out of the refreshments marquee, fumbling with a steaming flask.

"Psst, is that coffee?" she hissed across the top of Tove's tent.

DuBois startled, and the motion-sensing floodlight clicked on. His eyeballs shone like a fox caught snooping round the chicken coop. Only, unlike a fox, the dazzled rich boy kept walking, as if his richness could save him from retribution. A few floundering steps later…and he tripped smack over Tove's tent. A ripping sound echoed across the carpark as the flimsy canvas broke under his weight. Mulled wine—not even coffee—went everywhere.

Effie rapidly weakened at the stench of cloves. She should've known.

Tove's tent barked a rather un-tent-like word that sounded like "Fuck!", then spat up a tousled auburn head, static with rage. "How dare you! Imagine some giant, snivelling clown came and poured shite through your jewel-encrusted roof, soaked your silk bed and left your frescoed ceiling dripping! Would you like that?"

"I'm terribly sorry." DuBois shrank away, torn between mourning his mulled wine and appeasing the angry Santa. "You…uh, you can have my tent."

DuBois's tent was twice the size of anyone else's and brimming with cushions and woollen guernseys. Effie couldn't imagine what it was designed to house. Maybe an elephant. Maybe an elephant-sized dildo for one gigantic arsehole.

"Keep your effing tent," Tove scoffed. "It's not like you'll last the night without your five-star amenities."

DuBois shot a look Effie's way that said "help me out here," and although Effie didn't care much for his feelings, she couldn't let him take all the blame.

"Tove," she tried, "it's not his fault. I surprised him by—"

"It's done. I don't care. Please leave me alone."

And that was that. Tove returned to their (now sopping) tent with the ripped canvas and broken poles, DuBois sank into his, and Effie, too, wriggled in.

It was dark at first and smelled of damp—the dew had come down and condensation quivered on the canvas. But what made her gasp was the chill radiating from the ground. It was hard and cold, and her butt and palms burned under her weight.

She pulled on her gloves. This was going to be a long night.

It could've been ten minutes later or a whole sleep cycle when she darted awake to a sound. Blood crusted her chapped lips, and her heart pounded like that time she and Tove went to the aquarium, and their hand brushed hers in the luminous dark near the turtle exhibit. The sound was coming from her left—from Tove—and her first thought was what if they were being kidnapped. Using her phone camera as a periscope, she checked the world outside, careful not to let her sleeves jingle. There they were—not being kidnapped, but huddled on their flattened tent like Rose Dawson on that damn door.

Effie stuck her head out to get a better look. The noise that had woken her up was definitely coming from Tove, but with their head buried in their knees she couldn't tell if they were crying.

Their "leave me alone" still stung Effie's ears, but that afternoon's pact to help them through the pageant was louder.

"Tove, hi," she called. "Do you want to come and share my tent?"

Tove looked up. Their face wasn't wet, but windchill and streetlight lashed their nose red raw, and their teeth were chattering like pennies in a washing machine.

"You look like an iceberg," Effie said. "Come over here and let me warm you."

"No," they snapped. "The point of this thing is hardship. My tent got wrecked and it serves me right for buying a shit one. Sucks to be me."

"Don't be ridiculous. The point is raising money and awareness. How are you helping anyone by not taking care of yourself?"

They tipped their face to the light. "I suppose I'm not."

"So…join me?" She jingled her Santa sleeves invitingly.

"It'd be against the rules," they grumbled.

"There's no rule against sharing tents, we only have to last the night. Now come here, Ice Queen."

To her surprise, Tove unfurled from their foetal position and trundled over with sleeping bag in tow.

Moments later, they were lying together in a tent in the carpark Effie worked in. Staring at one another. In their eyes Effie saw a soul who'd been cold too many times and had no one offer to warm them.

They were shivering.

"Turn over," Effie ordered. "And hug this." She crammed her extra blanket into Tove's cold chest and throat. "Now, how about…" She undid the zipper on her sleeping bag, and then Tove's, and coiled her arm around them. She pressed her chest to their back and breathed warm air on the nape of their neck. They shook for a while, but eventually relaxed in her arms. Then they sighed.

"What's up?" Effie murmured. "Bad spoon?"

"No," they whispered back, meeker than Effie had ever heard them. "It's what I need."

And even though Effie knew they meant for the cold, she could almost kid herself they liked being cradled by her.

"The last few years have been tough," Tove said. "Christmas especially."

Effie waited for them to elaborate, but they didn't. "So where have you been all this time?"

"Germany. Living with my boyfriend."

Effie's heart ricocheted against her ribs, but it was too late. The arrow had already found its mark. "Your…?"

"We're not together anymore. That's why I came back to the Island. Six months ago."

The arrow was gone, but the pain didn't fade. "Aw, I'm sorry. Break-ups suck."

They were quiet for a few minutes, then said, softly, "You really believe that, don't you?"

Tuesday

6 days till Christmas

12

(a flashback)

"Break-ups suck," Tove commiserated with Aaron when their friends Jan and Berta broke up six days before Christmas last year. Tove was especially sad because Jan was *his* friend, which meant they probably wouldn't see Berta again. Tove owed Berta a bretzel.

"Which is why that'll never be us," Aaron replied.

Smugly smiling, Tove continued tying ribbon to their makeshift Christmas tree. They couldn't justify buying one of their own, but after the tree vendor left the square, they'd picked up a few fallen fronds and stuffed them into the spare mug back at the flat.

"We'll have the most successful relationship of them all," Aaron went on. "When they've all grown tired of each other and been through messy divorces, it'll be you and me outliving the lot of them. They'll try to pry us apart, but we're stronger. We can get through anything."

Tove took a sick pleasure in believing he was right. After all, if they hadn't broken up by now then they were never going to. Tove's life revolved around him. Outside this relationship was nothing but fear and emptiness. They'd built the relationship that way.

"I wonder," he was musing, "if Berta had a thing for me after all. She has this way of looking at me with those beautiful blue eyes of hers."

Tove's heart stilled. "Well, you are nice to look at." They pleaded, they pandered, they attempted to remind him that they liked him. *I like you. Me.* Tove didn't mind him thinking or talking about other people. All they wanted was for him to talk about them the same way. He had a habit of intellectually deconstructing Tove's weakness using others' strengths.

He crossed the room and flicked their shoulder, a morsel of affection. "Don't worry, Topping. It's always going to be you, even though your eyes are plain brown."

Tove's shoulder stung under their clothes, and they clung to the feeling, attached it to the words "always you…even though."

"So, Topping. Will we do anything and everything to avoid splitting up? It's my one goal: to be with you forever."

Despite a close-to-all-consuming urge to reach out and clutch this love, to wrap themself in it, the word "forever" rattled in Tove's brain like a headache. But they ignored it. They had already said yes, once and then every day since.

"I can't wait to make you my wife."

"Same," they said hurriedly, seeing an opening to the thing they had been psyching themself up to ask all week. "So have you booked the band yet?"

"Ah. No. Not yet."

"I can do it," they offered. "If it'll help take the load off."

"No. You've done everything. Let me do this one thing."

Tove had planned the entire wedding. They'd tried to involve him, they really had. But whenever they had a question, or asked him to proofread an email, it was "I'm so tired, can't we just watch TV tonight?" And then things got urgent, so Tove did them anyway. And then…well, then it became "These save-the-dates look like flyers for Sunday bingo" or "I should've said no to a church wedding in the first place."

"Well, how about we do it together? It's one quick email to see if they're available."

"They probably won't be. We're too late."

"Then the sooner the better."

"Look, if I'm being honest, I don't like the band. I don't want them to play at my wedding."

Another emotional thump in the face. "Why didn't you say so before?"

"You had your heart set on it. I didn't know how to tell you I want a string quartet."

Tove's eyebrows climbed. They said the only thing they could think of. "I already told my family it'll be a jazz band. My mum's obsessed with how I used to play the trumpet and she'll think it's weird if we have strings." They were terrified of their family—or anyone—finding out how hard they had to fight for every little thing.

"You really have to tell her sometime."

"What?"

"That you don't like playing anymore. Or she'll never shut up about it."

Aaron had been trying to get Tove to talk to their mum for years. They'd never understood what he wanted them to say. It seemed to boil down to "I don't like or respect you or want you in my life." Which was a lie. Sometimes Tove cried and cried and Aaron's arms could never suffice for their mum's.

"She is still trying to control you, like all parents do," he added.

Everything they liked, everyone they loved, he always found some way to call unhealthy or malicious. Tove's mind began turning blank, their insides to melt. Tears leaked from their eyes.

But as they crouched on the tile floor, Aaron remained standing. "Not again," he said, level and unaffected. "You absolutely have to get over this. Crying will not help you work through your issues with your mum. You clam up or cry every single time I challenge you to think for yourself."

Tove cried harder.

"I'm going to the pub to meet Jan." Aaron grabbed his coat from the back of a chair and opened the heavy door. "I hope you've stopped crying and had a think by the time I get back."

The door slammed shut. Tove bit back their wailing so the neighbours wouldn't hear. The band was not booked. Aaron got drunk at the pub and didn't come home till Boxing Day, without a word of where he'd been. It wasn't the first time he'd disappeared, or even the last. Christmas might as well have never happened.

"Sometimes breaking up is the impossible prospect that becomes the best thing you ever did," they whispered.

"Tove?" Effie murmured.

Effie's arms tightened around Tove's body, rousing them from their half-stupor. The thin canvas of the tent bathed them in a balmy blue lit by orange streetlamps. Effie's hand was curled under their ribs, palm flat. Her embrace was not quite like Tove's mum's, but it was the next best thing. Maybe it was better.

"Did you say something?" Effie asked.

"No."

"Well, I want you to know," she purred, her breath stirring the hairs on the back of Tove's neck, "I like you."

They gasped, cold air rasping their throat. Effie's crotch pressed against their ass. Despite the padding of their clothes, they wanted to push back into her, savour the resistance. The way cats wriggle to fill all the gaps, to turn two skins into one.

"What I mean is," she clarified, as if she felt their heart pounding in their back, stirring her own chest, "I like the person you are. When we ran into each other at first, I was too busy remembering the person you were. Grieving the time we lost together, maybe."

"I know what that feels like." Tove had been grieving themself as well.

"But I've begun to see you as you are now. And I like that you."

Tove's mouth dried out suddenly. "And what are they like? *That* me."

"They're sensitive to injustice and passionate about reversing it. They're stubborn about accepting help for themself, but humble enough to ask for it. And most of all, they're courageous. The world is full of scary things, but look at them go! Stepping out into it even though every day is uncertain."

Unbidden, Tove's hand darted for Effie's in the semi-darkness. They laid theirs on top of hers and let it shake till she clasped it and held them steady. It wasn't only her compliments, but the "they" pronoun she unthinkingly used… Tove felt whole when Effie spoke about them—held together with duct tape and determination, maybe, but whole.

"I've got you, Tove," Effie whispered.

For a moment she let go of their hand, and pulled the sleeping bag over both their shoulders, up over their heads. Tove wanted to tell her they weren't shaking because they were cold, but because of something else, only they were absorbed in guessing which touches on their cheek were from the slowly deflating sleeping bag, and which were Effie's.

Effie's touch, when it finally came, was unmistakable. A mind-blowing tucking of their hair behind their ear. The dusting of her fingertips, so fine Tove could almost pick out the whorls and ridges of her fingerprints, and then the hush of her warm breath beating against their eardrum.

"I've got you."

13

Sleep came and went, each snooze a slightly different shape, like a procession of cumulus clouds through an ever-moving sky. Each time Effie woke, she and Tove were pressed together, their mint and tea-tree shampoo rousing her to hug them tighter. Club-goers shrieked by, and seagulls, and the occasional pattering of padded feet she didn't dare think about. At some point there was a commotion in the carpark, but she knew her role too well to move: she was Tove's cardigan and their scarf, and it was her job to keep them warm and safe.

At length, an airhorn blasted them awake.

"Jesus," Tove muttered, rolling over. "This isn't *I'm a Celebrity*."

Lazy happiness washed over Effie. "I was thinking more *Love Island*."

"Don't say you watch that nonsense."

"What? Diss it if you dare."

Tove scowled in her face for all of two seconds before dissolving into a laugh. "Fine, don't tell anyone but I binged the last three seasons under my duvet this summer."

"Knew you weren't as romance-averse as you claim."

The scowl returned and Tove shuffled out their sleeping bag. "Speaking of duvets, which are you going to do first? Sleep or shower?"

Clammy cold enveloped Effie's body in their absence. It was hard to reconcile that scowl with this extremely personal question…unless she was taking it more personally than it was meant. "Bath," she responded. "You should see the wanky bath my landlord plumbed in. Giant tub with jets and fibre-optic lights. It's by far the nicest thing about my flat."

"I remember you saying." Tove bit their bottom lip like it was a big, soft apricot. Holy twat of Mary, they were cute even with greasy hair and eyebags. "I haven't lived somewhere with a bath since I was a child. Must be nice for you." Then they were gone, out of the mouth of the tent, and rolling up their sleeping bag on the dewy tarmac.

Effie was groggy from broken sleep, stiff from the hard, cold night, and entirely, *ineffably* dazed from so many hours clasping Tove's being to hers, like…like two pigs in the same blanket. (She'd think harder about that simile if she weren't now craving the bacon in her fridge. A big ole bacon roll with lashings of ketchup…alongside the beautiful human she spent the night with.)

It was irresponsible of her. But she did it anyway.

"Hey Tove, do you want to…come over and see my bath?" Effie emerged from her tent to the biting morning air, to find four Santas and a film crew staring at her, and no Tove in sight.

"I mean, it's the best way to warm up," she added, aware she wasn't helping herself.

Bryan #2 whistled, strolling over. "You're not fooling anyone, love."

"Friends have to stick together," she attempted.

"Sure, we all do." He closed one eye in a wink, revealing the trans sign tattooed on his wrinkled eyelid. A blink-and-you'll-miss-it revelation granted to Effie by the trust of a queer elder: Bryan #2 was a trans man.

"You're right," Effie relented, attempting to repay the trust in kind, "I'm nothing but a useless lesbian leveraging her fancy bathtub for a date."

"I'll be wishing you luck," he said with a laugh, and went back to packing up his things.

Tove materialised from the refreshments marquee with a mug of steaming tea. "I swear I heard my name. What's up?"

Effie floundered for a sentence that didn't include the word "date," and alighted on the empty spot where the rich boy was last night. "What happened to DuBois?"

"Didn't last, apparently," Tove growled. "Serves him right for ruining my night."

Words flit by like litter in the wind. So much for two pigs in the same blanket. They were one pig and one grumpy goat whose night was ruined.

"To answer your question," Tove added, "I *would* like to come and see your bath. But this isn't a date, okay? You're a romantic fool if you think it is."

"You heard that, huh?" Blood rushed to Effie's cheeks like it was Guy Fawkes Night up there.

"C'mon, it's a bath. There's nothing suggestive about using someone's bath."

Effie rubbed the sweat beading on her forehead. "Who are you trying to convince?" She might be a fool, but so was Tove if they thought coming to see her bath after a night of spooning was nothing. Unless they really did want a bath that much.

"What? I'm frozen and I need that bath. If you're going to stop me—"

"Tove," Effie said firmly, "I would love to run you a bath. Please let me."

Tove stared, before uttering a strangled, "Okay."

The cold in Effie's bones was making her feverish by the time she'd fielded her confessional in the green room and let Tove drive her home. They drank more tea as the bath ran, and Effie threw some hoodies and leggings on the radiator.

Melchior stumbled sleepily from the boiler cupboard as it rumbled to life, meowing.

"You finally have a cat!" cried Tove, attempting a squat. Every stiff joint in their cold body cracked as they extended a hand palm-down for Melchior to sniff. "I know your parents never let you get one."

Wow, they remembered! It was probably one of those annoying things that was hard to forget—Effie used to spend breaktimes scrolling cat pic accounts on Tumblr and moaning, "I want a cat"—but still.

"Living alone has its perks," she said. "This is Melchior. She's my number one."

"She's beautiful."

And Effie blossomed inside because someone called her cat beautiful. Melchior *was* beautiful. It was true.

In the end neither of them wanted to wait for the bath.

"Let's get in together," Tove suggested.

"Yeah?" Effie gulped.

"I'm wearing a shirt under my Santa suit and I don't mind getting it wet. We can be modest."

It didn't feel very modest, stripping together in the bathroom. When Tove unbuckled their belt their clothes fell in a great swathe, like a deity disrobing for a dip in the river. They were left in pants and undershirt—braless, Effie noted with a nod to small-boob privilege.

By contrast, she was torn on which way to face as she pulled down her trousers. It was either her jutting ass or her excellent cleavage.

Tove said nothing as she opted for a side-on pose, a hybrid butt-and-boob show. They were already in the water, T-shirt ballooning, flicking water at her with their forefinger and thumb.

Melchior left them to their weird water activity and trotted back into the boiler cupboard, and Effie joined Tove in the water with a groan. "It's good to get that Santa suit off."

"The bells on your sleeves kept waking me up all night long. It's well time you took that thing off."

Effie shot Tove a sharp look. Their mouth was a straight line, but a humourful one.

"If only I could get truly naked," she ventured, "then this'd be breathtaking."

Tove snorted. "Test me."

"What?"

"Take my breath away, why don't you?"

Effie was glad of the mounds of white foam that hid her hardening nipples. Even though she tried to keep her legs to herself, beneath the bubbles her leg-hairs kept prickling against what could only be theirs. "It's you who's testing me," she accused.

"If you want to be nude, I'm not stopping you."

Tove turned their palms to the sky, and Effie splashed them to keep from answering.

She wondered what they'd think if she really did it. Thanks to a haircut that suited her, some well-placed stretchmarks that showed off her good bits, and a carefully cultivated aura of queer bravado, Effie was hot now. Would Tove like what they saw? Effie hoped so, hard enough that it hurt.

They spent a while massaging the blood back into their (respective) limbs. Once Effie's extremities stopped tingling, she unwound the shower nozzle and washed her hair. Then she showed Tove how to use the jets and fibre-optics, explained her shampoo collection, and left them to enjoy the hot water.

Two minutes later, Effie was heating up a frying pan for her bacon when Melchior came skittering down the hall into the kitchen, peridot eyes wide. A yell echoed from the bathroom.

She ran to the door. Bubbles were piling up in the bath and spilling onto the floor.

"This isn't supposed to happen, is it?" giggled Tove. They emerged from Bubble Mountain, a spectre of soap with the white cotton T-shirt clinging to their curves.

"Shit." Effie shaded her gaze from their body, the dark shapes of their nipples, the enticing dip of their belly button. Tove's bare legs extended below the T-shirt, thicker than they used to be, with a hint of muscle that was sexy beyond belief. "Uh, it's the jets, I mean the bubbles, I mean both at the same time." Effie flicked the jets off and the piling bubbles heaved to a halt.

"So, what do we do?"

Effie fetched mixing bowls from the kitchen and together they bailed the bubbles back into the bath.

"Tove, you're shivering," she noticed when she dared look at them again.

"It's because my head's wet," Tove confessed.

"Get back in that bath and rinse your hair right now," Effie ordered. "I can finish cleaning up."

"Yes, ms." They swivelled to get back in, and their foot slipped on the soapy tiles.

Without thinking Effie caught their waist, cinching the T-shirt tight. And then her own foot slipped. She pulled as hard as she could, so Tove would be the one who fell on her, and they both pitched into the pile of towels she'd brought in to dry the floor. It was a soft landing, mercifully, and Tove came down hands and knees on top of Effie. Their breasts pushed against hers, small and round and firm in a way that defied even the horniest imagination. Their hair dripped cold into her face, their freckled nose wet. Their eyelids drooped, and with a jolt Effie realised they were staring at her lips. She couldn't help the puff of breath that escaped her lungs. But that was what made Tove's gaze flick up again.

"Effie?"

"Uhuh," she grunted.

"Are you okay?"

She blinked fifty million times and let out a hysterical giggle. "Yeah, I'm fine. I swear I didn't do that on purpose!"

Tove frowned, before splitting into a matching grin. "That's the second time you've caught me now."

"And I can't seem to do it without making a worse mess!"

"You'll get there. A bit more practice maybe, but I believe in you."

Effie chuckled, but the conversation lost meaning when Tove shivered so violently a new set of drips sprayed her face. "Come on, let's get you warm again."

Tove shifted stiffly onto their haunches and Effie hauled them back into the bath. While they sank into the deflating bubbles, she heated up the shower nozzle. Wordlessly, Tove offered their head, and it was Effie who got to run her fingers through the silky auburn waves and gently tug out the tangles as she washed the shampoo away. It was Effie who got to trace the contours of their head and map it out in her mind. She went softly over their ears, tracking behind them and rubbing the lobes lightly between her forefinger and thumb.

"Better?" she asked when she was done.

"So much better."

They took turns with the hairdryer and Effie gave Tove some dry clothes—a pair of leggings and a pastel pink hoodie with rainbow embroidery that swamped them.

"That's my best hoodie, you better take care of it," Effie said, admiring them.

"Effie, you're never getting this back." Tove winked snoozily. "It matches the hat you gave me." All their scowls were gone now. When they were tired they were less standoffish, as if they felt obliged to antagonise but their heart wasn't in it. It bothered Effie that Tove was so hot and cold, gentle now, sarcastic at other times. They might be holding a grudge against her, or worse, they might think she was weird and impulsive and overly familiar. But the way Tove responded to tenderness had Effie compelled to give her best over and over again.

She returned to her frying pan and toasted some bread for a crunchy bacon sarnie. Tove watched with slumping shoulders.

"You're falling asleep," Effie accused.

"I'm probably too tired to drive safely," Tove admitted. "Mind if I kip on your couch for a bit?"

"Have my bed," Effie said. "Come on. You deserve a mattress."

They didn't complain when Effie took their arm and led them to the bedroom, but they did murmur, "I can't believe you let me share your tent, your bath, and now your bed."

Effie smiled. "You're pushing your luck if you want my bacon as well."

"I am literally vegetarian."

"Oh, I'm sorry for insinuating you wanted—"

"Shush, you." They pressed a clumsy finger to her lips, then keeled into her bed. "Join me when you've eaten—if you like."

Effie could hardly speak for the print of their finger lingering on her lips, and the susurrus of their invitation in her ears, but she didn't have to say anything. Tove was already snoring.

After her bacon sarnie Effie made her special Christmas soup. She made it vegetarian—vegetable stock cube—with apples and chestnuts cut into chunks. Leaving it to simmer with the stick blender ready on the counter, she ventured back to the bedroom.

Tove lay on their side, mysteriously cuddling an ash-brown Guernsey Teddy sporting a pair of spectacles made haphazardly out of orange pipe-cleaners. Effie smiled and gave the bear a scritch under its chin, same as she'd do for Melchior. Tove didn't stir.

Then she climbed in beside them. It was hard to believe she could possibly fall asleep, but she did.

14

Tove woke with an arm as their pillow, and their own hand resting on the hand at the end of it. A warm pocket of air cuddled their back, evincing a second body behind theirs, insulating them. Tucked under their arm was Oberon, exactly where they'd put him last night after they retrieved him from their bag while Effie was out of the room. Effie must've seen him. And here she was, curled around both Tove and their bear as if it were the most natural thing in the world.

Tove tried to return to sleep, prolong this feeling of being together with a human who understood and accepted them, but the afternoon sun glowing through the curtains wasn't having it.

Sitting up, they took everything in. They were fully clothed in Effie's hoodie and leggings, wrapped in her scent from top to bottom. Their Santa suit lay in a pile of red and white on the floor—red and white and…furry. Effie's cat blinked and kneaded the fabric.

Tove crawled out of Effie's bed, praying they wouldn't wake her, and shooed Melchior off their stuff. Weirdly she was lying on their phone, which was bursting with notifications. Their heart rose to their throat as they checked the previews. **Hey, it's been a while.** Phew. No new messages in that chain.

They wandered down the hall, pausing at a mirror, then a painting, and finally at a corkboard of photos. Most were printed out on shitty paper, but there were also polaroids and photo booth strips.

Effie's life was laid out before their eyes. Her university social circles, her niece as a baby, her parents' unsmiling faces contrasted with her gigantic beam at her graduation. None of the photos were recent, Tove noted from her unbleached hair. What she did these days and who she hung out with was a mystery to the corkboard.

Tove almost missed the cluster of photos in the top right corner, of Effie's mid-teens. Oh, it was them. Their breath caught. There the two of them were, posing on the rocks near the bathing pools on a sunny day. They were both in bikinis, showing off how young and different their bodies were. Effie's arm looped around Tove's waist, and the way she grasped their bare skin had the blood rushing to their head in real time. It was an intimate touch, a caress.

God, if only Tove had figured out they were bisexual sooner. It was honestly astounding how they hadn't.

Yet the feelings inside the memory rushed back, no hindsight needed. Tove's toes gripped the granite, sea air tickling their skin. The sun beat down on their fair hair. And Effie's touch knocked the breath out of them. She had them firmly by her side. And Tove didn't voice, even to themself, how they were drawn to her in a way they'd never been drawn to anybody else.

Not even Aaron, though they'd taught themself to idolise him. How Tove adored Effie was different.

Back then, they didn't have the self-awareness to wish she felt the same. They didn't know they wanted her until she rejected them. Now, they did. They wished and wanted.

A delicious smell pricked their nostrils and their stomach rumbled.

In the kitchen they discovered a pot of something that smelled incredible. Stewed fruit? They lifted the lid and pushed their nose in. Mm, nutty. A stick blender lay beside the hob, on a freshly wiped countertop. Effie had made soup.

Without really thinking about it, Tove plugged the stick into the wall and blended the soup. There was something deeply therapeutic about pressing the stick into the pot again and again and letting the vibrations wiggle up their arm.

When it was smooth, they surveyed their work and second-guessed themself. What if Effie liked chunky soup? What if she'd left the blender out for another reason? What if she really wanted to blend it herself, or was possessive in her kitchen? That would be reasonable. Tove would understand if Effie berated them over this.

Panic churned their empty stomach. The desire to simply leave and not deal with it gnawed like a bruise, but they told themself to give Effie a chance. She'd been patient with them so far. More than patient. According to Tove's therapist, their habit to assume the worst was preventing them from connecting with other people. Here was a chance to practise the new habit. The one where they trusted others to have and express emotion as they themselves saw fit, and where they, as an individual, took appropriate responsibility for the same.

They returned to the hall, where they stared down Effie's door, bracing themself.

Okay, here goes. They pushed open the door.

Effie sat up in bed, her back to them, addressing her cat, who in lieu of Tove's phone had taken up residence in the warm depression they'd left on the mattress.

"And then I had a sex dream about Tove," Effie whispered loudly.

"Um, hello?" Tove said, stunned.

Effie jumped about three feet across the bed, disturbing Melchior with a yowl. "Whoa, what did *you* say?" With her head an unbrushed mess of flyaways and backcombing, it had never been more plausible that she was dreaming about sex.

Although they had no idea if they'd heard right, Tove snatched the chance to make their own confession. "I blended the soup you made. I'm sorry."

"Oh, cheers! Saves me a job."

They didn't know if they were more relieved or annoyed, or entirely disbelieving, that anyone could be so laid back in the face of their neuroticism. *Why are you letting me relax?* they wanted to ask. *What are you waiting to spring on me?*

"God, you didn't hear what I just said, did you?" Apparently, by her expression, Effie thought her dream was enough to drive Tove away.

Tove tamped down their whirling anxiety about the soup. *She's not acting angry. Maybe it's real. Maybe she really isn't angry.* "I heard you had a dream about me?"

"Yes." Effie's stare was heaven-piercing.

"What happened?" Tove prodded. "Where were we?"

"Right here. In my bed." Effie groaned. "Oh my *god*, why can't I keep my mouth shut?!"

Knots of tension began to unravel in Tove's brain. They felt like laughing. "What can I say, your self-professed superpower is eating pussy."

"Meow," protested Effie's cat.

"So you don't mind?" asked Effie.

"Shush, it doesn't mean anything. You can't help what you dream about."

"Ugh. You're so sexy and unavailable, I feel like an absolute fool."

"Hold up, unavailable?"

"You let me down literally moments ago. Or were you making fun of me? *It doesn't mean anything*, you said."

"Making fun of you yes, letting you down no."

"Sounded like a rejection to me."

Now Tove was back in the hot seat. They were still dazed at how Effie had called them sexy. "All I'm saying is, I've had my fair share of sex dreams and never intended to act on them. My ex used to say they didn't mean anything."

Effie snorted. "His dreams, or yours? Sex dreams don't mean *nothing*. At the very least, it means you're horny for *some*thing."

Tove wondered what Effie was horny for, but they didn't have to think too hard. They blushed. Then they wondered what Aaron had been horny for, and their mood went downhill very quickly.

"Being horny for someone doesn't *mean* anything," they insisted.

"Look, if you're polyamorous and you had some kind of arrangement, I'll say no more."

Why was she pushing this? Why was Tove pushing back? Was she that keen to make something of their attraction? Were they this averse to letting her? Everything was tangled up in the way Aaron constantly talked about women and joked about cheating as if it were really that outlandish, when in Tove's mind it had become sort of an unthinkable inevitability. The relationship *was* polyamorous; they *did* have an arrangement. And Aaron still pushed every boundary and gaslit Tove about where the limit lay. It wasn't supposed to be like that.

"I swear to god, if this guy cheated on you…" Effie mumbled. "Because that's what it sounds like."

"We just weren't right for each other." The cliché slipped out easily. Tove's gremlin poked out from its hidey-hole, recalling how last time they'd talked about their relationship, Effie had apologised. *I'm sorry. Break-ups suck*, she'd said. *Break-ups suck*, Tove had once thought.

"Don't you dare say you're sorry again," they cut in as her lips parted to speak. "It's not your fault my relationship tanked. Hell, I'm sure you would've done everything you could to keep us together."

Effie swung her legs over the side of the bed to face them, and their heart beat faster. Great, their gremlin had created another confrontation.

"What does *that* mean?" Effie demanded.

"You like people to be happy," Tove stuttered. "You like to see couples together. Right? You've never truly accepted your parents' divorce."

"Excuse me."

Her mouth was a hard line. Tove was suffocating. Effie's patience had finally worn thin and she was poised to get rid of them for good.

Like their therapist taught them, they questioned why they'd said what they said. It wasn't to hurt Effie, specifically—it was to provoke her into hurting *them*. Tove deserved to be hurt. That's what they believed.

Effie, though, didn't deserve to be hurt for Tove's self-destructive ends.

"Sorry," they choked. "That was out of line. It's been a long time. It's not okay to comment on your life as if I know a thing about it."

Effie folded her arms, a stern bedhead. "Alright, then let's get to know each other for real. My parents are back together. They remarried the summer I started uni."

Tove recoiled. Effie's parents used to keep her awake at night with their yelling. There was no earthly reason why two such toxic people should have gotten back together.

"I know my parents' divorce happened when we were friends, so it's about all you know about me these days, but it's not like it had a lasting impact. And it's not my fault you don't know anything about me. It was you that stopped talking to me when you met Aaron—who, if my maths is right, is the same person you broke up with six months ago. Am I right?"

"You're right," Tove gasped. "But it was you that—" The words dissolved on their tongue. They couldn't accuse her of ruining their friendship, by not liking them back. It was too unfair. For the first time, they saw clearly that it wasn't Effie's silence after the kiss that drove them apart. It was Tove themself. It was Aaron, taking advantage of how overwhelmed they felt in that moment to convince them that Effie didn't care for them, and that they needed a distraction. A nine-year distraction.

Just like their friendship with Effie—the tenderness in that photo—had recontextualised itself once Tove realised they were queer, their friendship break-up became recontextualised when shame and resentment and rejection started to cloud their worldview. Tove couldn't believe they'd ever thought their bond meant nothing to Effie, when here they were, in her flat after all these years!

"I mean," they said carefully, "*my* parents divorced the year I started uni. And they *didn't* get back together."

"Oh, I'm s—" She checked herself. *Thank you, Effie.* "Okay. This is a good start. So. Shall we see what you've done with that soup?"

Awkwardly Tove led the way to the kitchenette. They were just beginning to breathe again, when the pocket of the hoodie they were wearing came to life with the unmistakable octave-jumping synths of "Poker Face."

Tove halted in their tracks, Effie bumping into them. As the synths grew stabby, they pushed past and shrank back into her bedroom to let their phone ring out. They didn't check the number. They couldn't.

When it was over, they dabbed their eyes with their sleeve. They'd been awake for less than an hour and they were already close to tears.

"Are you…never mind." Effie lingered in the doorway.

"What are you looking at?" Tove snapped.

But before Effie could scold them for being such an arse, or whatever she was about to say, the nightmare began again. "Poker Face," again. Their ringtone, again.

Tove's eyes met Effie's. They felt like they'd been caught doing something they shouldn't. She was definitely wondering why the hell they wouldn't answer the phone like a normal person.

"I just want to know if you're okay," Effie said.

And for some reason, her concern bolstered them enough to retrieve their phone from their pocket and answer the call.

"Hello?" they managed to say.

"Good afternoon, Tove." Alice's voice boomed loud and clear—Tove kept the volume high to give them the best chance of understanding what the hell people were ever talking about. "I'm ringing to invite you to lunch tomorrow at my house. It's nothing special, just an opportunity to get to know the other Santa pageant contestants before the competition escalates."

Amid the panic roaring in Tove's ears, they scarcely heard what she said. "Sure," they replied.

"So tomorrow lunchtime, one o'clock sharp. I will text you my address."

"Yes, I'll be there. Thank—"

"Is Effie with you?"

They froze. Effie dawdled in the doorway, eyes wide, conspicuously listening.

"No. Sorry."

"No problem, I thought you might be able to pass on the message. I will phone her myself."

"Right. Goodbye?"

"Yes, see you tomorrow. Don't bring anything. I have it covered."

"G—"

The call dropped, and Tove grimaced at the phone. "Did that just happen?"

"Which bit?" asked Effie. "I, uh, heard it all. Sorry."

"I saw your elf ears twitching."

"Curious," Effie mused, "why did you say I wasn't with you?"

"This overachieving granny knows too much already."

"I would've told the truth."

"And we're not like each other. We've established this." Tove scowled. "I wish I hadn't agreed to go. She's so…"

"Self-assured? Steamrolling?"

"I dunno. I hate the phone. I'll agree to anything just to make them go away."

"I thought you hated your ringtone or something."

There was a question in Effie's voice, like she was fishing to see if Tove remembered bopping to "Poker Face" at breaktime in Year 8, clustered together as they shared Effie's cheap wired earphones and Tove's iPod Nano. They provided the tunes and Effie figured out how to do the dances in the music videos. The song was pure nostalgia.

"I changed it recently," they explained gruffly. "Was hoping a song I find comforting would make the experience of being cold-called less nerve-wracking. But I'll probably end up hating the song in association."

"Maybe you're doing it wrong. You said you'll agree to anything to make someone go away. So change your ringtone to, I don't know, *What Does the Fox Say?*, so you'll want to answer the phone to make it shut up."

"Wow Effie, that song could've stayed in the gutter and you *had* to drag it up." The corners of their mouth relaxed.

Then Effie's phone rang—her ringtone was a recent Carly Rae Jepsen song, the polar opposite of embarrassing—and she answered it. Her volume wasn't up as loud as Tove's, but there was no mistaking Alice's commanding tone.

And then…Alice asked Effie if Tove was with her. The question projected and Effie flinched away from the phone, like Alice had specifically raised her voice.

"No," Effie said evenly.

When the call disconnected, Tove gave her a look. "Why did you do that? I thought you said you'd've told the truth."

"I wasn't going to make you look like a liar," Effie argued. "You're right anyway, Alice knows too much."

Tove gritted their teeth against the tears encroaching once again. It was huge that when faced with an opportunity to make them look royally bad, Effie had their back.

"So you find 'Poker Face' comforting, eh?"

Heat flashed in their cheeks. "It's just a song."

Effie reached out and wrapped her fingers around their wrist. She tugged them out of the bedroom, to the kitchen and the soup, their pulse fluttering under her touch.

"Just saying, but I am the most sentimental person on the planet, but I'm not listening to tunes from 2008."

15

Effie didn't ask Tove when they were going to leave…

She liked their company and didn't want to spook them away. It was hard to know whether they were having fun on her sofa watching sketch comedy compilations on YouTube. Maybe they lived somewhere they didn't like. Maybe they struggled with task initiation. She didn't ask when they were going to leave…

But eventually they did. Around teatime, Tove said, "I should go soon. I've got…uh…knitting group." A little while later they stood to leave, still tucked up in Effie's favourite hoodie.

Effie paused by the door for a good few seconds, unsure of goodbye. It felt like a bigger deal than it should be, considering she'd be seeing Tove tomorrow for dinner and interviews. She wondered if the easy company they'd been enjoying would be gone by that time. She wondered what would've happened if she'd challenged the "knitting group" lie; would they have stayed longer or left sooner?

So Tove went, and Effie wondered if she should've hugged or kissed them goodbye.

And then Effie slouched on the sofa, cat in lap, and gave in to an explicable sadness.

Something she'd come to understand was that her inner world was always a little bit at war with the outside world. Inside, she was a sunny lesbian with oodles of love to give. Her sadness and loneliness came from outside, from the crushing effort of trying to live a sincere, fulfilled queer life.

At thirteen she was frantically saving up to visit her Tumblr crush in Ontario (at the time, she didn't recognise why she felt so frantic, but it didn't matter because she never found the money anyway); at fifteen, she struggled to tell her best friend how she felt, and it hurt even more that Tove hadn't stayed to listen; now at twenty-five all she wanted was a partner and a house full of plants, but she'd ended up on this painfully allocisheterosexual Island, where everyone was always shaming the things she wanted to like about herself.

Funnily enough, queerness was rarely the thing they tried to shame her for. But they didn't really validate it, either. Heck, she'd learned recently that PCOS met the criteria for an intersex condition. Nobody told her about intersexuality when she was in hospital once again with a phantom appendicitis that turned out to be ovarian cysts, and it felt like her body was rejecting itself, and the only thing that calmed the constant nausea was the tiny hormone pill she took when she remembered.

Add to that her birthday. "Beware the Ides of March," her parents used to say with wry grins. She was born on the day of betrayal, sandwiched between the millennials and generation Z, belonging nowhere. Impossible, invisible, incongruent.

Once upon a time she thought she had a chance at happiness. Now she was so deeply stuck, she wasn't sure she had a chance at anything.

But that kind of thinking wasn't going to help her, was it?

Effie shook off her mood and asked Lalla if she could come over and work on her craft.

She had to wait three whole minutes at the door until Lalla answered it.

"Sorry, had to make sure Heather was drying between her toes."

"Couldn't Liam…" Effie began. But a peep into the lounge revealed Liam with his feet up watching some esports tournament and gesturing at the screen like a dudebro watching the boxing.

"Don't ask." Lalla ushered her upstairs into the craft room, where Heather sat cross-legged in her pyjamas.

"Hi," Effie said. "Joining us?"

"Yes," said Heather at the same time as Lalla said, "No."

They stared at each other. Even a child who'd been raised by the internet was no match for Lalla's plucked and pinched eyebrows.

"I only wanted to tell Aunty Effie how sad I am about DuBois," said Heather.

"Really?" Effie recalled her role in the great mulled wine spillage of the Pollack last night with a smatter of guilt. Sure, that probably wasn't what drove DuBois out, but she could've been nicer.

"He was *so* cute."

"Do you know why he quit?" Lalla asked, gossip face engaged.

"Who knows? Likes his cushy lifestyle I suppose."

"You don't know that. Maybe he was cold," snapped Heather.

"Everyone was cold."

Effie was cold even while sharing Tove's body heat. An image popped into her head, of asking DuBois to join them too. The Bryans. Alice. The six of them spooning for warmth in her minuscule tent.

She shuddered and tried to change the subject. "So are you rooting for me now?"

Heather scowled and Lalla planted her hands on her hips. "You have something else to tell Aunty Effie, don't you, Heather?"

This time Heather crumbled. "I'm going to be on TV tomorrow. I'm your guest."

Oh no. Effie's guest for the interview segment. They'd invited her seven-year-old niece. "Fishsticks."

"Yep." Heather curled her glossy lips in a smirk that Effie didn't like one bit. "They rang Mummy up all proper and now I'm doing it."

"So I have you to thank?" Effie turned on her sister.

Lalla shrugged. "She wanted to. But this is on you, Effie. The reason you gave for entering the damn contest was your niece, when you were up on that stage at the weekend. Of course they invited her."

Those absolute geniuses. Effie wondered if Nowell had done this, or if they had senior producers calling the shots and trying to stir up drama.

Lalla scooped up Heather and popped her in bed, leaving Effie to contemplate her doom. Heather was going to ruin her on camera. She didn't know how, but Heather was honest and brutal, and if Effie weren't the one getting destroyed, she'd totally be hosting a watch party for the interview segment tomorrow.

"Have you told the parents?"

Effie looked up to behold her sister leaning on the doorpost.

"About the pageant?"

Lalla came in and shut the door. "They'll be delighted."

"If by that you mean they'll ridicule me."

Their parents weren't far away—in the West of the Island, so out in the sticks but still less than a mile from a main road. Effie and Lalla didn't see them often. Ever since they'd got back together when Lalla moved out and Effie was at uni in the UK, it had been clear they preferred being left to themselves. Their relationship worked best when they could pretend they didn't have children. Or the most perfect(ly infuriating) grandchild anyone could ever wish for.

"You're coming to Christmas dinner, right?"

"Yeah." Effie sighed. Christmas was the one thing their parents really felt obliged to make a family event out of. "I'd be surprised if they weren't watching the News, actually. They probably know what I'm up to, and they'll bring it up half a bottle of wine into the *festivities*." The word tasted like pickled cabbage, Dad's favourite, in her mouth.

Lalla eyed her like she was holding a grenade. "Effie… I've been thinking about what your Santa friend—Tove—said in the interview. Something about wanting to speak for the people who don't have good memories of Christmas. Do you think that applies to us?"

Effie startled. "Us? No, I love Christmas! It's only the Christmas dinner with the parents bit I dread. But it's never as bad as I expect. Why? Do you feel like that?"

Lalla shrugged. "Christmas was a weird time for so long. Don't you remember? Midnight Mass with Dad, Christmas morning swim with Mum, turkey number 1 at Mum's, turkey number 2 at Dad's. And now suddenly they're back together and doing those things together again? I don't know, it fucks with my head."

How could Effie forget being passed from one parent to another like hot rocks? Lalla was that much older that Effie assumed she was better able to process it. Perhaps she was wrong.

"I think your friend had a point."

Effie's now-or-never moment appeared, and she seized it. "I have to ask," she said, "what do you know about Tove that I don't? Liam mentioned a strange story. Is it something you can tell me?" Tove's reaction to their phone ringing, their snark and standoffishness…there had to be a reason.

Lalla sat on her backless swivel chair while Effie remained on the floor. She twisted back and forth as if deciding what to say. "I don't know how public it is. Especially if you were friends—right? Wouldn't Tove have told you?"

"It's…been a while since we were…close."

"Maybe Tove doesn't want you to know."

"Yeah, you're probably right. But can I ask one thing?"

"Shoot."

"Is it to do with Tove's ex?"

Lalla gave her a look that said *why did you put me through this?* "Oh, well, you already know then. They had their whole wedding booked and planned. And literally weeks before the day, Tove walked. Absolutely wild."

Effie couldn't look up from the carpet she was picking at. It was full of dust and hair and old staples, something like Tove's past. Tove, who basically ditched her after their one kiss at Winter Ball. Tove, who didn't believe in happily-ever-afters. Tove, who jilted their fiancé at the last moment. No wonder they were the way they were.

"Come on, let's get started on those wire animals for your craft fair thingy."

Before heading home, Effie stopped by the lounge to say goodbye to Liam. Tournament apparently finished, now he was sprawled on the floor mashing buttons on a Nintendo Switch with a thunderous face.

"What's up with him?" she asked Lalla.

"Heather keeps kicking his butt in *Surf's Up!* He's cashing in some practice."

"While she's asleep?"

"Of course. When else?"

Liam didn't look up. He was as engrossed as a grub eating a raspberry.

"Hey, the pageant segment is on in five, want to watch it here?" Lalla suggested.

After how it went on Sunday the answer was not really, but Effie did want to see it nevertheless.

"Won't we disturb Liam?"

"No, watch this." Lalla sauntered over and nudged his shoulder gently with her foot. "Hey, darling, would you make me a cup of tea?"

"On it." He quit out the game and leapt to his feet, nodding at Effie on his way to the kitchen.

"Christ," Effie swore as Lalla preened. She wanted someone to call her "darling." Someone to make cups of tea for.

Soon the segment on the sleep-out began. Most of the runtime was given to the fundraiser, but at the end was a recap of the actual night, interspersed with commentary from the

Santas in the interview room. The cameras missed the mulled wine incident, but there was a sneaky clip of Tove huddled on their flattened tent, and Effie beckoning them into her tent and them crawling inside. "Just gals being pals," said Bryan #2 in the interview room with the cheekiest of face-crinkles. (That old man was far too online for anyone's good.) There was also footage of DuBois packing up his things and leaving, but it was hard to pay attention with Lalla beaming eye-holes into Effie's skull from across the room.

"A while since you were close?" she exploded as the News rolled to tomorrow's weather. "It can get pretty close in a three-foot tent, Effie."

"Emotionally, sentimentally, I meant," Effie snapped.

She couldn't leave quick enough.

16

On the way home after knitting group, on a whim, Tove stopped by their favourite produce shop. It was run by Island folks and stocked local products, perfect for Christmas presents. They found what they wanted right away: handmade bath bombs. Effie and her absurdly big bath would love them. A present was the least Tove could do for how patient and accepting Effie had been over the past couple of days. She hadn't even kicked them out of her flat tonight; Tove really felt like she would've let them stay forever.

"You've been gone a while," Mum commented when they finally arrived home.

"Yes."

"You missed the pageant broadcast. It seems like a rather difficult night for you."

"It wasn't so bad." Guessing what they chose to show (probably DuBois's dramatic attack on their tent), Mum must be freaking out with motherly worry.

"Very nice of the other girl to take you under her wing."

Oh, they filmed that? "Yes, it was nice. Today she invited me back to her apartment to warm up. Sorry I didn't text you, I was napping at hers."

"I was worried," their mum confessed. "But I'm glad you're okay."

Tove flopped on the couch and kicked off their shoes, too worn even to make it to their bedroom. Mum loitered behind the armchair, expectant.

"I made Grannie Dot's gingerbread," she announced, producing from behind her back a Celebrations tin which contained a round brown cake.

"And? You do that every year."

"Actually, not since you stopped spending Christmas at home."

Tove kept their eyes on their feet. Even before moving to Germany, they used to spend Christmas with Aaron's family rather than their own. "Well, we were never much of a cake family," they reasoned.

"Your old friend used to eat most of it."

Now they caught onto where Mum was going with this. "Okay, it was Effie who let me share her tent. You saw it on TV. I get it."

Mum basically ignored them. "I always liked Effie."

"I thought you called her a bad influence on me. When you found out all Dad's vodka bottles under the stairs were full of water. You said she doesn't think before she does things."

"Oh, that was all your dad. You know what he's like when he's cross, he doesn't mean anything by it. I personally thought she was a good influence. She really brought you out of your shell, don't you think?"

Tove scowled. "It's been a long time, Mum."

"I know, I know, I'm very embarrassing and presumptive. All I want to say is, I would be pleased to see her if you ever wanted to bring her round."

"I wish you hadn't made the gingerbread," they grumbled.

"You do?"

They raised their gaze to meet hers, hating the wobble of her chin, recognising the same sensitivity to rejection and proneness to hurt in themself. "I know you mean well. But it feels like you're funnelling me into inviting Effie over."

"I have always tried not to funnel you." Mum's voice cracked. There had been many conversations over the years about "funnelling"; the word was hers.

"I know," Tove soothed. "Mostly you don't."

"You are too strong to be funnelled anyway," Mum comforted herself. "You've always known exactly where you want to be in life."

"That's not true."

"Well, I hope you are where you want to be now."

Tove's heart broke that Mum could ever find out how far astray they went, and how they no longer knew where they wanted to be. Still, they thought, reliving how it felt this afternoon to wake up in Effie's arms, in her clothes, and now coming home to a warm hearth, this could be it.

"It doesn't matter," they told Mum. "I'm safe and that's enough."

"I'm glad you feel safe here."

"When I...you know...moved back here, there was a bedroom all waiting for me. I wanted to thank you for keeping it. Even though you could've thrown out all my stuff and turned it into a study or a dining room or whatever."

Mum's brow pinched. "I wanted you to always have somewhere to come back to, if you ever needed it."

She surely understood that Tove wasn't ever supposed to come back. They'd made it clear they wouldn't even be back for Christmas. Yet she'd kept their room intact all the same. Almost like she was expecting their relationship to fall apart in a catastrophic way. Or perhaps it was her plain, self-avowed sentimentality.

Tove braved the question. "Did you think I'd end up coming home?"

"It's not a matter of what I thought," Mum said, "it's that I never want you to be left guessing whether I'll support you or not. You and your brother are the best things in my life and I'll always do everything in my capacity to support you, whether you take what I offer or not."

"Mum," Tove croaked. Occasionally their mum—the one who'd handled everything when they could do nothing, cancelling the venue, melting the rings, selling the dress, calling all the guests—outed herself as one of the best people in this world.

And then she ruined it.

"So, have you thought any more about carolling at late-night shopping on Thursday?"

"There's nothing to think about." Tove hauled themself off the couch and trudged to their room. To themself, they added, "I don't even think I can play anymore."

All the same, once their door was safely shut, they unlatched their trumpet case and stared down their golden nightmare.

"You've really got me in a bind, Felicity," they told their trumpet. "I desire you. You just intimidate me. I don't want to suck at playing you."

They polished the lacquer to give their hands something to do, imagining a spirit coming out of the bell and hovering before them.

The spirit would nod sagely. "Trust me. I've got you."

Tove stuffed the spirit back into the instrument and the instrument back into the case. Mum pottered outside their door, winding tinsel around the bannister. So close was Tove to opening the door and telling her everything, their heart accelerated to a drum roll.

Sweating, they stood up and peeked into the hall.

Mum spotted them immediately. "Tove? You look like you've seen a ghost."

Tove scuttled into the hall, feeling about four years old, and cannoned into their mum's waiting arms. "I love you, Mum," they said, holding a sob in their throat.

"I love you too." Mum squished them in a warm cuddle.

Tove buried their nose in her cardigan and imagined how her face would melt if they told her all the things Aaron said and did. She must never know.

When they returned to their room, they looked for someone who they could tell anything to. But they couldn't find him. And that's when they noticed they'd left Oberon at Effie's.

They drafted a text. **Hey Effie, I think I left my bear at yours.** Backspace. **Hey Effie, I think I left something at yours.** Better. Aaron would've never let Tove live it down if they were upfront about taking a bear to the sleepout. Easier to just drive over and collect him without specifying what they'd left behind.

But Effie replied almost immediately, with a photo of Oberon tucked up in her bed, paws on the duvet. He looked so cosy. Effie had captioned the picture, **It's his bed now.**

Tove stared at the photo for a little bit, overcome with affection for the way Effie had arranged him in her bed, with obvious care. They hadn't said anything by the time Effie's next message arrived.

What's his name?

Oberon.

An excellent name for an excellent bear.

Can you take care of him? Till I see you again?

I will take the most care. You can count on me.

And then Tove realised there was someone else they could talk to, someone who wasn't an inanimate bear. Someone who had been nice to them, who had shown kindness even when they snapped and snarled at her. Someone whose goofy smile had them envious enough to want to kiss it off her. Effie had offered them friendship…and Tove was ready to trust her with the truth about Aaron and their failed engagement and the wedding that didn't happen.

Tomorrow, they decided. Tomorrow, they'd tell her.

Wednesday

5 days till Christmas

17

Effie's wardrobe stared back as if to say, *They're your clothes. Don't look at me.*

She was supposed to be at Alice's for one o'clock. *Sharp!* she'd said, in the tone of someone describing the knife in their hand. It was currently eleven, and so far Effie had eaten, showered, and shaved her legs and PCOS face fuzz. It had been a long time since she'd had a reason to dress up nice, but today was the day. Not just because Tove would be there. After what she'd discovered from Lalla, and the subsequent sleepless night, heavy eyeshadow was a must.

An off-the-shoulder jumper slipped off its hanger and thudded to the floor, bringing her back to her wardrobe predicament.

If only she had a group chat to text outfits to. Moving away from the Island only to graduate into a pandemic and recession, and then moving back with a brain that perpetually forgot to reply to text messages, had not made for lasting friendships. Now she was tossed from temp job to temp job trying to avoid accountancy and failing to find anything permanent, mostly working with old guys on the fringes of the finance industry. How did people make friends in their twenties? Joining a Santa cosplay group, or whatever this was, seemed as good an attempt as any.

In the end, she texted Lalla three pics with the message **Show these to Heather and ask which she thinks**

She abandoned her phone to moisturise, and a minute later her cat buzzed. Melchior had taken up residence in her favourite spot, and she mewed as two more messages came in.

"Off you get." Effie swept her away.

The pokerdot dress is horible on you

Hate everything about the pink

U look hot in black

Effie texted, **Who's actually typing here**

Lalla's number spammed the eyes emoji, which said it all. Amazing that Heather had her own phone but still had unfettered access to Lalla's as well.

It wasn't black anyway. Effie pulled the *dark purple* top over her head. The cashmere glided soft as seawater over her skin, and the sleeves shrugged over her biceps, elastic pinching above the elbow. She picked some flared trousers to go with it, white with crimson vertical pinstripes, which made her look red-carpet tall. Her newly smooth legs felt fucking lovely in them. Gold hoop earrings, careful dark purple eye make-up, combat boots, oversized beige fleece, a spritz of vanilla and musk, and she was done.

The top wasn't black, but Lalla's phone gremlin-aka-daughter was right about one thing: she did look hot.

"Meow," said Melchior, agreeing, as Effie fed her to do.

"I should've asked you folks in the first place, not my sister," Effie said, addressing Melchior and Oberon, whose bespectacled head peeped out the top of her backpack.

A bus ride later, Effie strolled up Alice's gigantic driveway to her many-windowed bungalow. She wished she'd put on more scent to mask her sweating. It had been ages since she'd visited a big house, and Alice's reeked of middle-aged privilege in the special way someone who'd been on the property ladder for decades did. When she stepped up to the door, she caught a whiff of lavender cleaning product that sent her right back to her gran's house. It was startlingly visceral, considering how long ago her gran had passed away.

Before she had a chance to knock, the door opened to reveal a kid who definitely shouldn't be able to reach the latch.

"This one's an adult," the kid called over their shoulder.

An older kid glanced up from a thick hardback with yellowed pages. "Take 'em to the adult room, Raffi."

Raffi beckoned Effie inside all serious and proper, then proceeded to glower for no apparent reason.

"What?" Effie asked.

Raffi pointed at the wicker basket beside the doormat. To Effie's honest-to-Jesus horror, it contained about fifty children's shoes, all glitter and smallness and the scent of athlete's foot powder.

"Shoes off," said Raffi sternly.

Feeling terribly undignified and hoping no one arrived at the door while she was bending over and standing on one leg, Effie tugged off her size 9 combat boots and added them to the basket.

Raffi beckoned again. Effie followed, wondering what sweet hell they were taking her to. But Raffi led her past sweet hell—a big room full of screaming children—and down a hall lined with antique ornamental cabinets, towards a conservatory at the end of the corridor where she spied the two Bryans lounging around with wine glasses. But—wait up—Effie could swear she'd seen a familiar face in the roomful of kids.

It was a struggle to let go of the light at the end of the corridor, but curiosity won out. She retraced her steps—to Raffi's displeasure—and peeked into the doorway they'd passed.

Two lost brown eyes met hers.

"Tove?" Effie took a deep breath and crossed the threshold. The noise hit her like a train, but then there was Raffi screaming, "No adults in the kids room!" And about twenty—well, six at most—children looked up from their Duplo and glockenspiels and plastic food to yell, "INTRUDER! INTRUDER!"

And Effie, faced with an army of jammy kids, was forced to fall back.

She sank to the floor in the hall. How did Tove get in there? Or she supposed the real question was: how would she get them out?

She peered into the doorway again. One of the kids glared, but Effie swallowed and focused on a cross-legged figure buried in a mound of Duplo: Tove. A toddler presented block after block and Tove piled them in their lap, smile-less and forlorn.

Swiftly running some calculations in her head, Effie enacted Plan B. It was a fast crawl into the room, a grab of Tove's wrist, and a forceful drag into the corridor. Effie was in and out with her quarry before Raffi could sound the alarm.

"This one's mine," she told Raffi, firmly.

And Raffi, shrugging, returned to the front door. Now it was Effie and Tove alone in the corridor, contemplating the journey to the conservatory.

"Are you okay?" Effie asked, helping them up.

"They think I'm one of them," Tove sniffed.

Effie almost joked that Tove was on the small side, but couldn't bring herself to do it.

As if reading her mind, Tove groaned. "Whatever, I'm short. But it's not only that. I have a child's face. And style." They gestured at themself and searched Effie for a reaction.

Carefully, Effie looked them up and down. They wore avocado-patterned socks and denim three-quarter-length dungarees over a moss-green T-shirt that would look ordinary on anybody else, but was devastatingly hot on them. As for their face...well, Effie was no good at guessing, but she wouldn't peg Tove for younger than twenty. "You're stunning," she said, without really meaning to. "I mean, that's not really what you asked, is it?"

Tove sucked their lips, hollowing the dimples in their cheeks. "Sometimes I feel like I'm stuck at fifteen, still trying to puzzle together the pieces of a personality. But I'm not fifteen, I'm twenty-five. They say your brain is done developing at twenty-five. Terrifying, right? Like is this really it?"

"Doesn't everybody feel that way their whole lives?" countered Effie. "Anyway, you're thinking about it in a very fatalistic way. Our brains are never 'done.' We're always experiencing and learning and adapting. Think about how there are some cognitive things our brains literally *can't* do until we're in our mid-twenties. But now we can! We're actually getting stronger!"

"Then why do people treat us like shit because we're young? There's no point scolding a puppy for pissing on the furniture. They don't understand why you're upset and you can't make them understand."

"Who's scolding you for pissing on the furniture?"

"Maybe that's a bad analogy. How about when they parade you around in public and compliment your youthful looks, but bin all your croptops because apparently it's childish to show your midriff. It's the subtext. Calling someone childish is saying they're sub-human. Irresponsible. Unknowing. Incomplete. Probably a little bit gross."

"Uh, what the fuck?" cried Effie. "*Yes*, it's the subtext. Their goal is to call you all those things and they use the word 'childish' to accomplish that, while keeping the moral high ground because unfortunately it's socially acceptable to be an asshole to kids. It's nothing to do with you being or looking young and everything to do with that person being a piece of shit."

A suspicion snuck up on Effie: this, and what she'd discovered last night, were surely connected. It wasn't really about being put in the kids room, was it?

"This might be a bad time," she said, "but I brought your friend."

She twirled around so Tove could hopefully see Oberon peeping out of her rucksack. She thought they might laugh, but instead they retrieved him quickly and stuffed him into their own bag, red-faced.

"What's up?" she said.

"It's a bit embarrassing, isn't it?" Tove muttered. "Talking about wanting to be treated like an adult and then bringing a bear to all your social events."

"There's nothing wrong with bringing a friend along. You never know when you might need one."

"Huh. True." Tove sighed a little. "I guess I should be nicer to kids."

And so should Effie, she realised… It was second nature for Heather to treat her like a lesser being, mirroring Lalla's attitude

(Lalla having learned it all from Mum and Dad), and in turn, because Effie was indignant, she looked down on Heather. To invalidate it. To make herself feel better. To treat Heather like her elders had always treated her. To reinforce her shaky and besieged sense of self.

Ah. That was it. Every time Tove shrank back or lashed out, it was because of a slight or perceived slight to their personhood, autonomy, or identity. They were incredibly, extraordinarily sensitive to rejection. Perhaps—and Effie recalled the exact same struck-by-lightning look now from the suspended moments after they'd kissed at Winter Ball—they had always been a little bit this way.

But Effie didn't say any of this. Instead, she said, "Maybe the kids recognised you as someone who wouldn't give them any of this adult bullshit. Like a compliment. They take one look at me dressed up way too fancy and think, 'oh that person isn't gonna want to get her trousers dirty' and 'she obviously wants to drink wine and talk about nothing with people she doesn't know, and go home feeling emptier than when she came.' I feel like a fool thinking about what my life is."

"I don't want to take it as a compliment. That's reductive most of the time."

Good point. Effie's own adaptive coping mechanism when belittled—to convert what she could into a compliment and privately worry the rest was true—suddenly seemed less than sustainable. Maybe she should take her own advice: accept that the humiliation she endured from her family was less about her and more about them. But that was different. Effie's family were probably right.

She found herself lamenting her schooldays. When she and Tove used to hang out, there was always something to talk about, something fun to do. School wasn't perfect, but she missed that life—back when she still believed her life and dreams would all work out in the end. When she still believed she was or could be a good person.

Tove's thoughts were running along similar lines: "I honestly don't think I've been happy or relaxed in my whole adult life. But maybe I'm not remembering all the things I used to stress about."

Effie remembered a few of them: being in love with her best friend, for starters.

"It all feels different when you go away and come back," she said. "I feel smaller than I used to. More boxed in. Much more alone. I've seen what's beyond the Island. But it's hard to be ambitious when you're stuck and nobody believes you can unstick."

"I feel smaller too," Tove agreed. "I've been wrung out and hung to dry and forgotten about. Like I've failed and been banished to this purgatory Island to think about what I did wrong. I followed my dreams and they completely and utterly sucked."

Effie bit back a gasp. It was all too real. And Effie knew more about Tove than she should.

"But what do you do when you feel small?" Tove went on. "You find something that makes you big again."

Tove fished a mulberry lipstick from their dungarees pocket and crouched to apply it using a mirror in one of Alice's cabinets. They straightened moments later, smacking their lips. The colour popped with their moss-green shirt, all the more striking with their ginger, mascara-less eyelashes.

They tilted their head, charm incarnate, and Effie almost passed out.

"That's better. I feel up for this now."

"Colour gives you confidence," Effie said automatically. Tove had told her that one time she'd complimented their wardrobe. No, it was a brand-new pair of neon-yellow track shoes they wore to sports day the year they beat the entire class in the 1600m.

Tove shot her a curious look. "Hey, this lippy would go so well with your shirt and eyeliner, like you'd think we planned it. Do you want some?"

"Yeah, I'd l—"

Effie reached to accept the lipstick, but Tove didn't hand it over. Instead they stepped close, wielding it themself. "This cool?" they said.

As anxious as Effie had been to use Tove's lipstick, it being theirs and all, she ached now to feel their scrutiny of her lips. For them to be the one to touch her.

She nodded.

Tove's left thumb and forefinger clasped Effie's chin, pressing into the flesh softly, decisively. They wound the tube to their satisfaction, deft with their right hand. And they peered at Effie's lips.

"Pout for me," they demanded.

Effie did it. The lukewarm waxy stick pushed into her lower lip, bringing with it a waft of creamy sweetness. Then the upper lip.

"How's that?"

Tove detached abruptly from her chin and their heat receded. Effie caught herself swaying forwards.

"Good," she whispered, rubbing her lips together and trying to get her bearings.

Without stopping to let her recover, Tove gestured back to the kids room. "Where did these kids come from anyway?" They flashed a conspiratorial smile, as if they hadn't been chatting the deepest shit. As if they didn't just clamp Effie's chin and paint her purple.

"I don't know," Effie spluttered.

"Come on," Tove said, looping their pinky finger into hers, "let's join the party."

Alice's bear hug thumped Effie back to reality.

"Hello troops," she trilled, "come and make yourselves at home. We have Shloer—*two* flavours!"

Well, thank fuck Effie wasn't expected to get drunk. She was still stumbling from that moment in the corridor, when Tove stepped away and their celestial gravity nearly took her with them. Holy crap, was Effie falling for them. All the signs were there.

"I recommend the white grape and elderflower," Bryan #1 remarked cordially.

"Join me with the cranberry, Effie," Bryan #2 urged. "It'll match your trousers."

Effie surveyed his maroon chinos. "Is that why you chose the cranberry?"

"Naturally. It's all about aesthetic."

He really was a maroon chinos kind of person, maybe even the best dressed of the lot of them—although Alice, even in running gear, emanated such an air of class and competence that made Effie feel dowdy.

The sixth member of the party was Alice's husband, a beige-wearing man called Bill who washed pans in the sink while his wife ran the show. Effie asked if she could help with anything, to which he whispered, "Psst, do you want to see the crab I caught?" He took off his heatproof rubber gloves to open the cupboard under the sink, and Effie found herself staring into the beady dead eyes of the biggest crabby fucker she'd ever seen. "I'll be picking him later," Bill explained with a highly unnecessary wink.

And the seventh member of the party, who strolled in without warning right as they were scraping chairs at the table, was DuBois.

"Hello, everybody!" he called. "Did you miss me?"

He rolled up his satin Santa sleeves—he was put out that it wasn't a costume party—and reached into Alice's huge saucepan for some pasta.

Far from a bougie three-course meal, Alice had boiled two kilos of spaghetti and warmed ten jars of supermarket own-brand tomato sauce. To be fair, she was cooking for about five thousand people including the children—grandchildren, it turned out—who flocked in for their portions and vanished with tomato-stained faces.

Alice and DuBois hit it off at one end of the table, which made absolutely no sense and a lot of sense at the same time. Snatches of their dialogue included DuBois being a shameless flirt (towards both Alice and her husband), Alice flirting back while holding her husband's hand conspicuously on the tablecloth, and many, many stories about their respective world travels, a conversation Effie longed to join but where she had absolutely nothing to contribute.

When she glanced the other way to check on Tove, they were deeply engrossed in Bryan #1's monologue about the miniature piano he was constructing for his latest doll's house. Tove could do with a Santa of their own, Effie mused.

That left her and Bryan #2.

Their eyes met across the table and he pulled a dad-like shrug, all exaggerated as if they were both in on the absurd joke that was this spaghetti dinner party. "So Effie, you're a young lesbian with a physics degree, is that right?"

"Engineering," she corrected. "I wrote my dissertation about archways."

"Then," he said, "you can tell me how to deal with my *arch* nemesis." He cocked a finger towards Bryan #1. "I'll give you a hint, he has the same name as me, and all the kids are certain he's the real Father Christmas. If he joins me on TikTok he'll be unstoppable."

"You and I both know who the real Santa is," Effie rebutted, taking the same playful tone. She raised her own finger, and waggled it between him and herself. "Between you and me," she said meaningfully. It was a challenge and a threat and a joke all in one.

"Are you saying I have two arch nemeses?"

"Alright, so you've got your semi-circular arch, your classic, traditional archway," she explained. "But then you've got a parabolic archway—it's elegant, it's sexy, it's inevitable, and there is nothing you can do about it. Like, not in a sex way. In a Santa way."

"That is some way to tell me I'm old!" He leaned back with a guffaw. "Your humour reminds me of my husband's. He's strong and handsome and funny, and is very good at making smelly vegan soap—absolutely A-tier human."

"You mean S-tier," Effie said with the confidence that was in her nature, when she felt comfortable and respected. She described the S-tier to Bryan #2, who took a scruffy pocket notebook from his chinos and wrote the phrase down.

"For TikTok," he explained. "I'm shocked I could possibly describe my husband as A-tier, now I know there's a higher plane."

"One day I'll have a spouse or partner," Effie told him, "and they'll be S-tier as well. And our spouses will meet and immediately implode the universe because it would be untenable for two such excellent beings to exist in proximity."

"Are you in the market for a partner?"

Effie trained her gaze firmly on him and managed to keep her cheeks cool throughout the wildfire of embarrassment raging underneath. Partner? Please, just give her one friend or family member who truly cared.

"In a non-deliberate kind of way," she answered, a little hoarse. "I love loving people. But first I have to win the Santa pageant, so I can be worthy of being loved back."

"A word of counsel," Bryan #2 said. "Those who love you truly will not ask you to prove yourself."

Nobody had asked Effie exactly. In the end, she was here of her own volition. To prove something to herself, perhaps. With a precious hope of course for others' validation.

"You're certainly worthy of love," he added emphatically, "and that has nothing to do with the pageant. But for what it's worth, I believe you have what it takes. I confess I'm a little frightened of your competition."

"Thank you, Bryan #2. You're very kind."

"I'm just a normal guy," said TikTok Santa, "and I warn you I'm prepared to fight for my win. And so should you."

Effie absorbed his boldness. "I am. I *will* be the best Santa."

"Good. Now, did I hear you call me 'Bryan #2'? Number *two*? Who on Bezos's burning earth is Bryan #1?"

"Must've misheard me." Effie smiled expansively. Now she'd been exposed, she might start calling them B1 and B2 like the Bananas in Pyjamas.

After dinner, Alice's daughter-in-law, Claudine, popped in to fetch her kids and a box of books. As was the way, Effie found herself helping pack books and having a chat. Claudine ran the Island's first Black bookshop out of her porch, and kept most of her stock in Alice's spare room. She'd applied for a lot in the new shopping centre but had been outbid by the big chains.

"Alice thinks she's going to do something about it by winning the pageant, but we all know this is one thing she can't bulldoze her way into."

Back in the conservatory, Alice suggested party games. Excellent though Effie was at charades, her spaghetti stomach was not primed for prancing around, so when the Bryans announced they had to get home to their spouses before the interviews later, she excused herself too.

Tove tugged on her sleeve as Alice and DuBois settled down for loose-leaf tea and sour gummy sweets like the unlikeliest of friends.

"Hey, can I come with you? I can drive you home."

Effie couldn't blame them. Imagine being abandoned to the disarming charisma of Alice and DuBois? Or the volatile chaos of the kids room? No thanks.

"Of course," she said. It felt like a promise. One thing was certain: she absolutely had to come clean about what Lalla had told her.

They talked about nothing on the way home. Nothing as in: *Who's your favourite Bryan?* (Effie's was B2 and Tove's was B1.) *DuBois isn't so bad, is he?* (They agreed that he was harmless, and in fact nice.) *Could you make a better pasta sauce than Alice?* (They'd both made better pasta sauces at university, with hangovers, in pots that didn't belong to them.) They even wished they'd gone to the same uni, and hung out, and eaten each other's pasta sauces. ("Not a euphemism," said Tove, when Effie was about to make it one.)

And then the journey was over. Tove clammed up as they filed into Effie's flat. Effie wondered if they were thinking about last time they were here, how the two of them had bathed and napped and Effie dreamed about them… Unbelievably, that was only yesterday. The bathroom felt off-limits now; the bedroom even more so. They both pretended those rooms didn't exist, as if they held secrets they'd sworn never to tell.

Speaking of secrets, it was more than time.

"Tove," Effie began as she boiled the kettle, "my sister's husband knows your brother."

Tove, choosing a mug from the cupboard, froze as if struck by the icy wind of premonition.

Guiltily, Effie pressed on. "While watching the pageant broadcast the other day, he said something about you. And I asked for the whole story."

"What do you know?" Tove spoke slowly, either ominous or fighting to remain casual.

"I know you were engaged?" It came out like a question.

"Oh." They bit their lip, not looking up, then went back to shuffling and clinking Effie's mugs. "I suppose that saves me telling you."

It wasn't the reaction Effie had expected. "You sound like there could've been something else to find out."

"I was engaged, that's all anyone knows," said Tove evenly. "The way you said it made me think it was going to be something awful. Like I robbed a bank and didn't even know till you told me."

"How can you rob a bank without knowing?"

"I don't know." They were laughing now, but it was so self-deprecating Effie didn't know if she should laugh too. "Put it this way, if you told me I'd done it, I'd…believe you, I guess."

This was so not how Effie had imagined this conversation going. "Then you're not upset that I know?"

"Like I said, saves me telling you. Are you upset I didn't?"

"What? No. I feel bad for coaxing the story out."

"Look how much trouble you've saved us by being curious. Now you know everything there is to know about me. You understand me."

Tove's sly, sparkly half-smile took Effie right back. This was what she remembered: never knowing whether they were laughing with her or at her.

"Seriously," they added, "my failed wedding is my dark past. It's always at the back of my mind. But I'm oversharing if I talk about it and nefarious if I don't."

It was a bit of both: they were laughing both with her and at her. Effie relaxed. And because of that, instead of asking what, or why, she said, "That bad?"

Tove's smile wobbled like a branch under a heavy bauble. "It's a big deal. Some people say marrying young is foolish and of course it failed. Others think I'm the worst person ever for bailing three weeks before my wedding. The question is always 'Why?' But I'm not about to wring me and my ex's issues out in public. Do they think I don't wake up every morning with a guilty conscience? I'm drowning on the inside and I'm surely leaking bad vibes."

"Is that why you're so standoffish? To keep everyone away?"

"Duh."

"Well, it makes sense *now*. You're right. I think I do understand you better."

"Huh." Tove paused. "You're not going to believe this, but I'd decided to tell you today. It's almost a relief I don't have to find the words myself." At last they chose a mug from the cupboard—the Eeveelution mug, one of Effie's favourites. "God, I wish I could erase the past decade and start again from Winter Ball."

Hello, did they just say that? Were they finally going to talk about it? About Winter Ball? When they kissed? Effie panted into the space between them, waiting as the kettle rumbled to a climax.

Tove's brown eyes took her and held her with pinpoint pressure. Then they looked away. "I meant when I started getting to know Aaron. About to begin a nine-year relationship that ended badly. I wish I could have a do-over."

"Right?" Effie said, breathless. "If only he'd had one less beer at the pre-lash and not come and pissed all over our moment."

"Our moment? So that meant something to you?"

The kettle clicked. Done. Steam rose from the spout, Effie's hopes evaporating with it.

It was in their tone: Tove thought she was weird for treasuring that kiss all those years since they'd parted ways.

"Look, you found someone that night," Effie croaked. "I was happy for you. You were happy. *Weren't* you?"

It was a deadlock: they wanted her to confess, to confirm their suspicion that she was in fact the naïve and hopeless romantic they thought she was; Effie wanted them to reassure her it was a good thing she'd chickened out and let them move on with their life.

They muttered, "Maybe I could've been happier. I thought…never mind."

Unless…unless they returned her feelings after all. Unless they'd *wanted* Effie to tell them she liked them. To kiss them again and again no matter how many boys came offering a distraction.

"Thought what?" Effie pressed. "Thought what?" She leaned over so their faces were close, so they couldn't brush it off.

The stubborn hardness of Tove's cheeks untensed like they were melting. "I thought there was something between us. I thought you liked me. But we kissed and then you stood there like a lemon."

Wow, there it was. They *had* liked her. She knew it.

"Tove?" she said. "So did you."

A big wet tear rolled down Tove's face. And another, and another.

"I used to be a good actor," they sobbed. "If you thought I was happy not being with you, I must've been a really good actor. Not so much anymore."

Effie had seen Tove cry exactly one time. It was Year 9, they'd texted her halfway through first period: **Come find me?** Effie found them slumped against their locker. They'd started their period and were late to school, and got yelled at by Mrs Le Pelley. But they didn't burst into tears until Effie pulled them into a hug, and threaded her fingers through their hair, and rubbed their back while murmuring forgettable nothings.

After that, Tove went back to their mixed meek and abrasive self. A swirl of thoughts and feelings billowed about behind their brown eyes, coming out in snatches with their jokes, their laughter. They didn't cry again, or not in front of Effie.

Effie should probably offer a hug like she'd done that day by the lockers. But she said what was on her mind: "Tove, have you been incredibly emotionally repressed all along?"

Tove gazed between their wet, spindly eyelashes, and blubbered a laugh. "Did it take you this long to figure that out?" But their head dropped into their hands and they shook with a violence Effie couldn't begin to understand. "I used to be able to hold this in, I don't know what's happening to me."

Now Effie couldn't ignore it. She patted her shoulder and Tove fell into her arms.

"This is what I'm like now. I can go cold for days on end and then suddenly I crumble. Lots of nothing and then everything at once. It's scary, I can't control it. Like I'm finally learning to feel again, but I have no guideline for what's normal anymore. I'm doing it all alone." They broke on the last word and gasped for breath.

Effie took their hand and half-carried them to the sofa. Melchior trundled over, offering nuzzles. Together, Effie and her cat took Tove through some breathing, some counting, some grounding techniques.

"It's okay to feel," she said. "Tell me about it."

Tove talked and talked and grew more coherent, and the colour returned to their cheeks. They dried their tears and sat back, spent.

"How about we chill for a bit?" Effie suggested. "Maybe we could play some games? I have a Wii."

She brought out her little case of games and left Tove to peruse them as she splashed hot water into their abandoned mugs.

"Mario Party 8, I had that one." Tove flipped it over, hiccupping.

"Yeah, I literally bought a Wii because I had so much fun playing it at your house." Effie had no memory of the game itself; it was Tove who'd made it fun.

Tove crinkled into the cutest giggle. After crying they were like warm clay, all soft and kind of stripped back. They no longer had the energy to mask and hide.

"Effie, I think I understand something now."

"Yeah?" Effie placed their steaming mugs on the coffee table.

"You didn't do anything wrong."

Viscerally, something clicked in Effie's head. Tove's anger in the carpark on Friday. Their cynicism at the grotto on Saturday. Their rejection in the marquee on Sunday. Their exasperation in the car on Monday when Effie was trying to apologise—and, apparently, not for what they wanted her to apologise for.

"Wait, you were genuinely pissed at me for not telling you I liked you? You didn't give me a chance—you stopped talking to me altogether pretty soon after we kissed. I thought you regretted it. Hated me for kissing you."

"And I thought you led me on. I wanted to be with you, and when you said nothing, I was so hurt. I decided I might as well be with someone else. To get over you. And I think I've been holding this hurt for so long, maybe as a way to think about you even though you didn't want me."

"I never said I didn't want you."

"You never said you did. Not then, not the next day or the next. And I know I didn't say it either, and I'm sorry. I think we were both…too scared."

Effie's heart cracked like an over-glazed pot. Scared, no. Back then, after she'd chickened out at Winter Ball, she couldn't coexist with Tove's new relationship, in the same way as she couldn't coexist with her parents'. Couldn't coexist with any romantic relationship, in fact, even if it were her own.

"Tove, I cared about you so much. I'm so sorry you felt like I didn't like you as much as you liked me. I mustn't have been very good at showing it."

"It's not you," they said. "You were—you are—wonderful. Everything worked against us. My ex included."

They sat in silence for what felt like an age. Effie was stunned. Far too stunned to even wonder what Tove was feeling, until they spoke.

"Effie…" Their voice was meek, pleading. "Are you pissed at me? For being pissed at you?"

Pissed? Really? All Effie was doing was trying to process.

But when she looked, really looked at Tove, they were pale and shaking again, as if terrified. A few minutes of silence and they truly believed Effie was thinking bad things about them.

"I'm not pissed at you," Effie said.

It was as if her words unlocked Tove once again, and they unfurled. "Then…can I ask for something?"

"Sure." Effie would do anything for Tove if she only knew what they wanted.

"Can we kiss again? Like we did that one time at Winter Ball? Where it all started."

Effie hesitated no more than a split second. She stood up, took Tove's hands, and hoiked them to their feet, spilling Melchior off their lap and onto the floor, where she ran out of the room as if she knew what was coming next. Effie loosened one of their linked hands, placing it firmly on Tove's hip. She pulled them close. Her lips found their nose first, teeth grazing the tip in a tiny, greedy bite. Down, down, down to their mouth. Tove's lips parted without prompting and a gasp escaped…right onto Effie's waiting tongue. She lapped it up. Sweet corn on a stick, the *taste*!

"Fucking kiss me already," Tove growled.

Face first, their bodies crushed together. It was nothing like the kiss in the bushes. It was much, much better.

Tove's citrus perfume enveloped Effie in a fog of familiarity and hormones. They were feeling the same skin, sharing the same breath, wearing and ruining the same lipstick. Effie had never been so sure of herself. She was a being of sex, of sense, of surety. Ten years of kissing experience had brought her to this moment. Not because the bicurious girls and stoner lesbians who hit on her in clubs had taught her anything about kissing (though some of them were fun for a bit). It was more that after ten years of mediocre kisses, she had come home. To Tove's lips.

Effie broke briefly for air. She imagined going in again like they did in movies. There'd be a meeting of the eyes, a tiny nod, and then they'd go back in hungrier than before. This time they'd relish it, consciously log every sensation until they lost themselves completely. Maybe they'd fall back on the sofa and test how it felt to have Tove's weight on her, or to hold them gently beneath hers.

But that didn't happen. As she drew in, Tove shuffled away. Specks of eyeliner crackled underneath their shining eyes as if sprinkled there by a soot fairy. Effie's lips stung in the absence of theirs.

"It's too late," Tove whimpered. "It's too late for us to be together now."

"What?" Confusion twisted Effie's insides.

"I've changed too much. And so have you. It could never work."

First: pain. Tove didn't believe Effie could work with their heartbreak, meet their needs. Effie knew something they struggled to accept: even in their tears, their hurt, their anger, they were valid, normal, worthy of compassion. And Effie had capacity to offer them kindness. She wished Tove could see she was strong enough for them. But if they couldn't see it, she couldn't change that.

Second: a step back. Effie noticed once again the cynicism overshadowing Tove's thought process. Whatever their true hopes and beliefs, their defeatism wouldn't allow them to visualise a future where they got to be happy. Effie could relate to that, she really could.

All she could do for Tove was present a new possibility: a brief moment of pleasure. For a moment, perhaps, they could each feel truly loved.

"Maybe it doesn't have to be all or nothing," she soothed. "What if I kissed you again, and that was all?"

Tove hiccupped. Effie could almost hear the anxious cogs stop turning in their mind.

"I'd like that," Tove said.

18

Tove's waist tingled under Effie's circling hands. Her teeth nipped at their lips as she backed them into the wall. They were frightened—not of kissing her, although that was kind of the problem. They were frightened of this feeling of need filling their chest and throat. Of falling deep into someone, of trusting them and ignoring the red flags. What red flags? Were there any red flags with Effie? Could they find something, *any*thing that overrode their desire for her?

They would simply have to keep looking.

As their shoulderblades hit the wall, they surrendered their racing mind to the kiss. Effie's weight pressed the gloom clean out of their lungs. Her hands travelled up their body, thumbs ghosting sideboob where flesh spilled from their dungarees. Wetness flooded between their legs as she sucked at their jaw. The instant Tove let out a moan, Effie's lips were back, consuming their vocals hungrily into herself, playing with their tongue like a kitten with a feather.

And Tove, in kind, worked Effie's lips with the muscles they'd spent years building up in trumpet practice. For the first time in a long time, they craved the metal of a mouthpiece; they wanted to breathe their spirit into their instrument and excel there as they were excelling at this kiss.

Eventually Effie pulled back, alighting a final lick on the tip of Tove's nose.

"It was dry," she explained. "Speaking of, I need to hydrate."

Even with her weight gone, the pressure of her body remained. Tove luxuriated there against the wall until Effie took their hand and tugged them to the couch.

"Have a sit. Your knees are knocking."

They were, but it was from feverish euphoria, not the usual tremor of dread.

"Effie, I've a request," Tove said all in a rush.

"Another?" Effie gawked like they'd asked to sit on her—which Tove suspected, by the way she went on about her cunnilingus skills, might be all she truly desired. It was honestly not far from their mind either.

"It's nothing intimate," they clarified. "Or perhaps it's truly intimate."

"You've got me by the throat here. I'm slurping up every word that falls from your peony mouth."

"*My peony mouth*?"

"Consider me a bee, if you will, lapping at your nectar. Greedily trying to carry too much, as I get stuck in the sweet trickles."

Heat shot to Tove's clit, which pulsed unmistakably between their ever more slippery labia. They collapsed onto the couch as instructed, while Effie hovered above. "Only you."

"What?"

"Only you would say the horniest thing imaginable and attempt to disguise it as a normal thing to say."

Effie cocked her head and considered the ceiling, serious all of a sudden. "Hey, if you want me to turn it off, I can and will avoid all mentions of bees and flowers. I meant it when I said we could kiss and that's all. If I am making or if I have made you uncomfortable, I'm deeply sorry. Sometimes I struggle to read social situations. I zoom from zero to a hundred. Words come out, and that's how I lose friends."

Effie always spoke before she thought, so her reckless flirtation wasn't a surprise, or even something Tove disliked about her. What did shock them was the admission from Effie's own mouth. Self-awareness was something new to them both.

"I will never forget how the first time you met my dad you bragged about shoplifting a Twix from the tuck shop. *My dad*, head of store security at Goodfoods."

"No wonder he never liked me. I steam ahead with my inappropriate anecdotes and push people's buttons before I know a thing about them. It's a knack. But it was a bag of penny sweets, not a Twix."

"My dad's a stickler for etiquette bullshit, don't worry about it."

"I realise," Effie went on, "that saying you don't have a filter on what you say is often used as an excuse for being a bitch. And it's something white women, in particular, get away with. I need to work on it more."

"Are you in therapy?"

"No, I'm on a waiting list for adult ADHD assessment, hoping to get some help through the welfare system."

"Huh." Tove wasn't going to mention ADHD, but they'd be lying if they said they hadn't thought of it.

"And..." Effie said, breathing in as if bracing herself "...it might take a while to get to a place where I'm not a huge social turn-off. So it's cool if you choose not to hang out with me because of it."

"Wait, excuse me?" Tove cut in. "Who said anything about not hanging out?"

"I thought..."

"Effie, that's not even what I was thinking! I like the way you flirt, it makes me feel special. I like the way you say what's on your mind, it reassures me that you're not hiding anything. So long as you mean it."

"Every word."

"Right. So if you're aware of your, uh, poor impulse control, and you say you're working on it, I believe you. I believe *in* you."

"You do?"

"Yes."

"God." Effie combed her fingers through her hair, puffing it into a platinum halo. "It's nice to be believed in."

"You believe in yourself, right?" Tove prodded.

"Oh yeah, hundy P. Like, I *have* made mistakes and sometimes I *am* the problem. But if I thought I were truly unfixable it'd all be over for me. A soul can only take so much heaviness."

Tove knew that feeling well. While the last days of their relationship with Aaron existed in a fog, at some point they'd most definitely hit a limit on the crushing weight of hurt they could voluntarily endure. Because that's what it was: realising that it was, to some greater or lesser extent, voluntary, and with the wedding closing in they could put a counter on the days they had remaining to exercise what agency they had. When they pictured what would've become of them had they not left, they didn't recognise the person gazing up through the skylight in their one-room windowless apartment, dizzying at the snow-laden sky and unable to imagine any other life.

They'd come a long way.

"So...if it wasn't head, what were you going to request from me?" Effie gazed down, willing and expectant.

Tove blinked away the fantasies, the good and the bad ones. "Since my break-up I've been all over the place with my personality and identity." They paused, shaping the words inside their mind. They had to say this right. "And...my gender is one of the things that feels shaky."

"Totally, that makes perfect sense."

Relief unfurled over them like a morning sun. "It does?"

"Sure. Relationships can be intense. I can totally see a break-up being a catalyst for confusion, or, on the flipside, discovery."

"My relationship was super gendered," Tove said, "in the traditional misogynistic way, so sometimes I wonder if it's trauma rather than me being actually non-binary."

"What do you mean by 'actually'?"

The question caught Tove off guard. Their gremlin perked up, looking to cause mischief, to paint all those flags red red red.

Effie apparently spotted those pointy ears poking around the corner. "Sorry, I should've started by thanking you for telling me you're non-binary. I only meant to ask why trauma isn't enough. Trauma literally changes your brain chemistry. Of course it can be helpful to understand where things are coming from, but if you're non-binary then you're non-binary. There's no lesser non-binary experience for someone who started questioning their gender as a result of trauma. That might even be a common experience. I dunno. Not an expert."

Tove nodded speechlessly. For not-an-expert, Effie carried queer wisdom in bucketfuls.

"How would you like me to talk about you?" Effie asked.

Tove filed away her monologue for further perusal, and latched onto this, which they *could* answer. "I'm okay with a lot of gendered words. Girl is okay. You called me Ice Queen a few days ago, which was fine. But woman makes me cringe."

"How about pronouns? I've been meaning to ask since I saw your pronoun badge when we first bumped into each other last week."

Oh shit. Effie had known all along.

"Then have you been using my 'they' pronouns?"

"Only in private, when I was thinking about you, since I wasn't sure if you were out everywhere. She/her when talking to others."

"You think about me?" Tove's heart pattered in their chest, fiercer than the moments before they'd kissed earlier.

"Let me demonstrate the way I've been thinking about you, and you can tell me how you feel about it." Grinning, Effie crossed the room to sit on the windowsill, tugging the curtain around her like a blanket. "I'm daydreaming from my window, all alone, thinking about Tove. Tove, I think. God, Tove is wonderful! They have the most exquisite eyes I have ever seen. All shifting crepusculars of golden light, like tiger's eye gemstones blinking a warning to evil forces. The jungle is theirs, both the shadows they slink through and the sunlight they bask in. They hold the secrets of the wilderness: strong, courageous, and daring." She snapped her fingers. "How did I do?"

"Way too good," Tove mumbled. "You're so fucking nice to me. And I don't want you to stop."

"You're easy to be nice to."

Tove gasped. All this would be overwhelming, even corny, if they didn't know Effie as well as they did. They'd call her idealistic, even naïve, but no kind word she'd ever said had been a lie. Tove wanted her kind words with every bone in their body.

"Well, I've been doing a whole lot of mouth work," Effie said, "—by which I mean *talking*, you cheeky peanut—and I need to hydrate. Give me two secs and I'll bring you some water too."

"Are we onto pet names already?" Tove groaned. "This just-a-kiss business is biting me in the butt."

"I'd love to bite you in the butt."

"Go!" they ordered. "Get your damn water!"

Effie strutted to the kitchenette, laughing, leaving Tove to lounge in everything that had transpired. They'd psyched themself up to tell Effie about their past—she knew it already—Tove broke down in tears—the two of them kissed, *twice*!—Tove came out as non-binary—and now they were "cheeky peanut." Empowerment clenched their muscles.

Their phone buzzed.

They checked it out of habit, and their heart dropped into their stomach. A single message—**So?**—took the place of the unread message that had been in their notifications for so long. The one they couldn't open.

The feeling of empowerment from the day's events lingered. Tove had accepted that Effie wasn't at fault for what happened ten years ago. They felt appreciated and seen in a way they never had. Their ex's apology should barely shake them.

Before they could second-guess themself, they tapped the notification and opened the chat thread with Aaron.

Hey, it's been a while… I know you left in a hurry, and I understand why, after what I put you through… I hope

you are doing well, wherever you are. I am doing okay – I have a new coworker, a very sweet and timid lady, who reminds me a bit of you, hence I have been thinking about you. Now this may be a bit off the wall, but Christmas is coming up, and since it is a time to love one another, I wondered if you wanted to meet up. I'm visiting the Island for Christmas to spend time with my family and it would be good to catch up, smooth things over a bit. Closure is important. And even if we're not together anymore, I can help you through the break-up as a friend. I know what it's like to have no one to lean on and people are always weird about break-ups. Anyway, let me know. Perhaps I'll see you round either way, small island etc.

So?

A bone-deep shiver ricocheted up Tove's spine.

It wasn't what they'd expected at all. Not an apology in sight.

Here they were, readying forgiveness, when there was not and never would be any real admission of fault. Was their forgiveness worth so little that he didn't want it, or was it their hurt that paled into insignificance? Resentment crawled up their throat like acid reflux.

Aaron thought he was beyond reproach. He assumed Tove had nobody to turn to. He'd always talked shit about their friends and family. With smooth words, he painted over their memories by telling them others did not have their best interests at heart. He made Tove think they were all out to get them. And Tove, in turn, made the classic mistake of believing him, believing they were safe within the relationship, but not outside of it. When all along it was the opposite.

All of a sudden they were lonely, longing for those lying arms around them, the smooth voice telling them everybody else sucked.

But now there was Effie. Effie wanted to kiss them. Effie said they were easy to be nice to. Effie *liked* them.

Did she really, though?

Shaking, Tove reread Aaron's message. This time it was a threat. Was he here already? Outside Effie's place, waiting to ambush them with gaslighting and manipulation?

Effie returned with two glasses of water and a watering can, and busied herself with her row of plants on the mantelpiece while chattering about their stages of growth. Soon it was time to put on their Santa suits and leave for the interviews at the Pollack.

Tove put their phone away and tried to smile, and if Effie noticed any part of them had faded, she didn't say so.

19

The carpark was dark when Effie and Tove arrived for interview night; a deep blue sort of darkness, peaceful but starless; like halfway through an eco-horror movie where everything was briefly suspended before the environment started trying to kill them again.

Effie eyed the damp concrete warily. Tove lingered a pace behind. Maybe they were wary too, and letting her lead the way into the fray. That was fine; Effie could lead. If the carpark swallowed her up, she hoped they'd get away.

"There you both are." Nowell appeared with their signature clipboard. "Head to the green room—the other Santas are there. You'll be called up in turn."

The stage was already set up with armchairs and cameras. This time the live audience would be watching from their own homes.

"Nowell…" Tove started. They faltered, and began afresh. "Nowell, who's my guest? Nobody's told me."

"You'll find out when you come on stage."

"I really, really hate surprises."

But Nowell didn't hear—they were too busy yelling at a crew member who was rigging a floodlight wonky.

"See you both soon—and by the way, Effie, the interviews are live. That means no editing." They glared pointedly.

Effie raised her hands in surrender. "Got it."

"What was that?" asked Tove as they traced the edge of the stage towards the green room.

"I said 'effing' to Nowell when I signed up."

"You swore at someone you'd never met?"

"No, I said 'effing.' It was a pun on my name. Not a fucking swear in sight."

Tove uttered a limp "ha."

"You really don't know who your guest is?" Effie asked softly. Over the past hour or so, Tove had slowly retreated back inside themself. Effie suspected she'd caused it somehow, and she was scared to ask.

"It could be one of my parents, or my brother. It's not like I talk to anyone else."

"Hard to make friends as an adult, huh?"

"All my friends were my ex's friends."

"That's rough."

They shrugged. "It's on me. I realised that today—it was me who burned those bridges. Lost my friends one by one and never noticed till I was alone."

Yikes. Effie hadn't put the work into her friendships either. Thought it was enough—it had been enough for her—to send a few memes and video call maybe once a year, satisfied with the promise of more when she made it back to the UK. When all along, she was the one who hadn't moved on, hadn't faced the reality that she was stuck here now. No plans to move back; no plans to do anything, really. Eventually she got ghosted. Group chats were made without her, so she wouldn't have to keep saying *no, sorry, I'm still a plane ride away*. Of course, distance was the excuse. The fact was, she wasn't the kind of person people wanted to be friends with. She ruined the vibe. She'd known it for a long time, and her attempts to make new friends left her even lonelier, and more convinced of it, than ever.

"Hard to stop noticing once you've realised, isn't it?" she said.

Tove grunted. "Maybe I'm being too hard on myself. I guess a lot of things become your fault when there's no one else around to blame them on."

In the green room were the other Santas: Alice, B1 and B2. It was a relief to see them in their Santa suits; their lunchwear really was too much to compute. Tove clung to Effie's side as they were called up one by one. They barely laughed at her anecdote about the time Heather got her banned from the trampolines at Bungee World, at which point Effie realised they were spiralling somewhere she couldn't follow.

But before she could do anything about it, her turn was called. She stood, heart aching, planning how to tell Nowell she wasn't coming.

"Go on," said Tove.

"What?"

"I know you're worrying about me. But I'll be fine."

Effie studied them. "Is this an *I'll actually be fine* thing or a *Go! Leave me if you're going to do it anyway!* thing?"

Tove's beard twitched with a ghost of a smile. "The first one. Look. B1's going to keep me company."

As if by magic, B1 appeared at Tove's elbow, fresh from his own interview. Santa incarnate. Saviour of floundering queers.

"Good evening, Tove," he said in his big round Santa voice. "I'd love to tell you about my interview guest, if you'd be interested. He is my oldest friend, a bespoke cobbler who makes shoes with podiatric insoles."

Tove nodded, and Effie tried to convey her gratitude with her eyes.

"Are you ready for your big moment, Effie?" said B1.

Effie struck a pose, head tilted, peace sign out. "How do I look?"

"Very jolly," said B1.

Tove's eye contact was laser-beam intense. Effie's pulse sped up waiting for their response. What if they said nothing? Would that mean they didn't like what they saw? What didn't they like? This was the test of whether it was Effie that made them fade into silence, or something else.

It wasn't even a second's pause but she was close to screaming with impatience. *Please like me*, she pleaded wordlessly. If they didn't, there was no way she could go on stage.

"You're great, Effie," Tove whispered. There was a grin widening behind that beard of theirs.

Relief washed over Effie, but it was unsettling how much she'd needed their good opinion in that moment. And if it wasn't her who'd caused Tove's decline tonight, then what had? There was something dangling just out of reach, something very alarming indeed.

Before she'd grasped it, Nowell's assistant was pushing her under the lights, and she was cooking like a jacket potato inside her Santa suit. She left Tove listening to B1 talk about his excellent friend. Tove would have to wait. She hoped Tove *could* wait.

"Good evening, Effie!" called Nowell from the sofa. "Come and sit down."

Effie waved at the dark carpark, finding the cameras and memorising their locations.

"How are you today?" asked Nowell.

"Good, looking forward to seeing my guest."

"Then without further ado, let's get her up. Please welcome Effie's niece, Heather!"

It was a full-on cheesy chat show. How many people were watching this live on the News? A hundred? Half a hundred? Effie's clap echoed feebly across the empty carpark. She hoped production had their audio overlays ready.

Heather pranced on-stage with a smile that belonged in a toothpaste advert. She bunched the ruffled skirts of her black witch's dress and curtseyed, then perched on the guest sofa, legs swinging.

"Dressed as a witch?" said Nowell. "What season are you in?"

"If Aunty Effie can be Santa then I can be a Christmas witch," Heather retorted. She shot Effie a terrifying wink across the coffee table. At the best of times it was a mystery to what extent her cheekiness was performed, but right now she was exerting all her creativity.

"I understand you're the architect of Effie's transformation into Santa Claus," said Nowell. "Is that true?"

"I did say Santa couldn't be a lesbian, which is when Effie entered the pageant. But I took it back later, so between you and me I think there's another reason she's here."

"What do you think about that, Effie?"

Effie glared, glad her hat shaded her frowning brow from the cameras. "Girl talks nonsense, you should take everything she says with a pinch of salt."

"Truth is, I am the mastermind," Heather went on. "I wanted to be on TV sooo bad. And now I'm here, I can say whatever I want."

Nowell gave Effie a look that said, "Do I need to cut this now?"

Effie shrugged. She wasn't the one who'd invited Heather. Plus, she was getting some wicked enjoyment out of this. Apparently no one had predicted her niece would possibly be anything like her.

"I have one important question for you, Heather," Nowell said. "There's a lot of debate in the world over whether Santa really exists. Do you, personally, believe in Santa?"

Heather pointed an accusatory finger at Effie. "She's literally right there!"

Effie wanted to hug her for her support. But then Heather froze, slipped down from the sofa, and squinted in her face.

"Oh wait," she said. She looked at the fake audience and found a camera to stare into. "That's just my Aunty Effie."

Nowell guffawed and Effie felt a twinge of animosity. They didn't have her back in the slightest.

"And do you think the real Santa is in the competition?"

"He *was*. He was eliminated last round."

"Oh, really?"

"He was far too handsome not to be the real Santa."

"Perhaps we made a mistake eliminating him."

"You did. Awful mistake. This competition is a—" Effie gestured frantically, and she could tell by Heather's tiny pause she'd been seen. "—a real rollercoaster. And I've never been on a rollercoaster!"

"Thank you," Effie said under her breath, half to Heather and half to the gods.

Nowell wrapped up the interview, and Effie and Heather peaced out to the carpark where Lalla was raking greasy furrows in her hair.

"Neither of you should be on TV," she said.

"What? I think we were extremely entertaining."

Effie held her hand for a high-five. To her immense relief, Heather slapped it. That girl would leave her hanging just for the power play.

"They're lucky to have us."

Tove brushed past on their way to the stage and Effie caught their arm. They jumped at the touch, like a counterfeit ghost caught in the act.

"Are you okay?" Effie said, uselessly.

"Can you stick around while I'm on stage? Just for a minute?" In their eyes was the fear that this was too big an ask.

In Effie's mind, it was a small one.

"Of course, no problem."

She left Lalla and Heather arguing over whether it was bedtime or showtime, and crept back into the wings to watch Nowell welcome Tove to the stage. There was a scramble as the stagehands readjusted Tove's mic, even though it was obvious they weren't talking loud enough. The cameras cut for a soundcheck.

A man appeared at Effie's side, brushing her shoulder with his sports blazer. She held her ground, knowing first that she was bigger than he was, and second that he'd move away in a moment.

But he didn't. His arm clenched against hers, muscled as a hetero dream.

"I feel a spot underdressed," he commented.

Now she had to look at him, as if to say, *Why are you talking to me?*

He met her gaze with a charismatic smile, like a shorter, shabbier DuBois. And despite herself, Effie smiled back.

"Excellent job on the facial hair, by the way," he said, oh-so-charming. "I've been trying for years to grow even a stubble as full of yours."

"Luckily I don't have to try," she replied, laughing through her fake beard. "Polycystic ovaries and all, you get me. Real hack for thick and lustrous body hair."

Their eyes locked. Effie's heart sped up enough to let her know this was the closest she'd come to flirting with a guy, ever.

Her companion grinned, teeth like little stones. "Now I recognise a test when I see one, and you can't gross me out that easily. I'm sorry about your condition."

Huh. Most people would've jumped to the other conclusion: that she was trying to get rid of them. "No need to pretend ovarian cysts aren't gross, stranger."

"Ah well then, I'll respect that, Effie." And he stepped away from her, closer to the curtain.

Effie's stomach flipped. A whiff of pasta sauce puffed up her throat. Like always, she visualised a shoelace and untied it in her mind, till she'd relaxed enough to say, "You know my name?"

He half-turned. "Of course I do." Half-smiled. "You're on TV every other day."

Beyond his nose, a stagehand attached a new mic to Tove's lapel. They tapped it. *Thunk-thunk.* Nowell stood and gestured into the wings, towards Effie and the man who knew her name.

"And now without further ado, let's meet Tove's guest. A big welcome to Aaron!"

Effie's core went cold.

The man who'd brushed past, who spoke courteously and with humour, the man who now walked out past the curtain, was suddenly familiar. And when he sat on the guest sofa, facing Tove, facing Effie, she saw it. The reason he knew her name was because they went to school together. This was the boy who'd interrupted her and Tove in the bushes at Winter Ball, needing a piss. The boy who had Tove crying in her flat that very afternoon.

She hoped he'd held his piss ten years long, and hoped at long last he pissed his fucking pants on live TV.

20

Tove needn't have worried about their ex ambushing them with all his old unnerving and demeaning tactics. The real worst case was this one: where he ambushed Effie, and they talked and laughed like old friends, showing he could do all those things and more through the people Tove cared about. That's right, Effie, Tove had heard her fresh, golden laugh when he self-deprecated about his facial hair. (It was a lie, anyway. He could grow a beard if he wanted. He just thought it was hardcore to cheat death shaving dry with a cutthroat razor. Or liked Tove's terror when he did so.)

Now, welcomed by Nowell, he sat across from Tove, smiling like this wasn't a fulfilment of the threat in his messages. The springs of the couch snaked up like magic vines, trapping them in this torture. At least there was a low table separating them, keeping him at a physical distance.

"So, Aaron, you're an old friend of Tove's?" said Nowell.

He laughed. "You could say that."

Tove tried to scream, but nothing came out. It was the nightmare they had sometimes where when they finally picked up their trumpet again, they couldn't make a sound. That's what Aaron did. He stifled their screams.

"Have you been watching the pageant so far?" asked Nowell.

"Every night this week! It's very entertaining. It's nice to see Tove thriving, *making friends*."

Tove's insides clenched, a knot of sickness. He knew about them crawling into Effie's tent, sinking into her bathwater, kissing her lips pretending they were luxury pillows that could absorb the past. Aaron didn't need cameras; his eyes saw through theirs.

"Eh, Tove?" He leaned over the low table, breaking the barrier. "I just met one of your new friends, actually. Bit of a weird one. But what am I expecting, it's a Santa cosplay competition!"

His long-ago-voiced thoughts on Effie bled into their brain: *thoughtless, rude, inappropriate*, he used to call her. Any other time Tove would've chuckled to hear Effie bring up her ovarian cysts to disarm someone who wasn't expecting it. Now they were utterly, terribly embarrassed. He was mocking them both.

A locket swung out of his shirt as he laughed, and the oxygen in their lungs turned to grit.

"Frankly you're the one out of place," Nowell joked. "Where's *your* Santa suit?"

"I wanted to wear one," Aaron chortled, a laugh track on repeat, "but someone thought it fit her better."

No. Not that pronoun. Not from him. He had no right to refer to them at all. Words that were okay in others' mouths were like knives in his.

Tove looked wildly at Nowell, searching for some hint of understanding. Were they supposed to act like this was normal?

Was this some elaborate joke? The red lights on the cameras kept winking. Nowell seemed oblivious at best, complicit at worst.

Tove crossed their arms over their chest, their vitals. Aaron might be in their head, but they had learned, instinctively, to protect their heart. In this pose, they could bust out of this awful situation anytime they chose, shattering the air with their elbows. The world and everybody around wanted them there, but they didn't want to be there. And even though it was impossible to speak, let alone expose and denounce Aaron, they could exert that will.

They exploded to their feet and marched off the stage. Behind, Aaron launched into an explanation of their stage fright. Deft as ever in front of cameras and watching eyes, like a villain out of a psychological thriller. Nowell, ignorant, continued the interview.

Tove stumbled down the steps out of the wings…into Effie's waiting arms. The tender touch ignited their instinct to fight.

"Please, he mustn't see us together," they snapped.

Effie let go, desolation enveloping them in her absence.

"Did you know?" she murmured.

"Did *you* know?" Tove fired back. "I heard you there, bantering in the wings."

"I didn't recognise the bastard until the last moment. How was I supposed to guess? He seemed nice. He obviously doesn't like me, but he's probably right not to."

Tove tore their beard off and hurled it on the ground. "Why are you suddenly determined to think badly of yourself and therefore that excuses every fucked up thing this shitface has ever done to me? What happened to hundy P self-belief? Why is he right, and you and me are now wrong?"

A new fear grasped them by the ankles. Effie liked Aaron more than she liked them. Mere hours ago she'd waxed wise about trauma changing brains, and now was perfectly poised to take Aaron's side. Just because he said she was a "weird one," confirming an idea she clearly half-believed. But that was what he did. He pinpointed your weaknesses and exploited them in a handful of words.

Knowing that, Tove forced themself to listen to Effie's explanation.

"I meant he seemed okay before I knew who he was. It's shit form of Nowell and the producers to bring him on tonight."

Her answer calmed them, but not enough. Aaron had been vaguely nice to her one time, and now she probably wouldn't believe a thing Tove had to say about him. She doubtless thought they shouldn't have left him, wondered if it was them who was the problem.

Effie picked their beard up off the concrete and plucked out the rubble, before handing it back. "Hey, the man is a menace. You're better off far, far away from him."

You too, they thought. *You're also better off far away from him.*

They led the way to their car in silence, Effie following. The vortex of emotion was converging to a resolution. Betrayal, embarrassment, anger, they were all concentrating into a need to claim back the power that was taken from them tonight. And to show Effie that Aaron was a liar who'd only said those things to be mean.

Tove liked Effie so, *so* much. If she so much as said a word, they'd have to kiss all Aaron's shadows out of her.

"Tove," said Effie as they unlocked their car, "I'm here for you, okay? Tonight was wrong. If I can do anything to make sure this doesn't happen again—"

It was all they needed.

"Shush." They stamped their thumb on her lips. "It's done. It's over. Sorry I snapped at you."

Effie's eyes dipped unmistakably to their mouth. "It's fi—"

"We're kissing now." Tove grabbed a fistful of arse and pulled her to them. Her lips parted to their tongue, and they devoured her, uncertainty and all. Aaron would crumble to see this, after the shit that went down tonight.

Within moments Effie was returning their hunger with interest. She kissed down their jugular to the spot under their collarbone where the skin was coldest. Then, leaning down, she took them by the thighs and lifted them to straddle her. Their legs coiled around her waist, ankles crossing at the small of her back, their crotch resting clean on the belt of her Santa suit.

"Wait, I recognise this belt." Tove tugged the old, scaly leather. "This isn't the same Santa suit…"

"Bingo."

Tove appraised the fit, the fabric, the same Santa suit they'd touched before so long ago. "You're so much hotter now than you were back then."

"Good. That's the way it should be." Effie's hand stole between the folds of their jacket to cup their boob through their green undershirt. Since leaving Aaron they'd ditched all their padded bras and push-ups in favour of free swinging (without, in truth, much of the swing). "Want my hot mouth to keep your tits warm?"

Tove nearly swooned. "Get them out," they urged. "Tear my shirt."

Smattering kisses to their exposed throat, Effie undid their top two buttons. Their shirt was old and loose, and with a single, desperate yank and the rasp of ripping fabric, their boobs tumbled out.

Effie didn't let them feel the cold. One nipple was pinched between her fingers and enjoyed the warmth of her fist. The other got her mouth, sucking and biting by turns, tongue flicking hard.

"Are you a secret trumpet player?" Tove gasped. "You're better at double tonguing than anyone I've ever met. *Flight of the Bumblebee* would be a walk in the park for you."

Effie grunted into their cleavage. "I have an oral fixation. You've probably noticed."

Every puff of her breath, every lash of her tongue, was an electric shock zapping to the space between Tove's legs. Effie's arm, helping to hold them up, snuck down between their asscheeks, and her daring fingers curved under their crotch. The pressure caused a spurt of excitement to soak through their underwear and probably their trousers too.

"Someone's excited." Effie tucked their tits back into their jacket and hefted them higher, pinning them to the car with their legs wide open. Her arms were stirrups for their thighs, her gaze undressing them from the bottom up.

"This cool?" she asked.

"Yeah," they panted.

She dived between their legs, kissing and sucking. Tove pulsed into her buried face. Leaking through their trousers or not, she was wetting their crotch from the outside. Her eyes darted up every now and then, and Tove hung onto the sight of her cheekbones perfectly framed by the V of their legs.

They leaned back against the driver's seat window, elbows on the top of the car. "Fuck, Effie."

A kiss that started out of something close to spite had turned into a fully clothed face fuck against a car. Tove didn't come, but sure as hell, when they finally parted for the night, they took their arousal back home and fucked their own fingers to the fantasy of Effie's face between their legs.

When they were finished, they lay on their bed and thought about what they'd done. It had been so long since a pleasant emotion had consumed them like this passion for Effie's mouth, they almost didn't recognise the surge of power that came with it. They were unrecognisable from the fiancée who took all those taunts lying down, or even the tongue-tied ghoul on stage earlier.

While they were in the shower, a memory resurfaced as they imagined what Aaron might say about their masturbating to the thought of someone else.

"You can fuck anyone you want," he'd told them, "but it's me who holds a piece of you at all times, and always will."

And the locket around his neck would glint, exactly as it had on stage that evening.

The locket had a gold-backed case with a glass door and a clear jewel inside it. Tove and Aaron had found it at an antique shop the year they got together; the seller explained that you were supposed to wind a lock of your lover's hair around the jewel. That was how Aaron got the idea: he wanted to take one hair of Tove's every year and gradually fill up the locket—he loved the notion of having a living piece of their entire life, first auburn and then brown and then white around the outside when they were old. On the face of it, a romantic idea perhaps? To be wanted, to have a record of their whole self and history close to someone's heart.

In reality, Tove was quaking as they picked the hairs out of their hairbrush and burned them in the fireplace. That must be why Aaron was here. For his annual hair. He would show up in their life every year around this time, to pluck a fresh hair from their head like some vampire sacrifice nonsense.

Dair appeared in the doorway, summoned by the reek of the fire. "What the hell is that smell? Christ, are you burning your *hair*?"

And Tove knew what they had to do. Aaron would not get a single bit of them as long as they lived.

"Take the power back," they whispered to themself. To Dair, they said, "You have a razor, right?"

Half an hour of mysterious buzzing later, Tove was a new person. Dair held a mirror to the back of their head. "Are you sure this was okay?"

Tove stroked their head, relishing the even fuzz, the lack of irritation on their neck and shoulders. They were free. Freedom suited them.

"It's perfect," they said. "Thank you for helping me."

They dug Effie's bobble hat from the pile of clothes in their room and slid it onto their head. They retrieved Oberon from their bag and hugged him tight.

And then finally they unbuckled their trumpet case and blew warm air into Felicity. They filled the house with angry Christmas carols, feeling stronger than ever before.

Thursday

4 days till Christmas

21

Effie blew off Lalla and Heather and caught a bus home. She sat in bed well past midnight replaying the night over and over, and guiding Melchior, who had hairballs, away from the peace lily and back to the specialty cat grass.

Talking to Aaron was her first mistake. He had a point: she was "weird"—awkward and inappropriate and generally rude with strangers. When she thought about all the people she'd alienated in her life, the list was long: family, friends, more friends, Nowell, Aaron, and so on. Even Tove's dad didn't like her. For the first time, she wondered if maybe Tove's dad—or, more precisely, Effie's undeniable bad influence—had something to do with their friendship fizzling out. Earlier, the outrage in their voice when they'd pushed her off them, not wanting to be seen being hugged by her, had cut deep. They were embarrassed by her; on some level, even while they kissed her in the dark, they believed she was a "weird one."

The second thing she'd fucked up was letting Aaron on stage. She hadn't recognised him until it was too late.

To make up for it, she found the guy on Facebook and swiped through all his photos, so she'd never miss him again. Since school, he'd gained a sharp jawline and cruel tilt to his mouth, which made Effie appreciate Liam's baby face in a new way. Weirdly there was no record of his and Tove's relationship on Facebook, even though one of his older profile pics was him kissing his then-girlfriend at the very same Winter Ball where everything went down. He'd nuked all evidence that Tove ever happened.

Still, that didn't explain what he was doing at the interview.

Why was he there? Why was he flirting with her in the wings? Why was he smiling on stage as he said "You could say that" in the most indicative way possible?

Effie relived every word, every brush of his gross shoulder against hers. "I'll respect that," he'd said with a smarmy bob of his head. Like one of those losers with their "Don't worry, I respect women," like Effie needed someone to tell her why she was human. He assumed she was testing him with her polycystic ovaries and woman-with-beard-progressiveness and he was so desperate to pass. Anyone who really respected her would've either taken the lighthearted (although admittedly inappropriate) vulnerability as it was meant, or backed off immediately. God, he'd made such a big deal out of being accepting and sympathetic and it hit Effie now how odd that was.

Her thumb hovered over the Google search bar, wondering what she could be googling to make sense of it all. She even scrolled her contacts, wishing she had a close friend instead of relying on Yahoo Answers and Reddit. Eventually she slept, dreaming of creepy men.

In the morning, she woke to a text from Ranjula, the rep for the sponsor she'd completely forgotten about. **Can we meet**

before the craft fair? I have flyers and free sweatbands to display on your table.

Effie replied **Sure** and leapt out of bed to get ready. No one needed to know she'd intended to sleep late, forgetting she was supposed to be at the Pollack at ten. Not long later, she met Ranjula at Bonamy's coffee truck on the pier.

"You're the gay Santa." Bonamy, a local coffee roaster, handed Effie's paper cup over the counter. "My daughter, Natalie, she's assistant manager at Goodfoods now, she's one of the lesbians, she's been enjoying your run so far."

"Aw, thank you," Effie said. "Glad to be, uh, seen."

"Here's her card." Bonamy proudly extracted a slightly worn business card from his shirt pocket.

"Thank you," said Effie genuinely.

"Selling your crafts today, is it?" he continued. "Funny, they're making you sell your stuff on a trestle table like I'm doing right here, and yet you can bet the food lots in the new shopping centre will be chain coffee shops. Bit of a contradiction in kind, if you ask me." He shook his head. "All for show, all for show."

Effie shifted uncomfortably. Not only was she participating in an elaborate marketing ploy for the Pollack—which was all the pageant really was—she was standing here with a person whose employer was filling one of those lots, taking business away from roasters like Bonamy and jewellers like Lalla would be if she could afford it. Not to mention Effie's own involvement with the paid parking initiative. She too had her interests tied up in the Pollack. She too, as a member of the corporate workforce as well as a jobseeker, had to reckon with signing herself up to participate in the exploitation of the community, for the privilege of putting food on her own tiny table.

She joined Ranjula at the end of the pier, sipping coffee and gazing into the fog. The sea lapped gently at the granite and salty mist sprayed her exposed nose and fingers.

"How is everything going?" said Ranjula. "Are you enjoying the pageant so far?"

"Oh, I thought you wanted to talk about promoting Ultra-speed."

"Sure, but it's got to be mutually beneficial. I'm not going to flat-out use you."

"But you're in marketing," Effie pointed out.

Ranjula laughed softly. "We put these free sweatbands on the table, we're gucci. Between you and me, Ultraspeed is going to rake it in regardless of whatever exposure we get through the pageant."

Yeah, that's what Effie thought. An idea occurred to her, one she tucked away for later.

"So how are you?" Ranjula pressed. "I know we've only met a few times, but you seem down today. Is anything bothering you?"

Effie scanned her face for ulterior motives, but she was too desperate for a friend to care that much. It felt nice to be asked how she was. It was rare enough.

"I'm honestly in a pickle," she said. "You know Tove, one of the other Santas? We went to school together. We used to be really good friends."

"I wondered if there was something going on there."

"You did?" Something going on? Like last night against the car, Effie's mouth on Tove's crotch? Effie hid behind her coffee cup, sure her lips must be swelling with the memory of it.

"Tove spoke about you in a confessional after the sleep-out."

"Oh. Right!"

"She said she was glad you were there to look out for her."

"Wow." Effie coughed, a lump in her throat. She felt she'd done a poor job of that yesterday.

"I saw what happened last night. Couldn't not, I suppose, considering they continued to broadcast."

"They what?"

"Yep, after your friend walked off stage, they kept the interview going. Asking all these questions about her."

"Wait, asking Aaron? Questions about Tove? Even after she walked off?"

"It wasn't until the very end of the interview that he revealed they used to date. I'm shocked the producers invited an ex. Looks like the interviewer didn't know either, the way their face was. Horrible situation all round."

Effie tore the plastic lid off her cup and poured her coffee over the side of the pier. The dark liquid dropped through blue. At least the smell was gone. She felt sick.

"What did he say about Tove?" she asked.

Ranjula waved her hand. "This and that. Reliable, hardworking, wants the best for everyone, very tuned into people's needs."

"Yikes." Effie felt Ranjula's gaze but couldn't meet it.

"Yikes indeed. I'd understand flaming your ex. But being complimentary is something else."

"He shouldn't be saying a single thing about Tove," she muttered. "The pageant producers suck for inviting him on, but you know their goal is to ignite drama. Aaron agreeing to come on the show, though. That reveals an agenda."

"Yeah, I can't fathom an ex doing something so weird. Speaking as someone who literally had a kid with a guy I was never intending to stay with."

"Wait, you're not with your son's dad?"

"God, no! He's a great dad and shares the load of parenting super well. But imagine picking up his dirty socks for the rest of my days? No thank you."

"Doesn't that sound…nice?" Effie asked, wildly confused. "If I liked someone enough then I'd probably pick up their dirty socks."

"Oh, I'd do it. But would I enjoy it? I don't know. I've never liked anyone like that. The point is, we each wanted a child more than we wanted a relationship. So it all worked out for us."

"Don't people normally have a kid and then stay together because of the kid? Or have a kid deliberately as a reason to stay together?"

"Yeah, and half the time they break up later anyway. I'm not interested in prolonging the end. Raising a child as a single woman is my ideal situation. And with his dad's help I can also do my own stuff, like work my dream job and join the paragliding club. He allows me to be here getting coffee with you. So yeah, my boy's dad is a great dad, but I've never been in love with him. Mind you, my parents don't approve. Well, that's not entirely fair. My mum's all about women's empowerment, and she cheers me on, even if she doesn't exactly understand."

"Wow, that's so different from…what I know." Once again, Effie questioned her own impact on her parents' relationship. How having teenage kids as well as a stable relationship had been impossible for them. How much happier they were now she and Lalla had left the nest. *Why* they had her and Lalla in the first place.

"My point is, Tove's ex strikes me as someone who's desperate to watch *her* pick up *his* dirty socks. Like specifically."

"Sure, if that's your kink," said Effie.

"Do you think it's Tove's kink? Not judging, you know her better than I do."

Effie clammed up. Tove had straight up told her *I'm not into degradation.* Hypothetical dirty socks aside, how Aaron treated them was probably not how they wanted to be treated.

The more Effie thought about yesterday, the worse she felt for Tove. They'd literally cried because they were learning to feel again and didn't know how to control their emotions. It was more than a break-up; they'd been traumatised by a manipulative man who continued to haunt them even after they'd cancelled the wedding and fled the country. Tove shook last night in the green room, fearing what would happen. And their fears came true. Effie couldn't imagine what else they had to fear.

She had to head to the carpark for the craft fair soon, although she didn't want to. What she should be doing was quitting the pageant altogether and throwing a tantrum on whoever let last night happen, whoever let Tove's fears come true.

Would Tove want that? What would Tove want? They'd barely spoken after the interview. Just pushed her away with their hands and then pulled her back again with their mouth. It was all a bit confusing. Effie had worried all night about not doing enough for Tove in their moment of need, but now she considered if maybe she deserved a little more guidance on what Tove really wanted from her. They'd told her it was too late to be together. Realistically, any hurt Effie endured through taking on responsibility for Tove's actions or wellbeing was self-inflicted. Maybe all they wanted was someone to take out their frustration on. *They didn't really want her.*

Stomach roiling from the few sips of coffee she'd had, Effie followed Ranjula to the Pollack and began setting up her trestle table for the day. She'd be crafting wire animals for the first three hours, then there was a break for lunch, and finally an hour of selling. The carpark was lined with regular vendors and the ice-rink was open. Her every move had an audience, so she must swallow her nausea and follow the script.

"I'll be back after lunch with the Ultraspeed freebies," said Ranjula. She glanced at the empty table opposite. Tove's table. "Your friend not here yet?"

"N—"

Effie almost spoke too soon.

A dream of a human strutted between the tables on six-inch heeled boots. This was not the Tove of yesterday in the giant Jonah-whale Santa suit from the fancy-dress shop. Or even the Tove of Alice's dinner party in the dungarees. This was Ice Queen Santa, CEO of the North Pole. They'd ditched the too-big Santa trousers. Now fishnet tights climbed their thighs to roost under the short skirt of a little black dress which was barely visible under the Santa jacket. Hugging their neck was a tight choker. Red lipstick and winged eyeliner accentuated their sharp face. They bunched their usual Santa hat in a white-knuckled fist, their scalp bare. More than bare. Buzzed. Fuck, their head looked like it was chiselled by a woodworker making a nativity. Not any old head would look that good, only theirs.

Wow.

"Well, see you later." Ranjula's curious gaze corroded a hole in her skull. "Take care."

Tove didn't look at her, but Effie couldn't stop staring. She went to the Useless Lesbian Emporium and bought up all the stock. Ice Queen Tove intimidated the hell out of her.

Then Nowell appeared to announce the beginning of the crafting sesh. An hour in, Tove hadn't looked at Effie once, although Effie had stabbed herself at least four times with the wire-cutters while admiring the absolute pants off them.

God, her fingers ached like it was exam season. At least she could take a break, unlike in the middle of a three-hour civil engineering paper.

Abandoning the twelve wire mooses she'd managed to bend and solder, she stood up and considered what to do. She wanted to cross the aisle and talk to Tove, but they wouldn't catch her eye, as if they regretted kissing her yesterday. As if they were embarrassed by her. It was Winter Ball all over again, only this time they *knew* Effie liked them. So it couldn't be that they were shy.

Effie bought a hot chocolate from a vendor and meandered back to the Santa tables. She joined a throng of shoppers watching B1 assemble his doll's house. He explained to the huddle of spellbound kids that he'd pre-cut the pieces at home with a small saw.

On the next table was B2, chatting to his audience as he made little remote-control cars with cosmetic sleds on each side so they looked like sleighs. His fingers flew, deft and machine-like. He already had eight completed cars.

Alice warded off spectators with the AirPods in her ears. In front of her was a small crate of pebbles gathered from the beach near her house. She was painting pictures on the pebbles—holly, gingerbread, and so on. Before painting each one, she grabbed knitting needles and whipped up a miniature woollen beanie hat. They were adorable. Effie wanted one.

"Effie," said Alice as she passed, "we're going to the bakery on the seafront for lunch. Join us?"

It wasn't really a question—Alice didn't even remove her AirPods to hear a response—so Effie nodded, wondering who "we" was.

Now Effie only had to pass Tove's table to return to her own. Feeling suddenly self-conscious about how much she'd been staring, she kept her head down, although it didn't escape her that Tove was cutting notches in folded paper. Their craft was making paper snowflakes like they teach you in primary school.

"What?" they barked.

Effie swivelled. Finally their gaze was on her, but it was cold, unsmiling.

"I didn't say anything," she stammered.

"You were laughing at my snowflakes. I know it sucks, you don't have to tell me."

A few shoppers glanced over, so Effie went closer to speak in a lower voice. "Tove, what's up? Did I do something?"

"No, I..." They put their paper and scissors down. "I thought you were judging me."

"Why would I do that?"

Their eyes squeezed shut. "Maybe you think I'm ugly without my hair?"

That was *really* the reason they couldn't even look her in the eye? Effie didn't know whether to be amused, relieved or insulted. "You're emanating strength and sexiness. You seem like you've grown into a new skin." Bloody hell. They were all neck and head and thigh and cleavage. How could they ever be ugly?

Tove cracked open one eye and then the other, fake eyelashes flaring. "Do you think?"

"You're pulling all the light in for yourself like gravity. I can't see straight with you right there. Stop assuming what I'm thinking, it's annoying!"

"Okay. I'm sorry."

"Good. You should be." Effie poked at the pile of paper snowflakes. Up close, they were beautiful. "These are really good."

"I looked up some designs."

Tove had scorned art in school, because the curriculum restricted creativity and the grading was bullshit. Effie grinned at the memory. "You finally found your artistic calling."

"You *are* mocking me."

"It's not my fault you can't take a compliment."

"It's not mine either." They shot her a glare, the same way they'd once challenged her to eat a jalapeno sandwich. "You try being complimented by someone who's said the exact opposite to your face over and over again."

Heat flooded Effie's face. First she thought they were talking about her; then she realised. "Hey, I understand now why being complimented is uncomfortable for you. If you want me to stop, I will. I mean it."

In the space of about 0.01 seconds, Tove's eyes filled with tears.

"Dammit," they snapped, ripping their Santa hat off their head and using the pom-pom to dab their eyes. "This make-up was supposed to be a deterrent against crying, not a hazard!"

Effie fished the napkin she got with her hot chocolate from her pocket and handed it over, trying not to stare at their buzzcut again.

"Thanks. Look, like I said yesterday, I love it when you compliment me. So long as you believe it, so do I."

"Then I'll keep going," Effie said. "Your hair looks amazing."

"What hair?" Tove's lips tipped in a shaky smile. Holy crap, Effie had kissed those lips not eighteen hours ago… "Earth to Effie," they warbled. "Did you seriously zone out mid-tease? About the hair I don't have anymore?"

"I just fucking love your head, okay!"

"Taking a break, Effie?"

Effie jumped as Nowell appeared. They were always there when she said the absolute worst thing. Tove's head? Oh god.

"I'm going back to my table now," she said.

She returned to the wire robins she intended to make in hour two. Nowell loitered for a while, checking up on them all, but after they left, Effie and Tove kept giggling at each other across the aisle. They were good again. Everything was fine.

Hour three was crunch time. Later the Santas would have one hour to sell what they'd made. The stakes were high. Whoever made the least money would be eliminated from the pageant.

Effie swept her gaze over the other craft tables. The Bryans' spectators had wandered away and the two Santas kept their heads down, hands moving nimbly. Alice appeared calm, but she was doing step-ups on her overturned crate as she knitted her tiny hats, up and down, up and down. Tove cast away their scissors and scribbled in gold gel pen on a sheet of paper. Their table was littered with coloured gel pens. They did love their pens…at school they used them to jot down homework assignments, a different colour for each class, first in their planner and then in Effie's.

Today, somebody would be joining DuBois in the sleigh of shame where the losing Santas went. Looking at all the Santas' wonderful creations, it was surely Effie or Tove going home. And while Effie wanted to win more than she was letting on even to herself, she couldn't imagine continuing this contest without Tove.

This afternoon would be brutal.

22

Tove had just about decided to play their trumpet at late-night Christmas shopping that evening when the horn went, halting the Santas' craft work. They surveyed their snowflakes, poised to think despairingly about convincing people to pay money for them later, when Alice stomped behind their table and yanked their arm.

"Alright," she said, "we're taking you to lunch. Come along."

Tove's doom and gloom evaporated.

Flanked by the other Santas, Alice frogmarched them all the way to Nice Crumb, the bakery on the seafront. The Bryans claimed an outdoor table while everyone else queued for coffee and sandwiches. Effie ordered a crab sandwich and a flat white, then turned to them.

"What do you want? I can buy."

Alice's grip on their arm tightened. "No, I'm buying for Tove."

Alice and Effie had their little stare-off, till Tove flicked the back of Effie's hand and shook their head the tiniest bit.

"Excellent, excellent!" boomed ex-Santa DuBois behind the counter. He wore an apron and a badge with his name on it, along with the velvet Santa hat he never seemed to be without.

"What are you doing here?" Effie blurted out. "I thought you didn't need a job."

"I don't, but I do love to bake!" DuBois was all smiles. "Alice fixed me up with a position here, and I love it! It's my first day, in fact."

He had to be kidding, but Tove knew he wasn't.

They grabbed their spoils, a croissant and a cup of tea courtesy of Alice, and joined the Bryans outside. Tove's favourite Bryan magically produced two jam sandwiches from one of his big Santa pockets. "My wife always does triangles," he said. "Just as I like them." Then Effie arrived, and Alice, and then, inexplicably, DuBois, who leaned over the table with clasped hands.

"Tove," began Alice, "what happened to you last night was dreadful. Unforgivable. The producers should never have allowed it."

All of a sudden, Tove caught on. This was an intervention meeting. Their face boiled behind their make-up, the heat escaping at the hairline. Five pairs of eyes were on them.

"Yep," they responded, with as much brightness as they could muster.

"I want to fight that guy," snarled DuBois, making a fist. "He had no right. No right!"

"What happened happened," Tove said. "It's not a big deal."

"My dear," their favourite Bryan said gently, "it's okay to be upset."

"I'm not upset."

"We've started this all wrong." Alice took charge again. "How are you doing, Tove?"

Tove considered them each in turn, and was met with nothing but earnest concern. It was both their worst fear and greatest honour: all the Santas had noticed that something about last night was fucked up. And they didn't seem to think that something was Tove. With their range of backgrounds and experiences, maybe the Santas could help. Opening up to Effie yesterday had opened the door in their mind to being understood. Like Effie had said, they were strong and sexy. They were ready to engage.

"Okay," they began, somewhat shaky under the pressure of all the listening ears. "I'm really confused about what happened. What does my ex want from me?"

"That's easy," said Alice. "A way back in."

Tove scrunched up their nose. "He wants to get back together? But how can he trust me ever again?"

Beside them, Effie's fingers stiffened around her flat white. "You're not really considering getting back together though," she said.

Tove shrugged, irritated. What of it, Effie? If Effie had an opinion about who they should or shouldn't date, maybe she could actually come out with it this time.

"Sometimes it's not about getting back together," Effie's favourite Bryan suggested. "Sometimes it's about control. You can't control someone who's closed the door on you."

Tove passed him a silent gift of gratitude for moving the conversation on. "Aaron does like to keep people on his good side. He's playing the long game in life. Every person is an opportunity, he says."

"Gross," Effie offered. Tove thanked her, too, for moving on; fixating on getting back together with Aaron—which, they conceded, would be unconscionable in any stable state of mind—wasn't helping anyone.

They tipped a small smile her way, pushing away the ghost of the almost-guilt they'd felt last night about kissing her instead of engaging in meaningful conversation, as they said, "Honestly still feels like he can control me from the other side of the door."

"But it doesn't feel like that to him," added Effie's Bryan. "Controlling people are very needy. They want to know they're succeeding. So he arranged an attack at the one time you couldn't run or hide."

"It was very brave of you to leave the stage," said Tove's Bryan. "I was proud."

"But it still had the desired effect, didn't it?" Alice went on. "He's in your brain. Everyone who was watching the broadcast saw what there is to see."

"I *will* fight him," DuBois promised again.

The ever-encroaching tears stung their eyes once more, and they whipped out Effie's already sodden napkin for another dab. "Let me explain. I broke up with Aaron three weeks before the wedding. Moved country to escape him. Ignored his calls. I feel like in some way I deserve this for running away from my problems. In particular this one huge problem that I created, a problem called marrying Aaron."

"I want you to know," said Effie's Bryan with a touch of savagery, "you *can* cut people out entirely. There are some things you don't ever have to face if you don't want to."

"I tried," Tove said. Their voice snagged on the lump in their throat. "But he knows all the ways to find me and all the words that hurt me. And it's weird because all the nice things he said last night were designed to confuse me. He wasn't describing me…he was describing someone I aspire to be, and I feel drawn to him because he sees so clearly the me I want to be. I know that's part of his game, and he'd never let me be that person. And it hurts because I care about his goddamn opinion so much."

Out of the corner of their eye they caught Effie biting her lip.

"I mean," they tried to clarify, "I don't have many people around me to neutralise the poison he fills me with. Effie is basically my only friend—and we literally just met for the first time in a decade." It felt wrong that it had only been a week; Effie had quickly become the most important person in their life.

"Tove," DuBois butted into their thoughts, "we are your friends. Will you have us?"

A single tear broke barrier and made a run for it down Tove's cheek. Their ice, their cynicism, was thawing, thanks to these strange and lovely people. "I suppose I've already accepted you. This is the first time I've talked shit about my ex. Ever."

"Why's that?" asked Alice. She spoke softer than usual, as if moved by all this talk of friendship and hurt and manipulative boys.

"It feels disrespectful. We were big into sorting out our problems in private. Presenting the perfect relationship to the outside world. We were desperate to be a 'success' despite all the odds."

"The odds?" asked Effie.

Tove attempted to find the words. "Well, we were fundamentally incompatible. We both knew that. But also…it felt like nobody else wanted us to be together. So we made it our mission to spite them."

"What a dreadful basis for a relationship," commented Tove's Bryan. "Why would you stay together?"

"You see," Effie's Bryan explained, "there's a lot of social and cultural messaging that relationships are toil and trouble. In cisgender heterosexual allosexual relationships especially—or those where you're acting as such—there's an expectation that you will be unhappy no matter what. So if you're in that situation, you truly believe it's normal. You're playing a part every day. Is that close, Tove?"

Tove nodded. Jesus, what a mess it all was. "My name in his phone is 'ball and chain.' And he has a tattoo on his wrist of an anchor, which represented me. That was my role. The anchor."

Effie was quivering with rage as she said, "You're nobody's anchor."

"I was rusting at the bottom of the sea."

Everybody exchanged glances. The air was heavy and it wasn't just the rainclouds on the ocean horizon. But Tove's spirit was floating. It felt so freeing to say it all out loud.

"What can we do for you, Tove?" asked Alice.

"I don't know. This conversation helped. I feel like…I'm allowed to be angry?"

"Yes," all the Santas said together.

Tove took them in. DuBois's knuckles were white where his fists lay on the table. Their favourite Bryan's precious triangle sandwiches sat untouched in the Tupperware box. These were their friends now. They were no longer alone carrying the burden of their past. This was surely their turning point.

23

Alice created group "Santa Babes"

You were added

How do you bottle up a feeling? Capture a bubble without popping it? If she were to treat it like a joke, Effie could distil this elation into a milkshake on a hot day and the giggles of classmates as you snort it up your nostrils. But a joke like that would sacrifice the tearful loveliness of cold milk after a long drought.

"What's up? You're making the most unhinged face." Tove tweaked her elbow, sending a shockwave up her arm.

"I started the pageant with no friends, and now I have five?" Effie cried. "I'm in a group chat!"

Tove raised a doubtful eyebrow. "You sound surprised."

Something fussed at the periphery of Effie's mind—first Aaron calling her "weird one," and then how Tove, despite everything, still cared about his opinion. They'd admitted it out loud. Suddenly Effie didn't want to talk about her self-esteem with Tove.

The taste of milk faded, leaving it to her digestive mercies. Good thing she was gastronomically indestructible.

"What now?" she said. And if she meant more than Tove read into her words, nobody was any the wiser.

"We have to get back to the fair," said Tove. "Come on."

They finished their food and drinks and left Nice Crumb, waving goodbye to DuBois, whose heart of himbo gold Effie had begun to appreciate.

"How are you feeling about the fair?" she asked on the way back down the seafront.

"I'm in trouble. How are we competing with B1's gorgeous doll's house?"

Effie ached for Tove and her other new friends. It felt cruel to pit them all against each other so soon after cementing their solidarity.

"It's fine. If I raise a bit of money for the charity I'm supporting then I'll be happy."

"I don't want any of us to be eliminated."

"That's the game we signed up for, Effie."

"How are you so ready to let go?"

"Well, what exactly would I be losing? The Santas are great, but nobody sticks by you forever. And I never set out to win the pageant anyway. I'm done putting that much pressure on myself."

"Wouldn't it be nice if we could keep our friends *and* win the pageant *and* help others *and* have all the love and happiness we ever wanted?"

Tove sighed. "I guess I'm always waiting for the other shoe to drop. I envy how you always think the best of others and do everything you can for them."

Effie couldn't take the compliment. Not when she was always the one dropping the shoe.

"Come on. We don't have long to set up our tables."

Ranjula taped posters to Effie's table and produced a basket of free wristbands while Effie lined up her wire animals in a vaguely artistic way. Across the aisle, Tove and a middle-aged lady representing their charity looped string and ribbon around each snowflake so they'd hang like Christmas decorations. They had a donation bucket labelled with the charity's name and mission, not that Effie could read it from where she stood. Mysteriously, Tove also spread out their gel pens on the table.

Before Effie knew it, Nowell was on the loudspeaker announcing that the selling of the Santa crafts was about to begin. "The Santa who makes the least money from selling their crafts will be eliminated today, so make sure you buy from your favourite," they warned. And the horn blared.

Effie was definitely not everyone's favourite Santa, but she was surprised by the number of tweens and teens coming up to buy her Christmas mooses. Maybe moose was the new frog. The cute fashionable animal that could sell merch off its species alone.

When she glanced up from the initial rush, B1's doll's house was long gone, and he'd moved onto taking future commissions for houses and mini furniture with his sketchbook. Alice had a big crowd too, but they were mostly her family—women and men in their thirties with her same flawless skin, and grandchildren Effie recognised from the dinner party.

Then Nowell stopped by Tove's table. A quick, urgent conversation later, Tove, with a long face, removed their donation bucket from the table. Once Nowell's back turned, Effie scurried over.

"What's up?" she asked. "What happened?"

Tove leaned in to whisper, "Nowell said it was a bit on the nose. Like am I accusing Aaron of domestic abuse or what?"

"Domestic abuse?"

"Yeah, the charity I'm supporting. We run a knitting group for victims and survivors of domestic abuse. We knit hats and scarves on Tuesday evenings."

"So you really do have a knitting group? That wasn't a lie?"

"Why would I lie about that?"

To get away from me, duh. She pushed the thought away. "So you're part of a knitting group for victims of abuse?"

"Yes. *No.* Look. Aaron was the one who had to come and shove our relationship into the public eye last night. This wasn't supposed to be about me or Aaron or our break-up. It was supposed to be about people who are having a shit time. People who are, like, *not me.*"

"So now you have to put your bucket away to avoid what? Defamation?"

Tove shuddered. "I haven't said *any*thing! And so what if I did? This damn pageant doesn't give a shit about any of us. They were the ones who gave my ex a platform. All I want to do is live my fucking life."

An idea popped into Effie's head. "Hey, I'll be right back."

She ran to Lalla's stall at the fringe of the carpark, where she was selling her earrings. Lalla looked so happy, like she'd love the opportunity to do this more often. Her smile faltered a bit as Effie approached, but that was unimportant right now.

"Do you have space on your table for a donation bucket?" She swiftly explained.

"Jesus." Lalla nodded. "Of course, bring it over."

Effie raced back to the Santa tables, grasped Tove's hand and the bucket, and dragged them both over.

"I'll spread the word," promised Lalla. "I'm so sorry."

"I…you've got to know this isn't about me," Tove floundered. "My ex was shit but this isn't about me or him."

"Totally," said Lalla. "But there are plenty of types of abuse. Teenage me had a boyfriend who would get drunk and pee on my laptop."

Holy crap. No wonder Lalla was always fighting Effie for the family computer.

"It's hard to admit these things are real, let alone abusive," Lalla added.

Effie felt like an outsider. Lalla was charming and sympathetic like the girls you met in nightclub bathrooms. Effie had never been in a relationship. She couldn't commiserate about girls, let alone boys.

"On one hand," Tove was saying, "I recognise that conflict and abuse are different. But you start to question what's what when someone throws your phone down the stairs, denies it when you get angry, and then tells you you're making stuff up to get annoyed at. Even though the screen crack is right there."

"Jesus Christ!" Effie exclaimed.

They both stared at her.

"Sorry," she mumbled.

"He apologised eventually. But then he said I admired it secretly because I like a guy who doesn't give a fuck."

"Tove, I'm so, *so* sorry for telling you break-ups suck," Effie cut in. "Sounds like your break-up is the best thing that ever happened to you."

"Yeah," Tove said, "I was upset when you said that. And look, while we're here, you should know that although I keep saying

I left him because we weren't right for each other, there was…a lot more going on there. Sometimes I lean on clichés to get out of awkward conversations."

Effie was going to need a dark, quiet room to process all this. She guessed Tove had hardly scraped the surface of everything they'd been through. Not to mention *Lalla*!

"I deeply apologise," she said, "for all the insensitive and presumptive things I've said."

"Hey, you don't need to apologise. I can't expect you to know what I don't tell you. And that's on me. Come on, let's get back to our tables."

Over the next fifty minutes, something amazing happened. People came in droves to buy Tove's paper snowflakes. Some of them stopped to offer stories of unhappy Christmases, or bad exes, or reasons why they weren't looking forward to Christmas Day that year. Some of them said nothing, but bought ten 50p snowflakes, and slipped a tenner to Tove which they stashed in their pocket, presumably for the donation bucket. Effie noticed each person pick a gel pen and write something, maybe only one or two words, on a snowflake, before buying a different one. Some even wrote on a snowflake but didn't buy any.

It took her a while to figure it out, but eventually, as a teenager checked out her wire animals with one of Tove's snowflakes dangling from their wrist, Effie realised they were writing names. Maybe their own name, or maybe the name of a loved one they were thinking about.

She asked about it when the teen bought a wire robin.

"No, I don't know who Zachary is," they said, "but I'm going to hang this on my family's Christmas tree every year and think about him. I hope my good wishes reach him."

At the end of the hour when the horn went, and Nowell collected the Santas' earnings, Effie beelined it for Tove's table. Almost all their snowflakes were gone. Effie pointed at the ones that were left.

"Can I buy these?"

"Sure, but the money's going to charity."

"Of course." Effie shoved a twenty into their fist. "This is a gorgeous idea, Tove. Really."

"It's not really proper activism," said Tove, "but I hope it'll encourage people to think of others, and I think that's a good thing."

Tove's entire face sparkled with the glitter dispersing from their eyeshadow. Effie leaned on the table to steady herself, swaying closer as she did so. Good Lord of Lesbians! Tove smelled of ripped paper and citrus. Invigorating. Intoxicating.

"Would you..." she began. "Would you like to swap a snowflake with me?"

Tove understood. Effie could tell by the red flush in the roots of their hair and their smiling nod. "I'd love to."

Effie didn't have to look at all the gel pens to choose her favourite. She only had to find the hot pink one, her old favourite. Tove's was a metallic green. They each picked a snowflake, and Effie wrote her name in pink, and Tove wrote their name in green. And then Effie gave Tove her snowflake, and they gave her theirs, and their fingers brushed as they locked eyes, the two snowflakes dancing together in the restless sea air.

"Gather round the stage," called Nowell through the loudspeaker. "It's time to announce the results of today's Santa challenge."

Their pinkies were still touching. "Not looking forward to this," Tove murmured, and Effie felt their voice rumbling through the point at which they were joined. Would it vibrate the same if they moaned with Effie's lips on their throat? Would it feel stronger?

"Same."

Effie fully took their hand in hers and squeezed it. When she released, Tove didn't let go. They strolled to the stage linked together, the other Santas in tow, only detaching when Nowell's assistant waved them under the lights to await their fate.

"And now, the winner of today's challenge, who made the most from selling their wonderful craft," Nowell announced, "is Bryan Tanguy!"

Effie had no idea which Bryan was which. She glanced at B1, but he was clapping with everyone else. It was B2 the cameras were trained on.

"And the runner-up, it's Tove's snowflakes!"

Nowell gestured towards Tove. They both looked startled.

"Nice one!" Effie yelled over the din of the crowd.

"I know everyone bought them out of pity," Tove replied, "but we made loads for the charity, so I'm delighted!"

Now, as Nowell continued, panic began to knot Effie's veins. Tove was safe, which meant Effie wasn't. Her, Alice, and B1. She didn't want anyone going home. They'd only just created the WhatsApp group. She'd only just *made* these friends!

"In third is Alice, well done!" said Nowell. "Those knitted hats were so adorable, I had to buy a few pet rocks for myself."

The crowd tittered.

But now it was Effie and B1. Her naff wire animals…against his artisan doll's house.

"We're down to the final two, Bryan Bourgaize and Effie." Nowell glanced at Effie impassively. They probably couldn't wait to announce her demise. "I won't drag this out. The Santa who made the least money today, and who will be eliminated from the competition, is…"

They paused, dragging it out as they said they wouldn't. The sound team played a corny heartbeat sample over the speakers.

Effie was the first to admit she watched these moments on reality TV with bated breath, rarely caring whose name was called out but drinking in the drama all the same. But being in this position herself…she hated it. She desperately wanted to stay in this contest, with all her new friends, win it like she'd promised Heather. Yet simultaneously she couldn't bear the thought of B1 getting eliminated when he was manifestly the quintessential Santa. When his doll's house surely sold for more than her silly little zoo.

"Bryan Bourgaize!"

What did that mean? Was she staying or going? But B2 clapped a hand on B1's shoulder, saying, "Sorry, Bryan."

Holy crap. How did this happen? How was she still in this?

Nowell glared daggers at Effie. She didn't blame them.

"What's going on?" she said feebly as the crowd went wild and Nowell shooed them all off stage towards the green room for confessionals.

"Bryan here sold his doll's house for a tenner," B2 said, his hand still on B1's shoulder.

"I wanted to give it for free," B1 explained, as if that explained anything. "Three hours was hardly enough to put it together, and it's not even decorated or furnished yet."

"Free?" Effie glanced from one face to another.

"I'd usually sell them for around £100, to cover materials and so," said B1, "but this lovely lady didn't have that money. Still, she and her two daughters wouldn't take it for nothing."

"Oh my god," Effie groaned. "This is bullshit."

"Excuse me?" B1 inquired with a frown.

"You're literally Santa himself," she said. "Basically giving away toys to the kids who need them. And yet you got eliminated from the Santa of the Year contest because what? Money? This contest is rigged to make fools of us." A headache began deep in her left temple.

"So it goes. But I am satisfied with the way I did it." Behind his real beard, B1 let out a rumbling laugh.

Tove fell into step beside Effie and took her arm.

"I'm upset," Effie told them.

"Me too," they said.

"I'm going to rage at the camera in my confessional."

"They'll clip it down."

"You don't think the audience will be angry too?"

"Of course they will. But the producers will hit us with something really dramatic tomorrow and take their mind off it."

"You think?"

"I'm certain."

"I don't know why I'm still here," Effie said.

"Well, you won, I guess?"

"No, I mean choosing to be here. In the pageant. I could walk out anytime, right?"

Tove shrugged. "Well, what do you want out of this shitshow?"

"I want to show my niece I can do it. Be Santa."

"There you go. That's why you're still here."

Effie nodded, but it didn't feel enough anymore. Heather sat on that sofa last night and made fun of her to her face and a live audience. If she wanted a neat little package of her awesomeness, her worthiness, to show to her parents and her sister and her niece, to make them love her, this wasn't it. She supposed that was why she'd suddenly become more sensitive to Tove's opinion of her; they felt like her last hope at being valued. And she was so deep into her feelings for them already, that if they didn't feel the same way, it'd be more than she could bear.

"Hey, what are you doing tonight?" she asked.

Tove shook their head, letting go of her arm. "Sorry, I'm busy."

Disappointment twisted Effie's gut. "Maybe another time."

"For sure." Tove turned as they were called to the confessional booth.

"Text me…if you want," Effie stammered after them. God, desperation did not become her. She needed a new hobby.

Tove threw a smile over their shoulder. "Gotcha."

With every cell in her body cringing, Effie took herself to the refreshments marquee for a drink of water and a mince pie.

24

There was exactly enough time to drive home and wolf down some veggie lasagne before Tove had to be back in Town for late-night shopping.

"I'm so happy you decided to play," their mum said, tying tinsel to their trumpet bell with a huge smile on her face. "Now, if you feel uncomfortable at any time, you know you can text me and I will be there right away. I'll raid the piggy bank and put a copper in your collection after every song, set the example for others."

"Mum, please. I've been carolling since I was tiny."

After grabbing some warm clothes to go over their risqué new Santa outfit—fingerless gloves, Effie's bobble hat, and a denim jacket displaying their entire badge collection—Tove downloaded some backing tracks onto their phone and checked the charge bar on their portable speaker. They weren't nervous. Although their lip and lungs were out of practice, they could play serviceable Christmas tunes with their eyes closed. They'd always been much better at trumpet than talking.

Most of the good spots were already gone by the time they returned to Town, but the music coordinator was an old teacher of theirs, and he found them an unoccupied alcove off the High Street.

"I've been following you in the pageant," he said as he left them to set up. "My family are all rooting for you!"

Tove threaded their mouthpiece into Felicity and put her case on the cobbles as a collection pot for the knitting group. They placed the speaker on a folding chair and connected it to their phone.

As they began to circulate warm air through Felicity before starting, two things happened in quick succession. First, a wizened old woman came up and asked if they were the Sally Army. Second, their phone buzzed with a brand-new text in the message chain they'd been studiously ignoring: **You didn't seem pleased to see me last night.**

Their gremlin dashed to their aid. So when they barked "No, I'm fucking gay!" at the old woman and she scuttled off with a sour expression, even though it wasn't her fault she caught them at a bad moment, a surge of power tingled at their fingertips.

The desire to yell "No, I'm fucking gay!" at Aaron was overwhelming.

Tove typed **I wasn't** into the chat of doom, and pressed send.

Aaron typed and stopped typing several times over. Ha. Stumped him.

Eight bars into *Hark the Herald Angels Sing*, he finally replied: **You really hurt me when you left. I just wanted to see you and talk about it.**

Unbidden, the guilt climbed thick up Tove's throat, making them fluff their quavers. It was true. They had the last laugh. They'd axed him out of their life without giving him a chance, without telling him all the reasons they wanted to leave. They at least owed him an explanation.

They banged down their valves, trying to refute their own feelings. They wanted to be angry, not guilty. Anger was easier.

When they pictured his smarmy face from last night, the anger oozed back, but this time it had morphed. No matter what Effie's Bryan said about not having to confront people, Tove craved the pleasure of telling Aaron it was over for good, the way they always should've done. If he was hurt by last night, then, well, that meant the power was Tove's. They had the power—and the responsibility—to give them both some closure.

Meet me at the holly & ivy at 9:30, they sent between carols.

"Excuse me," said a voice.

Tove paused the playlist and turned to the voice's owner, a woman wearing scarlet lipstick and a furry hat like a rich movie villain. Effie's mum. She'd driven the two of them to Winter Ball all those years ago, Effie uncharacteristically sulky in her Santa suit in the back seat. The memory made Tove hesitate.

"Hi," they said uncertainly.

"Goodness, it has been a long time, Tove. Don't mind me saying but you haven't grown a bit."

Tove clamped their lips shut and breathed through their nose.

"I have been watching you on the news all week. A curious affair the pageant is, don't you think?"

"You're watching it?"

"Of course. My daughter didn't tell me she was entering—she's not the most communicative girl—but someone has to keep an eye on her."

There was something wrong about this conversation. Tove couldn't pinpoint what. All they knew was that if Effie didn't tell her parents about the pageant, it was because she didn't want them to know—at least, not on any terms but her own. That's why Tove almost hadn't told their own mum.

"She's doing a great job," Tove said, "really the funniest and sweetest of all the contestants."

Effie's mum sniffed loudly. "But rather irresponsible, don't you agree, for putting her face on the telly when she's trying to make her way in the world, find a stable job."

"She's job hunting?" Tove asked, surprised.

"Well, naturally, in her position. I fear she's never going to find anything if she keeps deluding herself with these fanciful ventures of hers. You know how she is. Flighty. Unreliable."

"I mean, I'm in the pageant too," Tove said, taken aback by the barely veiled rudeness.

Effie's mum had the nerve to laugh. "I'm sure you have other things to show for yourself than a pair of tits in a Santa costume."

Tove's latent anger flared up once again. Their unemployed, mentally ill self couldn't possibly measure up to Effie's mum's idea of success, unless—and this was hardly better—they passed simply by virtue of not being Effie. "Effie is a supportive, caring person doing her absolute best in a world full of people like you who will never accept her. Please take your opinions elsewhere."

They skipped to the beginning of the playlist and the opening bars of *God Rest Ye* pounded through the speakers. Tove tooted the first staccato notes into the face of Effie's mum, till she huffed and marched away. How the *hell* Effie had ended up so ready with a kind word when she'd probably never received one, Tove didn't know.

They played for an hour and a half straight, still angry, till their embouchure faltered and their unpractised cheeks ached, and till Aaron's response finally lit up their phone screen: **See you there**

They split their high G. Shit. It was really happening.

They couldn't play another note after that. While packing up their trumpet, Tove recalled Effie's adorably awkward offer to text tonight. What was on their mind was probably not what she'd had on hers, but there was no one else they could ask.

They began with something fairly neutral: **Hey what are you up to tonight in a non-flirty way?**

Effie, bless her heart and soul, replied within the minute: **Watching Shrek and finishing my soup, what's up? You okay?**

Can you come to the pub? Meeting Aaron at the holly & ivy to finally have it out

She took longer to reply this time, and Tove chewed their swollen lip to keep from descending into the dark realm.

Her message appeared with a pop. **Are you sure?**

Mustering some bravado, they typed, **Sometimes I get this little flash of self-love and I know what I have to do**

What do you need from me?

Moral support

They double-texted: **Is that ok?**

And triple-texted: **Totally fine if you don't want to be there, I understand**

It's cool I'll be there, Effie replied. **What time?**

I'm heading over now. Aaron is always late tho

See you soon ok, take care x

Tove pinched their nose and took some deep breaths. Effie was coming! They wouldn't be alone! The knowledge thrilled them, because with her support, and that little **take care x**, they truly believed they could face anything.

At this time of year, the Holly & Ivy was full of uni students catching up between terms. Tove clenched their jaw as the diamond-latticed windows twinkled into view. They hated these places. The likelihood of being recognised made them want to shed their skin and grow a new one.

They pushed the door open to a blast of heat and sweat and earnest chatter. Everyone near the door looked up, so they swept past without making eye contact. Effie and Aaron were nowhere to be seen, so they grabbed a table upstairs in the corner where they wouldn't be interrupted.

A minute later, Effie poked her head round the bannister. "There you are!"

"I'm so glad you came." Tove's cold, tight limbs untensed at the sight of her.

"I wasn't not going to come."

Unlike Tove, she'd changed out of her Santa outfit, and now wore nondescript jeans and a white croptop. Her face glowed with windburn from the day spent in the coastal breeze. She scampered over, touched their shoulder and leaned close enough to peck their cheek. Her hair brushed their temple, greasy, the brown roots showing through the blonde, but beyond gorgeous all the same.

Tove held their breath in anticipation of her lips, but in the end she switched tack, jabbing the pro-choice badge on their collar instead.

"Loving the pins."

She scanned their badge collection—a lizard in the bi colours, a vaccination badge, various political and social justice pins. Tove was all of a sudden self-conscious; when they picked this jacket and outrageous little black dress they weren't expecting to meet Aaron. Still, perhaps it was for the best. They could source confidence from all the things they'd gotten louder about since leaving him.

Then they noticed Effie's eyes had fallen between their lapels. Their nipples pebbled through their dress behind their jacket, swelling with the memory of her mouth last night.

Effie physically shook herself. "Do you want a ti—a tipple? I mean a drink. Tipple means drink. I totally was not about to say 'tit.'"

"D-definitely."

They moved to stand, and Effie waved them back down.

"My darling Tove, I'm going to *buy you* a drink. So sit down, you fool! What do you want?"

Heat rose to their face. How did she make them feel like the luckiest person in the world? Like it was easy to treat them well? How was she so perfect? "G&T. Any old gin, I'm not picky."

Effie returned with two tall glasses of clear, gently fizzing liquid. "G&Ts were the ultimate classy drink my last year at uni. Did you get into them around then?"

"No, the doctor prescribed tonic water to help my foot cramps. Because of the quinine. Only that stuff tastes like ass without alcohol."

Effie laughed. "I don't mind tonic water. Bit of elderflower cordial, a slice of lime, you barely notice the gin's missing."

"Still ass," said Tove.

"It's an ass I can get behind."

Oh god. Dirty-talking G&T Effie was hot. Just as hot as just-a-kiss daytime Effie or nipple-sucking carpark Effie. Tove pressed their cold glass to their temple, watching Effie gulp her drink as the flirtation floated between them. Her fingers tapped nervously on the side of her glass. Her nails were freshly cut and polished, they noticed, glossy as if coated in spit.

"Can I ask how this started?" Effie said abruptly. "Like, being here. Was this Aaron's idea?"

Tove blinked away the thought of sucking Effie's— Fuck's sake. They weren't here to get laid. The opposite, actually.

"No no, this was my idea."

"And do you…have a plan? Know what you're going to say? Or what you need to talk about?"

"Not really. All I want to say is how upset I am about the other night. And say it's over, for real, so please leave me alone. And say sorry."

"What do you have to be sorry for?"

"For leaving him three weeks before the wedding. It was so sudden. I never even explained why."

Effie drained her drink. "We're here because you feel guilty?"

"I want closure."

"Okay, and why do you want closure? B2 literally said earlier today that you don't have to confront things if you don't want to. You *can* simply cut this guy out."

"I don't know if I can. You know in books and movies there's always this big scene where they pour out their feelings, or write a letter? There's, like, some explicit statement of how things are going to be. I never had that."

Effie propped her chin on her hands and considered her empty glass. "It seems to me like a bargain that plays into the other person's agenda."

"You don't know his agenda," Tove insisted. "I think I really hurt him, and last night was his way of trying to get some understanding of my side. After all, I ignored all his texts and calls. That's got to be rough on a person."

"Your feelings matter too!" Effie argued. "But…you know him better than I do. Maybe it does make sense to lay down the law here. Express that you've moved on." She didn't sound convinced.

"I think it's the least I can do."

Effie splayed her hands on the table. "Well, however you want to play this, I'm here for you. Do you want another drink?"

Tove gestured to their two-thirds-full G&T. While Effie took her empty glass to the bar, they stole her beer mat and started tearing it up. There was definitely something to be said about playing into Aaron's agenda. No matter what they thought he wanted, he wasn't above playing the victim to find a way into their feelings. Still, Tove knew, as Effie didn't, that he wasn't the only one at fault. If only they'd been more vocal throughout the relationship, it wouldn't have ended the way it did, with them running away three weeks before the wedding. They'd been avoiding this for too long.

Effie returned with what looked and smelled like a vodka lemonade, her mouth a solemn line. Instantly Tove became a coin in a collection dome spiralling towards their doom: did they do something wrong?

"There's something I want to ask," Effie said. "I get that you care about Aaron's opinion and that's a hard habit to break..."

Tove inspected the shredded remains of the beer mat. Their stomach was full of stones. "Yeah?"

"Are you embarrassed of me?"

The question caught them by surprise. "Why would you think that?"

Effie hesitated for the longest of seconds. She ducked down to the table edge and blew slowly outwards, scattering the beer mat fragments. Some of them fluttered onto Tove's lap.

"I was wondering if you thought Aaron wouldn't approve or whatever. Like, of us being...friends?"

Well, shit. She'd hit on the exact thing that had been tilting their brain since last night. There was no denying that was one reason they'd decided to kiss her: because Aaron wouldn't approve. But also because they liked Effie a lot, and they didn't need Aaron's approval, and they wanted to show her that neither did she.

"It's not a you thing," they tried to explain. "He's the sort of person who wants to be in charge, so anyone getting close to me is a threat."

"Right. Yeah. He likes control. I should've seen that."

But the corners of Effie's lips tipped downwards. If anything, she looked more disappointed than before.

"Actually," Tove added, in an attempt to bring some comfort, "I lied. It is a you thing. Not because you did anything, but because you're a woman. He makes these meaningless comments about how he's glad I'm making friends, and I feel so judged. Even though me and you…we're not together. Or anything. But we did kiss right before that interview and it's always on my mind…"

"Then you *are* embarrassed of me?" Effie shook her head, sending her unbrushed hair into a frenzy. "Wait, the guy is a homophobe as well?"

"Only towards me."

"That's not…that doesn't…"

Tove glanced at the bannister. No Aaron yet. "Can I tell you something?"

"Of course. Please."

"I only came out as bi quite recently. Like, a week ago, to your niece."

Effie goggled. "What?"

"Your niece was questioning my right to be there in a Santa suit. And it slipped out."

"So what? Are you not out to many other people?"

"I'm pretty sure my mum knows. But it's tricky. Although I've been feeling the gay feelings for years and years, it took a long time to admit it to myself."

"Take me back to Winter Ball. What were you thinking then?"

Tove shrugged. "I don't remember feeling anything except confused. You know when you finally figure it out and everything gets recontextualised? In retrospect I know I wanted to be with you, and I got with Aaron as a response to that confusion. I assumed we didn't have a chance. But I didn't really understand back then."

"It's weird looking back with all this new self-knowledge," Effie mused. "I think I was 95% of the way there, but hadn't called myself lesbian out loud, if you get me."

"Yeah. It's not surprising neither of us said we liked each other. We didn't know what to call our own feelings."

"So what happens now we know what to call them?" Effie asked.

"Well, I tried to come out to Aaron."

"Uh oh." Effie went from biting her lip to gritting her teeth, and Tove realised she'd been flirting again. They'd entirely, mortifyingly missed it.

"I phrased it as, 'I think I'm bi.' It went badly."

Effie groaned like she'd never been less excited to be right.

"Long story short—you've probably heard it before—women are naturally more attractive than men so of course I feel that way. Blah blah. He concluded his lecture with, 'I don't think you're bi.' And that was that. I wasn't allowed to be bi. So I kept it to myself. I was resigned to never coming out ever."

"You could've—"

"No," Tove cut her off. "I couldn't. Going against Aaron's opinion is so radical, I'm shaking in my shoes thinking about it. Coming out to your niece was the ultimate rebellion."

"That was you defying anyone who wants to tell you who you are or where you belong. Or where you don't."

"Yes."

"And bringing me tonight…am I part of your rebellion?"

Tove hadn't considered it that way. "Um, I—"

"Hello, ladies."

They both jumped out their skins. A hand came between Tove and Effie, outstretched to shake. It was Aaron's, of course.

"Hi," Effie barked, ignoring the hand.

"Hello," Tove said carefully, looking down and trying not to get freaked out by the cookie-dough pallor of their own wrists.

Aaron withdrew his hand and tried, "Drinks?"

Tove declined, but Effie, ballsy as ever, handed him her glass and said, "Anything will do."

"Are you okay?" Effie asked while he was at the bar.

Tove gave a thumbs up, not trusting themself to speak. They used the time they had to gather their thoughts and motives. Self-truth was their strength, maybe their only strength.

Aaron brought back two pints of cheap lager, and Effie grinned as he set one down in front of her. It was a dig—imagine buying a girl a pint after she gave you a glass that clearly had a spirit and mixer in it. How could Effie have thought they were embarrassed by her? Effie wasn't the clown here. The clown was Tove themself, for bringing her here to be belittled once again by their piece-of-shit ex!

"Cigarette?" he asked, plopping himself on the stool at the end of the table. Only he didn't say "cigarette."

He slid a pack from his pocket and cocked it towards Effie.

She laughed, immediately copping that he was trying to get rid of her. "I prefer 'dyke.' But not from you."

"Get some air outside, then. You look"—he gestured at his own face—"warm."

"It's sunburn," said Effie.

"In December?"

"You're telling me you didn't see the sun rise today?"

They battled it out with their eyes, while Tove spoke a silent prayer of thanks to the Baby Jesus for granting them this stubborn ally of a woman with a wolfhound's nose for bullshit.

"Alright," Aaron said at last. "Then we'll pretend you aren't here. This is a private affair after all."

"Yup," Effie rejoined.

There was another pause, till Aaron realised this was the best he was going to get. He turned to Tove now, steepling his hands. "So, why have you summoned me?"

Tove's heart skipped a beat as their moment arrived, but Effie's eye-roll bolstered them.

"Well." They stopped. The crowd downstairs roared at a knockdown in the boxing. The wall lamps flickered. Everything was going black and white by turns. Aaron tensed as if to step in and tell them what to feel. This was wrong. They didn't want the last laugh, they didn't want to "win" the break-up; that would only be letting themself get drawn into his game, his agenda, like Effie said. Where was their anger when they really needed it?

They blinked away the dust swirls, and steeled themself. If they couldn't do this perfectly, they would at least conduct themself in a way Aaron couldn't criticise.

"I wanted to apologise."

25

"I wanted to apologise," said Tove, rigid as a pole.

Effie's heart splintered. Oh, Tove. Pure Tove. Tove who never learned to appreciate their own strength because they'd never had to reckon with somebody questioning it. Till Aaron.

She shot a murderous look at the man, who was nodding and going "Mhm" in a way that definitely wasn't disagreement.

"I'm sorry for the way I handled things. It wasn't very mature of me to run away like I did."

Mature, *really*? Even Tove's voice had changed, taking on a sombre, measured tone that Effie didn't like one bit. So this was how they'd coped, before they'd begun learning to feel again. They'd simply stopped feeling.

Effie gulped her lager.

"I'm sorry," Tove said again. They whipped their—well, Effie's—pink bobble hat off to reveal the new buzzcut.

Aaron's jaw dropped. "Oh, so that's how it is?"

"I'm different now," Tove said.

Aaron paused for the longest of seconds, recalculating. "I do think," he began, "there were better ways to tell me how you felt. But I'm glad we're having this conversation now. Funny how I had to surprise you the other day to remind you I exist."

Effie wanted to scream. "Alright," she cut in.

Tove held up a palm, a stop sign. "About your surprise the other day, I really felt like…there might've been…*better ways*?"

Effie mentally applauded them for throwing his words back at him.

"What else could I have done?" Aaron laughed. "You wouldn't answer my texts. You needed a little nudge."

Effie bit her tongue hard. Surely Tove would react to that.

"The way I did things," they said, placing every word as if tiptoeing around a minefield, "don't you think, maybe, I didn't want to be in contact with you? At all?"

"Well, we're here now," he pointed out.

Effie willed Tove to stop phrasing everything as a question. Inviting his opinion at every opportunity.

"Besides, you never said you didn't want to talk to me," he went on. "What happened to our communication? Nine years of stressing the importance of talking to each other, and then suddenly nothing. You got cold feet. You wanted me to find you, and finally I have."

Oh, there it was. He *did* want to get back together.

"It wasn't cold feet," said Tove. "I didn't want to marry you."

That must've been excruciatingly hard to say. Effie eyed Aaron as he reeled back in surprise. Maybe not at the statement itself, but at how Tove was pushing back.

"Well," he recovered, "like I said, nine years of working on our communication. I wish you'd told me."

"I did."

"No, you said you weren't sure if we were a good fit."

"I said I didn't want to get married."

"At the time, yes. Of course. And we could've delayed the wedding, figured it out like we figured out everything else. All we needed was time. C'mon Topping, we got through so many things together. We said every bump in the road made us stronger in the end."

Effie heard him growing flustered, frustrated. She heard Tove growing tearful.

"That's what you said. And I didn't *want that.* So I left."

Effie could see it, as if the break-up were happening again, a second time, before her eyes. He wouldn't listen. They couldn't muster the harsh, clear words they needed to escape his gaslighting. And so they had to disappear. Until now. Why now, Tove?

He had the same question. "Why are we here tonight?"

Tove wasn't crying yet, but it was in their voice as they said, "I wanted to apologise. But talking to you now, I don't think I could've done anything differently. So I take it back. I'm not sorry for what I did. And I don't want to see you or talk to you or be surprised by you on reality TV. Respectfully I would like you to leave my life."

"Tove," he chided, "I've moved on, I moved on months ago. It's you who can't let go of me."

The nickname was gone; now it was their full name, placed before them in gentle admonishment. His hard, calm eyes told the truth: he never had any intention of getting back with Tove. He wanted to make them think that was an option, to make them want him. And now they wouldn't play that game, he was turning it back on them.

"What's up?" he prodded. "At least I'm honest about my feelings. It's you who won't admit you regret leaving me. You're playing hard to win back, and I'm sorry but I just don't feel the same."

Effie caught Tove's face as the realisation set in. They believed it: they believed they were hung up on him. Their guilt was all-consuming, their hurt was unbearable. They were losing themself in the struggle to heal from this and the only possible explanation in their mind right now was the one he'd given them: *they* couldn't let go. They were experiencing his rejection all over again, exactly as he intended.

The tears fell. Tove's rebellion was over.

"You, Aaron," Effie found herself saying, and both their gazes snapped to her as if they'd forgotten she existed, "you are the smallest, stinkiest particle of poo I have ever laid nose on. Sewer rats look at you and say wow, we're never coming back here again. Seagulls have shat more appetising shits. You are the scum of the earth. I'd buy you a ticket to Elon Musk's space colony purely to see you go, and may the proletariat cut off your tech support and leave you to die."

"Those are strong feelings," Aaron remarked. "But this is none of your business."

"Is too," she countered. "Tove asked me here for moral support, you're being a manipulative, gaslighting piece of shit, ergo my business."

She glanced at Tove, looking for their blessing to interfere further. They were crying into their drink, unable to talk. It was up to her. She'd been a bystander to Tove's budding relationship last time. This time, she would speak up and whisk them away if she had to.

"Speaking of my business, how about yours? What made you think it was a good idea to show up to that interview last night?" she demanded.

His smile faltered. "They wanted someone who knows Tove really well, and I know her better than anyone."

"You wanted to check up on Tove, didn't you? See how things are going without you."

"And what of it?" he retorted. "I care about her and she gave me nothing."

"She almost gave you everything."

"Did you come here to argue about a relationship you know nothing about? Come on, Effie. What's your stake with Tove? Why do you care?" He laughed coldly.

Effie's body burned. How dare he talk of them like a prize bet? And was he wrong to call her out?

He knew…didn't he? He must know and he was about to use it against her.

"You like her," he said. And when she didn't respond, continued triumphantly: "You like her, and you can't accept that she'll never like you back." He jabbed a finger at Tove. "Look, Topping, you can't really believe this loser has your best interests at heart. She's a conniving lesbian who ruins relationships and can't keep her mouth shut."

Effie recoiled in shock. Not only that, her head spun as if she'd forgotten to oxygenate while talking. With sparkling clarity she realised she was drunk. The lager on top of spirits was having its effect.

"I like Tove so very, very much," she said quietly. "But whether it's reciprocated or not, I like Tove in a totally different way to the way you do."

"That's a relief," he chuckled. "Isn't that what we always said, Topping? That no one would ever love you the same. Us or nothing. Forever or not at all. I would never have given up on you. But everyone else will eventually."

Effie took a deep breath. She should never have engaged with this awful man. But she would indulge one more time. She would not let Tove go undefended.

"Tove was so brave to break up with you," she thundered. "You intended her to be hurt and lonely, just how you wanted, your perfect submissive fucking trad wife. You made her bottle up everything that made her herself. But she's way more than you ever gave her credit for. After all you took, you have no respect for how she's been striving to rebuild her life. I've seen all of this and I've only known Tove a week! You dated her for nine years and all you want to do is put her down? You disgust me."

"Ah," and he latched onto the obvious because of course he did, "only a week? Then how could you know anything at all? You're extrapolating from maybe a few minor disputes Tove has told you about, and filling in the gaps with your liberal lesbian outrage about how all men are bad. I *know* Tove, don't I?" He craned towards them.

"Enough!" Effie leapt to her feet, sending the table rocking and her empty glass to the floor, where it bounced uselessly on the carpet. She clamped her fists shut, quivering with rage.

Aaron sprung away: the desired effect. "What the hell is wrong with you, Effie? God, you always were a freak."

Her heart slammed into her ribs as if brought up short by a thick chain. She'd been called lots of things in her life. Weirdo, pervert, various homophobic slurs, and so on… *Freak* was a new one. It seemed to encompass all the sexism, ableism, and lesbophobia that had ever been hurled in her direction. Fuck, Aaron didn't even know her. How in hell did he find the one word that would hurt the most? It was like he did keyhole surgery on the darkest recesses of her brain to find her greatest insecurities, and fit a word to them like a puzzle maker. Sure, she was probably neurodivergent. And wouldn't it be great if people gave her a bit of grace sometimes instead of hurling slurs at her? Aaron knew how he was using the word; it was written in the smirk on his face.

"Effie..." Tove, no longer sobbing, swung away from the table and clutched their trumpet to their chest. "Can we leave?"

Flapping her own hurt away, Effie curled her arm through theirs and together they marched down the stairs.

"Follow us and I'll deck you," she snarled over her shoulder.

Aaron folded his fucking arms and death-glared them all the way out.

They decided to walk back to Effie's flat instead of driving to Tove's mum's house. For a start, they were in no state to drive. For a second, Effie was tipsy and should probably be in her own bed. And for a third, Tove begged to stay, saying something like, "Please, my bedroom is full of ghosts. I can't go there." And they tugged Effie's sleeve between their finger and thumb, like a gnome at a giant's coattails.

They both stared at Effie's sleeve for all of a second before they dropped it, and Effie uttered a "Yes" to whatever they said; she couldn't remember exactly.

Truth be told, Effie's flat was beginning to feel full of ghosts too. The bath, the bed, the sofa, all touched by Tove's beauty and presence. Melchior was asleep in the boiler cupboard and not interested in saying hello at that time of night. Her snores echoing down the hall were a little ghostly too.

Effie turned all the lights on and went to the sink to pour herself some water. Her head was clearing, but not enough to process what happened in her brain when Tove flung their arms around her from behind. They snuggled their head between her shoulderblades like an affectionate backpack and whispered, "Thank you."

She choked on her water, catching herself in time that Tove didn't notice. Wiping her mouth with the back of her hand, she grunted some kind of acknowledgement.

"Thanks for standing up for me," they added. "That must've been hard."

She relished the press of their stomach on her ass, the way their strawberry nose squished and tickled her back. A treasure chest labelled "Tove's touches" built itself in her mind and the lid parted from the body briefly to welcome these memories. In her mind she decorated the chest with the pieces of Tove she'd grown to know: strings of ivy from the Santa grotto, smiling avocado socks, the catalogue of exquisite shapes their eyebrows could make.

"Effie?" A twinge of uncertainty rattled their voice, the same as the other day when they'd interpreted her brief silence as disapproval.

Effie wanted to pump them full of love and assurance so they never had to fear that ever again. Tove brought nothing but warmth and light. She could never disapprove of them. If only they knew that.

She took their hands from her shoulders and twisted to face them, then tucked their arms around her waist. It felt right. Safe. In her alcohol-addled brain she couldn't remember a time when she didn't love Tove.

"It was easy," she murmured. "I'm not the one he bullied into silence. Though I probably didn't choose the right words."

They shook their head, eyes shining. "Why? Why do you care?"

I love you teetered on the tip of her tongue. But Effie kept those words, stashing them in a secret pocket down the side of the treasure chest. Words she would like to say to Tove one day.

Instead she blew softly across the crown of their head, then, as they shivered, pulled her Santa hat from her pocket and tugged it over their ears. Their buzzcut prickled the blood out of her capillaries, yet was soft as pussywillow to stroke. Her fingertips lingered, perhaps too long, till she lay them to rest at the nape of Tove's neck. "I'm going to look after you from now on."

"You've been doing a really good job," they almost purred, stirring the fabric of her shirt and the skin beneath. They must've noticed how she was holding their head, but they made no move to detach from her clasp.

"But let me know if I'm overbearing. I need some help knowing what you want and need sometimes, okay?"

Tove burrowed their head into her chest, smack between her boobs. The pins and badges on their jacket dug point-sized dents into her skin like fork pricks in uncooked pastry. "Course," they mumbled.

Effie's nipples began to throb. She longed to rip her bra off to give Tove's head a better resting place. She clung to them, wanting them to stay there, to roost there, to make it their home if that was what they desired.

"Do you like that?" she murmured.

Tove's golden-brown eyes rose, deep and gaping as cauldrons of liquid gold. Effie melted right into them.

"It's safe to say," Tove breathed, "that when I'm crowned Santa of the Year, you'll be my top Elfie."

"Still think you're going to beat me, Mistletove?"

"It's Ice Queen to you." Their hands snuck over her shoulders and around her neck.

Effie was centimetres away from kissing them, moments away from absolute exhilaration. She bent and their foreheads collided. She hovered there, testing the hard boundary between them, gently pushing but balanced all the same. She shuddered and shut her eyes, her lashes grazing theirs.

"To me?" she whispered. "It's darling Tove to me."

She leaned into their stretch and their mouths smashed together. Tove's body arched into hers and she supported their spine as she pressed them against the kitchen counter and kissed them and kissed them again. If she was drunk on drinks before, now she was drunk on Tove. The ravenous way they nipped at her bottom lip, the soft bunches of skin she found on their ass and the slope up to their neck, the moans rumbling in their throat that escaped the corners of their mouth as they gasped for breath.

"Effie—" they cried out.

Effie sprang away. "Too much?"

"No, not that." Tove adjusted their dress straps where they'd slipped down into their jacket sleeves. "I want you to kiss me. More. I want more."

Effie's throat wobbled. "You know I had three whole drinks?"

"You're mildly tipsy at best."

"Even though I'm…saying all these things? Darling. Beloved. Cheeky biscuit." Again the *I love you* bobbed to the tip of her tongue. She didn't say that one. But was she saying it without saying it? She searched Tove's face for the answer.

They were shaking their head and smiling right up to the eyes. "You're one of those people who doesn't need alcohol to say what you're thinking. The only thing that's different is your confidence. You aren't questioning yourself when you kiss me."

"Well, that's you, not the alcohol." The tipsy haze from earlier had faded into a blistering clarity. "You are so brave, so determined, you're rubbing off on me."

Tove crumpled, a complimented bottom if ever there was one. "Me?" they squeaked.

Alcohol still fizzed through Effie's veins—it surely must—but far from hindering, it was infusing her with conviction. It was more than courage; there was nothing to be brave about when you were so completely certain of yourself and what you were doing.

"I would like more than your determination to rub off on me," she growled. "But I'm not completely sober, so that brings up some dubious issues of consent."

Tove shut their eyes at *rub off* and moaned. Their smooth hands flew to their face and they raked their knuckles down their cheeks.

"I have an idea," they said, holding up a long finger. "One pint."

"One pint?" Effie's brain measured the length of that single finger. Something absolutely feral was going on between her thighs.

"One pint." Tove grabbed her glass and filled it at the sink. Water spilled from the brim in a smooth sheet, till they shut off the tap and handed it back. "One pint of water, to hydrate your brain and body. I'll match you. After all, I had a drink too. *Then* you can kiss me again."

Effie didn't need telling twice. Halfway into the pint in a single glug, she began to feel ill from the volume of liquid in her stomach.

Tove caught her look. "And a slice of toast. For soakage."

They untwisted the plastic-wrapped loaf on the counter and popped two slices into the toaster, one each.

As they ate their toast, something occurred to Effie. "Tell me if I'm overstepping, since we didn't discuss where we want to go tonight," she rambled, "but I should probably ask, do you have any protection? I mean, for safe sex and such. A condom would do, like you only have to cut it down the side and ta-da, a dental dam!"

"No, I didn't… I mean I didn't expect…"

"That's cool." Oops. She had overstepped. Pushing back the fantasies crowding her mind, she finished her toast and licked her fingers, only to find Tove gawping. "What's up?"

"I want," Tove said with heavy emphasis, "to have sex with you. Do *you* have any protection?"

They knocked the breath out of her every time they spoke. Her body ached for theirs. And it ached worse to know she didn't have any protection either. "I don't," she groaned. "It's been forever since I got laid. Imagine wanting to screw a single person on this sapphic-starved Island before running into you again? I was not *prepared*."

"Well," said Tove calmly, "if you haven't gotten laid in forever, when were you last tested?"

"Oh." The frustration faded and Tove's lips came into sharp focus once again. "Just before I left the UK. The clinic was converted into a vaccination centre and the nurses were giving out home STI testing kits at the door. How about you?"

Tove spread their hands, grinning. "I went to the clinic in the summer." The grin soured. "I'm sorry I flew off the handle when you asked if Aaron cheated on me. I don't think he did, but it's true I didn't trust him not to. And he knew it."

"Getting checked is responsible, not necessarily an expression of distrust."

"Well, it was true. I didn't trust him."

"He didn't give you much reason to trust him though, right? If you're distrustful, that becomes another way to control you."

Tove sighed. "I don't want to think about it. I don't want to remember. Remembering makes me want to never have sex ever again. And that's not how I feel. Looking at you, Effie… I want to have you. I want to mess. you. up."

Effie hesitated long enough to register their pupils dilating, their nails scratching at the tabletop. Tove wanted this. They could be about to have the best sex of their lives. In fact, she was sure of it. But they needed to take the requisite precautions, bearing in mind that they were two people with needs and baggage.

"Tove, before we… I mean, if you want to stop at any point, if you feel yourself falling into a bad place, or thinking things you don't want to, or zoning out or anything, anything at all, you tell me or tap out. And we stop. And I'll make some tea, or more toast, or hug you, or you can leave, or anything you need. Alright?"

"And the same for you."

Effie breathed through the joy of how equal this felt, how even, how Tove would consider her needs exactly as she would consider theirs. They'd both grown so far past their old friendship, which, although balanced, never felt as honest as this did. They'd both been holding back so much of themselves.

Now she was ready to lay everything before them. Herself included.

Tipping her head, Effie chugged the last of her pint of water. She scraped back her chair and stood over Tove. "Can I take you," she asked, her voice growing in gravelly texture, "to the bedroom?"

A flit of amazement that this was really happening passed over their face, then there was only *want*. "Yes." They placed the word in the air for her ears to devour, a syllable of desire and sexy, sexy consent.

"Come on then."

26

Tove surrendered themself to Effie's arms. They wrapped their legs round her waist. Their body hummed, clit thickening on Effie's hip, as if picking up hers on radar, inches away through their clothes, vibrating at the same frequency.

Effie picked them up effortlessly and strode the ten steps down the hall. Ten steps of purposeful deliberation amid the desperation driving Tove almost to fury. Ten steps and they were in the bedroom. Effie kicked the door closed and bent to let them roll onto the bed. They pulled her with them, craving her weight on their body.

"I don't want to wreck your badges," Effie said as she tore off their jacket.

"I don't want to come on your shirt," Tove retorted as they ripped her croptop over her head.

Effie groaned. "You are so much sexier than you were in my dream."

"I fucking hope so. Your imagination has never come close to a cunt like mine."

"How do you make that word so hot?" Effie palmed their ass, searching for a way to their skin.

"At my pace, Little Ms Eager." Tove slapped her away. "And the word's only okay when I use it. It's only okay when I'm sitting on your face and your tongue is too busy making me come to speak it. Is that alright?"

She panted like an animal in their mouth. "I want it. I want you. So badly."

"Soon," they promised, tugging at her bra to let her soft, round boobs spill down her front. "And you'll have to say *please*. Didn't you say you liked that?"

"I do," Effie moaned, and Tove bent to kiss her again.

And then it was their tits and her tits, their hips and her hips, their lips and her lips, moving and tasting and devouring. "That's good," they murmured, or "More of that"; and over and over again, "You're so fucking beautiful."

The zip of Tove's dress foiled them both, but they managed to get their arms out, so there was nothing the straps and skirt could do to cover them. Effie cupped their breasts as they lay entangled, squeezed them, pinched the hard nipples to make Tove mewl. Her mouth pressed their temple, then their cheek, chin, neck, across their collarbone, and then she took their flesh in a gentle, hungry kiss. Her tongue circled their nipple and Tove's breasts had never felt so good, so seen and cared for and enjoyed. Tove had never liked them as much as they did now.

Effie continued down Tove's trembling body, their ribs and stomach through the dress, peeling off their tights as she dipped to kiss the hollow of their leg joint. Quick and mischievous, the kisses pattered down their leg to their foot, where she slipped their big toe into her warm, wet mouth.

Tove propped themself on their elbows and beheld her beyond their puffing skirts. Effie's big eyes locked on theirs as her mouth clung to its toe hostage, her body and legs now off the end of the bed.

"Effie," Tove called, "what about my clit?"

"You said at your pace," Effie whined, muffled, mouth full.

"I said you can have my *cunt* at my pace," they replied. "Now, give the toe back."

With a reluctant air she gave up their toe—which, to be frank, was sending bolts of arousal straight to Tove's clit anyway.

They swung off the side of the bed and made their way over, kicking their underwear away and standing before her. Almost naked. Completely certain.

Effie scrabbled on the floor, nipping at their thighs with her teeth. "Please, Tove," she begged. "It's my superpower."

Tove made her wait a moment longer, till they knew she was serious, till they could hardly contain their anticipation.

They splayed their fingers through Effie's hair and edged closer, holding her head centimetres from their pulsing pussy. "Lie down," they ordered.

She obeyed. Tove hovered over her, slipping their fingers through their folds to check they were wet. Effie's eyes widened. Tove needn't have worried; they were slick, nearly dripping. They had been for a while.

Tove lowered themself, kneeling up at first. Their skirts spread to cover Effie's face, trapping her in the dome of their desire. And then her tongue whipped out and needled their clit from below, impossibly long, incredibly accurate, and so dextrous they choked on a gasp. Effie was right; this was a superpower.

They paused to figure out their zip, and ripped the dress away to reveal her, tongue out, mid-lick, about to make them her own. Their eyes met. She gaped and so did they. And then she grabbed them, one hand to clamp their thigh and lever them closer, the other with two fingers angled to part their labia. For a second Tove lost balance as a shudder of pleasure gripped them, but Effie's strong arms caught them immediately, holding them just where she wanted.

Nobody had ever done this for Tove.

As they grew more comfortable with the extreme intimacy of looking into Effie's eyes, her face a triangle between their legs as she ate their pussy, they made a mental note never to agree to marry anyone without first verifying that the marriage would include this. Lots of this. Lots of…fuck. This. *Fuck.*

Effie's arms snaked up and she pinched their nipples hard.

Fuck!

Almost without comprehending, they came on her face. Their eyes shuttered and they could barely stay upright, every muscle in their body simultaneously clenching and unclenching. Magic poured from their pussy like a fountain of welding sparks, and when finally they rose up on their knees again, thighs tremoring, they saw themself painted all over Effie's mouth and chin…and nose.

"Wow," Effie chuckled. "You came on my nose." Her tongue, red and swollen, swiped at her lips. "Mmhmm. I taste of sex. I *smell* of sex. Yum."

"Oh god, your nose?" Tove cried, falling sideways off her. "Are you okay?"

"Darling, my nose has never been happier. The nobbly bit was made for your clit to grind into. The sweet mouth of your pussy pinches the tip as you come."

Tove couldn't help it: they blushed as if they hadn't just rocked themself to orgasm on her willing countenance. Her speaking it aloud—"as you come"—reminded them how few people had seen this part of them, and how they never knew if any of those people liked it.

"So?" Effie said expectantly. "How was it?"

"I feel like I should be asking you that."

"I'll tell you. You're perfect. Your clit feels like a cherry drop, made for licking and sucking, that tastes sweet as sugar and fresh as fruit. I think your labia love me; they'll simply undress at my touch. Your vagina is a work of art. It is a pleasure to be sat on by you, Tove. I enjoyed every moment. Thank you."

Tove was blushing from their toes to their tips. "I liked it too," they croaked.

Effie's grin split her shimmering face. "Oh good! I really hoped you would."

"You did?" It was a small yet momentous thing: to be amazed by the idea that someone had done something specifically to make them feel good.

"Yes, of course. You're all I can think about. Being under you, under your body and your feelings."

Tove had to turn away from the deluge of her sexy servility, just to keep from throwing themself back at her. They grabbed a box of tissues and helped her dab her face.

"That said," Effie mumbled through a tissue, "I didn't expect you to be so...dominant. The way you held my hair and told me to lie down, I nearly expired. I thought you'd be way more of a bottom."

"I'm not sure I felt dominant," Tove said, "with you going to town on my clit."

"But did you feel like you had autonomy? You weren't just there because I wanted it?" Effie was frowning slightly.

"No, I fucked your face on my own terms."

Effie shivered. "You're so goddamn hot when you do things on your own terms."

It was a new idea to Tove, and a powerful one.

"I'm glad you made me beg. I tend to take charge in the bedroom because I'm five foot eleven, and didn't want that to be our default without seeing where your role would naturally take you."

The words "our default" kicked a switch in Tove's brain. They'd had sex! With Effie! For the first time! And if she was talking about "defaults," maybe not the last time…

The thought only made the wetness still clinging to their pussy and legs burn hotter.

"You tend to take charge?" they spluttered. "In the bedroom?"

Effie got to her feet and shed the rest of her clothes. She towered over them, naked and smoking hot. "Yeah, what about it?" She grinned.

"Will you…show me?" Tove suggested.

Before they'd finished speaking her mouth was on theirs, and she crowded them onto the bed. She kissed them, running her hands up and down their sides, under their breasts, between their thighs. She pressed the heel of her hand against their clit, finally giving them the pressure they needed. Without warning two fingers slipped inside and plucked at the soft, sensitive spot on their inner wall. Tove cried out into the kiss but Effie kept them pinned down till they came a second time, wailing into her, and the kiss ended with them both gasping for breath.

"You like being penetrated, huh?" Effie purred against their cheek, fingers still curling gently to keep them on their high.

"I do," Tove huffed.

"Then do you want to try something? Hm?"

"I'm down for anything."

There was a rush of cold air as Effie leapt away. Seconds later she was back, holding a bottle of lube and a purple silicone object. The object had two ends, one long and one shorter, angled like the two shafts of a saxophone. The long end culminated in a slight bulge like the head of a cock. Between them was a smaller, thumb-like appendage tipped slightly towards the short end.

"Is that a dildo?" Tove asked, breathlessly.

"Yep, but not just any dildo. You see, you're not the only one who likes being penetrated."

Tove now saw it clearly as a strapless double-ended strap-on dildo. The short end penetrated the wearer and the longer end penetrated the receiver. The little thumb must be a clit stimulator for the wearer.

Tove wanted it inside them. Immediately.

"Effie, please fuck me," they breathed.

"Yes, darling."

First, Effie pushed the long end inside herself, thrusting a few times to coat it with her own wetness. Tove's eyes watered to watch her bite her lip and groan as she brought herself close to the brink. Then she took it out and put the shorter end inside, positioning the clit stimulator so the dildo held in place without her touching it. It jutted out from her crotch, rigid and gregarious. She grimaced for a minute and grumbled about slacking on her pelvic floor exercises.

"You're taking *so long*." Tove squirmed with anticipation.

Effie laughed. "What's that, do you want to come again? Do you want me to make you come again?" She squirted the length with lube and deftly spread it down and around.

"Yesssss," whined Tove.

"Yes, what, my darling?"

"Yes, please and fucking thank you!" Tove nearly screamed.

"That's right! That's right!" Effie's eyes flashed with hunger as she crawled on top. She leaned close, hard nipples scraping Tove's neck. "Get ready," she growled in their ear. "I'm about to fuck you till we both come."

Tove snuck a hand to their clit, unable to bear the anticipation.

Effie let them keep it there as she guided herself inside. Tove almost wept. They'd missed this comforting fullness. It had been so long.

"How does it feel?" Effie's voice caught, almost as if she really shared nerve endings with the dildo. "Being connected to me? Does it feel good?"

"It feels incredible," Tove whimpered. Effie hadn't started moving yet and they were already squirming around the purple silicone cock, already on the cusp of another orgasm.

"Alright, Tove." Effie cradled their cheek in her hand and pecked their lips, somehow sweet and chaste while being the sexiest person Tove had ever known. The only person they'd let inside who, they felt, truly belonged there. "Will you let me make you feel amazing?"

Tove let her.

Friday

3 days till Christmas

27

Effie and Tove lay panting, cuddling. They couldn't let go of each other. Effie reached for her phone and put on MIKA, unable to think about anything except how Tove used to love MIKA. She retrieved the emergency Hobnobs from her bedside drawer and made Tove snack while she stretched her quads, energised and planning. *We'll brush the crumbs onto the carpet*, she thought. *I can clean the room and these soaking sheets tomorrow.* Or today, she supposed…the sun was already casting shadows between the blocks outside, flickering behind swooping seagulls. She should sleep, or she'd never make it to the pageant's secret challenge tonight.

She returned to bed, blinking at the sight of Tove lying alongside her, crumbs freckling their face, a peaceful look in their eyes. How could she ever have thought those eyes were empty? Tove's gaze was deep and luscious, framed by those spidery eyelashes Effie had always admired, the eyelashes the teachers used to tell them to go and take off, only they'd say defiantly, "Bump off, they're real." And right now, with a different kind of defiance, they were looking at Effie herself, taking all of her in.

"You're so beautiful, Effie," Tove whispered.

The way they said her name set all Effie's nerves tingling. She felt as special, and yet as tongue-tied, as she had been when they were teenagers sleeping over at each other's houses—only never in the same bed, and never, she noticed with a fresh jolt, completely naked as they were now.

"I want to kiss you all over again," she breathed.

Tove booped her nose with their finger. "I thought you'd never ask."

They closed the gap, all mint and tea-tree and smoothness and precious handfuls of wanting, willing flesh. They rocked together, till Effie wasn't sure what parts of herself were her and what parts of herself were them.

"This feels so right," Tove murmured into her ear after she came on their fingers.

"Yeah," Effie agreed, dozy with dopamine and encroaching sleep. Nothing existed but her and Tove and the rumpled covers.

"My ex…Aaron…only felt wrong in snatched moments that I mostly ignored. But he never felt right like you do. You feel right every second we spend together."

Effie roused herself to pay attention. "Mm, maybe that's because it's true."

"What is?"

"Me and you, maybe we're right."

Tove uttered a low giggle. "Maybe."

"The other day you said we were too late. To be an 'us.' I know this is kind of a loaded question, but what's stopping you from believing we could work out for real? Because I think together we could be unstoppable."

Tove slumped against the bedboard, puffing air between pursed lips. “I’m scared, duh. I’m scared you’ll give up on me. I’m fragile and weepy and would rather flip you off than let you see that.”

“Maybe that was the you of a week ago. But now? You couldn’t do anything that would make me support or cherish you less. I’m strong enough for you. I promise.”

Tove’s ginger eyelashes shimmered in the sunrise. “Well. Maybe.”

“Will you think about it?”

“Yes, I’ll think about it.”

They kissed sleepily and shuffled under the covers. Effie lay blinking, as the ceiling whirled with ways she could prove to Tove that she could help them achieve their wildest dreams.

Tove wriggled their hand into hers. “Thanks, Effie.”

“For what?” she asked.

But they were already snoring.

Mere hours later, Effie’s cat vibrated with a phone call. She flinched awake and rolled over, tugging Tove with her. They were still holding hands from last night, so safe and sound they’d never let go. Effie did not want to ever let go.

She glowed at the thought, and at the memories they’d made last night.

She couldn’t detach from Tove, so she stretched her other arm to grab her phone from underneath Melchior and take the call.

“Effie?” It was Lalla, and she sounded pissed.

“Hi,” Effie murmured. “Keep it down, would you?”

"What's up, entertaining?" teased Lalla. And then, as Effie said nothing, "Oh, okay."

"Relax," Effie drawled. "Why the call? It's so early."

"It's 11 and you promised to bring my supplies back. My soldering iron? My wire reels?"

Tove stirred beside her.

"Ah, whoops."

"Come on, Effie, I'm off work for Christmas and wanted to start restocking from yesterday's sale."

"Yeah, yeah, how did it go?"

"Really well, nearly sold out. So I need my stuff? Now, please?"

"I'll be there soon," Effie promised with a sigh. She hung up.

Tove blinked awake. "What was that?"

"My sister wants me over. I was supposed to give her stuff back from yesterday."

"She sounded cross."

"You heard? I hate how she talks to me. How about starting with, 'Hi, dear beloved sister. What's up? How are you?'"

"What do you want, a gold star for getting laid?"

"Yes, actually." Effie laughed. "I have to shower and get going. Or she'll give me actual hell on Christmas Day in front of the parents."

"Is that your plan? Christmas with the family?" Tove followed her to the bathroom.

"Yep. It's the one time our parents want to see us." She climbed into the bath under the showerhead. "Lalla thinks you're right that we have unresolved trauma about our parents. But less about their divorce, and more about how they got back together."

Tove arched an eyebrow in the rapidly fogging mirror. "And what do you think?"

Effie hesitated too long, till the shampoo stung her eyes and filled her mouth. "I won't say it doesn't bother me. How happy they are without me."

"Their loss." Tove's matter-of-fact voice reached through her soapy haze.

"How about you? How are you spending Christmas?"

"Chill day at home. Dad's spending Christmas with his girlfriend's family but me, my mum and brother are going over for dinner on Boxing Day. My parents are still kind of friends and my dad's GF is decent. I spent the last few Christmases wandering around the Strasbourg markets, so I'm glad there's not too much pressure on me on the actual day. It's weird enough being here at all."

"How do you mean? Doesn't it feel, like, familiar? Being here?"

"No, it's dissonant. I'm stuck between memories of loneliness in the Christmas capital of Europe on one side and fading childhood memories on the other. I can't return to either of those Christmases. My relationship and break-up took all sense of home and self and friendship and family from me. I don't know if I'll ever escape this empty, homesick feeling."

They spoke levelly, but their words pumped sadness through Effie's heart. Six months was hardly any time to heal from the loss of both their future and the things they'd taken for granted in their past. They were probably still grieving the life they'd thought was before them. Effie wanted, beyond anything, to make Tove's present worth having. Could she give them a Christmas that was nothing like any Christmas they'd had before, that supported their vision of the Tove they aspired to be? Oh, dear! She had so many ideas already!

"Unrelated, but can I ask," she said, "are your family nice to you? You've said barely anything about your parents except that you didn't want to go home last night."

"They're really nice to me."

"Really nice?"

Hair rinsed, Effie soaped her body, enjoying how each tired limb responded to her touch with a tactile memory of Tove from last night. As if feeling it too, Tove beckoned, and Effie bent to let them do what they wanted—which was to reach up and grab her tits. Tove kneaded the soap into them, thumbing her rapidly hardening nipples, and sliding to the underboob which they massaged as if they knew, they *knew* how sweaty and sore it got under there.

Effie was getting turned on all over again, and she sighed when Tove finally retreated and rinsed their sopping hands in the sink.

"Way nicer than I deserve after what I put them through."

Effie tried to remember what they were talking about before. "What does that mean, your parents are nicer than you deserve? You deserve all the things. All the niceness and tenderness and kindness and—" *Love*, she nearly said. There she went again. This expanding feeling in her chest had nothing to do with last night's alcohol, because look at her now, wholly sober and it was still there and growing by the hour.

She caught Tove smiling in the mirror.

"Aaron charmed my parents' socks off. They were delighted when we got engaged, delighted to sink five grand they didn't have into a wedding that didn't happen. And like, when I turned up home three weeks before they were supposed to fly to Germany for the event, and shut myself in my room at my mum's house for a month, they were just like *yes, okay, what do you need doing*. They did everything for me and we still haven't talked about it."

"They don't know what happened?"

"Nope. They must be deeply confused."

Effie finished rinsing and gestured to the shower. Tove nodded so she left the water running.

"Will you ever tell them?"

"Doubt it. I don't want to break their hearts any more than I have already."

"Is there a possibility you're projecting?" Effie towelled off her nooks and crannies and decided to air-dry the rest of her while she combed her hair. "Like, not to pretend I know anything about *their* relationship, but if they're divorced, they must get it to some extent."

"Oh, for sure. I'm just so embarrassed and ashamed. I nearly married someone who didn't like me. At least my parents acknowledged they had a good run and still appreciate each other as humans."

Effie shrugged. "You're doing the best you can with the information available to you at each step. And it'll take time to heal and regain your empowerment and stuff. If your family aren't pushing you about it, then they probably think the same."

"Yeah, you're probably right."

While Tove showered, Effie stepped out the bathroom to make another phone call, this time to Natalie, Bonamy's daughter. There was another Grand Plan in the works.

Afterwards, they dressed in clean clothes, Tove in Effie's second favourite hoodie, which said FRONT on the front and BACK on the back. Effie packed Lalla's supplies into a bag along with her Santa costume, which was really beginning to smell, ready for the secret challenge that evening, in case she didn't have time to go home beforehand. Then, at around midday, they left the flat and retrieved Tove's car from Town so Tove could drop Effie at Lalla's.

"I meant to mention something while we were talking about our parents," Tove said as they pulled up in Lalla's estate. "Your mum turned up last night while I was busking."

Effie cracked open the car door. Cold air bore into her ears, making them ache. "Oh?"

"She came up to talk to me."

Her ears struck up a terrible ringing that eked into her skull and teeth. "What did she say?"

"She said she'd been watching the pageant."

Fantastic. Her parents knew. Of course they knew. She hadn't even won it yet and they'd already formed opinions. "And?"

"She, uh, wasn't very nice. About you."

A groan rumbled deep in Effie's bowels. She'd dreaded this. The pageant would not impress her mother. Maybe nothing would.

"Well, I guess there's something wrong with me no amount of Christmas cheer can fix," she said with forced joviality. "So long as you like me, right? Unless you were only in it for the sex. My personality, I'm afraid, is utterly fucked, according to my mother, but at least I've got a strong tongue."

"What? Yeah, the sex was fantastic." Tove yanked the handbrake on as if preparing to prolong the conversation.

Effie swung out of the car. "Good. Glad. Great."

"Hey, should I not have told you?"

Effie paused. She'd forgotten how Tove flew to an assumption of fault and rejection whenever something went wrong. "It's not you," she said, bending back into the car. "I'm upset my mum doesn't love me, which is for me to get over in my own time. Sorry I took it out on you."

"For what it's worth, I don't think you're either irresponsible or deluded."

Was that what her mum had said? The words stung. Could she be right?—if Effie was deluded *and* a freak, like Aaron had called her, then she probably wouldn't see it. But everyone else would.

Tove mustn't see the tension in her face, because they asked for a goodbye kiss.

"Are you sure?" Effie said, half-sarcastically. "Are you sure you want to be seen kissing a weirdo like me?"

"I do. So help me I've gotten over that hurdle."

"So last week, when I asked you weird good or weird bad…?"

"Why does that matter? You have to make peace with yourself regardless of what other people think. That's the only reason *I'm* not still in Germany chewing my fingernails. Now come over here."

Effie's thoughts were far away when she crawled back into the car to press a kiss to Tove's lips. Every time they addressed her insecurities, it was roundabout. Incomplete. Unsatisfying. They wanted to kiss her yes, but they also thought she was weird. Now she'd learned that taking backhanded compliments as genuine ones might be unproductive, Effie was noticing more and more that Tove, like everyone else, had no answer to the question she was asking. Was she a fuck-up? An oddball? A freak? What, really, was wrong with her?

Lalla was waiting at the door, staring after Tove's retreating car.

"What are you thinking?" Effie asked, expecting a less-than-kind reply.

Lalla shrugged. "That you're cooler than me."

Effie froze. Literally anything else would've surprised her less. "What?"

"Look at you, going out, kissing your friend, finding yourself. Wish I had your courage."

Effie shrank at the word "friend." She would've taken affront if it weren't for the hint of wistfulness in her sister's voice, and something else she couldn't pinpoint.

She asked, "What's the difference between me kissing my friend and you kissing Liam? Aren't you married to your bestie?" The real question, though, was what did Lalla think "finding yourself" meant, that she wished she had the courage for? She was *married to her best friend*, what had she yet to *find*?

"That's not what I meant. You're...exploring."

"I don't know what you think I'm exploring. I know what I like, I know what I want." Effie liked Tove, she wanted Tove. She wanted Lalla's marriage and her house and her stability, although maybe not her corporate job. "If you think I'm cooler than you for pursuing what I want, well, you could do it too. Just saying."

"I'm...married," Lalla huffed. Effie seriously doubted Lalla wanted anything other than to be monogamously married to the baby-faced e-boy of her heart, which is why *I'm married* sounded more like *I'm in deep denial about something I can't possibly tell you because you're a total weirdo and you'd never understand.*

Effie watched her sister's discontented eye-roll and let the frustration wash in. "I meant theoretically, abstractly, you *could*," she said. "What makes us different, you and me? Seriously?"

Lalla pinched her nose like whatever she was about to say was unsavoury to her. "You're free. You're unbound. No one's relying on you to do something or be something. You're not beholden to anyone for your life and worth. You don't need to worry that one wrong move or one wrong word could cost everything."

It was a punch to the gut, but Effie took it like she took everything. Firmly and invisibly.

"Do you really think that?" she asked her sister. "That I'm cool and free?"

Lalla let go of her nose and sighed. "Probably not. Being free is its own shit to deal with."

"You know 'free' doesn't mean anything? Whether I'm outside your cisheterosexual, takeout-and-football-on-weekends, live-to-pay-the-mortgage society by choice or not, I still live in a world where I'm constantly being rejected and left out. You don't think I'd rather be part of something? I want to live in a community. So then why wouldn't I care about my interconnectedness with other people?"

"I didn't say you didn't care. I said it didn't matter."

Ouch. Ouch ouch ouch.

Lalla, like everyone, couldn't answer Effie's question in any way that made sense. Effie knew within herself that she was no different from Lalla, at least not in the ways Lalla thought.

It was, as it always had been, a question for herself.

"I super don't want to talk about this," Effie managed to say.

She didn't really want to stay after that—after all, it apparently *didn't matter*—but she still found herself offering to start the bean jar for dinner to give Lalla a chance to start on her jewellery. Maybe she didn't have dependents or responsibilities, but her help mattered to Lalla, and therefore it mattered to *her*. *Honestly.*

"Mummy says you're late because you were seeing someone last night," Heather chirped.

Effie had never made bean jar. Good thing Heather, sitting on the counter in front of the saucepan cupboard, was there to witness her poison them all with improperly soaked beans.

Effie swept Heather from her perch, but she lingered in front of the hob, which Effie now needed to turn on.

"Mummy didn't say so, but I think the person you're seeing is that other Santa."

"Yep," Effie said to make her stop pestering.

Heather erupted into smiles and applause. "Ooh, did you kiss?"

Effie kept her head down as her face flamed. But she was desperate to brag, and couldn't resist saying, "A bit."

"Are you girlfriends now?"

Effie's heart fluttered, but she couldn't kid herself. They hadn't even discussed whether there would be a "next time." "No, we definitely aren't."

"Why not?"

"Sometimes…" Effie began. Then she decided to be frank. "You saw Tove's interview on Wednesday night, right?"

"Yeah, we watched the rerun."

"Right, and Tove's ex turned up out of the blue. They recently ended a long and serious relationship. It might not be a good time to begin anything. It's up to Tove."

And Effie herself… Well, she was beginning to wonder if she was or would ever be fit to be anyone's girlfriend. Maybe she wasn't built for being a girlfriend, or a friend, or a sister, or a daughter.

"I'll tell her to date you," Heather said as if it really were that simple. "The clouds this morning told me today is destiny. I bet all she needs is a little reassurance."

"You can't intervene!" cried Effie. Bean toxins and cooking failures faded in light of this new, devastating threat. "What I need to do," she said forcefully, "is support Tove the best I can. And then they will decide on their own if they want to be my partner. And I'll decide the same thing in my own way."

"Okay, so how do you support them?" asked Heather, switching pronouns effortlessly.

Oh dear. Effie would have a few things to tell Tove later. Outing them to their menace niece, said niece's matchmaking plot...and then there was the dilemma itself. How could Effie support them? How could she prove she was in this thing for the long haul?

28

"Tove. You're humming."

Tove's head snapped up at their brother, and they hunched over Effie's Christmas present to hide what they were doing. "I don't hum."

"You were humming *Deck the Halls* two seconds ago."

"Impossible." The song stuck in their head was *Christmas Tree* by Lady Gaga and Space Cowboy, but Dair didn't need to know that.

He eyed them with a contemplative curl of the lip. "You're happy."

Tove tried to deny it, and ended up smiling. "What about it?"

"Nothing. It's nice seeing you like this."

As Tove gasped like a fish, they accidentally let go of the wrapping paper covering Effie's bath bombs, and it flopped over to reveal them in all their scented glory.

"Hey, what's that?" Dair advanced into the living room.

"Nothing."

"Is it a present for me?"

"No, it's toiletries. For mum," Tove lied. Reluctantly they held up the bath bombs for inspection.

"I'm offended. I like baths too." Dair sniffed, then stared. "Wait. We don't have a bath. Are we getting a bath for Christmas?"

"Oh my god. We're *not* getting a bath for Christmas."

"Right, right. So either Mum has somehow sourced a friend who lets her use their bath, or—and here's what I think—*you've* sourced a friend with a bath."

"How does it feel being god's nosiest fleshsuit?"

"All I'm saying is, you haven't been home two nights this week."

"I was camping in a carpark for at least one of them."

"And last night?"

Tove scowled. Saying they'd met Aaron at the pub would shut him up. Last night had been a monumental mistake. They'd opened both themself and Effie up to his abuse. Instead of retaining the resentment they'd felt when he texted, Tove's gremlin had ended up absorbing blame and oozing shame. It could be harsh and standoffish with everyone, *except* the one person who'd caused all that pain in the first place. Poor thing. Maybe their gremlin was hurting as much as they were.

But last night was irrelevant, thanks to Effie. Aaron was over. Effie was now. In Tove's head, they and Effie explored the great beyond together, hand in hand. She made them believe in happily-ever-afters.

"You're smiling again."

When they'd told Effie they were scared she'd give up on them, it wasn't a lie. With the awful, awful things Aaron had said last night and the furious hurt plastered across Effie's face, Tove had their doubts about Effie's "hundy P." Even her mum had called her unreliable, and while Tove wouldn't have used that word, there was no way Effie could commit as hard as she claimed she could. Tove wouldn't have willed it so. They knew well enough what it was to bury your own vulnerability in an exhibition of valour and commit yourself body and soul to another person. Till all your deepest insecurities surfaced at once and everything slipped through your fingers. And your falling apart looked like betrayal to those around you.

As much as they wanted to say *yes* to Effie in all ways, they were wary of committing, and wary of letting her do the same.

"Fine! The bath bombs are for Effie," they confessed. "We're getting on really well. Like...I honestly..." Heat crowded their head. They must be blushing.

Dair squatted cross-legged on the rug, searching their face. "I'm going to tell you something, and you don't have to say anything in return, but in case you're interested in knowing... I'm pansexual."

Tove reeled a little. "I didn't know that."

"'Course you didn't."

Tove swiftly calculated whether Dair had anything to gain from knowing they were queer, and decided little enough to take a chance. "I'm bisexual. And non-binary. And I have been kissing Effie."

"Oh, shit! Go get it!" Dair offered a fist bump. "Proud to be your brother."

"Thanks." Tove blushed harder.

"So...does Effie have a sibling?"

"Yeah, and she's married to one of the guys you play D&D with, so suck it."

"Dang, I forgot about that." Dair ran his fingers through his gelled hair. "Guess I'll have to date Shane."

"I mean, do you even date?"

He huffed. "Pffft, imagine being brave enough to put yourself on a plate and offer it round like *hey, do you want a taste?* I couldn't possibly. Way too adventurous."

"Coming out as pansexual is adventurous."

"Come on Tove, I'm not brave like you. I'm a twenty-eight-year-old who still lives at home."

"I'm twenty-five and I live at home."

"You went on this whole adventure though. And look, maybe you didn't *want* to do it—I don't know how you feel—but you gave it a go, and had the courage to say no when you knew it wasn't for you. That'll always be impressive to me."

A seed of pleasure rooted and grew and blossomed in Tove's heart. "Wait, so you don't think I'm a hot mess?"

"Hot mess?" Dair laughed. "I think you're the coolest person I know. You're always putting yourself out there and trying things out, even if they'll be tough, like the publicity aspect of the Santa pageant. What happened to you earlier this year sucks, but I can't tell you how happy it makes me to see you giving people a chance again. You're doing your best at every moment. I admire you."

This rare moment of sincerity from Tove's clown of a brother had them wheezing into the cup of tea they'd left on the mantelpiece. What had Effie said earlier? "You're doing the best you can with the information available to you at each step. And your family probably think the same." It was exactly as she'd predicted. Good, sweet, wise Effie.

"That's very nice of you," Tove said, completely baffled as to how to respond.

"You ever need anything…say the word."

"I mean, there's one thing only you can do right now."

"What?" Despite everything he'd just said, Dair's expression turned from generous to faintly terrified in an instant.

Tove beamed at him. Their brother was still their brother, ever cautious about what he agreed to. "Put your thumb on this paper so I can tape it up."

They folded the wrapping paper over the bath bombs once again, and made Dair help with the fiddly bits. They even tied a ribbon around the package, taking several tries to make the perfect bow. They hoped Effie liked it.

Afterwards, they brought their trumpet to the living room, because Dair begged them for a concert before they had to be at the Pollack for the secret challenge that evening. The concert soon devolved into a lesson, and they spent a good hour teaching Dair to play *Silent Night*. Since their last lesson—maybe two, three years ago—Dair had kept a segment of PVC pipe on his desk, which he buzzed into while he worked as a mouth stim, so his embouchure was almost in better shape than Tove's.

"Why don't you learn for real?" Tove said when he finally produced that high F without splitting it. "You've always been interested."

"Ah." Dair shrugged. "It's too late to learn."

And that was the moment Tove's phone decided to ping with a message from the person they should've blocked months ago.

Effie will never love you

The world shrank to their phone screen, a sharp glow surrounded by dullness. The edges of their brain shrivelled like paper burned by a match.

"Tove?" said Dair. "Are you alright?"

"Um," they quavered.

Effie's crisply and lovingly wrapped present taunted them from the couch. Their trumpet glinted in Dair's grip.

"Sorry, I—need a moment." They clasped their phone to their chest and rushed to their bedroom, banging the door behind them. Once they were safe, they opened the push notification. There: the message was real.

Effie will never love you

With shaking hands they tapped out a reply. **What do you mean?**

Aaron was typing immediately. **I cannot believe you had a secret girlfriend the entire time we were together**

They crumpled to their bed. **That's not true**

I know you kissed at winter ball before we got together. I thought it was nothing. I was so naïve.

Who told you?

One of Tove's parrot plushies faceplanted onto their lap from the side of the bed. They tucked him under their arm. They needed all the support they could get.

So it's true? You and Effie have hooked up?

Great. It had been nothing but a bait.

Well? Is it true? Aaron repeated.

Yes, Tove replied, trembling.

Have you had sex?

Why do you care? I'm sure you've had loads of sex since we broke up. All the sex you wanted while we were together. So what if I sleep with one person one time?

Pretty different to the sex I've had

How?? they challenged.

Because you promised that no matter what, you loved me and would always love me. Nobody else. And now you're hooking up with a woman? Can you imagine how this feels for me? To find out I was about to marry a lying, cheating lesbian?

Frustration seared at Tove's fingertips like the skin was being peeled off strip by strip. **I'm bi, not lesbian. And I've never cheated.**

Then what am I supposed to think?

Whatever the fuck you want, Tove typed. **It's none of your fucking business.** They pressed send. God, they had come so fucking far. **I tried to tell you I was bi, but you said you didn't think I was**

Then why didn't you tell me I was wrong? This is what I always hated about you. You could never tell the fucking truth. This fucking proves it.

Tove rolled onto their stomach, the parrot beneath them. Their vision had begun to blur, their mind to empty.

Tell me the truth just this one time. Did you ever love me? Or was it all a lie?

Of course they'd loved him! Ridiculous, really, when all he did was berate them. That and sprinkle in the perfect mixture of "I would be nothing without you" and "you would be nothing without me" to keep them grateful and guilty and resolved to do their best to satisfy him. They'd done their utmost to love him in all the ways they could. *Maybe he had done the same for them.*

They squeezed their eyes shut against the creeping shame. He was manipulating them. Just like he had been last night. *But what if he was really hurt?*

Aaron, of course I loved you, they texted back. **I know I can never convince you to believe me and I'm sorry about that.**

There was silence on the other end for the longest time.

Tove, I understand and I'm sorry I was aggressive

Tove stared at the new text. A wicked curiosity pulsed in their neck. He *never* apologised.

I know I have no influence with you anymore, and you can do what you want, but please be careful. Your friend Effie is more unstable than you think. I could see in her eyes last night she wanted to hurt me. She'll hurt you too in the end. Please listen to your gut on this one.

If their experience dating Aaron was anything to go off, Effie couldn't be trusted not to hurt them. But Effie wasn't like Aaron. And what, they thought, if she never hurt them at all? What if they were worried about nothing? In the end, everything he said was a dirty manipulation.

They smiled. They'd entered the pageant and opened up to Effie, hoping and willing to change. And Effie had changed them. With her brute-force optimism, she'd changed everything.

Let me know when it happens, Aaron said. **I'll be there for you.**

Thanks, they told him. **But I'm good.**

29

The Pollack was dark once again. Nowell strutted up and down the stage testing the lights, and even though she was dying to see Tove, first Effie beelined it for Nowell.

"Can we talk?" she called.

"Sure, one minute." Nowell finished their tests and let the crew go for a break, then vaulted off the front of the stage to land beside her. "What's up?"

Effie went straight to the point. "There's been a lot of bullshit in this contest so far and I wondered if anything is being done about it."

Nowell didn't need prompting. "You're talking about Tove's ex?"

"That, and how Bryan was eliminated yesterday despite being the most Santa-like of the lot of us."

Nowell sighed. "I don't know what to tell you. The pageant is promotion for the new shopping centre. Nobody's really interested in finding the best Santa. At least, the people who hold the cash aren't interested."

The truth sat in Effie's stomach like a ball of chewing gum accidentally swallowed.

"I tried to talk to the producers about what happened at Tove's interview," Nowell said. "They obviously didn't realise what they were stirring up, but suffice it to say they don't care either."

"Do we have any hope of starting a revolution? Leading a media campaign against them? There must be lots of angry viewers as well."

"*You* can try. I'm afraid this is my job."

"You'd choose your job over other people?"

Nowell eyed her quizzically. "As a trans person trying to survive on a small Island, I believe my own path here is to do my best from the inside. Do you judge me for that?"

Effie tried to imagine what Tove would say, but her conscience wouldn't let her get that far. "I can't judge you." After all, she worked for the Pollack too. She accepted money to work on a paid parking system in place of the free parking currently enjoyed all over the Island. "Out of curiosity, what have you done on the inside?" she asked. "What *can* you do?"

"I do my best to keep everyone happy. Like allowing Tove not to have a sponsor."

"But you wouldn't let Tove fundraise yesterday. To us, you seem more like the producers' lackey than our representative."

Nowell had the grace to look away. "It's tricky," they said. "I'm sorry about what's happened, and what's in store. Believe me, I'm doing my best to give you a chance."

"What does *that* mean?" Effie demanded.

But a crew member was calling Nowell's name, and they were already turning away.

"I'll catch up with you later, Effie," they said. "Confessionals in the green room in five, yes?"

It was about the nicest Nowell had been to Effie, but about as satisfying as a mousse without gelatin. Fists balled in frustration, Effie marched to the green room, where B2 and Alice slumped glumly on the bench. They both looked as small and powerless as Effie felt.

She made her complaints known to the audience during her confessional, ignoring Nowell's glares. It didn't matter; her words would be chopped up and edited harmlessly into the broadcast later.

Tove turned up flushed and anxious just in time for their own confessional. Effie couldn't hear them talk behind the Perspex screens, but she watched the tremor of their lips and the hint of a frown suggesting the stress they were under. She wished she could take it all away. Clear the path for them. Maybe she could.

Confessional over, Tove tucked themself under Effie's arm with a tiny smile. Effie warmed. She snuggled them close, pressing her nose to their hatted head.

Then it was showtime. After Nowell's intro, the four remaining Santas filed onto the stage, where four little lecterns and microphones awaited them, one each.

"Our contestants know nothing of tonight's challenge," Nowell announced to the cameras. "We have kept it a secret all along that tonight they will be voting off one of their own. Oops, did I say that?"

They put on a stricken expression and Effie imagined the editors pinging a laugh track in there. God, it was humiliating.

Wait...voting off one of their own? Was that what they'd said?

"Each of our contestants will name the Santa they want to eliminate. The contestant with the most votes will be leaving tonight. In the event of a tie, we'll ask quiz questions until somebody gets one wrong."

If yesterday had been brutal, this was something else. Effie, B2 and Alice were looking aghast at each other. Tove looked like they'd been hit, backing away from the mic, squinting under the lights. Effie wanted to hold them. They were so sensitive to rejection, this must be agony.

"Let's begin!" said Nowell. "Effie, you're first. Who would you like to eliminate?"

Effie's lips parted but no sound came out. "Are you serious?" she hissed. It zipped through the mic, too loud.

Nowell's face morphed from a thunderous frown for Effie into a grin for the cameras. "It is rather a surprise, isn't it?"

"I don't want any of them to go," Effie said simply.

"Cut!" yelled a producer.

"It's the nature of competition, Effie," said B2.

She glanced at him, at Alice, at Tove. They had all recovered and were nodding. Wow. They were really prepared to do this.

"Okay." Effie gulped. They were right; she'd signed up for this. Was eliminating one of her fellow Santas by her own hand so different from watching the producers push B1 out for being a nice guy? She was already complicit. The others knew it. Nowell had tried to tell her. But god was it a cruel trick, right after Lalla had dangled her detachment from an interdependent existence over her head. "I'll do it," she said. "But can I go last?"

Nowell huffed a little, but flipped the order and went over to B2. The cameras started rolling once again.

"Bryan, which Santa would you like to eliminate?"

"Effie," said B2 without missing a beat.

Effie turned incredulously. Really? *Really?*

"Sorry," he mouthed.

There was no explanation…no possible explanation. Even after all their bonding, he must see through her façade to the "freak" underneath. All along, he had been the kind and supportive parental figure Effie lacked. Now his good will had run out. Now she was nothing but a bore and a burden in his eyes.

Tove, beside B2, had also jumped in surprise, and was now staring at him with vitriol in their gaze.

"And Tove, who would you like to send home?" Nowell asked.

"Bryan," said Tove stonily.

Effie's heart ached. *No, don't defend me!* she wanted to wail. *You don't need to fight for me. I'm not worth it.*

She breathed in through her nose, out through her mouth. What had Tove said that morning in the car? *Weird good or weird bad…why does it matter?* They were right, of course. She was weird. Everybody thought so. She would accept herself the way she was. Frankly, she wasn't worth defending, when a screw-up like her didn't belong in the pageant at all.

"Alice, you're next. Who's it going to be?" said Nowell.

"Tove," said Alice.

Rage poured into Effie's belly to hiss and burble as it met the self-loathing within. *Nobody vote Tove! Nobody touch them!* her insides screamed. Maybe Effie wasn't meant to be in the pageant, but Tove was! That was what they'd said all those days ago when they went to buy tents together: "I want a shot at winning the final vote." Nobody got to take that away from them.

"Effie, at last," said Nowell, finally coming around to her. "Yourself, Tove, and Bryan each have one vote. You can be the tie-maker or the tie-breaker here."

Effie felt sick. The metaphorical chewing gum in her gut was dragging her to the ground. She could pick Tove, which was out of the question. She could pick B2, which even despite his betrayal was unthinkable. She could pick Alice, who'd invited her into her home and fed her spaghetti, found DuBois a job he loved, and planned an intervention for Tove in their direst hour. In that case, the four of them would go head-to-head in a sudden-death quiz. Then nobody would be safe.

"Who's it going to be?" Nowell asked again.

Effie didn't need the corny heartbeat edit because her own heart was doing it for her. *Boom-boom. Boom-boom.* It shouldn't be this loud in her ears.

"So?" Nowell pressed.

Effie looked at Tove, their beautiful, chapped lips parted in a silent cry. She looked at B2, his eye-twinkle dim. She looked at Alice, fit and stoic, poised for any eventuality.

And this time, the perfect solution found her in her love for the other Santas. She would not let what happened with B1 happen again. She would speak up rather than let her friends down.

She parted her lips. Her stomach was tight. She visualised her shoelace and tried to pull it loose, but it didn't work, it didn't work. The time had come to give up on her own dreams. Today, Heather had said, was destiny.

"Me," said Effie.

Nowell gasped, but recovered quickly. "Who, sorry?"

"Me. Myself. Effie." Her own name dropped from her lips like a stone into water. This was her own sentence. Her own elimination.

Nowell's announcement of her demise didn't reach her brain. Effie left the stage feeling dizzy with the effort of hurting herself. Was she happy? Relieved? Or numb? It was hard to tell.

30

Tove couldn't believe it. They needn't have worried about Effie giving up on them. She'd given up on *herself*! It was so painfully obvious now that she'd been building up to martyr herself all along. And Tove had *let her*! Encouraged it, even, every time they sought her aid and leaned on her strength. Effie wasn't unstable or unreliable. She was *too* stable. *Too* reliable. To her own detriment!

When Nowell dismissed them with instructions to be back on stage in half an hour, and the other Santas dispersed into the refreshments tent, Tove traipsed down to the fishing pier and cried and cried and cried. Moonlight made snail trails of their tear tracks. The still sea made a mockery of their tumultuous heart.

Eventually Effie found them there, because of course she did.

"Hi, Tove," she called softly. "What's up?"

"*You!*" Tove yelled, losing it at the softness Effie was so determined to give them. "You can't do shit like that and expect me to applaud you."

Effie winced. "I don't understand. Did I do something wrong?"

Tove leaned back on their hands and turned their tears to the stars. Effie hadn't meant to hurt them. Had she even meant to hurt herself? She deserved compassion. She deserved understanding. She was *exasperating*!

"I am *so* cross with you."

Effie sat on the pier beside them, long legs dangling towards the dark ocean. "But why? I was only trying to show you how much I care."

"You care too much!" Tove exploded once again. "You didn't need to do that. I never *asked* you to do it. But you did. Why? Am I really so broken that you had to sacrifice yourself so I could go on? Or was this all some pumped-up self-flagellation stunt?"

"What? No! Neither! I couldn't vote you or anyone else. So I had to vote myself."

Tove eyed her disbelievingly. "Why couldn't you vote anyone else? The rest of us played the game. Why couldn't *you*?"

Unexpectedly, Effie's eyes dampened. "Because I'm weird, alright? Weird and different and outside. Everyone says it. And I accept it. I'll make peace with it. I'm a weirdo and nobody wants a weirdo as their Santa. This was the best outcome."

"Oh my god!" Tove scrambled to pick up the seeds they'd sown. "That's not what I was saying at all! I meant you're too selfless. Generously, excruciatingly, infuriatingly selfless."

"And you don't want me to be?"

"No, I want you to love yourself as much as you love everyone around you. I want you to tell the people who love you what you really want and need so we can care for you as you care for us. I want you to stop taking to heart the mean things other people say."

"But maybe they're right," Effie said miserably, lonesomely.

"Effie." Tove slapped both hands on her shoulders. "You are worth everything in the world. The sun and the stars. You're fun and sweet and kind—and this Santa stuff comes naturally to you in a way I frankly envy. But only some things are within your control. If someone doesn't like and support you, that's their problem, not yours."

Effie shuddered as the ocean wind picked up at their backs. "I don't know if that helps me."

Tove let go. They couldn't reach her. Panic wound like lace around their lungs. Effie was going to keep martyring herself again and again. For someone, if not for Tove. Realisation bloomed like a bruise. The pain of what they had to say tightened around their windpipe.

"I can't," they choked out. "I can't watch you hurt yourself while telling yourself it's for others, or that you have no other choice."

Effie stared in shock. "Okay," she said. Then she repeated louder: "Okay."

They sat for what felt like forever, wrapped up in their own individual torments. Through the silence, a horn went off in the distance.

Effie leapt to her feet, all springs and jitters. "That didn't sound like a ship."

Tove got up more languidly. They pulled their Santa hat over their bare head, at once defeated and resigned, broken and uncaring. "It's Nowell's challenge horn. Time to get back to the stage. Come on."

"I'm out, remember?" Effie said, bitterness now ghosting through.

"Weren't you listening? Nowell told us to stick around."

"Oh." Effie brightened. "You think there's a twist coming? Maybe I can fix this."

Her optimism was unfathomable. But this time Tove wouldn't let themself be pulled in. They had plenty of their own demons. Watching Effie, at close quarters, burn and douse, burn and douse, time after time again, was not something they could put themself through. Because if Effie's optimism was a front and a lie after all, then what had Tove really learned from her?

31

Effie followed Tove back to the Pollack, where she was swallowed by the other Santas coming out of the refreshments marquee and carted back to the stage she'd left in shock half an hour ago.

They were soon live once again. Nowell interviewed Tove, B2 and Alice about why they'd voted the way they had. Effie couldn't listen; she and DuBois and B1, mysteriously clad in their Santa suits, waited in the wings. For what, she didn't know.

"And now I have the pleasure to announce a twist," Nowell announced at length. "This is where you, the audience, can take the fate of the contestants into your own hands. You may vote one eliminated Santa back into the competition. You love them, you've missed them, let's welcome our hopefuls to say a few words!"

Stagehands swept the three of them under the lights and they were forced to wave at unsmiling cameras.

Nowell invited them each to speak.

"I'm delighted to be here," declared DuBois. "I do love a good contest twist, and I hope you'll all vote for me!"

"I'll always be here whether you vote for me or not," said B1. "These Santas are all top-notch and I know someone very deserving will win."

When it was Effie's turn, she tried to temper her simmering anger. "Thank you to everyone who has ever believed in me. I'm sorry to have disappointed you."

But who, really, had ever believed in her? Maybe her dissertation supervisor, who'd read her first draft at 2:30am three days before the deadline. Maybe her Year 9 PE teacher, who'd let her sit out swimming every week even though she could only conjure up a period note once a month.

"Phone lines open now!" cried Nowell. "They'll be open until midday tomorrow, when we'll be back to announce the results. Please text or call the number on your screen."

Effie left as soon as she could and caught the bus home, where a dark figure sat on the kerb outside her door.

"Hey," said Lalla.

"What are you doing here?" Effie grunted.

"I saw the broadcast." Lalla's mouth drooped.

Effie punched in the door code. In her flat, she put the kettle on and retrieved her Piglet mug from the cupboard, the one Lalla had always coveted. Lalla settled on the sofa with her tea and Effie took the window sill, not wanting to go near the sofa where she'd sat with Tove only two days ago.

Lalla peeked over her steaming mug. "Do you want to talk about it?"

"No."

"It must've been rough, what you did up there."

"It was the right thing to do." Effie still believed it, even if Tove wouldn't.

"You have another chance, at least. Liam texted me about the second half of the broadcast. You and the doll's house Santa and the rich dude."

"Yep. It's the worst. Everyone likes them better than me, even you guys."

"What do you mean?"

"You and Liam will vote for Bryan and Heather will vote for DuBois."

"I don't know why you'd think we wouldn't support you."

Effie gave Lalla a look. "I was there when we watched the original interviews together. You really went out of your way to treat me like a chump and sing the praises of the others. I don't even know if you like me."

Lalla sipped her tea and made a face, probably at the heat of it. "I do like you. You're my only sister."

"If you have to say it like that..."

"How could you think I don't like you?"

Effie set her tea down. It was about time she told her sister what she wanted and needed, like Tove had suggested. Then she could support Effie if she chose.

"You make me feel bad," she began. "You are constantly putting me down and talking as if I'm not there. Just because I don't have a kid and a house and a steady job like you, I'm apparently not worth shit. You call me 'free' but what does that even mean when all I want is to belong to someone or something, to love and give and be loved in return? You ridicule me in front of Heather, who by the way imitates you because she's seven. She's ruthless to me."

"Shouldn't you be able to handle that? It's what comes with having kids around."

"First of all, she's *your* kid—although I choose to be a part of y'all's life so I respect the argument. But as for handling it? I can't rebut like I would with any other person because she's fucking seven! How about teaching your child to be nice to others and respect them as autonomous human beings?"

"She's not that bad, Effie."

Maybe she wasn't that bad. Maybe Effie was too fucking sensitive to be around other people.

"You asked me why I could possibly think you don't like me, but I'm telling you and you're still not listening! At the bare minimum, you could actually be nice to me once in a while."

"I'm here, aren't I?" Lalla gestured around the flat.

"Why are you here anyway?" Effie snapped.

"Empty flats can be…lonely."

"If you know I'm lonely, and you're here when I'm at rock bottom," she said carefully, "why aren't you here for me all the time? Why won't you listen when I tell you how you hurt me? This all feels…not good enough."

Lalla didn't respond right away. "I have been trying, Effie. I help when you ask me to. But when I try to reach out and have a real conversation, you always push me away."

"I don't want to talk about the things you're always probing me about."

"Well, maybe I do!" Lalla flung her arms in the air. "Maybe the reason I start those conversations is because *I* want to talk about them, *with you*. You're the only one I can talk to about everything that happened with our parents. Are you there for me in the way you want me to be there for you? I don't think so!"

Effie darted through the tunnel of their last few conversations in her mind. Lalla was dead right. In return for Lalla's sharpness, Effie was evasive. They each had their barriers. Effie was not blameless. She lapped at her tea to soothe her raw throat. "I'm sorry," she croaked.

Lalla sighed. "I'm sorry for making you feel lesser because you don't have a house and a job and a kid. And I'm sorry I said you're free of all that and what you do and say doesn't matter. Of course it matters. That was never supposed to be a reflection on you. I think it's my frustration spilling over, because it's hard juggling all those things and I feel a lot of pressure to keep everything running smoothly. And that's on me."

Wary, but somewhat comforted, Effie settled back into the window seat. Wrapped up in how Lalla's attitude was affecting her personally, she'd been oblivious to the fact that Lalla's reasons had nothing to do with her. There was still no excuse for Lalla's unkindness. But it helped to know Effie wasn't the cause.

"But we've gotten side-tracked. I'm sorry I made this about me. Tonight I was supposed to be here for you. Not me. So. What's going on?"

In front of Effie was an open door to beginning to repair her relationship with her sister. She had to brave the door. She must.

"I have no friends," she said, because that seemed most important. "People keep calling me weird and rude and inappropriate. I get that I make mistakes. I wreck people's trust in me. I know I have a long way to go and I try to take on board what I've learned. But am I fundamentally repulsive? It feels like nobody wants to be around me or support anything I do. I'm always on the outside and the thing is, I don't want to be. I just want someone to let me in and make space for me." Even Tove couldn't accept her in the end.

Lalla beckoned. “Come here. Remember my neck rubs?”

Effie crossed the room and sat on the floor. Tween Lalla had a phase of wanting to become a massage therapist and Effie had been her guinea pig. She relished the sensation of gradual unravelling as Lalla got to work on her trapezius muscles.

“I don’t think you’re repulsive,” said Lalla soothingly. “I think you’ve been through a hard time and haven’t found your feet yet. You didn’t see yourself coming back to the Island at all, did you?”

“No,” Effie admitted. “I thought I’d be in the UK for good. And when I did come back here, I didn’t think it’d be for long.”

“So why are you still here?”

She huffed a rueful laugh. “Fifteen months of hunting for a job in a country you can’t travel to, followed by a global recession… Like you said, it’s been a hard time.”

“What does your ideal life look like?”

“I want a job in environmental or structural engineering that pays a living wage. I want a partner and houseplants up the wazoo and maybe a few more cats. I want to hang out with people who care about me. A lot to ask, I know.”

“That’ll happen for you.”

“I was with Tove for about a day before I fucked it up.”

“You can’t rush these things.”

“Easy for you to say, you married your sweetheart straight out of Sixth Form. Some of us are out here jilting our school boyfriends at the altar or pining for our friends who we kissed once—well, a few times now.”

“I’m serious.” Lalla was working a tough knot in Effie’s neck. “And you absolutely can’t force it either. Maybe you have to let this person go.”

Effie gritted her teeth. "Well then what am I? A sad lesbian who keeps getting rejected."

"So what if you are? How can you be a sad lesbian *best*?"

"That is an absurd question."

"*Well*?"

"Alright, alright."

Effie thought for a long second. Tove had been right: voting herself out hadn't just been about being a martyr, although for that reason she didn't regret what she'd done. Really, she'd given up on herself.

But Nowell had proffered a second chance—to get voted back in. She would give it one more try, and see if anyone truly cared about her, once and for all. "Say I get voted back into the pageant, beat them all, and show everyone I can do it. Santa can be a lesbian and I can be that lesbian."

"Right, then there's our goal." Lalla twisted Effie to face her. "Let's get you back in!"

"How do we do that?"

"I have a plan. Get your stuff, you're coming back to our house tonight."

"I am?"

"Oh please, this flat is lonely as hell! We're going to plot tonight, and face tomorrow together! And bring your cat, I know she comforts you."

Effie didn't have much stamina for any Grand Plans, but she was, genuinely, grateful for her sister.

Saturday

2 days till Christmas

32

Effie woke on her sister's sofa to raised voices. She crept to the foot of the stairs and listened to Heather and Lalla screaming at each other in a way that rattled her canines in their sockets.

"How could you betray your aunt like this?" yelled Lalla. "She is counting on us to get her back in that pageant!"

"I didn't think you'd care," Heather snarled. "You keep saying the pageant is stupid."

"Well, I was wrong. It's not stupid to her!"

"Meow," said Melchior worriedly at Effie's feet.

After a lot of shouting and banging doors, Lalla stomped down the stairs. Heather had snuck Lalla's phone in the night and stayed up texting **DUBOIS** to the pageant number. She was grounded.

"It's two days before Christmas," Effie said groggily over her morning coffee. "Go easy on her."

"She's a menace." Lalla groaned. "You were right. I'm sorry I shut you down last night when you were trying to tell me. I *am* anxious about her. I *do* want to be the nurturing and guiding force she needs. It's just… Ugh. This is all my fault."

"Yelling on my behalf isn't going to make you feel better. You should apologise."

"Aren't you upset?"

Effie sighed. "Heather followed her heart. She did everything she could for the person she wanted to champion. Who am I to be like, 'support your family no matter what'? It doesn't work like that."

"But after last night…"

"At the end of the day it has to be your choice," Effie said. "Tove didn't choose me because they can't accept the way I am. Heather didn't choose me because she didn't want to, and I have to respect that equally as a reason."

Lalla grabbed chunks of her hair and groaned again. "Alright, I'm going back up to apologise for yelling. But I'm not ungrounding her. My phone bill isn't going to pay itself."

After breakfast, Effie changed into her Santa suit and they left the house to enact Lalla's canvassing plan. Heavy with emotional hangovers, they paced the High Street and tried to talk people into voting for Effie. Everyone was doing last-minute Christmas shopping and no one wanted to talk, let alone spend 20p on a text for a thing they didn't care about. Effie didn't blame them. But it was nice that Lalla was there, and she was trying.

At midday they gave up and went to the Pollack. The ice-rink was open again and throngs of people gathered to hear the results of the vote-in. Effie spotted a flash of purple hair, and caught sight of Heather's friends holding a banner with DuBois's name painted across it. They avoided her studiously.

"They were all in on it," Lalla surmised crossly.

Effie soon found herself back on stage before an audience of kids and teenagers who only had eyes for one person. DuBois had money, a vast community of contacts, *and* eye candy appeal. How could she or B1 hope to beat him?

Nowell announced the results with their usual corny gusto and dramatic pauses. The winner was DuBois. Of course it was.

The sight of the crowd going wild, their hopes and efforts vindicated, was the final blow. A chorus of "Happy Birthday" struck up because apparently it was DuBois's twenty-ninth birthday on top of everything else. Effie was not wanted here.

She slipped behind the stage and marquees to shed her gay Santa outfit, and stuffed it in one of the skips lingering behind the new shopping centre. (Then she retrieved it, because she couldn't throw anything out for the life of her.) She gazed up at the shopping centre's dark, shiny windows, knowing she wouldn't be the one to cut the ribbon with the big pair of scissors, knowing nobody cared.

She shivered despite her thermal shirt and leggings.

Where are you, texted Lalla.

Effie met her down the road, away from the festivities, and Lalla lent her coat so Effie could carry the Santa suit under her arm.

"Thanks for being here," she said. "Thanks for trying."

Lalla just nodded, and took Effie back to her warm house. Effie holed up in the lounge and let her sister feed her juice and biscuits like she was nine years old again when she tripped in the relay race in front of the whole school and their mums.

The Grand Plan was over.

Lalla popped her head in to announce she was going to the shop for some final Christmas supplies. Liam hovered in the hallway, padded up in a winter coat and grimacing. They left together and the car engine thrummed to life and faded away. Apparently Effie was babysitting.

It was really a no-brainer, now nobody was around to watch her being sad, to climb the stairs and knock on Heather's door, Melchior at her heel.

"Hey Heather, it's me," she called.

There was an almighty groan from within the room.

"You alright there?" she asked.

"What do you waaant," Heather drawled.

"I dunno," Effie answered, truthfully. "See how you are or something. I heard the argument earlier."

"Are you going to tell me off?"

"I mean, that's not the plan. Do you think you need telling off?"

"No!"

"Well then."

There was a pause while Effie considered how this was going absolutely nowhere. She was about to go back downstairs and re-enter her own funk, when Heather stirred in her room.

"Do you want to come in?" Her voice vibrated the wood of the door slightly; she was right up against it.

"Sure," Effie said.

The door clicked and cracked open. Effie squeezed through the gap alongside her opportunistic cat and was confronted with the chaos that was Heather's room. Everything was on the floor, except for the things that were in the air. Even Effie's depressed housemate from her final year of uni, whose room she'd helped clean every so often, had nothing on this seven-year-old.

"Wow, is it usually like this?" she asked, ducking to avoid a low-hanging scarf. There were a dozen wispy scarves with one end nailed to the ceiling and the other in her eyes.

"It's my new technique," Heather explained. "The scarves catch your hopes and fears and then tell me what they are."

"Wait, mine personally?"

"Yeah, duh. If I'm trying to predict your fortune I might as well have an idea of what you're aiming for. Makes it more accurate, you know."

Effie shook her head to clear the brain fog. Heather was making no sense at all.

"For example—now hear me out," she went on, "—you're not interested in winning the Santa pageant. Not really. So I didn't bother helping you get back in."

Effie snorted. "Excuse me?"

"If you're going to be like that, I'm kicking you out my room."

Effie stared at Heather, and Heather stared at Effie.

"Fine," Effie said. "Please explain. I don't understand."

Heather nodded, satisfied. "Right, so Mummy doesn't get this, but I do. You're not in it to win it and you never were."

"And there's another reason?"

"Yeah. It was all to prove you *could* do it."

"Yes, that I could win it."

"No. It's not about winning. It's about wanting to be noticed by the people you care about. Me, probably Mummy, definitely that other Santa who you want to kiss."

Effie was speechless, thwarted by a mouthful of scarf. "You're calling me an attention seeker," she mumbled.

"It's okay to want attention," said Heather oh-so-matter-of-fact-ly. "We all have needs and it's normal to develop maladaptive behaviours if our needs are not being met."

"*Where* did you learn the phrase 'maladaptive behaviours'?"

Heather shook her head. "My room, my words!" she said. "Well? Say you won the pageant but none of us bat an eyelid, what then? Hm?"

Effie tore the offending scarf from her teeth. "You're wrong."

"And you suck at admitting the truth!"

"Alright, how's this for the truth? You're always scorning me—like literally saying I suck. It feels bad. It feels like you don't respect me."

Heather pouted. "Respect is whatever. What would you do with my respect? Put it up your butt? Like *oh my god, why don't you guys respect meee.*"

"I guess I don't want to be that person."

"And? What person do you want to be? It's not about respect at all, is it?"

Now Effie was stumped. She gave up swatting the scarves away and sat cross-legged on the floor.

"Oi, mind that shirt, it's my favourite."

She tugged Heather's reversible sequin shirt from under her. "This one? It's on the floor though."

"Leave it, you're spoiling the fabric mosaic." Heather glared till Effie put it back where she'd found it. "Well? What do you really want?"

When Lalla had asked last night how she could be a sad lesbian best, Effie had thought the answer was to win the pageant. She'd also thought she wanted Lalla's life and stability. But those things were only ever the means to an end. The real answer had been there all along.

"I want to be liked," she said simply. "And…loved."

"Wow, I thought you were going to get all deep or something. All anyone wants is to be loved."

"Well, I'm pretty bummed," Effie went on, "because I have all these cool people in my life and none of you give a damn about me."

"That's not true."

"Then tell me honestly, do you even like me? Or am I looking for love in the wrong place?"

"Of course I like you! You're fun and cool and you don't treat me like a child like most people do."

"Wow," Effie said drily, "I never felt that from you."

"I think you're waaay sweating it. You're not gonna find out someone loves you and be like *ooh now I have ascended to happy, this is it for me now.*"

"Why not?"

"You have! to love! yourself!" Heather chanted. "*That* is your happily-ever-after."

Effie reeled from the sweet, sore truth of it.

"Look, I've been thinking a lot about happiness this week," said Heather. "And it's not simple, not like I wanted it to be. First I wanted to make people happy myself and take my own happiness from that. Then I realised I couldn't, because there are reasons people are unhappy that I can't fix. Like sometimes Mummy is unhappy, and although I wish she could just be happy, that's the way it is. Then I realised you can be happy and unhappy at the same time. Happiness doesn't always take away the unhappiness. *But.* It works both ways. Unhappiness doesn't always take away the happiness. So if you can find something good, maybe you can get through the bad. And I got to thinking, where can you find happiness that you can't get anywhere else? What can you always rely on? And I thought, me! Myself! If I love myself, I can always find some goodness when I need it."

And wasn't that the hard part, Effie thought. Loving yourself. Relying on yourself. Believing in yourself. Taking care of yourself even when nobody else could or would.

"So do you love yourself?" pressed Heather.

God she was relentless. "Yes. That's not the problem here. The problem is I'm too weird for other people to love."

"That's not the problem either! Didn't I just say you're cool? Isn't Mummy doing everything she can to prove she cares? You know what I think? I think this is about a particular person and you're not being honest with yourself."

"What of it?" Effie did *not* want to talk about Tove.

"Give me a sec." Heather crouched on the floor and jumped up to touch a sequence of scarves. "Hm," she said eventually. "Someone said something really mean about you and you can't get past it. It's clouded the way you see yourself."

Wait, the "particular person" wasn't Tove? It was Aaron? Effie couldn't accept the scarves had told Heather a single thing, but who was she to deny the occult? If she didn't come clean, who knew what other techniques Heather would employ to divine into her life?

"Tove's ex called me a freak," she confessed.

"Oooh." Heather winced. "Ouch."

"Right? Everyone hates me. I wish I knew why."

Heather scoffed. "Why do you think?"

"I don't know! I keep asking everyone and they can't explain anything."

"Yeah, and the reason is, there's nothing to explain. Nobody hates you. Except Tove's ex, but that's because he's poopy."

"So why use that word?" Effie argued.

"If you're looking for some deep truth about yourself, you're not going to find it," said Heather.

And that was when Effie understood. Aaron didn't come on the interview to re-establish control, though she was sure that was a part of it. He wanted a reaction. Any reaction, good or bad, was fuel for his fire. If someone was thinking about him, feeling about him, he existed.

When he called her a freak, it was not about her.

"But what if they're right?" Effie said miserably. "What if I am irresponsible and deluded?"

Heather had been watching her closely. "Aha! So now can we talk about the real person who made you feel this way?"

Effie startled. About thirteen things happened in her brain at the same time. Structural supports clicked into their foundations. Cement pooled and solidified around them. Beams lowered into place. For the first time in ages, the framework inside her head felt stable. The wobbling stilled.

She knew who she had to talk to.

33

Tove didn't leave their room till late afternoon, when their stomach clenched with hunger and their phone ran out of battery from doomscrolling social media. They used to think break-ups sucked; then a break-up saved them. Now they were back where they'd started: break-ups sucked. Even this not-really-a-break-up-because-they-were-never-technically-together.

They snuck into the kitchen when nobody else was around, and retrieved the malt wheats from the tall cupboard. The oat milk was half poured when disaster struck.

"There you are," their brother said.

Tove jumped and milk slopped onto the table. "Crap."

His usually innocuous five foot six managed to take up the entire doorway, arms braced against the doorframe. "Pyjama day, is it?" he said.

"Leave me alone."

"Don't you have to be somewhere? I thought they were voting one of the Santas back in."

"Yeah, that's the others. Not me."

"Isn't your Effie one of the hopefuls?"

"She's not *my* Effie."

Dair chewed his lip as Tove slapped some kitchen roll onto the milk spill.

"It's been like a day since you said you liked her. What happened?"

"I was wrong."

"About what? Her?"

"Yes. No."

"Then what?"

"I was worried she'd betray me. Everyone always does eventually." *But in the end, she'd betrayed herself.*

"Whoa, excuse me? Have I ever betrayed you?"

Dair's earnest gaze implored Tove to answer honestly.

"Well…no."

Brotherly mockery notwithstanding, he had always been nice to them, ever since they could remember. If you were to line up every candidate in the world and ask Tove to choose a brother for themself, they'd choose him. Every time.

"And do you think I will in the future?"

"Maybe."

"But what are you basing that on?"

"It's a consideration, a possibility, a likelihood."

He frowned at the ceiling. "And such a likely one that all my years of not betraying you aren't any kind of reassurance?"

Tove tossed the sopping kitchen roll into the bin and finished making their cereal. If they could end this nonsensical conversation soon they'd have time to eat their wheats before they went soggy. "Not really."

"Gosh. Aaron really hurt you, didn't he?"

"*What?*"

He spread his hands. "Correct me if I'm wrong."

A hard stare had no effect on him. And nor, apparently, did any of Tove's lies or evasions. He knew they were queer without them telling him. That should've been the tip-off. He'd guessed everything.

They ragdolled into one of the kitchen chairs. "I failed at hiding it, didn't I?"

"Even if Aaron weren't a huge asshole, it was obvious."

"Wait, you didn't like him? I thought everyone did."

Dair laughed. "No. Mum used to ask me questions about him. Like 'Does Tove want to spend Christmas with his family or are they just doing it to please him?' As if I knew."

"She did?" Tove's spoon weighed as much as a shovel.

"Yeah. But I ignored the warning signs. I didn't pry like Mum maybe wanted me to."

Dair left the door to come and sit opposite. Tove's desire to escape had evaporated. Now all they wanted to do was eat their cereal, so they had the energy to process this. Or perhaps avoid it altogether.

"I'm sorry," said Dair.

"It's okay," Tove responded automatically. "It wasn't yours or anyone's job to save me."

"Oh yeah?" he returned. "Was it Effie's job to save you? Did she fail to do it?"

Tove's spoon clattered into the bowl. The cereal was already going soggy and there was no stopping it. "No, she did and I didn't want her to."

"An unusual definition of betrayal."

Now they thought about it, Tove had been rather harping on about helping other people—asking Effie to help them, in particular. It had become a sort of need for them, as if they couldn't save themself from Aaron, or even Aaron from himself, so now they were duty bound to find other people who needed saving and encouraged everyone around them to do the same. But Effie didn't need to be compelled to care for others. She was good enough at that already. She needed to be reminded to care for herself and helped in doing so when she struggled.

"Actually, it wasn't that she betrayed me. That was what I was afraid of. What she really did was betray herself. And it hurt so much to watch."

"Well that's not confusing at all," said Dair, sarcastically.

Tove spilled the whole story—how Aaron called Effie a freak, how scattered she'd been in the car the next morning, and how she'd voted herself out of the pageant.

"She's nothing but kind and soft and I can't handle it," they said. "She's too good for me. She's always been too good for me."

Since the moment they'd met, Tove had been a little bit in love with her. Effie had moved schools—Tove was never sure why, bullying maybe—and on her first day Tove's form tutor asked them to look after her. But it was Effie soon who was looking after Tove. Tove adored and depended on her. Effie went through friends like phases of the moon, but Tove was always at her side. They wouldn't have dreamed of being anywhere else.

"I'm not sure I'm seeing the problem here," said Dair. "Effie is great and treats you like you deserve. What would you have her do differently?"

Tove scowled. They scraped their chair loudly as they got up to bin their ruined cereal.

"She doesn't treat *herself* like she deserves! She thinks she's unlovable. Which…makes me feel…" They had to pause for breath. "Look, Aaron *crushed* me. I can't watch Effie do this to herself. Is it me? Why do people break shit and then tell me I'm the reason? Or teach me one thing about myself and then treat themselves differently? It's not fair! I can't take it anymore!"

"You didn't deserve what happened to you."

"I know. I know Aaron was a shithead and *he* was the one who hurt *me*. I know Effie thinks she did a good thing and is putting it on me because she can't accept her own low self-esteem. I *know* I'm not the problem."

"Tove, it doesn't matter who is and isn't a shithead. What matters is how you deal with the chaos Aaron left you with, and how it's informing the way you feel about Effie's decision. Whether you're the problem or not, you need to find compassion for yourself as the person that you are, with the feelings that you have."

For a moment, the gremlin in Tove's chest crept out into the open and sat to listen. Their tight muscles loosened, flashing a vision of how they could untie the knot inside.

"But what do I do about Effie?" they asked.

"Well, she's human. She has weaknesses and wants and it sounds like Aaron—or maybe someone else—really hurt her feelings. What's with saying she's too good and expecting her to be perfect?"

Malt wheats slipped out Tove's bowl as they tried to pour the milk down the sink.

They swallowed. "I'm horribly sensitive. How can I be with someone if they're not perfect? How am I supposed to handle someone else's flaws as well as my own? All I seem to do is hurt, hurt, hurt."

"That's a question for you." Their mum's calm tones filled the kitchen.

"Mum," they choked. How much had she heard?

Their mum entered the kitchen. Taking the bowl and spoon away, she sat them back down at the table. Tove was too stunned to protest.

"When you've been hurt by a romantic partner," their mum told them in the same tone as she'd describe how to clean a washing machine, "everyone tells you to stay single and focus on yourself before anything else. But I think the emphasis should be shifted to healing, rather than on remaining single. It is possible to heal with the help of and in conjunction with others. We were not meant to live in isolation. It is possible to move forward and use new experiences to fill in your gaps of self-understanding, and let others cover for your weaknesses, so long as you are doing it alongside the work of finding compassion for your true self. I don't say any of this to funnel you one way or another, but I want you to know you don't have to do the work alone."

Involuntarily, Tove met Dair's eyes across the table. He had the same long eyelashes as they did, which gave him a starry, half-afraid look. His words from yesterday rang true, how he admired them for putting themself out there, giving people a chance again.

"It's okay to retreat when you need to," their mum continued, as if reading their thoughts. "In fact, healthy boundaries are essential. But always try to know what you want, and understand whether your present hurt might be pressing on a deep wound you've patched over time and time again. Will your actions keep patching the wound, or will you begin to uncover it so you can finally feel that pain as it is and let it begin to heal?"

Tove's gremlin froze in the spotlight, and with their defences suspended, they noticed how they organised their life around avoiding new hurt and covering up the sensation of inner defectiveness deep within. For a brief moment, they wondered what it would be like to not have that sensation. Without it, perhaps the new hurts wouldn't disturb the old pain over and over again.

Rather than holding onto their anger, or shame, or any semblance of control they had over their feelings, there was another option, the one their therapist talked about. The one where they meditated on their own pain and found a way to love themself through it, with the aid of good therapy and medication if they needed it, till they no longer needed either their gremlin or an external source of value.

"The crux of the matter, though," their mum went on, "is that your life is your decision. It's not about the other person or their needs or their flaws or their own hurts. This is about you. Do you want to be with them? Can you understand and accept them? Are their faults compatible with your tolerance? *Those* are still questions about them. The real resolution is within yourself. Will you dissolve the bed of betrayal that new hurts and frustrations land upon? Are you willing to see what happens if you try?"

She paused, grinned.

"Now, more cereal? You haven't eaten all day."

Speech failed Tove, so they nodded, head whirling.

Their mum made another bowl of malt wheats, asking no questions, not prodding into their life and psyche at all. When it really came down to it, she would never push them to say more than they wanted to offer.

Dair poked their arm, lifting the reverie. "For what it's worth," he hissed, "I didn't like Aaron, but I do like Effie."

Mum and Dair left them alone in the kitchen. Tove worked their way through the box of malt wheats bowl by bowl, chewing on everything they'd said, and on their own question: how could they be with someone who wasn't perfect?

Here was the thing: they wanted to pick up the phone and call Effie and tell her they understood why she'd done what she did and they admired the hell out of her for it. But would she listen? Last night on the pier, their compliments couldn't get through to her. It was a slap in the face that Effie's dislike of herself overshadowed Tove's good opinion. That only proved they were right to be cautious.

Then again, they hadn't done much to help her either. In fact, they suspected they had unwittingly contributed. So maybe they owed her an apology first. They couldn't make Effie understand herself. They could only give her the benefit of the doubt, and as many reasons as they could think of to value the radiant person she was.

A plan began to take shape.

They could never trust anyone, Effie or Aaron or even their mum, to act exactly the way they wanted or expected. They *would* get hurt. Confused. Rejected. It was inevitable.

It was hard to imagine having the strength to go forward knowing that was true.

But they must. And they could.

After all, their life was better with Effie in it.

They paced back to their room, where they'd left their phone on charge. It glowed with the hope of a broken heart that wanted to be mended. Opening their contacts, they decided, all over again, to let Effie help them in the ways she could, forgive her for the ways she couldn't, and try to understand her as she'd tried, over and over and over, to understand them.

Tove decided to heal, within themself and for themself.

34

After leaving Heather's room, Effie did what she never, ever did. She texted her mum: **Hi can I come over?**

And then, because she felt bad leaving Lalla out, she texted her too: **Hey I'm heading to the parents after you get back from the shop. Any interest in coming?**

Lalla replied almost immediately, **Fuck you but sure, I'll be back in half an hour**

"So what's this about?" she asked as they loaded Christmas gifts into the car beside a giant box labelled "Heather." It made sense to take them over now, so they wouldn't have such a full car on Christmas Day.

"Not sure," Effie answered. "I can't do anything about Tove, so I thought I'd do something else instead. Maybe I'm looking for comfort for my broken heart."

Lalla side-eyed her. "They're not going to offer *comfort*, you know that?"

Effie knew. "I miss the mum and dad we had when we were little."

Lalla didn't say anything to that, though she took one hand off the steering wheel and squeezed Effie's knee.

Their parents' house was as unfamiliar as a white cucumber: it felt like they should know it, but Lalla still had to use Google Maps to find it in the maze of country lanes. Eventually the car skidded onto a gravel driveway. The obnoxiously large house stood beneath a pine tree at the crown of a hill. Beyond a gloomy lawn and overgrown banks, the sea sparkled black in the distance.

Effie and Lalla stood side-by-side on the gravel, considering the house. It loomed over them, all darkness and windows. A slice of light peeked between heavy curtains, the fabric flickering from a TV program.

"Did you tell them we were coming?" asked Lalla.

"I texted Mum. No response though."

"Then let's leave the presents in the car for now. Till we've announced ourselves."

Lalla strode to the door and flicked the doorbell. A sterile rendition of "Oranges and Lemons" played behind the granite walls. Nothing happened.

"We'll give it a minute," said Lalla.

"Then what?"

"We try again."

And they did exactly that. A minute later, Lalla pushed the bell a second time. Now the flickering between the curtains stopped, and footsteps clonked down the hall. The door creaked open and there stood their dad, ringed with light from the LEDs above him. The fuzzy outline of his jumper burned like a solar eclipse.

"Girls, hello! What a surprise, I didn't think we'd see you till Monday."

The dewy night felt starker and emptier than before.

"My dear!" Dad called behind him. "Laura and Felicity are here!"

Effie clenched her fists. Nobody needed to know that the names she and Lalla used day to day were nicknames they'd given each other as kids. Effie's first syllable was "la" and her first word was "Lalla," and it stuck. As for her, Lalla always knew she was too spiritually large and physically strong for her soft, delicate birth name. "Effie" suited much better.

Dad's use of their birth names now was doubly wounding because he used to make an effort to use the names they liked. Since getting back with Mum, he'd made an effort in the opposite direction, as if putting on a show for her.

But Lalla, ignoring all this, marched up the step to barrel past their dad with a forceful, cheery greeting. He stood back to let her in, and after a brief hesitation, Effie followed.

Mum appeared at the living room door now and waved them to the kitchen. "Goodness, this is quite a deputation," she said. Effie peered at the TV on the way past but her mum was solidly in the way.

"It was supposed to be a passing visit to drop off a few things," Lalla explained. "Effie did text ahead."

"Yes, yes, what do you need?" said Mum. "A drink maybe?" She was in her dressing gown with her hair in a towel, probably in the shower when Effie had sent that text. A smidgeon of guilt snuck up Effie's spine.

"Really only passing," Lalla repeated. "I did want to make another request, though."

Mum and Dad exchanged glances. And Lalla and Effie did the same to check that neither of them had missed it.

"Let's hear it," Dad said easily, slugging a can of lemonade.

"Effie and I have been struggling. Things are tough at the moment."

Mum rasped a laugh. "Come along, you didn't really think this Santa business would work out for you? What is there to be upset about?"

"Don't do that to her!" Lalla snapped.

Effie opened her mouth and closed it again. Her tongue seemed to have been exiled from her brain.

"Well, what about you, Laura? Please regale us with your grievances."

Lalla's hair lifted slightly, as if rising by static. She spoke in a clipped, irritated tone. "Work is busy as always, which makes it hard to keep on top of housework, as well as trying to raise a kid who's getting more and more, how do I put it, headstrong? And it's not that I want her to be a cardboard cutout child. It's how I feel an increasing need to keep tabs on her, make sure she's not getting dragged into…certain internet spaces, for example. And really, on top of all that, I…"

God, it was so obvious now. Lalla had been struggling to grasp all the pieces of her life this whole time, and Effie had never noticed.

"To be sure, the internet is a very hostile place nowadays." Dad picked up Lalla's dropped sentence with a joking smile on his face.

"Very left-leaning," Mum added.

Lalla blanched. "Well, actually—" She tossed Effie a panicked glance.

In her sister's need, all the power came flooding back to Effie's tongue. "I think Lalla was going to ask you to help with minding Heather. With childcare." Effie looked to her for confirmation, and she nodded. "But on second thoughts—"

"Childcare!" Dad roared with laughter. "Oh dear. We've raised two entire children of our own. It's your turn now."

Lalla's white cheeks flushed now like cocktail blinis left in the pan for too long. "You have no idea what it's like to be a young mum in late-stage capitalism. You had the money to pay a childminder and a cleaner to ease the load. And you weren't working sixty-hour weeks."

"We helped with the deposit on your house. We help with your sister's rent. What do you think that's for if not to allow you to spend your excess on making your lives easier?"

"No, that's what allows me to eat as well as pay rent," Effie corrected. "That's how Lalla and Liam could afford to buy a house at all. There's no excess."

"Well, if you settled down with a real job then you wouldn't have any trouble paying your bills. We won't be around forever to finance your breaks between jobs."

Rage bolted through her. She didn't *want* to work temp jobs, she'd hated every one of them. What she wanted was a stable position doing what she was good at, that would hopefully make the world a better place. And yet, thanks to her parents—they were dead right about that—she had enough money. Fuck it, she could even afford takeaway coffee and the occasional G&T.

"That's not why we're here," she said instead. "My heart got broken yesterday and I was hoping for some sympathy. Lalla needs a helping hand with raising your grandchild. That's it."

Their mum sighed a sigh that would have spun a thousand windmills. "My dear, don't you think relationships are a little hard for you? You are making quite a habit of becoming involved in other people's break-ups—it is not really surprising that you can't hold anything down yourself."

Every word was a stone to her body. Bones cracked. Bruises bloomed under her skin. Effie stumbled sideways into Lalla, who squeezed her hand and hissed, "Stay strong. It's all lies!" into her ear. Effie bolstered herself; their unkindness was *not about her*. Exactly as Tove could expect nothing from Aaron, she could expect nothing from her parents. Like Tove at the pub, she'd been looking for closure and reconciliation. But forgiveness was an internal process. It was the work she must do to resolve the feelings of inadequacy her parents had left in her.

"And as for Laura, I don't think childcare is what she really wants from us. Is it, darling?"

"Do you know, forget it." Lalla rapped her knuckles on the kitchen counter. "What I wanted was a bit more of an effort from you. I'm struggling, I'm exhausted. Most of my friends have their parents helping out with childcare, meals, lifts, anything they can do to help. I'm the only one who doesn't have that, even though you're both *right here*, and I want to know why."

Liam's parents had retired to Norfolk, but although they weren't around to help with the practical stuff, they kept up their grandparent duties with regular, enthusiastic phone calls, and had never missed any of Heather's birthdays. Effie couldn't say the same for her and Lalla's parents.

"Darling, don't you think it's rather degrading to have your parents running around after you even once you're grown up?"

"It would be *really* helpful—"

"To us, dear," Dad said. "I've never been anyone's dancing monkey—your mother will attest to that—and I'm not about to start in my middle age, when things are beginning to get more fun again."

The rejection hit Effie across the chin. The reason Mum and Dad weren't present in their lives wasn't because they didn't think to help or didn't know how to help, but because they didn't *want* to help, even when told how, even when asked outright. Plain and simple.

"Wow, you *suck*."

Lalla coiled like a venomous snake at Effie's side, holding her stomach.

"Monday is Christmas Day," she snarled. "You have always insisted on this one day as a family. Do you still want us to come over?"

"Of course, darling," Mum said as if everything so far was totally normal. "I think it's a time families should be together, don't you?"

"Yes, the one time, according to you. I'll say this once: if you want us on Christmas Day, you'd better put in the work all year round. Your granddaughter is seven now and hardly knows you. You're missing out on the best years of her life and, if you care, you'll do something about that."

Once again Mum and Dad looked at each other with impassive faces and implicit understanding. They'd gotten meaner since getting back together. This was a relationship which they sustained only by being the worst versions of themselves. Maybe they didn't belong together. Maybe they did. Maybe what they wanted from life really was this insular toxicity. Maybe Tove would've gotten by in some fashion if they'd been able and willing to become the submissive wife Aaron wanted them to be.

Effie read her parents' look and all her pain boiled to the surface.

"So that's it? You're seriously considering the idea of never seeing us ever again, purely because you can't take your blinkers off and choose your family? The daughters you birthed are asking you to care and you're happy to let them go forever. Is that how it's going to be?"

"Felicity…" Mum began. "We chose you girls all those years ago when we divorced. Well, now we're back together. And it's time to choose ourselves."

The fire drained from Effie's belly. She'd always known she was the reason they'd divorced. Finally, it was explicit.

"How dare you!" Lalla screamed. She'd uncoiled now and was shaking both fists, Big Sister Mode activated. "How dare you put that on us! It's not our fault you don't love us."

"Of course we love you—" Dad cooed.

"No." Effie cut him off. When Lalla and Heather said it, she believed them, because they were willing to engage with her beyond the empty words, when she'd asked them straight up.

"This year," said Lalla, "I don't want to spend Christmas Day with people who make no effort. You get in touch if you want to change that, and maybe next year will be a different story. Now, I hope you have a merry Christmas. We'll be going."

Lalla grabbed Effie's hand and stalked back down the hall. She yanked the front door open and pulled Effie outside. Right before slamming, she turned briefly back to their parents, who'd pursued them under the LEDs, and said quietly, "I was going to tell you I'm having another child. I thought you'd be happy."

Next thing Effie knew, she was back in the car. Lalla revved the engine with tears streaking her face. Their parents didn't come after them.

"Good thing we left the presents in the car," Lalla said shakily. Her tears receded as the house disappeared from view. "I'd totally have stormed out and left them there, and then Heather wouldn't be happy."

"Hey, um, congratulations," Effie said. "About the baby. I'm really excited for you."

Lalla shot her a smile. "Thanks, Effie. I'll announce it again on Christmas Day and then we can all celebrate for real."

"Christmas Day?" As far as Effie could tell, Christmas Day just went tits up.

"Yes, at our house. The four of us, and I'll invite Joan from next door. Her husband passed away a while back and I don't know if she'll have plans."

Effie swallowed the sudden lump growing in her throat. "Yeah, that'll be good. And Liam will be fine with it?"

"Definitely. He'll be so pissed when he hears what happened tonight."

"You go home," Effie said, "and tell him everything. And if he doesn't start pulling his weight, I'm going to deck him."

Lalla laughed. "Liam's good, honest. It was Mum and Dad who I wanted to step it up, not him."

"Well, I intend to be here from now on, okay?" Effie said. "Anything you need, ask me. Except Christmas morning…I'm busy then."

"Wait, you were going to bail on Christmas Day swim with the parents, *again*?"

"They don't want us there! My original plan was to win the pageant so I'd have to be at the Pollack early to cut the ribbon. No way Santa can fit a freezing swim into her busy schedule."

"More imaginative than faking a hangover like you did last year."

"If you ever want help with bad excuses, I'm here for you."

Lalla stopped at some traffic lights, and regarded her seriously. “Thanks, Effie. I appreciate the offer of help—not the excuses, you can keep those. With the parental ship sailed, I’m going to need you in other ways. I don’t know if you remember…last time…when I had Heather. You helped me so much simply by being there, keeping me company, doing a bit of laundry. Our parents were barely there at all, so I was really hoping this time… Anyway, that’s not going to happen.”

“Hey, it’s going to be better. I’m way more grown-up than I was then. I can do more than laundry. Cooking, cleaning, nappies, you name it. And I know emotional maturity is underrated compared to domestic prowess when it comes to grown-up-ness, but I might have a bit more to offer in that department too.”

“Thanks, you’re the best.”

“Well, I owe you. Thanks for standing up for me. Standing with me.”

“I’m your sister, aren’t I?”

Effie decided to stay at Lalla’s another night. The evening was early yet, but she curled up on Lalla’s sofa with Melchior, a deep ache in her bones. Tonight’s sleep would be heavy and blissful. It was all over now. All the drama, all the heartbreak. She could rest tomorrow, and then it’d be Christmas. And then she’d be back to work, and the grind, and the boredom.

As her head hit the arm rest, her phone bleeped with a text. She wondered if it was Lalla, or Heather on Lalla’s phone, or possibly Ranjula.

It wasn’t any of them. When she checked her phone, the last thing she intended to do before giving in to sleep, Tove’s name was on the screen, with a single, short message.

Turn on your TV

A few minutes later, Lalla swept in and grabbed the remote. "Wake up, sleepyhead. You might want to see this."

35

If Nowell was annoyed to be called by Tove on their evening off, and then to have to orchestrate a grand romantic gesture with the Pollack Committee and the pageant production team, they didn't show it *much*. The vein in their forehead only ticked a little as Tove faced them under the stage lights once again. Tove, for their part, was sweating through their dress and jacket.

"Action!" yelled the director.

"Good evening! I hope you enjoyed the recap reel of today's events in the Santa of the Year Pageant. But today's excitement isn't over yet. I'm sitting here with Tove, who wants to say a few words to the listeners. Take it away, Tove."

"Hey, everybody. You know me as the Santa who walked off stage after being cornered by their ex on live TV. I had big aspirations for what I'd do with my public position in this pageant. And instead I've become the dramatic Santa. So it goes.

"But I didn't come here tonight to talk about myself. I want to talk about one of the other Santas, one who's had a much bigger impact than I ever could. I want to talk about Effie."

Tove took a shuddering breath. No going back now.

"She introduced herself with jokes, and she left the pageant so the rest of us could go forward. But I don't think anyone really saw all the things she was doing behind the scenes.

"On Monday, we went to buy tents for the sleep-out together. Effie convinced the outdoor store to sponsor us for the night as well as donate supplies to the homeless shelter. That night, she shared her tent with me when mine got destroyed. On Thursday, she helped me fundraise for a charity I work with for victims and survivors of domestic abuse. Effie doesn't know I know this, but she's also been hard at work with the contacts she met through the pageant to cook Christmas lunch for the homeless shelter on Christmas Day."

Tove paused to smile at the camera. They'd found out from DuBois that Effie had somehow made friends with the assistant manager at Goodfoods, the Island's main supermarket, and arranged for a huge donation of vegetables and turkeys. Effie and DuBois plotted to take over Nice Crumb on Christmas morning, where they'd cook a roast and take all the food to the shelter, so they wouldn't have to rely on microwave meals.

"And that's not including all the little things she's done to care for me throughout the week, from apple and chestnut soup to 'Grace Kelly' by MIKA."

They blushed at the memory of that soft, perfect night.

"Yesterday, Effie couldn't bring herself to vote any of her fellow Santas out of the pageant. So she took the fall for herself. She is more generous than I can ever understand. And for that reason, I was initially angry and jealous. I couldn't accept that anyone could possibly be that selfless.

"But that's just who Effie is. To me, she is the perfect Santa. Kindness and giving come more naturally to her than anyone

I have ever met. She brings joy and jokes and Christmas cheer with every word she speaks.

"I think a lot of us know that doing the right thing often comes at a price. Effie is one of those people who does the right thing anyway. She gives her all, every second of every day. However, I want her to know that sometimes, there doesn't have to be a price. Sometimes, you can have everything you dream of. She taught me that herself! She *changed* me. You can be there for others *and* you can be the best Santa this Island has ever seen!

"So that's my proposal. I want to share my place in the pageant with Effie. I want to do tomorrow's gift delivery challenge together as a team. I want our names side by side on the ballot when you vote for your favourite Santa. The pageant is kindly letting me do this. If Effie agrees."

"And you're not the only one who wants to share their place, right, Tove?" asked Nowell.

Without any more prompting, Bryan #2 marched on stage and took up residence on the other side of the couch Tove occupied.

"I would like to apologise to Effie for voting her out last night," he announced. "I'm glad she has a friend like you, Tove. And similarly, I want to share my own place with Bryan Bourgaize. Bryan brings something special and nostalgic to the table that none of you young'uns have. Besides, we old men must stick together."

"Thank you, Bryan," said Nowell. "I think we are just about ready to wrap up. Tove, is there anything else you would like to say?"

Tove's voice wobbled a little as they said, "Effie, this is all possible because of you. So what do you say? I'll be waiting for your answer at the starting line tomorrow."

Sunday

1 day till Christmas

36

Melchior slept on Effie's phone and managed to turn off her morning alarm, but fortunately (or not), Effie's irrepressible niece sent a barrage of texts at god o'clock in the morning. So many texts that Melchior uttered a loud yelp, waking her up.

You didn't text me last night

What happened

I saw this morning

It's all on TikTok

Wake up!!!

Not stopping till you answer

Hey, what did the apple say to the prime minister?

Effie grabbed her phone from under the cat and responded, **I don't want to know**

She was too late.

Grow a pear, big guy

Did she know what that meant? Did Effie even know what it meant? It was a mystery. She'd never find out.

Effie was awake now, and it was probably a good thing considering how much she had to do today. She'd arranged almost everything after the broadcast last night, unable to sleep after all the mindblowing things Tove had said on air. Still, she fired off a few more texts as she picked the sleep out her eyes.

So? texted Heather.

Then followed about ten thousand emojis, the notifications making Effie's phone completely unusable.

Why are you texting, I'm literally in your house right now

She braced herself as Heather came thundering down the stairs and proceeded to rant about love and friendship and Christmas and whatever else. Half listening, she washed her face in the kitchen. The Effie she wanted everybody to see today didn't have bags under her eyes. She was washed and moisturised and put-together.

Lalla soon appeared and with a big smile pulled Effie's Santa suit out the tumbledryer.

"Thank you," said Effie quite genuinely, while secretly hating the scent of lavender that now clung to the cheap felt.

When she was ready, she took the bus to the seafront. DuBois was wiping tables outside Nice Crumb, and he served her coffee and croissants and sat down to chat as she ate them.

"Surprised you're working before the delivery challenge today," Effie commented.

"It doesn't start till eleven," he explained, beaming, "plus I couldn't not come into work. There's bread to be baked!"

Next Effie went to the Pollack. As expected, Nowell was there already, decorating the stage as a starting line. The delivery challenge was, after all, a race.

Effie offered a pain au chocolat courtesy of DuBois, which they gladly took as she explained another piece of her plan. When it was all sorted, she caught Nowell's arm before they could get back to their team.

"Hey, I'm sorry I was so risqué when we first met. You've been terrified this whole time I'd say something inappropriate in public, and that's my fault. I'm sorry."

"Risqué? Gosh, what did I miss?" Nowell pushed the wispy hair back from their forehead and laughed.

"I said 'effing.' Remember? You told me it was a kid-friendly contest over and over again. Like you were scared I'd swear on TV."

"Oh, that!" Nowell's hazel eyes widened. "No, no. I overheard you tell DuBois to go fuck himself and was concerned you'd cause trouble with the other contestants."

Effie was stunned. "When did I ever tell DuBois to go fuck himself? Like, I wouldn't put it past me, but I don't remember it."

"At the sign-up table. You were talking about his birthday, and then out of the blue you snap 'Go fuck yourself.' To be fair I don't know if he heard, he was counting months on his fingers."

"Oh!" Effie remembered now. Her mum had texted asking if she was still vegetarian. "That wasn't at DuBois, it was at…somebody else." She caught a flash of anxiety in Nowell's eyebrows and specified, "My mother, to be precise. DuBois is actually a delight. I can't believe you thought I was so rude."

"From my perspective you did tell him to go fuck himself for no reason. And you act quite familiar with strangers, so it didn't seem out of character."

"God." Effie was mortified. "I need to work on that."

"Well," said Nowell, pushing to their feet. "I'm sorry I didn't trust you. Maybe I have been too harsh and too cautious."

"Maybe," Effie agreed. But who was to say what other things Nowell had to be harsh and cautious about in their life?

Effie's next stop was meeting Ranjula at Bonamy's coffee truck on the pier.

"Are we all set?" she asked Ranjula as she paid for their flat whites. It was her second coffee in an hour and she was growing giddy.

"All set and sunny," Bonamy responded from behind the counter, flashing a giant smile.

Effie returned it in kind. "Thank you, Bonamy."

"The answer is yes," Ranjula said as they strolled down the slipway to the water. "But what was that about?"

"I have a whole bagful of plans," Effie boasted. "But the cat's out the bag on that one. Bonamy's daughter is helping me organise Christmas lunch for the homeless shelter."

"I admire your…elasticity," Ranjula commented.

"My what?"

"You've really bounced back from the past couple of days. How are you doing?"

"Doing my best." Effie smiled. "It feels good. Maybe I'll do more of this. Just…let myself do all the things I want to do without worrying about what people think of me."

"You ever want a job, there's an opening on my team."

"Marketing, me? Nah. I'm an engineer."

"You are? My dad's the project manager for the tidal energy dam they're trying to get set up in the Channel. They don't have the funding to start yet, but I'll ask if there are any spots going for when they do."

They stood on the slipway long after their takeaway cups were empty, chatting not even about work or anything in particular, but about life. The struggle of spending their twenties in a dying economy post a pandemic that had traumatised the world. The pieces of their souls they'd lost along the way. The lies and outrage they'd internalised to fill the void.

Effie could imagine texting Ranjula once in a while and meeting up for a meal or a movie. She'd made a friend.

Ranjula left when the Pollack carpark speakers began to blare across the water. She tapped her nose sideways and went up towards Town, and Effie retraced her steps to the Pollack. The crowds were thick, but a small hand grabbed hers as she approached the toffee apple stand and tugged her round the back. It was Barney who pushed her under the tent flap, and then she was surrounded by Heather and her friends, in their hideout in the wings of a marquee that stank of melting sugar.

"How did you get in here?" Effie demanded, feeling like Princess Atta ensnared in Dot and the Blueberries' daring plot.

"Chill, my cousin runs the toffee apple stall," said Avril.

"Then why are we hiding? And aren't you supposed to be grounded, Heather?"

Heather scowled. "Mum ungrounded me because it's Christmas. She's literally right there helping sell toffee apples." She jabbed a thumb to the front of the tent.

"Good to know."

"So, we found Tove before you got here," Heather continued, business mode activated, "—don't worry, I told these guys all about the plan—and arranged everything."

Effie smacked her forehead. "What did you say?"

"Just that you'll be there at the start line."

"And?"

"You want to be her girlfriend," snickered Zooey.

"It's not funny," Barney retorted. "Effie is a lesbian. She falls in love with women."

"And non-binary people," Effie added. "Seriously though, who gave you permission to talk to Tove? I was hoping to do that myself."

"You were late," Heather complained. "They're all up on stage already."

"But it's only—" Effie checked her phone and swore. Curse Ranjula for being so fun and interesting.

"Don't you have somewhere to be?" Heather prompted.

"Whoa, who was it kidnapped me and dragged me in here?" Effie backed out of the tent.

She pressed through the crowds. There Tove was, in their powerful Santa suit—the one whose skirts had smothered Effie three nights ago as she'd licked their clit. Holy fuck. Effie squeezed the taste out of her mind and tried to focus on making it to the stage before the race began.

Alongside Tove were DuBois, who was waving at the crowd, Alice, who was jogging in place doing bum-kicks, and B1 and B2, who'd made a little camp on the stage with folding chairs and cups of tea. B2 spotted Effie and gave her a thumbs up. Effie sent a thumbs up back. She couldn't blame him for voting against her, any more than she could blame herself for doing the same.

That's when Tove followed B2's eyes and found Effie's. They held the gaze over the tops of a hundred heads. The chatter muffled till all Effie could hear was her heartbeat, and she imagined she could hear Tove's as well, *one-two, one-two*, steady as a reindeer's trot.

Effie elbowed her way through the last of the crowd, making it to the stage just in time for Nowell to announce the count-down.

"I thought you weren't coming." Tove seized Effie's hand and gripped it fiercely.

"Of course I was coming! But I had to plan our route first."

"Our route?"

"You think I was going to let you run me ragged all over Town without a plan to win the race?"

The contestants could use any means necessary to deliver five presents to five prespecified locations around Town, and the last Santa to complete their deliveries would be eliminated. There were maps on big display boards in the carpark, with five Xs marked in red, so everyone knew the locations: the Castle, the top of Town Church steeple, the War Memorial, and the Pavilion in the Gardens, and then finally the stage back at the Pollack. They could visit the first four in any order, but that was the order Effie had planned for herself and Tove. Effie wouldn't admit it to anyone, but she'd been plotting their route all week.

Almost before she'd finished going over it all in her head, the horn screeched and the race began!

37

"This way!"

Effie tugged Tove after DuBois, who'd dashed down the side of the refreshments tent.

"Town is the other way!" Tove pointed back to the coast road, which had been pedestrianised for the long weekend, and the huge crowd that had turned out for the race.

"Trust me." Effie flashed her signature grin, the irresistibly cocky Cheshire cat one that had charmed Tove from the get.

The noise of the crowd faded till it was only them and DuBois and the loudspeaker faint in the distance, and the drawstring sack of presents thumping up and down on Tove's back, and the December sea lapping at the breakwater, and now the juddering surge of a diesel motor. Effie had brought Tove to the pier behind the Pollack, where DuBois was starting up a motorboat called *Da Boi*.

Tove couldn't believe their eyes as Effie clattered down the pier and vaulted into the boat. For a split second Tove heard

Aaron in their head saying, *They're going to leave without you.* Then they banished him.

"Get in!" Effie yelled over the revving engine. "This is our ride to the Castle!"

"It's my boat," DuBois boasted from the rudder. "Effie's idea, though. Isn't she a genius?"

Effie extended an inviting hand. She smiled and Tove felt like they were the only person in the world.

Tove relaxed. "Take my sack." They launched their Santa sack into the boat.

"Kinky!" Effie said, as only she would.

The sack of presents fell into her arms at the same moment as Tove's feet hit the boat, and without a moment's delay they parted company with the pier and cruised into the bay.

"Sit down!" DuBois ordered as they picked up speed.

Wind streaked past Tove's ears. They clutched their hat with one hand and the bar in front with the other. The sea grew rougher and they rode the waves. Up they went…there was a suspended second when they were airborne…and then down they came with a thump that went right up their spine. It almost sent them flying.

"Can I hold your hat for you?" Effie screamed over the roar of the wind and the waves and the engine.

"No, just hold me and make sure I don't fall out!"

Effie slunk an arm round their waist and clasped them to her side. Pleasure darted up Tove's body. She'd touched every piece of them with her lips, and with her caring, generous soul. They braced for the next bump, but Effie sat firm. With her holding them, they were going nowhere she wasn't.

Far too soon they were slowing down once again. The Castle, which in reality was only on the other side of the marina, loomed into view. Canons like iron telescopes peered through the walls. A cameraperson waited at the portcullis, lens gleaming at their approach. A local ten-year-old jumped up and down on the battlements, waiting for his Christmas gifts.

DuBois docked the RIB on another slipway and grabbed his sack of presents. Effie and Tove helped one another back onto dry land and raced up the iron ladder to the main pier.

"Can you handle the delivery?" said Effie. "I want to check the next leg is sorted."

Tove dashed under the portcullis and into the Castle. Five minutes later, and with the first delivery checked off, they jogged back out. DuBois had finished first, and he idled with Effie by the yacht club building.

"Thanks for waiting," said Tove.

"I wasn't waiting for you. You're on your own from here."

Tove looked askance at Effie, but she smiled encouragingly. "We have to part ways eventually if we're going to beat him."

DuBois laughed. "You're welcome for the ride."

And then, to Tove's astonishment, a lemon-yellow four-door Ferrari pulled up. The windows rolled down, blasting EDM, and a bevy of rich kids with far too many arms tentacled out.

"Godspeed." DuBois slid into the back seat half on top of his friends. With a wave, he was gone.

"Fantastic," Tove groaned. "He'll be done in no time with a car at his disposal."

"If only I'd thought of using a car," Effie lamented. "It's so obvious."

"Town is pedestrianised today, surely it's against the rules?"

"The roads were cleared for the race, plus Nowell said we can use 'any means necessary.' I'm sorry if we lose to him."

"It's okay. We only have to beat one other Santa to make it to tomorrow."

Effie ushered them back towards town. The Castle used to be an island, so the pier was very long. It was nearly a kilometre to the Town Church.

"Get the right present in the end?" she asked, panting. "DuBois said that's why you took so long."

"I think so." Tove warmed to her attention. "The kid liked tabletop war games, so I gave him a model aeroplane. Thought he might be able to paint it like his soldiers and use it as a prop on the battlefield."

"Wait, do you have more than five presents in that sack?"

"So many. They're mostly small."

"What did DuBois give?"

"He literally chucked the first present he found at the kid and ran, and guess what it was? A teething toy, like for a baby. The kid was ten!"

"Get out!" cried Effie.

"He was faster though."

"Here's another way of looking at it. The winner will be voted by local children. And DuBois has just lost a vote."

Tove's affection for Effie was impossible to contain, almost on a par with what they felt for their mum and brother: peace in her presence; appreciation and gratitude for the wisdom and kindness she brought, both gentle and aggressive with its confidence; recognition that even Effie could not be optimistic and resilient all the time; tenderness in acknowledging her vulnerability; yet trust that she would do no wrong Tove could not forgive; and, finally, joy for the process and nature of loving her.

Tove loved Effie.

Fuck. They'd learned to love again.

A long-forgotten sensation welled deep in their soul. It rushed like a dam unblocked. And it kept going and going, and it didn't stop. *Watch out, Effie. It's going to catch you if you stay close.*

She stayed close.

Together they made it to the warehouse along the pier where the tourist train, *Le petit train*, roosted in the winter. But when Tove rounded the corner, there it was in all its bleach-white glory, a uniformed driver waiting in the tractor that towed the open carriages.

"All aboard!" he called.

Effie hopped into the nearest carriage and pulled Tove and the sack of presents with her, and the train jerked off.

"Welcome aboard *Le petit train*, Tove and Effie," the train speaker announced. "Today we're doing a little speed-sightseeing. It's a new route, so bear with me as I make these tight corners."

"Oh my god." An incredulous giggle bubbled up and out Tove's mouth. "Effie. You didn't."

"Oh, but I did! You better sit back and catch your breath, because we've got a church tower to climb, and then the next leg is a sprint—sorry."

"At first I thought we'd have to do the whole thing on foot. Thanks for…not making me do that."

"Not my idea of a date," Effie remarked. "I mean— This isn't a date. I'm helping you with the pageant like I promised. And accepting your offer to team up. And also trying to win. Together."

She pulsed like the beam of a lighthouse, swivelling from *haha* to *oops* in an instant. Tove believed every word—not because they were idolising her, but because she had never given them cause to doubt her sincerity. That was the evidence they ought to be relying on, rather than Aaron when he told them everyone would hurt them in the end.

"Relax, Effie," Tove told her.

And they placed their hand on hers where it rested on the bench.

She froze, sneaking a sideways glance like she thought it was an accident, but Tove wrapped their fingers around hers. They were glad they'd let Effie in. With her hand in theirs, everything Mum and Dair had said yesterday was clicking into place.

They coughed to break the tension. "Did you see Alice?" they said as if they weren't holding her goddamn hand. "Shoved her sack in a hiking rucksack and went off at a lightning pace. I think she went up the hill first."

"She runs marathons. This'll be a piece of cake to her."

"And here we are, Town Church!" called the driver over the speaker. "Thank you for your patronage, I hope you enjoyed the ride! I'm rooting for you!"

Tove slid out the trailer and Effie thanked the driver.

"Delighted to be of service," he said. "I wouldn't be where I am now without the kind acts of people I don't know. Thank you for allowing me to pay it forward."

They ducked into the church, where the next delivery awaited. As Tove climbed the steeple, a familiar whirring sound irritated their ear. They reached the top in time to see a large drone leaving the tower, a sack of presents dangling from its claws. It buzzed into the distance, towards the Castle, like a big mosquito.

"Should've known," Effie said behind them. "The Bryans are delivering their presents by drone."

It made sense—how else would two old men compete with a bunch of young folks and a marathon-runner? Effie's Bryan must have built the drone specially to have carrying capacity and a long remote communication distance. It must have some kind of functionality to deliver each present too, like a microphone, or maybe it was supposed to be a lucky dip.

Once again, Tove was grateful for Effie and her Grand Plans. Without her, they wouldn't have had a chance against the talent and ingenuity of the other Santas!

Despite the hurry, they tried to take the present-giving as seriously as they could. A few open questions from Effie ascertained that the kid liked watching TV, so after a long think Tove dug out the first volume of the *My Hero Academia* manga and explained that it was very exciting and cinematic and there was even a TV show if they were interested.

"What happened to the grumpy Tove from the Santa grotto?" Effie said affectionately as they left the church together. "Telling my niece happiness isn't worth having."

"You misunderstood me! All I meant is things aren't always perfect. We have to find compassion for the imperfect people we are, with all the pain we experience and the insecurities we face."

"You said it *really* badly."

Tove laughed. "I guess I was a bit pessimistic about my chances of being able to handle the world at all."

Tove had expected to pass Alice along the High Street, but they jogged up the steep cobbles to the War Memorial without seeing her. Perhaps she'd taken a different route and passed while they were on the train.

The girl at the Memorial wanted to become an astronaut, so Tove gifted her a model moon made of a special plastic that absorbed light and glowed in the dark.

"Why do you have the perfect presents?" Effie asked. "Doesn't everyone have the same stuff in their Santa sack?"

"We each got a budget," Tove explained. "We all went to the toyshop at the crack of dawn and got what we needed."

"And you bought a whole lot of different things so you'd have more choice?"

"Yeah."

"And what did the others get?"

"Bryan got Lego, and Alice bought five handmade woollen guernseys. DuBois went to the childcare and baby section. I don't think he realised how old the kids were going to be. He looked at the stuff I bought and was like, 'Aren't those for adults though? I'd love to get any of these for Christmas.'"

"God, he is adorable. I can't stand him."

With the Memorial done, it was another haul up the hill to the Gardens. Effie took the sack for this stretch. She must've noticed Tove was getting tired.

"Are you hungry?" She pulled a pack of jelly cubes from her pocket. "Here's some fast sugar if you fancy an energy boost."

Tove gasped. "You remember?"

"Of course I remember."

Tove ripped the packet open and tore into the raspberry jelly with their teeth. They were supposed to be melted in boiling water, but when Effie and Tove did their Duke of Edinburgh practical expedition together in Snowdonia, they'd eaten them like this. They'd open a packet every few hours and share it as they hiked up exposed ridges and down slate scree hills.

"Those are some of my happiest memories," Tove murmured.

"Mine too. And I'm delighted to be making new ones."

"Same."

By the time they reached the holly-endowed gates of the Gardens, they were both rosy and sweating. Snowdrops winked from the flowerbeds and frost crackled under their feet. Tove touched Effie's arm and they paused at the gates to catch their breath.

"Hey," Tove began, "thank you for doing this. I'm sorry I bit your head off the other day."

"You were protecting yourself. There's nothing wrong with that."

"I think I didn't understand, or want to understand, why you voted yourself out."

"There were different reasons," Effie mused. "But…I think you understood me better than I wanted to admit. I was hurting more than I knew."

"Aaron, um…did he really hurt your feelings?" Tove used Dair's words.

Effie shot them a shrewd look that told them Dair was right. "Yeah. He got me smack bang in the place it hurts."

"I'm sorry."

"It's okay. The funny thing is, I feel so much better now. I have to cut out the people who make me feel like garbage, who will never be satisfied with anything I do to make myself better, and focus on the people who will actually be there for me."

"People like your parents who treat you like shit?" Tove asked softly.

"Yeah. People like them. They made me feel weird and different and unlovable. Like I'm not meant to be around other people."

Tove's chest ached for Effie. They'd been through something similar—constant belittlement from the one person who was supposed to care most.

"You thought you broke up your parents," they stated, realising this as they said it.

"I did," Effie responded. "They basically told me so."

"No. Your parents broke up because they are selfish people. They gave up on you. Anyone could've been their kid and they still would've broken up. And breaking up is okay. But how they treat you isn't. None of that is your fault."

Red rimmed Effie's eyes. Unusually, she was close to tears. "I really thought they were the perfect couple. And I ruined that. And then they found each other again, like they were meant to be together forever and I'd nearly sabotaged it. I think that's why they hate me."

"If they do hate you," Tove said, "I'm so sorry. You're exciting and hilarious and kind and sweet! It's on them if they can't see that!"

Effie bit her lip through a chuckle. Tove hoped she believed them. "And what about you and Aaron? Were you soulmates? Did I wreck that as well?"

"God no!" Tove grabbed her shoulder and gave her a shake. "That shit is over." Once upon a time they would've said they didn't believe in soulmates anyway. But now, Effie made a close case for their existence. "Hey," they began without a plan or a reason, "I was thinking…"

"Ahoy!" At the crest of the hill, on the grass beside the Pavilion, a figure waved their arm in a wide arc.

Effie shot them a glance, but turned back to Tove. "What's up?"

Tove shook their head. It could wait. "Never mind. We'd better get this fourth present done."

They reached the Pavilion, where the next present recipient awaited. This child was smaller than all the others, with big eyes in a small face and a tatty hand-me-down coat.

Tove dropped down to the decking and introduced themself.

"So what do you like to play with, Lainey?" they asked.

"I like my sister's Barbies," said Lainey, "but most of their heads fall off. And I like my brother's fire-truck, but he says I play with it wrong."

"It sounds like you don't have many toys of your own," said Tove. "I don't have any Barbies or fire-trucks, but would you like a friend for Christmas? I've been carrying a friend round all day with me, and I think he belongs to you."

They took the Guernsey Teddy out of their Santa sack, and Lainey's face transformed as she took in the lush mahogany fur and shining eyes of the handmade bear. Inspired by Oberon, Tove had knitted the teddy's jumper themself at knitting group. It was green and they'd stitched a clumsy red heart into the wool.

"He's beautiful!" Lainey said, hugging him to her chest.

"He's yours," said Tove. "Take care of him. You might need him someday."

Their throat began to choke up as they left Lainey with her new bear. They took a few big, quick breaths and were feeling better by the time they joined Effie and her companion—the person who'd waved earlier—on the hill.

"Tove, this is Ranjula. Ranjula, this is Tove," Effie introduced. "Ranjula is a member of the paragliding club and she's going to help us get back to the Pollack."

Tove took in the parachute paraphernalia scattered all over the grass. "Wait, is this what I think it is? Are we paragliding down the hill?"

"That's the idea! But you don't have to do anything you don't want to."

"The day's good for it," Ranjula commented, friendly and brisk. "My friend Tom is down at the Pollack and will help you land when you get there."

"You're not coming too?" Effie asked.

"I am! I'll follow, though, make sure you get off okay."

Tove heart sped up imagining how it would feel to stand on nothing, to trust themself to the air. "I've never done this before."

"Neither," said Effie.

"If you like it you can join the club," Ranjula offered.

"Right." Tove surveyed Effie, her nervous excitement and fidgets matching theirs. "Yeah, okay, I'm ready."

"You are?" Effie's face split into a beaming grin. "You really want to do this? You don't have to. My other idea was to get a go-kart or something and roll down the hill, although I wasn't sure how we'd get it to stop. So anyway, this is totally optional and—"

"Effie." Tove laid a finger across her lips.

Effie stilled.

"I want to do this. I'm ready. And…I trust you."

"I hate to interrupt," Ranjula intervened, "but is that speck that other Santa's drone?"

Tove followed her gesture out over the hill, over town and the sparkling bay. The other islands glowed blue in the distance. A tiny moving object hovered near the Castle, heading back towards the Pollack.

"You're right, we have to get going," said Effie. "What do we have to do?"

Ranjula strapped them into the paragliders, tying Tove's Santa sack securely to their belt so there were no loose strings. She explained how to take off, what to do in the air, and how to land, assuring them her friend would help on the way down.

"I'll be right behind you as well. Any problem, or if you don't feel good at any point, you yell at me right away. I'm highly trained."

So now they were ready, standing on the grass, ready to launch into the distance on the home stretch. Tove's knees knocked.

"Will you go first?" they begged Effie. "I'm sort of scared."

"Anything for you."

Effie muttered Ranjula's instructions under her breath, did a small run-up, then jumped at the point the hill got steeper. The canvas billowed above her as the wind filled it, and she turned towards the Pollack as Ranjula instructed, so she was going in the right direction.

"This is awesome!" she yelled over her shoulder, all infectious exhilaration and freedom and openness. "Come and join me!"

Unexpectedly, Tove didn't want to be left alone on solid land. They wanted to leap into the sky by Effie's side, and go into the future with her, uncertainty and all. They poised to begin their own run-up.

Suddenly, there was a shout from the bottom of the hill. Someone was running up through the Gardens in huge, loping strides.

"Tove, Tove!" He screamed their name. "You can't jump! They've cut the strings! They're out to get you!"

Aaron.

He glared up, the whites of his eyes vast and full of hatred. But nothing he said could make any difference to Tove now. They were going to jump of their own accord, and then he'd lose them forever. He clawed at the grass in the effort to get up the hill faster.

"No, Aaron!" Tove's refusal sliced the air, pinging the strings of their glider. "You're the only one out to get me!"

They jumped.

There was a moment of dread, then their feet touched nothing. With a clamping sensation around their waist and hips, the harness held them suspended in the sky. They were in the air and cruising down the hill. Aaron dived to get out the way, but as Tove passed—and it was between accidental and deliberate—they kicked him dead in the face. He fell. Then he was in the distance, too small to see, and all they could hear was him yelling insults, and then he faded away.

38

Effie saw the whole thing over her shoulder. As Tove caught up with her, and they were zooming side by side over the trees and the rooftops of town, she called into the rushing air, "Hey, nice one back there!"

Tove was fiddling with their hands, overflowing with an energy Effie had never seen in them before. "Effie…can this be a date after all?"

Everything stuttered, even the wind in Effie's sails. "A date? Really? Is that what you want?"

"Yes. I'm in love with you."

A gigantic bubble expanded around Effie's heart. "You are? With me?"

"I've always loved you."

"I've always loved you too."

"Fuck, now you're going to make me cry."

"That's not me, it's the wind. It burneth thine eyes to tears."

"No, Effie, it's you. It was always you."

Effie's bubble took in Tove. It took in Ranjula, gliding behind them. It took in Tom, who called instructions to help them land on the asphalt and unclip from the gliders. And all the spectators, who clapped and cheered as Tove took Effie's hand and dragged her in the sprint to the finish line: they were in it too.

But most importantly, Effie herself was inside it. In fact, she was the centre. The origin. The point at which her own happiness began. It had always been her.

39

While Tove leapt onto the stage, tearing open the sack of presents for the boy waiting there, Effie counted the presents already at his feet. One, two… Two Santas were already there. She and Tove were third! Their place in the pageant was safe!

"Hi Effie, good to see you again."

Effie swivelled to find B2 at her elbow. He held a remote control, and wasn't even out of breath. Of course; he'd never left the carpark. B1 sat in his camping chair to the side, sipping hot cocoa with his wife.

"I loved your strategy," she said.

"Had to use my strengths." He shrugged. "Looks like Tove did too."

He inclined his head in a meaningful way, and all of a sudden Effie was embarrassed. She was Tove's strength. That's what he meant.

"Tove has her own strength," she pointed out. They'd kicked their ex in the fucking face.

"No one could deny that. What I mean is sometimes we're stronger together. But I think you always knew that. I'm glad you both made it through."

"Who else made it?"

"Someone else who used his strengths—friends with a fast car." B2 nodded at DuBois, who was giving autographs in the crowd.

"And that's our third Santa team back from their deliveries!" cried Nowell into the microphone. "Bryan Bourgaize and Bryan Tanguy, DuBois, and Tove and Effie are all safe from elimination today! Which means they'll be going into the final vote for Santa of the Year! I've just had word that Alice has dropped out of the race, and won't be making it back. So let's have a round of applause for our remaining Santas!"

"Oh shit," said Effie. "Hope Alice didn't get injured. Those cobblestones are lethal on the ankles."

"No, not her. She got a call that one of her grandkids fractured his wrist on the monkey bars at the park. She ran to the hospital instead of the Memorial."

"Ouch." Effie winced. "So we were safe from elimination all along."

"Didn't you see the WhatsApp group? Alice messaged into it so we'd all know we didn't have to hurry."

Effie checked her phone. There was a flurry of activity in the group chat. "I was so distracted, I never thought to look."

They both laughed.

"Phone lines open now! Don't forget to vote for your favourite!" declared Nowell.

"I have to ask," Effie said with a touch of nerves, "why did you vote me out? You never did say."

"Ah." B2 coughed into his fist. "The truth is, I saw you as my greatest rival. If I wanted to win—which, I'll be honest, I do, and I'm allowed to want things—I needed to vote you in that position."

"Isn't Tove your biggest rival? She's so great." And cute and hot and brave and interesting.

B2 shook his head with a smile. "Tove is great, it's true, but she doesn't have your presence. You're funny and charismatic and know how to captivate your audience. As far as I'm concerned, you absolutely had to go."

Effie completely disagreed. Tove's presence was undeniable, electrifying, encompassing.

"I thought I was the weird one nobody liked," she said in half-hearted self-deprecation.

"Nonsense. I like you. The other Santas like you. Tove likes you. Right?"

Effie nodded, tears in her eyes. She'd struggled to fit in all her life, but that didn't mean there was anything fundamentally wrong with her. And the bubble around her heart kept growing and brightening.

"Hey." Tove's hands appeared on her shoulders. "That's it. We'll see if it was enough."

They perched on the stage and wrapped their legs round Effie's waist from behind. Effie swivelled so they were straddling her hip.

B2 raised his eyebrows. "Had a good trip?" he inquired.

"Rather productive," said Tove. Their eyes dropped to Effie's lips.

"Before you go, I have one more announcement," Nowell called.

The crowd quietened once again, and all eyes turned to the podium.

"DuBois and the Bryans have switched their sponsors, with full approval of all parties involved. Would you each like to come up and say a few words?"

B2 took to the stage to introduce his new sponsor: his husband's vegan soap business. B1 explained that he'd partnered with his friend, a maker of podiatric insoles for people with arthritis, lower body pain, diabetes, and other disabilities. If the two Bryans won the pageant, they'd split the money: half to secure a regular stall in the foyer of the new shopping centre for B2's husband, and half to help B1's friend take on a paid apprentice.

DuBois then came on to talk about his initiative. If he won, the prize money would go towards running a regular soup kitchen out of Nice Crumb's facilities.

"What's going on?" Tove said.

"Oh, this is the other thing I've been working on, me and the others and Nowell," Effie explained. "We've agreed that whoever wins will split the prize money six ways, although we haven't told Nowell that part yet."

"Wait, are you for real?"

"Of course. The amount is huge; there's plenty to go around and it's not like our sponsors need it. Not to give you a big head or anything, but we liked your idea of refusing to get a corporate sponsor."

Tove's smile could've launched a thousand ships. "None of this would've happened without you, don't even pretend."

"Yes, and you paved the way."

Tears sprung to the corners of Tove's eyes. "Go on then. What are you and Alice supporting?"

"Alice is supporting her daughter-in-law's Black bookshop—you remember we met Claudine? They need a shop space and better deals with UK suppliers. And I want to help my sister do what she loves, which is make jewellery. The shopping centre is happy to give them each a stall in the foyer, so that's a start. Guess they realised the value of supporting local businesses, since they'll be poaching so much from the economy."

"Wish we'd done more to oppose the shopping centre before it was built."

"Me too. But you know what? We're going to do our damnedest to give our local talent a chance."

They wandered the fair all afternoon, Tove's hand swinging loosely in Effie's. They tested various handholds and they were all perfect, like their hands with all their bumps and knuckles were made to fit together. People noticed and nodded at them like the local celebrities they'd become.

Effie remembered, barely, to stop by the toffee apple stall, where Lalla threw her sticky arms up and hugged her tight, and Heather and her friends gathered round to make judgemental comments.

"We always had to come to this stall," Tove whispered in Effie's ear as Heather & Co. were momentarily distracted finding the juiciest apples to skewer. "It's our ship name."

"What?"

"Toffie."

"Oh my god, did you just come up with that?"

"My mum used to call us Toffie, years ago."

"Your mum has been shipping us before you even knew you were bi?"

"I mean, she doesn't understand ship names, but yeah, basically."

Effie couldn't believe it had taken them this long to get together.

Monday

Christmas Day!

40

"Oh, Effie," yawned Tove, stirring her from a blissful, dreamless sleep.

"Oh my god," Effie croaked. "I can't believe you're in my bed again." Her tongue felt thick and swollen. She was so out of practice.

"Good, isn't it?"

"Nothing compares. I'm exhausted, though."

"Serves you right."

Effie laughed, and sat up. "Hey, it's still dark outside. Are you telling me we didn't oversleep?"

"You're literally the worst at setting alarms, so I set one."

"It's not my fault my cat sleeps on my phone and turns off my alarms." Effie showed her phone, with the 5:30am alarm dismissed a little while ago.

"I should've got you a hardcore alarm clock for Christmas."

"What *did* you get me for Christmas?"

Tove knelt in front of the bed and produced a small cuboid package wrapped up in red paper and a pale blue ribbon from their bag. "Here."

Effie didn't need asking twice. She tugged the ribbon loose. There were only three short bits of tape on the paper, but she took her time unfolding each flap and enjoying the unwrapping process. The first visible end was the wooden slats of a miniature crate, painted and distressed in a shabby chic style. Effie slid it out, and a barrage of vanilla and pine and marzipan zipped up her nose. The crate was full of small powdery balls.

"Bath bombs!" She erupted into a grin. "Made by Bryan's husband!"

"I *knew* I recognised the company name when Bryan announced it yesterday. So, do you like them?"

"I'm delighted! But I'll only use these if you'll join me."

"In the bath?" Tove squeaked.

"Wouldn't be the first time."

"Effie, you tease..." Tove squeezed their eyes shut and whimpered.

Heat spread from Effie's ears to her toes. She shoved the bath bombs to the side and snatched Tove into her arms. She pressed her lips to theirs and now they were moaning into her mouth. She'd already forgotten the fantasy of making out in the bath, and was fully present in the tremendous reality of kissing the person she loved.

Eventually she pulled away. "I have to get dressed and head to Nice Crumb. I have so many potatoes to peel before the winner of the pageant is announced."

"Five more minutes?" Tove wheedled. "I'm coming to help, remember. So it'll only take half the time."

"You're so persuasive."

But Tove stopped her as she leaned in.

"Hey, Effie. I'm proud of you."

"I haven't done it yet. My potato peeling might suck ass."

"Oi, no more putting yourself down! They might be the best potatoes someone's ever tasted. And I was talking in general, not about the potatoes you haven't peeled yet. I'm proud of you for being you. It suits you. I think you should stick to it. Being you."

After five—well, maybe ten—more minutes of kissing, they finally got dressed, Effie into her now-shabby-looking Santa suit with its bells and lesbian colours, and Tove into their little black dress and choker necklace and fishnets.

"Win or lose, I want to feel like a queen today," they said. "Zip me up, would you?"

"Yes, Your Highness!" Effie cooed with a curtsey.

"And touch my ass while you're about it."

Effie obeyed. "You've got a great ass, Your Highness."

"Maybe I'll let you see it sometime," Tove purred, "if you're good."

Roleplay aside, Effie was close to swooning.

As she gave the zip one last tug and Tove turned, she saw they'd pinned all their badges from the denim jacket to the front of the dress.

"You're stunning," she told them.

Tove beamed. "Do you think we'll win?" they asked.

"The pageant? Probably not. DuBois has already proved his voting potential and the Bryans are all over TikTok. Will you be disappointed if we don't win?"

Tove tilted their head in thought. "No. I'm satisfied. My goal was to give some visibility to people who weren't looking forward to Christmas, and while it turned out much harder than

I thought, the number of people I spoke to at the craft fair blew my mind. I got what I wanted at every step of the way. Except Aaron's intrusion. And even then, I got the closure I needed—by realising that the only way forward is to shut that door myself and keep marching on." They stopped. "How about you, babe? Will you be disappointed?"

Effie's eyes pricked at that one intimate, affirming word: *babe*. What she'd wanted was a friend to support and validate her. What she'd found was a person she loved with her whole heart, who could make her feel special with a single syllable. And alongside that, she'd found that she didn't even necessarily need another person's love to be whole. Only her own.

"I got what I needed," she said carefully. "But I think it would be pushing fate to win the pageant as well. Nobody's that lucky!"

"You're wrong!" Tove laughed. "Luck is whatever, but always remember you're deserving and worthy of all the good things in the world. You *can* have it all! That's what you told me at the fair."

"And you believe that now?"

"Yes. You've changed me. Irreversibly and for the better. Don't you believe it?"

Effie smiled. "I really want to."

They met DuBois at Nice Crumb, along with Natalie, Bonamy, and a carload of food.

And then they peeled, and chopped, and cooked. Around eleven, they loaded several dozen trays of roasted vegetables, stuffing, four turkeys and a soup warmer of gravy into the car of the shelter volunteer who collected it. Effie's Santa suit no longer smelled of Lalla's lavender detergent, but of turkey and gravy. Much better.

Then she, Tove, and DuBois headed up to the Pollack. Incredibly, even on Christmas Day, it was packed for the end of the pageant and the opening of the shopping centre. B1, B2, and even Alice were already in the green room, and Effie relaxed to see them. She'd grown to love this liquorice all-sorts bunch of Santa wannabes.

Nowell smiled through their stress-lines, looking uncharacteristically sheepish. "Before we go in front of the cameras, I wanted to thank you all. When I took this job, I didn't realise everything it would entail. I'm sorry I didn't advocate for you as well as I should have done."

"No hard feelings," Tove said softly.

Nowell then led them all to the stage and began the show. There were speeches to broadcast and voting lines to close, a highlights compilation to show as well as commercials for the shopping centre. Eventually two stagehands brought on a trestle table and a colossal pair of scissors, at least the size of Effie's two arms and probably bigger. Nowell clapped their hands to get the audience's attention.

It was time.

"And so, without further ado," they called, voice ringing over a thousand faces upturned to the stage, "our Santa of the Year, by popular vote of this Island's children, is—wait for it—our team of Effie and Tove!"

The crowd roared. Tove's eyebrows climbed into their hat and Effie clasped their hands. The others leapt to their feet to join the Santa pile-on.

Now the stagehands were trotting onto the stage, one at either end of one of those giant lottery cheques with an obscene amount of money written on them.

"Effie and Tove will split the money among a charity and a small business, is that right?" said Nowell. "Would someone like to come and receive the cheque?"

Effie yelled something over the absolutely chaotic reaction of the crowd.

"What?" Nowell yelled back.

"Is the cheque real? Will it be rewritten?"

"Oh, it's fake. Why?"

Effie strode to the humongous pair of scissors on the table. She hoiked them into her arms and presented them, amidst cheers, to Tove. Then the two Bryans took the cheque from the bewildered stagehands and everyone screamed and laughed as Tove chopped the motherfucking cheque into six pieces. Now each Santa took one piece and held them up, and the six recipients—B2's extremely handsome silver fox of a husband; the lady from Tove's domestic abuse survivors group; Alice's daughter-in-law Claudine; B1's shoemaker friend; DuBois's boss from Nice Crumb; and finally Lalla, Effie's sister—came up to receive them.

Nowell's expression was pained, but they let the Santas have their moment to stick it to the corporate nutjobs. Eventually they announced that Effie and Tove were going to cut the ribbon on the shopping centre, and then everyone would be free to roam it thereafter. They began a procession towards the gate, headed by Tove and the hazardous scissors.

"Told you so," said Tove as they were pushed forward by the current of the crowd. "You can have it all."

Blood rushed to Effie's face.

The crowd stalled as they reached the shopping centre entrance, where a red ribbon stretched between the gates. Tove brandished the giant scissors once again, and they beckoned Effie over.

Now the blood was rushing elsewhere. Effie snuck an arm round Tove's waist and put her hands over theirs on the scissors. "How much do you care about this shopping centre thing?" she breathed into their ear.

"After the ribbon's cut, not at all."

"Well, we've got some time before Lalla's Christmas dinner. How do you fancy…a bath?"

And as they cut the ribbon together, Tove's beautiful brown eyes crinkled up like they always used to, no longer empty, but full full full of joy.

Epilogue

1 year later

"Ready?" asked Effie.

The Atlantic wind swept over the dunes and into Tove's face, bringing grit that stung their eyes and buried itself in the hair they kept tidily buzzed.

"Not even a little bit," they replied.

It was late afternoon; they'd spent the morning with Effie's sister, taking turns holding the baby and playing with Heather. Lalla had wanted to name the baby Torquil, and Liam had wanted to name him Dougal, but they'd settled on "David" as a compromise. Now it was time to hang out with Tove's family, and they'd traded Lalla's noisy house for a cosy dinner in the cottage on the coast.

The house was warm, with a fire crackling in the living room.

"Happy Christmas!" Mum burst from the kitchen and cannoned in to hug them, clutching both Effie and Tove to her chest like two of her precious Kilner jars. "I have been waiting for you. Effie, Grannie Dot's gingerbread is here on the table. Please dig in while I finish up the dinner."

Mum plugged them with plates and forks and offered the tin of gingerbread.

"Wouldn't miss Grannie Dot's gingerbread for the world," said Effie.

Mum bustled back into the kitchen, and Tove hissed, "Sorry, she's a lot."

"I love it. Incredibly, someone is pleased to see me. And likes me. And is vocal about it. It's the greatest compliment."

"You're like each other in that way. Effusive," Tove said.

"Effie-usive." Effie giggled through a mouthful of gingerbread.

Mum and Effie got on well. They were both brimming with warmth.

"Forget that cake for a minute and come to my room," Tove said. "I have something to show you."

Effie brought her plate across the hall to the back of the house. Tove's box room was emptier than it used to be; most of their possessions were in Effie's flat, which they shared now. But some things remained, like the bed, and the wardrobe, and the fucking graffiti they'd found under the wallpaper while helping Mum and Dair strip the room for new paint last week.

Effie took one look at the wall and guffawed.

"I completely forgot about this!"

"Dair was scandalised when he ripped the wallpaper off."

"Oh god, your poor brother. And your poor parents, back then. Weren't you grounded?"

"Yep, and I had to do the wallpaper cover-up myself. That's why it was peeling off."

"Why didn't you paint over it?"

"Do you know how many coats it takes to paint over black writing?"

They were supposed to be making signs for the class assembly. Instead, they'd feasted on Tove's dad's tequila and painted the wall of their bedroom. They'd drawn Effie and she drew them—two naked figures with exaggerated genitals and body hair. They'd labelled them "Effam" and "Teve" in huge black letters, and laughed themselves through to the next morning's hangovers and the fallout from Tove's parents.

Memories were the worst thing about Tove's life. Knowing they had a past where they were treated differently was so distressing that they often wished they could erase everything before the present moment. The happier and safer they became in their new existence, the more confusing and frightening the memories were when they bit them out of the blue. But then...then there were these other memories, of their and Effie's mischief, of childhood family outings, and reminders that the past wasn't all bad. These memories saved them.

"This is the deepest lore," Effie said, snapping a photo on her phone. "I'm getting this framed."

"Don't you dare!"

"I want to gaze at this while I work. You're so fucking beautiful, even as a blobby apparition, and I want to shower you with love all day and every day and for all time."

She wasn't looking at her phone or the wall now, but at Tove themself.

"I love you, Tove."

It wouldn't ever get old, the way her tongue shaped their name, the way her gaze drenched them with a tingling joy. The rake of her half-circle fingernails on their palm and wrist as she pulled them close and her touch slid up their arm. It still blew their mind, even with all the therapy and journalling they were doing, that they were with Effie, and Effie was with them.

"I love you, Effie." Tove could say it again and again.

It was all they could do to get out of the bedroom and stumble back to the living room.

"Slipped away, did you?" Dair said. "I was about to knock. Dinner's almost ready."

"You could've called," said Tove.

"Everyone knows what a closed door means."

"Oh no. I was showing Effie the wall," they retorted.

Dair turned pink. He had such a shock when the wallpaper came off, he refused to go into the room again.

"Gingerbread?" asked Effie, offering the tin, a devilish grin on her face.

"No," he stammered. "Bit adventurous. Too much taste."

"You're going to love the present Tove found for you," Effie said. "It's like, controlled adventure. Nothing dreadful."

Dair's eyes rolled in his head like a frightened rabbit. "I'll die if you don't tell me immediately."

"It's nothing, just some music lessons. Tove found this wonderful teacher who's starting a brass band for adults, and who's looking for people to teach. They're extremely cool."

"Effie!" Tove exclaimed. "Presents are supposed to be *after* dinner!"

"They have purple hair," Effie added. "You'll like them."

Dair tapped his fingers on his cheeks. "Couldn't you have just gotten me new dice like I asked?"

"We got dice too," said Tove. "Hey, you don't have to learn the trumpet if you don't want to. Only if you're into it."

"Screw you. I'll think about it." Dair smiled, and Tove knew he wasn't upset. The ball was in his court now.

"Come on and serve yourselves! Nothing's eating itself," called Mum from the kitchen.

They ate at the kitchen table, Christmas music blaring from the radio. With Effie at Tove's side, her toes nibbling theirs under the table, they could only devote about 30% concentration to the conversation. They were in love, and god knew they couldn't hide it.

It was in their mum's eyes, flicking between them as she smiled knowingly at the short and conscious sentences Effie and Tove managed to utter to each other. And it was in her voice when in the late evening they all stood by the door in the whipping wind, and she told Effie, "Thank you for looking after Tove."

Tove brought it up in the car on the way back to the flat.

"She used to worry herself sleepless about me," they explained. "I know she rests easier knowing I'm with you. Mum really likes you."

"No pressure!" Effie laughed.

"Don't think about the pressure. Trust yourself. I trust you."

"You do?"

"Yes, you silly! How could I not? Look at us—moving in together, you're about to start a new job with the tidal energy company, I'm training as a counsellor and joining a band. We run a soup kitchen with our friends at the weekends."

There were some things Tove didn't say, because they were more personal. The healing process was rough. For a long while, they'd felt worse, stripping back the trauma and the resentment, the wound and its gremlin caretaker. They were working on un-identifying with all of it, and finding themself in the mess. Because what were they left with, when the pain was all gone? Their name was Tove. They were non-binary. They were brave. They deserved kindness and they were easy to be kind to.

With their therapist, they were also learning healthy boundaries, and that was why they'd blocked Aaron on all social media. They thought about their gender more often than they thought about their ex these days!

"We're moving forward," said Effie. She, too, was in therapy, and was learning to re-parent herself now her emotionally immature parents were out of the picture, as well as come to terms with her recently diagnosed ADHD.

Tove realised it as she said it; while their goal for the year had been to get to a place where they could imagine moving forward, they'd gone further than that. They were taking the new steps already.

The realisation knocked the breath out of them, so much that they pulled over onto the side of the road so they didn't wreck on the dunes.

"Are you alright?" asked Effie.

Tove turned to meet her gaze, and took her in. They loved every piece of her, from her mussed-up hair to the way gifts and secrets spilled from her soft lips. The bond they'd formed long ago had repaired itself like a vine, growing ever stronger, ever sturdier. Tove couldn't see it ever breaking now.

"I'm fine," they replied at length. "I just… I want to kiss you."

Effie grinned, the cocky, intentional Cheshire cat grin. "Wish granted."

And they kissed and kissed and kissed in the wind-battered car.

Acknowledgements

Writing was always a solitary endeavour for me; as a child I was paranoid my family were reading over my shoulder as I wrote, and I'd close my document every time anyone came near. Ten years of query rejections, book after book, didn't make me any more eager to share my work. And when I did, there were people who told me my writing was stiff and belittled the genres I have always felt most comfortable in. But despite all this, crucially, I let a few of the right people in at the right time! Thank you to all of those people, and I am sorry to those I have missed:

Alexandria, for picking this book for Pitch Wars in 2021. I was new to writing romance at the time, and insecure about it, and you were one of the first people to read my rough, too-short draft, let alone see something to like. Thank you to the other mentors who have shown me kindness over the years and now; I hope to pay it forward someday.

Pitch Wars introduced me to the loveliest community of writers I could have dreamed of. Thank you to all my positivity readers during the awful months post-showcase, and for sharing your wonderful books in return to take my mind off all the rejection. Thank you to the kind and supportive souls in the

"Romance Discord" and in the "Big Discord"—there are too many of you to name! Thank you to the mods who created these spaces and keep them running.

Anya, for reading an early draft and figuring out Effie and Tove's star signs (for anyone wondering, Effie is a Pisces sun and Libra moon with Aries rising, and Tove is a Leo sun and Scorpio moon with Scorpio rising).

Ali, my editor, for your interest and good humour and compliments. You helped me polish up my book and gave me the confidence that I had a product good enough for this wild, passionate self-publishing plan I'd dreamed up.

Annalise, the artist who designed Effie and Tove's Santa outfits and illustrated the cover. I cannot fathom how you created something so perfect. You're amazing! Thank you!

Kaylynn, for the most magical audiobook narration, for bringing all the feelings back when I thought I'd read the book too many times for it to affect me any more.

And Harry, for playing and recording the trumpet parts and generally always having my back.

Thank you to my sensitivity readers. I value and appreciate your help. Any remaining errors in judgement are my own.

Old writing friends, and people who have read old books and kept me going over the years. I've met many wonderful people in the ten years since I sent my very first query. Although trad pub hasn't happened for me thus far, I am now self-publishing a project I'm proud of, and your continued encouragement amid changing goals and changing milestones means the world. You know who you are. I love you all. Thank you.

Thank you to the person who mistook me for someone else and thus gave me my pen name.

Thank you to wolfeglicksdad on Twitch.

My family and friends. Especially my brother, my cousins, my best friend from home, my jazz band, my maths buddies. Everyone who has been there for me in the times I was hurt and alone, and who reached out even when I couldn't. Thank you to my partner's parents, for welcoming me into your home and looking after me when everyone else is far away. Thank you to my parents for giving me the best start in life and continuing to support me. I miss you.

Thank you to my beloved partner. You changed everything for me. I couldn't do this without you.

Finally, thank you to readers who decide to pick this book up. I hope you like it.

About the author

Lillian Barry (they/she/he) writes in short spells when the world stops spinning, which, when you have vertigo, isn't all that often. Every word that makes it onto the page feels like a small miracle. But that's the way they like it—progress in small miracles like the smell of the sea through an open window or putting a name to a feeling you've always felt or a small kiss that says *more, later*.

They write until the world spins again, only this time it's a different type of spinning, the kind you get from creating love stories, a love you don't want to ever end. Other things Lillian loves include playing brass instruments, watching anime, and getting sucked into the microcosm of a niche video game. A Channel Islander by childhood, they currently live in Ireland with their beloved partner.

Find me!

Follow me **@SoLillianBarry** on social media.
For news and updates (and a free ebook of short stories introducing the Santa contestants around Halloween), please subscribe to my newsletter at **lillianbarry.com**, I'd love to see you there!

www.ingramcontent.com/pod-product-compliance
Ingram Content Group UK Ltd.
Pitfield, Milton Keynes, MK11 3LW, UK
UKHW040004200726
13854UKWH00001B/32

9 781739 530006